MW00586817

THE
LIES
WE
CONJURE

THE
LIES
WE
CONJURE

SARAH HENNING

**TOR
TEEN**

TOR PUBLISHING GROUP
NEW YORK

THE LIES WE CONJURE

Copyright © 2024 by Sarah Henning

Art by Shutterstock.com

A Tor Teen Book
Published by Tom Doherty Associates / Tor Publishing Group
120 Broadway
New York, NY 10271

www.torpublishinggroup.com

Tor® is a registered trademark of Macmillan Publishing Group, LLC.

The Library of Congress Cataloging-in-Publication Data is available upon request.

ISBN 978-1-250-84106-3 (hardcover)
ISBN 978-1-250-84107-0 (ebook)

Our books may be purchased in bulk for promotional, educational, or
business use. Please contact your local bookseller or the Macmillan Corporate
and Premium Sales Department at 1-800-221-7945, extension 5442,
or by email at MacmillanSpecialMarkets@macmillan.com.

First Edition: 2024

Printed in the United States of America

0 9 8 7 6 5 4 3 2 1

To Whitney—who helps me keep the magic going,
one book at a time

This family is truly desperate.
And when people get desperate, the knives come out.

—Benoit Blanc, *Knives Out*

Just think of the story we're going to tell.

—**Wren Jourdain,**
who's super pissed Ruby got to tell it and she didn't

PART ONE

THE
PARTY

CHAPTER 1

RUBY

SIX DAYS BEFORE

The old woman arrives at the Ye Olde Falafel Shoppe not with an order, but with a question.

"Are you sisters?"

As usual, Wren is manning the register and flirting her way to much bigger tips than I can get, while I fulfill the orders as they slide through the kitchen window of Grand County Renaissance Festival's most popular (and only) falafel stand.

"Yes, my lady." Wren smiles at the woman, her festival-mandated British accent sweet in air equally scented with all things fried, excessive sunscreen, and the stink of more than one horse decked out as a knight's noble steed.

"How old?" the lady presses, lifting huge sunglasses into her cloud of silver hair. Deep set and large, her dark eyes sweep between us, and it's like she's checking our features off on a list—tall, pale, brunette, check, check, check. The lunch rush is over, and the moment I slide an extra vat of hummus to a man dressed as fox Robin Hood—tail and all—and he disappears with a tip of his cap, we're alone. No customers stack up behind her as she continues to peer at us instead of choosing off the menu printed on a medieval "parchment" hanging behind Wren. "Sixteen? Seventeen? Irish twins?"

"Yes, my lady," Wren answers again, jabbing a thumb in my direction. She announces in her perfectly posh accent, "Ruby's older, but don't let the age gap fool you, I'm the brains of this operation."

The woman chuckles, her attention lingering on our faces with building excitement. I can't explain why but my gut tightens.

"Their accents are just like yours. Tepidly British and put on for an occasion," she says mostly to herself before turning to me and ordering, "Let me hear yours."

For some reason it feels impossible to tell how old our nosy customer actually is—she could be sixty or pushing a hundred. Either way, I realize I've seen her before. I've *served* her before. At least two weeks in a row.

I gesture at the menu, and prod in my fake accent, which is way less impressive than Wren's, "Is there anything I can get you? You ordered the number two with jalapeños last week, didn't you?"

Wren mutters "Pushy" under her breath. Yet rather than answer my question or agree with my sister's assessment, the old woman's obvious elation only grows—her heart-shaped face expanding and elongating in such a way that it resembles an exclamation point.

"Good."

She then precedes to plant her elbows on the counter and gesture for us to lean in close.

Wren, happily coasting on her four semesters in high school improv class, does so without hesitation, but I must admit to being a little less enthusiastic. The only reason I'm slinging falafel in a wench outfit is because I need more money for my pitiful college fund, and this is *far* outside the parameters of what we're paid to do. Not to mention this is the last weekend of the Ren Fest and we literally have five hours left on the job. Our customer ignores my frown, and greets our combined attention with an eager smile outlined in matte maroon lipstick.

"Girls, my name is Marsyas Blackgate. I'd like to hire each of you to pretend to be my granddaughters at a dinner party at Hegemony Manor—do you know it? It's just outside of Wood Rose."

Wren's eyes nearly pop out of her head. "*The* Hegemony Manor? Of course we know it! Gothic perfection on the hill, with the turrets and the windows and the Wednesday Addams moodiness. Our mom just *loved* it."

My breath hitches at the mention of Mom. She did love that place. There's no way this woman—Marsyas?—could know that, but something unsettling plops in my gut.

Beyond the old woman's rounded shoulders is a steady stream of humanity wandering by, gnawing on massive turkey legs, crinkling maps, and brandishing kiddie-sized wooden swords. Not a single Ren Fest guest is looking our way. I drop both my hideous accent and my voice. "You want us to impersonate your granddaughters? May I ask why?"

She blinks as if it's obvious. "You look just like them."

"But we *aren't* them."

Marsyas straightens and, with a dignified sniff, draws a photograph from somewhere beneath the voluminous fabric of her black caftan. In it, she beams at the camera, bracketed by two tall, pale brunettes. Their heads are smooshed together, the iconic pyramid of the Louvre in the background.

I have to admit, we *do* look like them.

"My girls live abroad with their mother. I miss them dearly and though they miss me, they haven't been back stateside in a decade. I'm invited every year to a special dinner party at Hegemony Manor, and every year the other families expect to see Lavinia and Kaysa. Every year they're disappointed, and I'm disappointed too."

Marsyas's chin wobbles, her dark eyes shine, and suddenly she looks like she might be a thousand years old. If it's an act, her improv lessons have been far more extensive than Wren's. "This year, I want to show off my girls."

Wren immediately claws at my hand, her expression pleading. I know my sister just wants to help, even if it's some next-level psychological bullshit that this woman is propositioning us to pretend to be her living, breathing granddaughters for a night so that her friends will think that they love her enough to cross the Atlantic.

"I—" I start. That tremor of unease in my gut is now a 5.0 on the Richter scale.

But before I can put that into words enough to pull Wren aside to discuss it, Marsyas lays out twenty one-hundred-dollar bills on the counter.

"I'll give you each a thousand up front and another thousand after dinner." Her gaze sweeps between the pair of us, that spark returning. "I'm sure you will find that reasonable."

My jaw drops.

That is more money than we've earned—combined—in our six-weekend run at the Ren Fest.

More than I alone earn in a month at my part-time job as a bookseller at Agatha's Apothecary & Paperback Emporium.

More than enough to pad my college fund so that it isn't completely laughable.

It's enough that it's too good to be true.

So, of course, Wren immediately accepts the offer for both of us.

"Why, that's more than reasonable, Miss Marsyas. When's the party?"

In answer, the old woman says, "Call me Nona," and lays a handwritten card atop the cash advance.

Saturday night. Formal. Wear solid black. I'll be in touch.

"Wait, what—" I glance up, a new line of questions forming and then immediately dying on my lips.

Marsyas Blackgate isn't there.

I lean on the counter, craning to see farther left, then right, ready to chase her down for more information, a contact number, more specifics about the deal.

But she's vanished.

Wren eagerly gathers the bills and stuffs them into the inside pocket of her wench's apron. She's neglected the card, and I snatch it up and flip it over, hoping for at least one answer to the flood of questions in my churning mind.

Instead, I find one final order. Or maybe a threat.

Tell no one.

Chapter 2

RUBY

The lie isn't ours.

But we wear it as overtly as our new party dresses and shoes. As our drugstore lipstick and mother's pearls. As the accents that sit, awkward, upon our tongues, waiting and ready for polite conversation over the course of one gilded evening.

"Fuck, it's haunted."

That's the first thing Wren whispers to me after slamming the chauffeured SUV's door shut with a decisive echo. She doesn't use her accent.

Before us, the western sun is hanging over the Continental Divide like a blowtorch, a line of fire trailing along every nook and crick of the Rocky Mountain peaks. It's beautiful—magical, even—the perfect backdrop for literally any story the night wants to tell. It also lies in stunning juxtaposition to the gothic mansion staring back at us.

Painted a flat black across a solid three-story construction, its windows are stacked like the eyes of a spider, while turrets akin to spindle wheels reach up, eager to prick the sky and send it to a deep sleep.

Hegemony Manor.

We've never been so close to it. It's been perched on the edge of Mom's tiny mountain hometown for a century and counting, vast enough to house every resident within its walls, its grounds larger than the city limits, all roped off by barbed wire strung for acres until they become miles.

For a few years after the divorce, we lived in Wood Rose with Mom, and drove past the manor on our way to visit Dad and our stepmom, Karen, in Grand Lake. Mom almost always pulled onto the shoulder for a moment's appreciation of the moody lines of the manor, wishing the Hegemonys would open it to visitors or turn it into a bed-and-breakfast operation. Anything for a peek inside. Then three years ago a drunk driver took Mom away from us. We moved in with Dad and Karen, and the drives past Hegemony Manor became a relic of the past.

In this moment, I can't believe we're just feet from the front door. I wish we could tell her.

Inside the barbed-wire perimeter and massive gates, there's a beautiful brick drive that loops in a teardrop up to the manor and back out to the private road that leads to the property from the highway. I stand on that drive now, wedging my brand-new stiletto heels between the bricks as I stare back at Hegemony Manor, trying to find solid ground. Suddenly feeling nervous about this plan.

About what we're about to do to the people who live here.

People who've been more rumor than reality in my life up until this very moment.

The rumors at school went like this: Three kids lived behind these great gothic walls and towering, treacherous gates. Two boys and a girl, orphans all. Cousins, adopted by their grandmother. Kept by nannies and tutors before calling boarding school home.

With a collection of rumors like that, as big and bold as the mansion that bears their name, it's strange that we're about to make rumor a reality and then *lie*.

I wouldn't have said yes to tonight if Wren hadn't already done it—my sister and her habit of hoovering up experiences to fuel her dreams of stage and screen.

"Do you think they name their ghosts?" Wren's amber eyes pop wide, false eyelashes like fireworks as she leans in. "Like, 'That's just Old Imelda, crying in the foyer again'? Or maybe they just ignore them—too numerous to bother?"

"Please make sure to corner an honest-to-God Hegemony and ask."

The sarcasm in my voice practically drips onto her dress but she ignores it.

"I just might. They'd probably find that kind of innocent interest endearing after spending all semester with walking icicles in sweater sets and pearls." Wren adds a self-indulgent hair toss while disparaging the entire female population of the Hegemonys' boarding school of choice, Walton-Bridge Prep, before a shade of anxiety flashes across her face and she clutches my wrist. "Wait, what do *we* wear at the Baxter Academy for the Arts?" That's where the real Lavinia and Kaysa go to school. "If they have some sort of awful green plaid as a uniform, I need to know about it for character development reasons."

Wren is living for this.

I am not.

She whips out her phone. I pull out mine too, and my palms immediately slip with sweat around my phone case. I resist the urge to wipe my hands on the silk of my dress and try again, swiping away a "Made it to Boulder" text from Dad that I missed on the group thread twenty minutes ago. When my lock screen disappears, it reveals the document I have about the dinner party guests. It's something Marsyas sent us after we'd accepted her opportunity—details on the families in attendance. Names, pictures, and surface information—employment, schooling, hobbies. Totally creepy, actually.

Evidently, no one besides Marsyas is related to "us," which was much to Wren's relief as she'd tagged literally everyone under the age of twenty attending as "so hot."

Hot or not, these are people who need to believe we're Lavinia and Kaysa Blackgate, at least for tonight. According to Marsyas, none of them have seen the sisters since the pair of them learned how to read and write. The girls aren't allowed on social media, and, like everyone at this party, the internet has never heard of them.

"Do you have reception? This won't load." Wren stabs at her phone screen as if that will make it do anything. Looks like I don't have a signal either. "I know, I know, if I'm quizzed on the specs of the Baxter Academy uniform, it's my cue to recast the small talk to something far more interesting." She waggles her eyebrows into her thick fringe of bangs. "Perhaps the ghosts."

She's about to laugh—until she sees my face.

I'm fairly certain I've begun to go green underneath my makeup. My heart is rabbiting against my breastbone, and when Wren ditches her phone to snatch my hands, they're clammy against her dry grip. "Look, just because you're allergic to fun doesn't mean you need to be nervous. You're going to do fine."

I shake my head and try to put words to the unease uncoiling in my belly at the thought that this is actually happening. "I just don't like this."

Wren rolls her eyes. "It's not *actually* haunted."

It's not that Hegemony Manor seems *scary,* per se, it's just . . . too *right*. Too stately, the grass too green and lush for the summer drought, the air too still. It's like the whole thing is a mirage, and a little dose of reality will slough off the perfection like dead skin.

"I know, it's just—" I tug on Wren's hand. Pinky to pinky. "Promise you'll leave with me if I need to bolt."

Wren's lips purse into a lopsided smirk. "Only if *you* promise not to panic and at least make an effort to have a good time. It's a party, not a funeral."

"Girls," calls a voice with a whisky-warm rasp—Marsyas, or tonight, Nona. Appearing from around the rear bumper of our SUV, Marsyas is a bowling ball of a woman punctuated by a tight chignon. She drops the keys into what truly looks to be a handbag fashioned from a decapitated raven. Like, with feathers and a wing and everything. Satisfied, she flashes that eccentric grin of hers, a mile wide and as treacherous as a canyon. "Let me have a look at you."

Marsyas addresses my sister first—"Kaysa"—and Wren frowns. She isn't a fan of the name she's been given. The old woman's fingers tug at Wren's neckline, straightening the drape of silk across her collarbones and the flash of skin at her shoulders. At first I think she's going for the price tag we left tucked under her collar, but then she removes the string of white pearls at Wren's throat and deposits them into my sister's open palm, the meaning clear—*put these away.* "There."

As Wren drops Mom's pearls into her wristlet without a word,

Marsyas hits me with the full force of her critical eye. My dress is less complicated, an ankle-length A-line and belted, and it must pass the test because rather than a single adjustment she hums out a "mmhmm" and smiles again, teeth tea-stained and surprisingly wolflike for a grandma. I suppose I'm allowed to keep Mom's pearl studs. "Perfect, girls. Now, take my hands."

"Yes, Nona," we answer in our accents now, as she's instructed us to do, and sweep our hands into hers, stepping to either side. The black rabbits' feet she's clasped on delicate gold chains about our wrists tap gently into her own matching ones.

I'd declined my bracelets when she'd foisted them upon me, but I was informed wearing them was nonnegotiable. A Blackgate necessity.

My bracelets might go missing the moment Nona starts drinking.

This close, Marsyas smells of layers of expensive makeup and roses, and like us is dressed head-to-toe in black. Along with her own dead bunny bracelets, she accessorizes with an elaborate cascade of natural black pearls cloaking her considerable décolletage like a mass of tiny beetles. Her earrings have the unsettling swing of a spider weaving webs through the too-still air, stark against her pale powdered skin.

Marsyas doesn't lead us toward the gravestone steps rising to the ornately carved doors of Hegemony Manor. Instead, we walk entwined down a strand of star-shaped stone tiles leading around the side to a massive manicured garden that hugs the rear of the house like a cape, its hem disappearing into the Rocky Mountain wilds.

Voices hum under the melodic whisper of stringed instruments, though the way the hedges bracket the space, no guests can be seen from where Marsyas's steps have halted.

The old woman seems to be gathering herself, straightening her thoughts like she did Wren's dress with a deep breath and an upturned tip of her heart-shaped face.

"Girls," Marsyas whispers as her grip on my hand tightens impossibly, "two final rules, and it is imperative that you follow them."

Her dark eyes are no longer mischievous as she finds each of us before continuing. They're sharp with seriousness. My heart churns back up to racing speed as if a gun has gone off. I swallow and stare at her, focusing on every word.

"First, we need to stay together. Second, we must do whatever Ursula Hegemony says. Do you understand?"

My speeding heart skips and my stomach drops. Yet I match Wren as she answers, so that we're in near unison. "Yes, Nona."

Marsyas tosses back her shoulders, points her chin toward the garden, spiderweb earrings swinging, the pins in her hair glinting like the clustered eyes of a housefly. Her grimace curves upward with a heave and a new proclamation. "Smile, girls. Blackgates always smile."

Grins in place, we enter under the bough of baby pink roses arcing above the privacy hedges. Though it's still bright enough, small lights bound the garden like so many fireflies strung into position.

A clever trick.

In fact, floating, enchanted light seems to be a theme, as at the center of the garden is a line of seemingly hovering chandeliers, gold with taper candles illuminating a long table. Apparently, gravity doesn't exist if you're rich enough.

It's so perfect it's disconcerting. There's not a single flaw.

The party is small—fewer than ten guests. And, as they all turn to assess our arrival, I catch Wren's attention over the top of Marsyas's intricate chignon, and soundlessly mouth, *Promise me.*

Wren's response is yet another eye roll and a flash of pale lipstick and white teeth as she mouths back, *Live a little.*

Chapter 3

AUDEN

All rumors are assumed to be lies until proven true.

They're created on assumptions, fed by a lack of knowledge, spiked with jealousy, boredom, and unease. Or, made for a purpose.

The Hegemony family lives by this understanding. We've used it to our advantage for nearly five hundred years. For our protection. As a weapon.

And yet, tonight it slips my cousin's mind.

"I'd heard they weren't coming."

Evander tracks his prey from the solarium windows high above the garden. His shark's smirk distorts behind the icy remains of a finger of scotch on the rocks. I don't need to guess what "they" to which he's referring. I also don't need to move closer to catch the procession of two girls, tall and raven-headed, locking arms with a shorter, silver-haired matriarch.

"Don't believe everything you hear." Undoing a button at the throat of my dress shirt, I return to my reread of *Leaves of Grass*—the deathbed edition of 1892. Like almost everything else I own, this rare Whitman and the rest of my poetry collection were my father's.

I'd known the Blackgates would come. I'd seen our grand-mother's request before she'd sent it—not an invitation this time, an order. And no one, not even the Blackgates, refuses an order from Ursula Hegemony.

"They've never come before."

"No," I correct, "they haven't come *since*."

Winter enters the room and our conversation with a frown and a waft of perfume as perfectly floral as the briar rose pattern ab-stractly beaded into the rich fabric of her low-cut kelly-green dress.

We've been waiting for her—getting ready always takes her twice as long when we're home as when we're away at Walton-Bridge.

This, exactly this, is what we do on nights when we must be Hegemonys.

We gather, assess the situation, prepare in our own ways. Evander drinking; Winter preening; me reading until the very last moment; and, when our armor is firmly in place, we act as Ursula Hegemony's generals.

Winter arches an eyebrow, first at our guests, then across the room to me, where I'm propped against one of two Italian marble fireplaces, embers snapping merrily and throwing fire lines across the sheen of my polished dress shoes. She studies me with an expression as tight as the ribboned choker bear-hugging her throat. "Why are the girls here? Now?"

"More like, what do the Blackgates know about tonight's itinerary that we don't?" Evander answers, thumb aimlessly rubbing the rim of his glass as the ice clinks. "They wouldn't just fly in from London after ten years. The Blackgate sisters are kept offshore like illegal funds, everyone knows it."

Uncharacteristically droll but correct.

The moment their father, Marcos, died, Lavinia and Kaysa Blackgate were shipped to Europe under the cover of night. That left old Marsyas playing matriarch stateside and mastering redirection whenever their mother, Athena, or the girls themselves became the topic of discussion. I'm not even sure if they've officially oathed Lavinia as heir. At seventeen, she's older than Kaysa by a year, but age doesn't always determine a would-be matriarch or patriarch among the Four Lines. Character matters too, though considering the predilections of the Blackgate family, perhaps having the personality of a snobbish feral cat is more desirable than detestable.

Honestly, despite the fact that the Blackgates and I have never seen eye to eye, I don't blame them for putting an ocean between themselves and Hegemony Manor for the past decade.

"Illegal is that eye makeup," Winter mutters—disdain typically manifests when she's jealous. This is exactly how Winter always sizes people up—by tearing them down before extending her hand with a firm smile. She doesn't bother to be anything other than direct with me. "But seriously, Auden. *Spill.*"

They expect me to know for good reason.

I'm the one who has been home with Ursula the longest since boarding school let out in June. The one who didn't spend the first weeks of our summer gallivanting about. The one who is objectively her favorite. I'm also the one who spent my childhood inventing sly and increasingly devilish ways to tempt the claws out of dour Lavinia Blackgate.

"Perhaps they wanted to see what they've been missing all these years," I suggest as dryly as possible, audibly turning a page in my book, though I haven't been able to comprehend a single written word since catching visible proof that the Blackgate girls are indeed back on the manor grounds.

Evander wheels around, frustration deepening at the fact that I at least appear to still be reading. Nonchalance annoys my older cousin to no end. "What does *she* have planned?"

I don't answer.

Evander steps away from the bank of floor-to-ceiling windows. I set the book atop the mantel—I can't have it ruined in the crossfire of his rising anger, fueled by both his annoyance and insistence—and lift my eyes to his. They're green, stormy, and all his mother's, just like his warm brown skin. He's taller by an inch, and heavier by a good twenty pounds of hard-earned muscle. Like his status as oathed heir to every title our grandmother holds, he wields those advantages as overtly and often as possible.

"It's a reunion with old friends. They're simply dressing the part for a nice evening." Evander glares at me and Winter joins him. I hold up my hands. "I know nothing beyond the usual triad for these annual meetings: convey what's important, reaffirm Hegemony power, scatter to the winds for another three hundred and sixty-five days."

Winter looks like she might chuck something at me if she had anything reasonable nearby to throw or otherwise fling my way. "Auden, you're the worst liar."

"He is not lying, Winter Elvire."

We're too practiced to gasp, but all three of us stiffen at the addition to our party pregame.

There, in the wide, arched entry to the solarium, is our grandmother, our guardian, matriarch of the Hegemony Clan, leader of the Elemental Line, High Sorcerer of the Four Lines, and general no-nonsense woman of a certain pristinely obscured age.

Ursula Hegemony.

She was soundless before—one of her many gifts—but now that she wants us to know she's here, Ursula enters the stately beauty of the room on steps as sharp as the stab of a knife on the parquet. Her posture is perfect, her expression discerning, her eyes, as usual, miss nothing. She notes the book discarded at my side, Winter's blush at the admonishment, the remaining scotch sweating it out in Evander's spooked grip.

"The annual meeting is necessary to our continued success as the leaders of the Four Lines. Tonight is no different." Evander visibly relaxes—if Ursula had heard his side of the conversation, she'd certainly say so. "That being said, I expect all of you to treat this as what it is from our point of view. It's not a social hour, it's a *campaign*."

Ursula pauses at that, and I don't believe it's a coincidence that her forefinger taps the four inset gems of her High Sorcerer's ring. A wealth of power is tied to that ring, and she's tied to that power simply by wearing it. The ring and the title have been ours for nearly five hundred years—the control, the influence, the authority—and like anything of worth, it becomes harder to grip the longer you hold it. Something our grandmother is keen on reminding us. The last of a line has a duty to survive—or go out in a blaze so bright it leaves a mark.

"I want you on your best behavior. You are leaders, not simply hosts." She frowns. On the unnatural planes of her smooth, unlined face, the movement is slight, but holds enough weight that my heart skips a beat. "A fact I see each of you has conveniently forgotten."

Without a moment's hesitation, our grandmother turns her laser focus on Winter, her clever cerulean eyes striking on the rich fabric of my cousin's impeccably tailored gown. It's an ankle-length column that highlights the lithe strength her upper body has acquired from long hours on the tennis court and in the weight room at Walton-Bridge Prep. Ursula's tightly held scrutiny sours further. Instantly, the heart shape of Winter's neckline unfurls, elongates, and crawls up and around the back of her neck, transforming it into something much more modest.

When she's finished, the emerald hue of her magic evaporating, Ursula announces, "Cleavage is unnecessary and impolite."

Winter dips her chin in acceptance before fussing to straighten the bow now settled underneath her long, strawberry blond hair and probably at odds with her choice of necklace, now swathed in fabric.

Our grandmother turns her attention to Evander. The barest flicker of a grimace crosses her face.

The final dregs of his scotch burst into flame.

Evander nearly drops the glass but catches himself and it just in time. As the green hint of magic flares, his wits kick in and he smothers the fire with a wide palm atop the rim. With a muttered curse, he rips it away from the tumbler, a ring burned into the skin. He waves it violently in an attempt to sooth the pain, and meets Ursula's stoic expression with glassy, red-rimmed eyes.

"Sobriety is crucial for the case we are to make for continued Hegemony supremacy. The libations tonight are for our *guests'* enjoyment, not yours. You may take a glass as it encourages others to imbibe what is offered, but recreational and excessive liquor consumption is unbecoming and steals from both our family credibility and your own as my oathed heir."

Evander discards the tumbler without a word.

Ursula turns to me.

I'm dressed in the suit she chose and standing so as not to wrinkle the fine Italian craftsmanship. The open button at my throat could hardly be classified as unnecessary and impolite, and it's obvious I haven't had a drink, not to mention Ursula knows me well enough to be sure I don't intend to.

Still, I've violated her expectations, the same as my cousins.

Turns out it's not what I've done, but what she expects me to do.

"The High Families are our peers as much as they are our responsibility. You are no longer children—I expect you to be polite, courteous, and respectful to *all* of our guests, but most especially to the Blackgate heirs." I think that's it, but only when our grandmother continues and adds the use of my first name does it truly dawn on me how much of a liability she must believe I am. "Auden, I do not have to remind you, I'm sure, that a renewal of your previous little *animus* with Lavinia Blackgate will not be tolerated this evening."

"Understood," I answer with a drop of my chin that I hope appears remorseful.

I wait out Ursula's appraisal for what seems like several moments too long before she inhales thinly.

"Now that we're all reacquainted with our expectations, I must finish my preparations." I raise my gaze just in time to see her spear Evander right through the heart. "Because, yes, Evander, *she does* have something planned tonight."

With that, Ursula Hegemony turns on her heel and walks out.

The moment her steps are swallowed by the plush hallway carpeting Evander crumples. *"Shit."*

The side of Winter's mouth lifts ever so slightly at his mortification. "You got roasted *and* you didn't even learn anything. That takes some talent, Evander."

He grumbles at her but makes it a point to glower at me. "Wipe that smug grin off your face, Auden."

"I didn't say anything."

"Exactly the point and the problem."

Winter rolls her eyes and sweeps a ribbon of strawberry blond behind her ear using her watered-down reflection in the windowpane.

"If she won't tell us, I'm just going to go ask the Blackgates myself why they're here—politely, courteously, and respectfully, of course."

Evander fusses with an impeccably turned cuff at his wrist, clearly already wishing to rip off his jacket. The man cannot stand to feel confined. "Win, you're wasting your time. Marsyas wouldn't fly those girls forty-five hundred miles and not prep them."

"I suppose I'll find out, won't I?"

At sixteen, Winter's the youngest of the three of us, and appropriately stubborn. Especially when Evander tries to play patriarch at eighteen—he's just graduated high school, after all, and we're only a year behind him. Winter spins and heads for the doorway that leads from the solarium onto the sprawling elevated stone terrace, down the steps to the gardens and the Rocky Mountain wilds beyond.

"Be nice," I shout at her back.

"I'm not the one who was given a direct warning," she *tsks* before pausing and turning around, one immaculately sculpted brow mischievously arched. "Anyway, I will be—to them. To Hex? I make no guarantees."

"Nor should you."

If Hex Cerise is still standing by the night's end, it'll only be because Winter is making him suffer instead of putting him out of his misery. The guy's basically been pulling her hair for attention since they were both in diapers. It's as pathetic as it is predictable. And it makes her cling harder to the people she likes best—namely Infinity.

As Winter vanishes, Evander stalks away from the windows, heavy footfalls pointing toward the serpentine halls of Hegemony Manor. "I'm going to the source."

"Ah, yes, because interrogating Ursula during her stated preparation for the most important gathering of her calendar year after she already roasted you for being uncouth is a most excellent plan for both obtaining the truth and going unscathed."

My older cousin pauses to glower at me yet again, thick brows lowered to match his frown. "I'm not stupid, I'll start with an apology.

But I am *the* oathed heir and do have the right and obligation to know her plans as part of my training."

I don't tolerate his infantilization any more than Winter does. If I'd been born six months earlier, I might be the patriarch-in-waiting. If Ursula preferred me as much as my cousins believe she does, those few months might not have mattered anyway. I smirk at Evander and raise an invisible glass. "Top-notch argument. I'm sure that'll go over swimmingly."

"Shut up, Auden."

With that, Evander straightens his jacket and leaves. His foot-falls echo down the hall, and I have no doubt he'll stomp the whole flight up to the third floor. A fool's errand and tantrum rolled into one, in my opinion. Not that he'll get anything out of it.

When I'm alone, I finally step to one of the many floor-to-ceiling solarium windows and peer out onto the grounds. Everyone is accounted for, as commanded by the mighty ink and envelope of Ursula Hegemony.

The Cerises. The Starwoods. The Blackgates.

The Blood Line. The Celestial Line. The Death Line.

And us—the Elemental Line.

Here, now, together again, and with a full two generations of each High Family of the Four Lines—for the first time since Marcos Blackgate was alive.

My cousins are wrong. I don't know what Ursula has planned.

Ursula does everything by her own rules. No compromises. No mercy.

I don't know why the Blackgate heirs were ordered to make an appearance after a decade away. I don't know why they complied.

But I do know both my cousins are wasting their time.

It doesn't matter what Ursula has planned and it doesn't matter why the girls have finally appeared. We'll have answers soon enough. Ursula Hegemony will make sure of that.

CHAPTER 4

RUBY

The partygoers descend like vultures. Swooping in, all speed and precision, talons extended toward the fresh meat.

Wren and I—Kaysa and Lavinia.

The Cerises take the left flank. The Starwoods the right.

Ostensibly, Marsyas is clutching us for support, but in that first moment I feel that if I weren't holding on to the soft swell of the woman's forearm, I might float away altogether.

Because, as they close in, I am sure beyond a shadow of a doubt that these people will know we're total fakes. And then we'll really be in trouble.

I brace myself as Hector Cerise greets us first. Like his wife and seventeen-year-old twins, he has the air of old Hollywood, as if they were made to be in black and white. To wit, Hector is all slicked-back hair and cigar smoke clinging to his navy suit coat and pants as he crashes into our three-person line with a showman's gravitas. It's impossible to miss a large ruby ring on his right index finger as his hands press together in front of his chest.

"Marsyas, you've enticed your girls into coming!" he exclaims—bowing to Marsyas like she's royalty and not an old lady dressed in dead animals. "After all these years? Bravo!"

"And what fine young ladies they've become," crows Luna Starwood from the elbow of her grandchild, Infinity. They're both wearing gauzy white, paired with brilliant grins on their dark brown faces. They look about a thousand times more comfortable than I feel. Luna's midnight gaze meets mine. "You must be Lavinia?" I nod automatically, wondering how she got it right on the first guess. Really, for all our differences, Wren and I look alike. Similar height, bone structure, coloring. "And Kaysa, how lovely are those hazel eyes?"

And now I know. Something subtle. The smallest of tests passed.

"They're just the spitting image of Marcos's gaze, Marsyas," agrees Sanguine Cerise, Hector's wife. Every one of her attributes is best described with a "very"—very tiny waist, very big boobs, very sharp cheekbones, very blond hair, very red nails, all wrapped in a very tight long-sleeved dress. And apparently, she's *very* pointed in her commentary too.

Sanguine doesn't mean to be unkind—*I think*—but under my grasp, Marsyas tenses at the mention of her late son's name. Wren catches it too, immediately giving "Nona" a loving pat while cooing, "Such a compliment, Mrs. Cerise. Why, thank you so much."

"Call me Sanguine, darling. And Hector is fine for my love." Sanguine gropes Hector's bicep as if we'd have some sort of confusion over whom her heart adores. They seem like the type of couple that mistakes codependence for affection. "Kaysa and Lavinia, please meet the twins, Ada and Hex."

Wrapped in a dress with longer sleeves than a hem, Ada is her mother without all the extremes, soft and natural, like a museum painting of a girl frocking among wildflowers. Or maybe poppies. Something poisonous. Hex—short for Hector Junior according to Marsyas's document—is tall and dapper like his father in a matching navy suit. He has the bearing of an athlete—the kind named team captain not out of talent but out of fear. Given that he's a varsity linebacker, he probably shoves kids into lockers as a pre-practice warmup at the fancy Pinault Day School the twins attend.

"We know each other, Mama," Hex scoffs, his coal-dark eyes pinned on me. My heart gives a little kick.

"Prancing around in your nappies a dozen years ago doesn't imply knowing them as they currently are," Sanguine insists with a dismissive wave that has me noticing that it's not just Hector—all four of them are wearing matching rings on their pointer fingers. I don't know the first thing about gems but these aren't costume jewelry. Rubies, garnets, or whatever they are, they have the weight of a family heirloom. I wouldn't know. The pearl earrings I'm wearing are the closest thing I have to my own and they're not even real.

Ada frowns at Wren. "I thought you preferred 'Kay'?"

Shit, I think, but Wren handles this little snag like a pro with a shrug. "I grew out of it. Kaysa fits me better these days."

Ada's lips twitch as she accepts my sister's outstretched hand, but she doesn't comment further. Phew. Keeping to my current plan of smiling and saying as little as possible, I accept Ada's hand next with the barest of pleasantries.

Meanwhile, when I move to Hex, there's a sharp edge to his features, and his long fingers are far too cold for the summer night. His unfortunate nickname does his general air of presentation no favors.

As I'm doing everything I can not to rub my clammy, and now chilly, hand against the lovely silk of my *very expensive* dress, a musical voice calls to us from somewhere in the vicinity of the manor.

"Are those the long-lost Blackgate girls I see?"

We all turn, and there, approaching, is not so much a person as a living, breathing candle flame.

Winter Hegemony.

Like the perfect grass, the floating chandeliers, the soft air too still for the mountains, her outward appearance feels aggressively manufactured—a mirage with a pit crew.

Honestly, it's absolutely unnerving.

"Best get your eyes checked, Winter Hegemony, because we're *all* here," Luna shouts in her direction, with a cackle that shakes her frail frame as she hangs on to Infinity's strong arm for dear life. I immediately like her—Mom's favorite patients were exactly like Luna, ornery broads whose love language was subtle verbal decimation.

"There's no missing you, Luna—how are you?" Winter makes a point of enveloping the ancient woman in a gentle embrace the moment she reaches our circle.

"Not dead yet, which is pretty great when you're ninety-seven, I'd say."

"Pretty great, indeed," Winter agrees, smoothing the old woman's ivory caftan as she disentangles herself, careful to make sure Luna is still well balanced against Infinity. Winter greets the younger Starwood with a gentle embrace that doesn't upset the balance of their grandmother, and an enthusiastic compliment about the cut of their ethereal jumpsuit.

Then, with the practiced precision of someone painstakingly trained in the social arts, Winter precedes to welcome each guest warmly, proxy to the hostess, promising her grandmother's imminent arrival. She gives everyone their due, their time, working with both class and efficiency before concluding, most likely purposefully, with the three of us.

"Can you believe it?" Marsyas asks, pointedly squeezing us close in a remake of the Louvre photo she showed us at the Ren Fest. "My Lavinia and Kaysa, in the flesh!"

Winter agrees that it's so wonderful she *can* believe it, and then pulls us each into a warm, rose-scented embrace. "So lovely you've decided to join us this year," she muses to the pair of us. "It's been so long—whatever changed your mind about attending?"

"Yes, Marsyas, what spell did you put upon them to do your bidding?" Hector asks, hopping in with a grand laugh. "Mine are starting to weasel out of my instructions." Both twins flinch as he claps them heartily on the shoulders. He squeezes, his large gemstone ring outshining the plain gold wedding band in the floating light with the movement. "It's quite infuriating as a patriarch, honestly."

I don't think I've heard a person outside a Regency novel describe *themselves* as a patriarch. Maybe he does belong in another time.

"Nonsense," Luna insists with a wave of an elegant ebony hand, "these charming young ladies needed no convincing to attend a party." She winks at me. "It's your mother who needs convincing. We know, girls, no need to pretend."

Wren's mouth pops open to give the stock answer we'd agreed upon about "our" attendance, but Marsyas lets out a practiced chuckle, insisting, "It was high time, nothing more, nothing less."

"Speaking of time, I want to hear where you've been, what you've been up to, all of it." Then, before either of us can object, Winter claims our wrists, dislodges us from Marsyas, and aims us toward a fountain gurgling merrily among the expertly shaped topiaries.

I look back at Marsyas for some clue as to whether a directive—and a physical assertion, no less—from Winter Hegemony counts as doing what her grandmother says, per her final set of instructions. In answer, Marsyas pointedly tugs Sanguine down to sit on a nearby bench, and waves over a waiter bearing a tray of gleaming crystal flutes bubbling with champagne.

Wren uses that as her cue to happily launch into the story she's concocted over the past six days.

A manor house just outside London, a penthouse in Barcelona, a walkup along the river in Prague, a little cottage in Bavaria to retreat to when we please. Boarding school, complete social media ban, everything directed by our mother, Athena, and Nona Marsyas.

Reveling in their undivided attention against the hum of string instruments being piped in from somewhere discreet, Wren clearly finds this part of tonight exhilarating, while I find it completely and utterly exhausting. So good at putting on a show, my sister, while I can barely hold up the curtain.

Sometimes, I'm not sure how we're related at all.

Wren is in the middle of a very spirited tale about the time "she" chucked a scone slathered with clotted cream at a boy's head in the Baxter refectory, resulting in an explosion on contact if her hand gestures are any indication, when a voice appears in my ear.

"This story isn't about her."

There's a wryness to his delivery, as if he's in on a joke, and a weight to his presence that hangs between us in the thin mountain air over my shoulder.

I turn toward this boy—bracing because he could mean that sentence and humor in any number of ways, including seeing right through our sister act—and my breath catches. I immediately recognize the lacrosse-star build and clean lines of his classically handsome face from Marsyas's files.

Auden Hegemony.

I know who he is. And yet, I'm so startled—by him, by his droll accusation, by the stupid way my breath hitched—that I *laugh*.

"Um, what?" I grasp for my accent, which slid away in my surprise, and clarify with a questionable British lilt, "How do you mean, Auden?"

A wry smile lifts now to go with his delivery, and there's just something a tad bit dangerous about it. Like black ice—hardly visible and deadly all the same. Still, his eyes, blue rimmed in brown, twinkle in a way that signals he seems pleased not to have needed an introduction. "You're the kind to bean an adversary with a perfectly good pastry. That's all."

"So . . . you think this story is actually about me?" I ask, slowly, hoping I'm understanding this whole bizarre tit for tat correctly and that he hasn't just casually dismantled our entire ruse.

"Yes."

I squint at him, a small, confused smile tugging at the corners of my mouth because whatever the heck is going on here was not outlined in his file. "Is that some sort of compliment?"

He tips his chin. "Please consider taking it as one."

"Auden Hegemony," Winter's voice breaks in, chiding and insistent, "what kind of host are you?" She flourishes her mostly filled drink at him with a very toned arm. "Reacquainting yourself with one Blackgate but not the other. Don't play favorites, it's rude."

I would not call his attitude toward me any sort of favoritism because what in the name of rich people was *that*? But I'll happily accept the benefits of Winter's instruction and Wren's enthusiasm as she hops to her feet from where she'd settled in on the fountain's edge for story time. "Kaysa," she announces. "Lovely to meet you again, Auden."

Wren's tone is tickled—like she just can't believe she's meeting him at his very own home. And, as Auden is shaking her hand, I realize he didn't afford me the same hospitality. Or even greet me really. Yet, as I watch, he goes through the same routine Winter executed, spending time talking to each and every person like he's a politician or something.

Apparently, he doesn't need or want my—Lavinia's—vote.

With a delicate quirk of her brow and a pointed perusal of the garden, Wren announces, "I've collected two of the three Hegemonys. Now, where is the—"

"We're not a set."

My head whips around as a brooding, broad-shouldered boy steps into view. Warm brown skin, close-cropped dark hair, eyes the color of the shadowed depths of a forest floor, and the unmistakable air of Hegemony in his refined features.

Evander. The oldest cousin.

Eyes twinkling, Wren smiles at him like he's exactly what she's been waiting for. "That's not what the collectors say. Hegemony sightings are very valuable on the black market."

He doesn't laugh, but Winter does. "Come now, Evander, isn't it nice to be sought after? I won't bore our guests with the travails of your love life but suffice to say your reputation as a sourpuss is not as sexy as one would assume."

Evander simply meets Wren's delighted expression, and deadpans, "I'd say sightings of the Blackgate heirs are much fewer and farther between."

Heirs. Again. Used in a sentence by someone who just graduated high school. So formal. So weird. Maybe rich people *are* a different species.

"Well," Wren says, a sly twist to her lips, "if there are stories to be had about Evander Hegemony's love life travails, I can guarantee you'll be seeing much more of us."

Wren winks at Evander, her dark eye makeup shimmering in the floating glow of the lighting arrangement. This makes Winter laugh, Auden smirk, and Evander scoff.

No one, not even Evander, can deny it. They're an obvious set.

And just as I've determined that, their final piece arrives.

In that moment, the volume of the party bleeds into nothing

but prim footsteps as the matriarch of Hegemony Manor appears on the stone veranda above the garden, framed by a slate of massive windows ablaze in reflection of the setting sun.

Ursula Hegemony is straight-backed and prim, a tall woman, who, even if not stationed above the party, would have no trouble looking down her nose at everyone around her.

That much I'd expected. What I don't expect is her age. She should be a contemporary of Marsyas or Luna. But whether it's a trick of genetics, the distance, or, perhaps, her obvious fortune, Ursula Hegemony doesn't appear a day over forty.

"Welcome, welcome to Hegemony Manor, all of you." Ursula's graceful arms sweep wide and warm, even as she stands purposefully above and apart.

I realize this is her dinner party, but it *is* a dinner party, not a presidential address. Yet as I glance around, no one seems surprised, except for Wren, who mouths to me, *Revival of* Evita? She gestures like she might burst into "Don't Cry for Me, Argentina" before winking and returning her attention to the balcony.

Ursula continues in a strong, clear voice. "I have summoned you here as allies and friends, our most unusual and unbreakable family, for a night that is wholly ours."

I wait for Ursula to launch into a full speech, but instead our hostess simply gestures to the long, beautifully appointed table.

"Please be seated—we will feast and then tonight's business will begin."

I am extremely happy to take that as my cue to start moving and latch myself back onto Marsyas's arm as quickly as possible. Wren is more leisurely about doing the same, but she eventually pries herself away from Winter and Evander, who she clearly finds intriguing.

We've made it two steps in the direction of where the table is set under those gorgeous, glowing, floating chandeliers, when I feel Marsyas stiffen under my grasp. "Ursula, hello! You look as stunning as ever."

My gaze snaps up and there, indeed, is Ursula Hegemony.

I have no idea how she arrived so quickly, but she's only feet away now. This close, her eyes are as blue as tropical water and Ursula wields them with an intensity that confirms, without a shadow of a doubt, that she sees everything. I immediately regret prompting Wren's *Evita* reenactment.

Marsyas's grin stretches to the point where it might fall off her carefully powdered face and turns to us. "I'd like to reacquaint you with my granddaughters," Marsyas announces. "Lavinia, my oldest, and Kaysa, my youngest."

Wren offers a hand and a grin. "It's fantastic to see you again, Mrs. Hegemony."

Ursula's eyes flick to Wren's pink-polished nails and the swinging rabbit's foot, and she sweeps her own hands together, lacing her elegant fingers in a clear, stunning denial.

Wren, ever the actress, drops her proffered hand as if it had never been raised at all. Ursula's attention returns to Marsyas's face. "I see you've prepared them for tonight, Marsyas."

The old woman forces a chuckle at Ursula, even as her nails dig into my skin to the point where they'll definitely leave a mark. "I've only had my heirs back a day. Their skills are still quite raw."

"I do hope Athena is taking the heirs' grooming seriously, Marsyas," this woman says as if we're not standing right here. "With Marcos gone, they are the Blackgates' future."

Marsyas swallows so deeply her spiderweb earrings sway, and I swear her eyes mist at this mention of her son. Unlike when Sanguine referred to Marcos, I'm fairly certain this allusion was meant to hurt. When Marsyas answers, her words are carefully etched. "My Marcos's absence will forever be a chasm, Ursula."

"A feeling I know quite well."

Something passes between them. The losses of Ursula's own children, most likely, though there's an edge to that buried pain I can't read. "Fortunate we are to have the next generation." Ursula regards the two of us again and I would not be surprised if I glanced down and found my flesh burned straight through.

"We are so very happy to be here, Mrs. Hegemony," Wren pipes up. Clearly trying to prove she's perfectly pleasant and not bothered by the extremely precise, extremely coded small talk. "Your estate is lovely, and your grandchildren are so very welcoming."

Ursula eyes my sister. Then, she extends her own hand—not to Wren, but to Marsyas.

"Come, Marsyas, we have much to discuss."

I automatically take a step forward.

But Ursula's mouth quirks at the sight of my assumed inclusion. "Just your matriarch, Lavinia."

Marsyas drops our forearms and steps forward. Our hostess beckons to the party at large. "Auden? Evander? Please see to it that the Blackgate heirs are properly entertained at dinner."

Great, we're being assigned handlers.

As they arrive, Wren immediately latches onto Evander's elbow, pleased as punch at this turn of events. An opportunity to flirt at close range. She'll probably tease him about ghosts.

Meanwhile, Auden turns to me and offers his crooked arm—we apparently needed to add Regency-era actions to go with the Regency-era word choices. Then, he goes further, twisting his palm skyward so it's open for the taking.

My brain short-circuits because this whole thing is so bizarre and when I know I've spent too long deliberating, I reach for my terrible accent and a bit of humor. "Such a gentleman, and only moments after accusing me of being a scone-throwing maniac."

Auden smiles, but I have the distinct feeling it's not for me. Something he seems to confirm when he admits, "I'm sure you of all people will understand that when my grandmother tells me to do something, I oblige."

"That I do. I'm here because I wasn't in a position to say no—to coming to this dinner or to my grandmother's fashion choices."

I lift the wrist nearest to him in demonstrative presentation, the black rabbit's foot swinging morosely. It's possible that I've waved it too hard because on the upswing, the taxidermic animal appendage grazes the side of his offered bare hand.

Auden jerks away as if I've bit him.

"It's dead, Auden. It can't hurt you."

I attempt a smile. If he has an actual phobia, I've made things worse, and I have no idea how to remedy that.

But Auden simply tugs at his very expensive suit sleeves. "It comes with the territory. Part of what makes you a Blackgate."

I have no idea what he's getting at but I nod, because that seems like the right thing to do. But even that seems all wrong, and I have the suspicion that I'm trying so hard to be someone else that I've literally lost my grasp on how to be a normal human being. In an effort to reset, I turn away from Auden's extremely handsome face and make it a point to watch the others situate themselves at the long rectangular table. Ursula at the head, the adults filling in up at the top. The kids round out the rest.

Then, Auden surprises me and offers his arm again.

Because he's a gentleman and this is how gentlemen human, apparently.

"You know," I say, "I think I'm good to walk on my own. Very kind of you to offer. Very regal."

He pointedly slips both hands into his trouser pockets. "Suit yourself."

I have no idea if it's me, or if it's him, or the combination of the two of us, but there's a thorn buried somewhere beneath this Auden and Lavinia relationship. If I'm going to survive the next four hours, I need to steer this ship in an entirely new direction.

"Auden," I begin as we finally start strolling across the beautiful, star-shaped ceramic tiles of the garden, "I think we got off on the wrong foot. Can we give it another go?"

I hold out a hand to him, hoping that starting over at a proper handshake will do some symbolic heavy lifting to get us out of our apparent social death spiral. "I'm Lavinia, nice to meet you again."

Auden eyes my peace offering and for a small moment, my heart drops at the thought of him delivering the same clear admonishment his grandmother dealt Wren. I know Ursula Hegemony is watching us from her seat at the head of the table. And though she turned her nose up at us, Auden's own admission is that he must do what his grandmother says, and she instructed him to take care of me.

It's a small gamble. A tiny, little dare.

Auden sets his very nice mouth into a line, a decision made.

He reaches out and accepts my hand.

His fingers are warm and dry, and carefully still—a clasp rather than a shake, which keeps the offending bunny bauble from swinging his way a second time. His eyes lift to mine, narrowed slightly, as if they're trying desperately to read something that isn't there.

Because I'm not who he's looking for.

I breathe as shallowly as possible, trying to stave off my panic at the idea that—again—Auden Hegemony can see right through me.

But then his face breaks into that classically handsome smile.

"Auden, and likewise, Lavinia."

CHAPTER 5

AUDEN

This Lavinia Blackgate is not the one who lives in my memory.

That girl never would've smiled at me. Never would've admitted fault or started over. She certainly wouldn't have apologized or tried to make me laugh.

Too sanctimonious. Too snobbish. Too thorny.

Too much of a Blackgate.

Even ten years ago, at age seven, I knew exactly the type of woman she would become. Several bouts of our *animus* relationship made sure of that. Lavinia Blackgate was destined to be arrogant and beautiful enough to believe she was entitled to everything she desired, and when she inevitably didn't receive all she thought she was owed, she'd be propelled by vengeance at the smallest perceived slight.

And though the deaths of my father and hers had to have changed both of us in ways that we're still processing and might always process, I can say that even with the distance, even with the decade between, this Lavinia Blackgate is not at all what I expected.

"Um, what *do* you remember about me from the last time you saw me?" Lavinia asks. Her accent, word choice, even mannerisms are still very American despite her upbringing abroad. "What . . . ten years ago?"

That's a loaded question considering what happened on these grounds the last time she was here, and because I'm a nicer person than her younger self ever gave me credit for, I skip the worst and go for the most inane.

I point toward a swell of greenery at the very western edge of the manor's manicured garden, before it sprawls into more wild, natural vegetation. "The last time we were together, you found a dead skunk under that bush and wanted to resuscitate it."

Instead of a well-timed quip, Lavinia promptly trips over the lip of a star-shaped tile in her ridiculously high heels. She nearly falls into the approaching table but rights herself without my help—though perhaps taking my arm would've been advisable.

Still, gentleman that I am, I don't comment on Lavinia's regrettable choices as I pull out a seat for her. She thanks me, exasperation clear against her now-pink cheeks as she pins me with her sable-dark eyes. "You remember that, of all things?"

No, I think, *I was simply kind enough not to bring up the worst of it.* Lavinia blinks at me, the blush delicate as she watches me, waiting—earnest and honest enough, it seems, though this is yet another unexpected expression coming from the thundercloud of a girl I once knew.

As I smooth my suit jacket and drop into the chair beside her, I feel the familiar heat of Ursula's gaze on my profile. I meet Lavinia's parted lips and wide eyes with the polite smile my grandmother expects.

"It's seared into my temporal lobe." I tap my temple for good measure. "Very memorable to have nearly had a skunk séance in my backyard. Went horribly with my grandmother's choice of annuals that year."

Went horribly with what came after.

I watch the memory soak into Lavinia's mind, her full mouth quirking as if it isn't sure if a frown or a grin is the appropriate answer.

"Are we retelling the skunk story?" Hex barges into our conversation, brandishing a half-eaten brioche roll, steaming and glistening with butter, from where he's been relegated—the far end of the table. No doubt this is Winter's doing. "I love the skunk story."

"Oh, good," Lavinia mumbles, snatching her water glass and touching it to her lips. "I'm infamous."

"At Hegemony Manor, we're all infamous," Infinity assures Lavinia with a tip of their champagne, clinking Winter's glass.

Ada lifts her own flute. "As we should be."

"That skunk looked like roadkill. Bloody as hell," Hex ruminates after downing the remainder of his bubbly. "I swear someone planted it to see what one of us would do with it. A little test for the kiddie set."

"We're not retelling the skunk story," I announce tightly, Ursula's astute gaze now burning a hole in the side of my face. Beside me, Lavinia is having a wordless conversation with Kaysa across the table, all dinner-plate eyes and delicately furrowed brows.

"Why not? Reanimating a skunk? It's classic Blackgate."

"Because it's disgusting and we're about to eat, Hex," Winter snaps from her spot between Kaysa and Infinity. She reaches out to touch Lavinia's wrist. "No offense."

"None taken," Lavinia assures her. Yet another polite aside from someone who used to relish in any chance to take offense and be absolutely ghastly about it.

Just then, the waiters arrive in a white-suited mob. We lose several moments to the delivery of our soup course—a delicate watermelon gazpacho studded with fragrant sprigs of mint. Ursula's favorite.

When they've buzzed away, Winter leans into Kaysa, who, along with her sister, seems uneasy about the presence of non–High Family members. "Ursula takes care of the staff. You don't have to speak in code. It's fine."

"It's fine," Kaysa parrots, very interested in her soup, raising a questioning brow. "What's fine?"

"Seriously, you don't have to play," Winter assures her, fishing an unwelcome sprig of mint out of her soup with a swipe of her spoon. "We're here to discuss Four Lines business."

The Blackgates' discomfort is palpable. We don't know how careful they have to be, living abroad with the weight of their family's legacy across an ocean. It's probably not far enough, honestly.

Lavinia squints at Winter as if trying to read between the lines. "Okay. Sure. Thanks for reminding us about the staff."

The sisters pointedly dig into their soup when Evander leans back in his chair, eyeing them both. "I, for one," he begins, "think it would be quite useful to know how the American High Families are perceived over there."

Again, the Blackgates exchange a look.

"You don't have to talk about it," I assure them, though I'm not clear why I'm helping at all. "You didn't come all this way to gossip about our European counterparts."

Kaysa demurely dabs at her mouth with a corner of her cloth napkin, a lush green like the rest of the table treatment. "If there's one thing we've learned from the Brits, it's to have the utmost discretion."

"This is true," Lavinia adds, almost in a rush, a new blush creeping across the heights of her cheekbones. She clutches her water glass like a social life raft. "Mum doesn't want us being the big-mouthed Americans."

"A fact I'm sure our grandmother appreciates," I answer. Ursula is now deep in conversation with the other elders, but one should always assume she's paying attention. "Discretion is her favorite quality."

"Oh?" Kaysa asks, leaning in, brandishing her spoon with a grin. "Is that why your cousin here won't put me out of my misery and confirm that Hegemony Manor is haunted? Inquiring minds deserve to know."

"It's not haunted," Evander barks out gruffly.

"So you *claim*. But you can't deny the general sense of malaise hovering over the building." Kaysa waves a hand at the manor now, as if it's a painting and not a nearly 150-year-old mansion. She waggles her eyebrows into her bangs and addresses the table at large. "And we all know what malaise means: specters, grays, ghosts—"

"There aren't any ghosts," Evander insists, and I'm quite amused that he's entertaining this at all.

"I don't know, man, you've got to admit there's a whole Darth Vader vibe to the entire building," Hex interjects from the table end, the first roll devoured, a second palmed in his hand like an apple. I realize he's a football player but that doesn't excuse him from eating like a goddamn bear.

"Especially as you approach on the highway," Infinity adds. "Objectively. As a visitor. There is a certain Blackgate vibe to it."

At the mention of her name, Lavinia wets her lips, looks her sister right in the eye, and announces, "My understanding is that there's a ghost in the foyer named Imelda."

"That's not even remotely true," Evander replies, punctuating the irritation in his tone by dipping his spoon decisively into his gazpacho.

I catch Lavinia's eye. Maybe this version of her likes ribbing Evander as much as I do—as much as Kaysa apparently does. Both sisters have a playfulness that ironically was not present when they were actual children.

"Come to think of it, didn't we have that maid named Imelda several years back?" I straighten, as if a memory is flooding in. "With the hair and the smile? Always wore perfume like peonies, before she fell down the stairs while carrying a teetering stack of your meticulously folded boxer briefs?"

Evander rolls his eyes and grunts out, "No."

I rub my jaw. "It's probably in your own self-interest to forget the woman who died under a pile of your underwear, though pretty inconsiderate, if I do say so myself."

"Shut up, Auden."

"I'm just answering our guest's question," I insist innocently. Then, I lean in such a way that I collect both Blackgate girls in my purview. "While I've never seen a ghost in Hegemony Manor, I must admit that every time I've been away and return, the foyer does greet me with a floral scent that is distinctly peony-esque."

"I *knew* it," Kaysa exclaims, and though he's trying very hard to have all the personality of a secret service agent, there's a softness at the corners of Evander's mouth that tells me he's actually maybe sort of enjoying this. Kaysa was happy to live in Lavinia's skunk-reanimating shadow when we knew them ages ago, but now she seems to be the sister who prefers the spotlight. She taps Evander again with her elbow. "I demand a ghost tour after dinner. I want to meet every single one, starting with Imelda."

"Are you serious—"

Evander is cut off by the elegant rise of Ursula at the head of the table.

The rest of the party goes silent as well—conversations stop mid-syllable, soup consumption mid-sip.

My pulse spikes because this isn't the normal rhythm of our annual meeting.

Ursula's speech happens after dessert.

Is this part of her plan?

It must be.

I know it, Evander knows it, Winter too. If the others suspect something, they don't show it. Just as with everything Ursula Hegemony does, we follow along. That's the way it's always been and the way it always will be until Evander inherits control of the Hegemony family titles and the corresponding influence.

Ursula looms over us with her usual aristocratic benevolence, smile drawn tight, as she addresses every turn of the head, steady gaze, bated breath. Even the ley line beneath our feet seems to halt, its power frozen in proximity to Ursula in High Sorcerer mode.

My heart kicks up a drumbeat in my chest.

"My friends," Ursula begins, "we have yet to enjoy the main course but I'm afraid we must move swiftly to the business of tonight."

Someone is staring at me, and I don't have to check to confirm it to be Evander. While I watch my grandmother from my spot toward the center of the long table, I note a flash of crystal in my periphery. Winter, taking a steadying sip of champagne. At my side, Lavinia is still, as she soaks up the formal opening to the business of the Four Lines.

"I started this evening by calling you my unusual and unbreakable family," Ursula intones in her clear, unwavering voice. "We are exactly that, even as we are tested. Even as the world grows more unforgiving to us. It is not the worst we have ever faced across the centuries, it is simply new, and change is always a threat."

That's an understatement. It's been that way since Salem and only worsens with every passing year.

"Change is always a threat," Ursula repeats. Strange, and throaty, as if she's buying time, forgetting what to say next.

She starts again. "Change . . ."

The word dies on her lips.

As if a puppeteer has yanked all the strings, Ursula's head snaps up as the rest of her sags. Her mouth is a gaping, silent vacuum, wide to the night. The muscles in my legs constrict, I'm ready to spring out of my seat, to run to her, to steady her, to—

She falls.

Slamming first to the solid wood slab of the tabletop, then all the way down to the stone tiles, grass, and the ley line buried deep beneath. The magic thrumming in the earth below us can do so much but it can't do a damn thing in this one terrible moment.

Above, the chandeliers flicker. Every light in the house too. The mountain wind kicks up, the sounds of the night flooding in for one eerie moment until the winking lights snuff out completely. The three chandeliers crash to the table, shards of shattered porcelain and crystal flying through air filled with gasps of surprise and shrieks as Ursula's magic fails.

Then I'm up—muscles firing finally—and diving to her crumpled form. Winter and Evander too, but I get there first.

I scoop my grandmother's head into my arms. Her eyes are gone and glassy. Lips gagged open. I bend my ear, listening for breath I know isn't there.

No sight. No breath. No mistake.

Ursula Hegemony is dead.

CHAPTER 6

RUBY

Condensation sweats from my cold glass to my trembling hand, and a blast of pain radiates up my arm. I'd shot to my feet when the light fixtures fell, knocking over my chair, and leaping away from the table.

In a blink it's no longer pitch black—the flickering chandeliers lie on the table, beached on their sides like burning whales in a sea of spilled pink soup, crushed tableware between them. It's dimmer than before, the floating lights that'd lit the rest of the garden still out, the house an obsidian void, absorbing the weak illumination like a black hole.

Swallowing, I can see now what I felt before—shards of fractured porcelain embedded in the meat of my arm, pinpricks of blood surfacing like beads of sweat between globs of pink gazpacho.

Bile burns the back of my throat as I catch sight of a slick of red on the corner of the table and seeping out from beneath Ursula's fall of dark hair. The wind kicks up, carrying the scent of pine, mingling perfumes, and the coppery tang of blood.

Plunking down my ice water with unsteady hands, I scramble for my purse, furiously digging for my cell phone. I get a grip on the phone and yank it out so forcefully I nearly drop it. The screen comes alive. Still no bars of service. No Wi-Fi. No emergency call button.

"Does anyone have a signal?" I have no idea the volume of my request. My tone feels both meek and frantic, panic billowing out of me like a mushroom cloud as it rises above the garden. If I remember my accent, I don't hear it. "Anyone?"

No one answers me. Everyone is staring at the knot of Hegemonys. Sanguine whispers something to Hector, but no one else is saying or doing anything.

I pivot toward Marsyas, ready to run for the car—if we can't call an ambulance, we can drive Ursula to the hospital. *I* can drive Ursula to the hospital. I know Marsyas has the keys. I saw her slip them into her bag.

But Marsyas isn't there.

I find Wren across the table, and she's frozen on her feet, just like everyone else. Then the stunned silence breaks with another sound. A mournful wail.

Winter crying.

Balanced on her teetering heels, she's sunk into a squat, her shiny floral dress tight against her calves—she's clutching her grand-mother's hand. They've got her prone now, Auden cradling Ursula's head in his lap. Beside Auden and opposite Winter, Evander has removed his jacket and is rolling up his sleeves. Workman-like, he applies two vigorous pumps to his grandmother's sternum, before bending to blow air into her lungs.

Ursula's chest doesn't expand. My heart lurches. As Evander goes in for the next set of compressions, Winter reaches over and roughly shoves him backward. Evander is basically as muscled as a Greek god, but her fury and his surprise tips him back on the heels of his dress shoes. "That won't work!"

I want to argue with Winter. I'm on Evander's side—this isn't over. It isn't too late. Ursula fainted. Hit her head. We can get her breathing again; we can get her to a hospital. Hook her up to every machine available and bring their grandmother back to life.

"Evander, no! Let me do it! It's my choice!"

Winter's voice is shattered and pleading. I see now that she's trying to get both hands on her grandmother's body. Evander is pulling her away—maybe they've switched positions on life-saving measures? But Auden has a forearm up too, physically blocking his cousin's desperate reach.

Evander yanks Winter to her feet and away from the body, hold-ing her tightly by the shoulders. "Win, I won't let you pay that price. Not—"

Across the table, a waiter pitches over into Marsyas's empty seat with a sick thud and shattering clatter of the second course he'd been balancing on a tray. Remnants of arugula salad litter the lawn around him as he stares up, limp and glassy-eyed.

In the distance, more bodies fall—another waiter, the bartender, the security guard. All around, people drop—*thud, thud, thud*. Not a scream or complaint. Just the muted sound of bones and flesh hitting the grass or stone.

Suddenly a massive *clang* reverberates off the sleeping mountains.

The iron gates. Slamming shut.

Then, another collective gasp, soft and sharp.

A wisp of something like smoke *rises* from Ursula's still form.

The Hegemony cousins watch—Auden tense as he cradles his grandmother, Winter batting at her mascara-bleeding eyes, lips trembling, in Evander's firm grip. Yet none of them wear an ounce of surprise.

The plume of smoke shifts and swirls, until it forms a ghostly rendition of Ursula. The likeness hovers high above our heads, easily visible to everyone.

It's . . . like nothing I've ever seen.

The apparition's mouth opens, and Ursula's voice fills the night, as clear and strong as just minutes before, when she was upright, powerful, and missing exactly nothing with those blue eyes.

"I, Ursula Elvire Muscatel Hegemony, High Sorcerer of the Four Lines, commit that this is my soul's truth, for any and all living creatures to witness."

Gooseflesh erupts on my forearms, peaked with specks of blood.

"My truth is this: I have been murdered."

Something cold drops in my gut.

She—it, the voice—sounds so real. My brain tells me this is some sort of effect, maybe a type of audio/visual combination. But there's no tinny feedback from hidden speakers, or misdirected sound. It's from her. Clear as a bell and loud as before.

"The staff have been bodily quarantined. The Hegemony Manor Estate is locked down."

I shoot a glance at that waiter, his white suit jacket stark on grass that seems less lush than before, suddenly brittle, sapped and faded under his weight.

"To the ears left hearing my truth, know this now: to leave the estate, you must complete my final requests set out for you within my last will and testament."

The image pauses, its vibrant eyes seeming to take in our reaction as if it can truly see all of us staring back at it. Somehow satisfied, it continues, every word measured.

"If these requests are not completed by midnight on the third day, you will be locked upon the grounds of Hegemony Manor forever."

My fingers begin to tremble. I try to stamp my numb feet, to will my flesh and blood still.

Nothing works.

Then right there in Auden's lap, the body *shrivels*.

Ursula's refined features suddenly wrinkle and spot, her lovely raven tresses graying and thinning to nearly nothing at all. She ages in rapid time—thirty, forty, fifty years added on to her corpse in a matter of moments—until she's more of a husk than a human.

I blink once. Twice. Again.

The body is still there, skin and bones, as if every ounce of fluid fled with her life, her beauty, her soul.

It looks like magic.

It has to be a trick.

"I haven't seen an honest-to-Merlin soul's truth in twenty years," Luna announces as if she's just spotted a bald eagle in the trees. Then the old woman waves a hand at the Hegemony cousins. "Best move, children, the earth's about to claim what's left of her. Preservation is necessary when murder is involved—the soul will seal her up to avoid tampering."

Auden, Winter, and Evander silently exchange looks, and, strangely, more than one set of eyes falls to me. To Wren.

What do they think we'll do?

A low rumble rises in the air. First just a warning, then the lawn beneath our feet begins to tremble worse than my panicking body. The smashed porcelain on the tabletop clatters, bubbly sloshes against crystal.

The sound sends the Hegemonys scattering, Ursula's shriveled corpse in the limp embrace of newly dry grass blades as Winter's shoulders heave into another sob. Auden attempts to tuck her under his wing, but she slinks away on unsteady feet, preferring to wind her own limbs about her quivering frame in comfort. Evander withdraws and then thinks better of it, leaning down and removing something from Ursula's hand before backing away for a second time.

The earthly trembling becomes an all-out shake as a seam forms from Ursula's well-appointed heels to the cottony ends of what's left of her hair. Her body slumps inward, as if the seam will rupture into a true, gaping crack and devour her corpse in one earth-rattling gulp.

Instead, the opposite happens.

Flecks of soil as fine as sand rise from between the weak blades of grass, shimmering darkly in the golden glow of the downed chandeliers. They swarm together like starlings, dancing and swirling above Ursula's body.

Like the "soul's truth," it's completely magical in effect. I've never seen anything like it. There's no sound, but if it's a projection, there's no visible source creating it. It really does appear to be bits of dirt, balletic in the bite of a rapidly cooling night.

Then, with one sweeping, coordinated movement, the grains dive toward the body. They knit together, as tight as drying cement, about an inch above Ursula's form. In a matter of two breaths, and nothing more, the collected earth particles have encased the corpse in a protective shell, not unlike the volcanic ash forever swaddling the bodies at Pompeii.

Ursula was there. Now she's not. And yet she is.

This isn't an illusion. If I walked up, I could run my fingers along the earthen surface that curves around the newly skeletal lines of her body. The covering is as solid and smooth as molded plastic.

"It's true then. She was murdered," Evander says, almost as an aside, staring at the encased corpse as if it's proof. Maybe it is.

"Of course she was," Luna replies with a mixture of sage wisdom and pure annoyance. "Souls tell the truth whether anyone is around to hear them or not. Even if we'd all been sleeping off our champagne when she went down, the victim's shroud confirms foul play. And her last will and testament will prove it."

It's an explanation but I'm even more confused.

Luna juts a birdlike arm out to her grandchild, who's still at the other end of the table. "Infinity, help me up, we best get reading that will. My bones have other plans for eternity than rotting in a guest room at Hegemony Manor."

CHAPTER 7

RUBY

Eternity.

Somehow, I've gone from frustrated by inaction and jittery with panic to completely numb. All sound has dulled, the scent of earth and blood muted, the returned mountain wind nothing on my skin or in my ears.

I must be moving because Wren and I come together at the base of the wide, ornately beautiful stairs that lead up from the garden to the balcony terrace—the place where I first saw Ursula, welcoming us to her home, only an hour before her last breath. Some light has returned to the house, the wide, glass-banked room off the terrace glowing with warmth.

Wren's fingers threading within mine grounds me.

"You're bleeding," she says, dabbing at my arm with a cloth napkin, the white fabric already dotted with her own blood. I am. My porcelain-nicked skin is weeping in thin tracks of crimson between the running pink of watermelon gazpacho.

Infinity has guided Luna all the way to the top of the stairs, the Cerises nipping at their heels behind. Evander is a stoic sentry watching everyone pass with a critical eye. Like it's his job. And maybe it is.

Someone was murdered here tonight. The Hegemonys will need answers.

That's when it hits me.

All of us are suspects . . . but *we're* the only imposters.

That icy numbness cracks and shatters. Suddenly I feel the burn of the climb in my tottering heels, the warmth of Wren's grip, and the tickle of her breath in my ear. "Too much to hope we're at a murder mystery party?"

If only—Hegemony Manor is certainly the perfect place for one.

But that death was real. As was every strange moment that came after it.

"Yes, too much." We're nearly to the top of the stairs, and everyone, not just Evander, is watching us ascend. I concentrate on my feet. "Act normal."

When we land upon the veranda, Wren immediately captures and cradles the eldest Hegemony's wrist, her true, tender heart immediately on display. "Oh, Evander, I can't believe this is happening. I'm so very sorry about your grandmother."

Evander stiffens under her touch—no one has consoled him. No one has consoled any of the Hegemonys, in fact, save for Infinity squeezing Winter's elbow while passing by where she and Auden hold court on either side of the main entrance to the house. "Yes, we're very sorry for your loss."

When Evander answers us, it's with a curt nod and a direct question.

"Where's your grandmother?"

Oh. God. That's why everyone is staring at us. Marsyas is unaccounted for—which is immediately suspicious. Which means we are too, without them even knowing the rest.

"I—I, uh," I fumble, accent on sideways.

"She bolted for the loo," Wren answers with a little shrug. *Genius.*

"Where *is* the loo?" I ask Evander, and it takes everything I have to keep my words level over the rising drumbeat of my heart. "I think we should perhaps check on her—and clean ourselves up."

I hold up the bloodstained napkin apologetically. Wren shifts her wounded shoulder into the light streaming from the endless bank of windows before us. How we seem to have been the only ones hit by flying shards of ruined dinnerware, I don't know.

"You're bleeding?" Hex asks, stepping away from where his family is clustered and whispering near the doors, oddly concerned for how contrary he's been with us.

"Don't touch them," Evander snaps, wheeling on the other boy, and sliding his broad frame firmly between Hex and us.

The twin immediately halts and holds up both hands. "I'm just trying to help, man."

"You are not," Evander spits.

Hex rolls his eyes but retreats. Evander waits for the other boy to join his family, who are being led into the house by Auden and Winter, the Starwoods already inside, before turning his attention back to us. When he does, his mossy-green eyes are as fierce as the cut of his jaw and slice of his words. "I know you've been away but don't let him—or anyone in his family—ever touch your blood."

My heart skips.

"Understood," I confirm, almost mechanically. Even though I don't understand at all. The Cerises own some sort of medical conglomerate, per Marsyas's file, but they clearly aren't doctors or they surely would've come to Ursula's aid—I think.

But nothing is making sense at the moment.

There's a ringing in my ears and I try to focus. We need a second alone. I need to try again.

"The loo?" I prompt, this time glancing past Evander to search what I can see of the ornate room he's mostly blocking from me with his brawler's body.

A muscle ticks in his square jaw. "It's through the solarium, down the hall, to the right. I'll escort you."

"That's very polite, but not necessary," I tell him, both because he has a myriad of more important things to worry about than us finding our way to the nearest bathroom in this massive estate, and because Wren and I really need to talk.

"I'm not being polite. I don't want three Blackgates missing."

That . . . is not a jab at us—that's an outright bludgeon. I offer a stiff smile and follow him over the threshold from the stone terrace into the house we've wondered about since we were little girls.

It's everything I can do to put one foot in front of the other, but Wren, she can't help it—she's soaking in the sight before her despite the circumstances.

"It's exactly how I thought it would be," she whispers, "right smack between Wednesday Addams all grown up and Edgar Allan OH, NO."

Wren isn't wrong.

Replica gas lamps ring the room, cozying up to wallpaper lush enough to upholster a chaise lounge. The furniture is exquisitely polished and on par, as we weave through an almost endless maze of antique pieces. I'd gawk if I wasn't scared shitless.

After a quick check of the progress of others, bottlenecked at a threshold along the room's opposite wall, Evander gestures toward a door. "I'll wait outside."

Nodding, I haul my sister through the door and close it with a quick, and hopefully not suspicious, wave to Evander. Luckily, there's a lock on our side, and I turn it as silently as possible before surveying the space. The washroom has a large parlor with red velvet fainting couches, more ornate wallpaper, and a chandelier that looks to be actually attached to the etched, paneled ceiling. The "loo" is bigger than my bedroom.

"What the fuck, what the fuck, what the fuck?" Wren whispers on agonized repeat as I detach myself and bang around, checking for any sign of Marsyas.

I fail. "No Nona."

"No shit. She did it and ditched us," Wren answers from the glistening antique porcelain sink, where she's wiping drying blood from her arm. She shakes her head and launches into a low rant, aimed at the running water. "I really, really believed it was a murder mystery party and Marsyas was in on it—classic red herring for her to go missing and then turn up as victim number two. But then Ursula's soul gave us literal orders before the earth breaded her body like a chicken tender. That was magic, wasn't it? It had to be."

Her eyes flash to mine in the mirror and I nod.

I can't say it—*magic*.

Magic is the only explanation and yet, that word and what it means has lodged in my windpipe as if it's too much of a reach.

Nothing computes. Well, other than that this situation is *all wrong* and the dead body is only a small factor in that equation.

"And no one batted an eye. What the fuck are we supposed to do with any of that?" Wren continues, whirling around. She thrusts a hand out in frustration. "I'm about to pass out on that fainting couch right there."

"Definitely don't do that. We already look guilty enough."

"That's what it's for."

"Not when we're suspects."

On furious, uneven steps, my sister crosses the room, lower lip wobbling. She sweeps both hands into mine and her whisper drops until she's nearly mouthing the words. "We shouldn't be suspects at all. We're not actually related to Marsyas."

"Yes, because *we're imposters,* which makes us look like bigger suspects, not lesser ones."

Wren's hazel eyes bore into mine, striking under the curtain of her dark bangs and the smoky sheen of her makeup. "Then we vanish too. We run. That's what you wanted to do before we walked into whatever the cursed hell this is. Let's do it. Let's go."

She's suddenly craning her neck, searching for an escape route that's not there. No alternate door, no window, no fireplace flue. Dropping my hands, Wren strides forward, eyeing a vent above the coffee table. "Watching all those action movies with Dad is about to pay off. I just hope the Hegemonys clean their air ducts. Give me a boost."

"I—"

"Are you all right in there?" Evander pounds hard enough to rattle the lock.

Shit.

"Yes! Just a minute!" Wren calls sweetly. Then, to me, she whispers, all shiny eyes and trembling lips, "We're *so* screwed."

I place my hands on her shoulders and lean into her ear. "This is what we're going to do. We're going to go back out there, and when the opportunity presents itself, we run. No hesitation, we just do it. You and me. If Marsyas suddenly reappears, she's on her own. Got it?"

Just as I did when we arrived, I tug on Wren's hand. Pinky to pinky.

She nods, watching our fingers twine together. Then, she pastes her Blackgate smile straight back on, and paws the fresh tears away from her eyes. When she answers, it's in her accent, prim, proper, and lip-curling.

"You and I just spent six weeks doing festival falafel improv, we know how to exit a scene." She sniffs and draws her shoulders back. "And how to enter one."

I tug at her hand.

"Flirty but respectful," I remind her in a whisper because we both know over-the-top is her comfort zone. "We feel sorry for him—"

"I do."

"You do. And you're worried for Marsyas—"

"I am."

"You are. You can do this, Kaysa."

Wren nods. I breathe a thin sigh of relief. Together we unlock the door.

Evander is waiting for us, propped against the wall, just as he was before—and I'm relieved he wasn't leaning in, eavesdropping. Wren greets him with a worried smile. "Nona isn't in there, I'm afraid. Is another washroom nearby? Somewhere else she would've gone?"

His handsome features are as taut as a bowstring. As if he surfaces the feelings underneath, he'll snap.

"There are sixteen bathrooms in this residence, and we have a will reading to attend. While I would prefer all parties be present for the reading, we must be going. We'll search in more detail for your grandmother after our conference in Ursula's study." Then with the politeness of a request but the urgency of an order: "Please, they're waiting."

"Yes, of course," Wren replies. "Lead the way."

I squeeze my sister's hand as we follow Evander into the mysterious halls of Hegemony Manor.

Chapter 8

AUDEN

The finality of it all roars in my ears.

My grandmother is dead. The High Sorcerer of the Four Lines, the woman at the heart of our brand of modern magic in North America, is dead.

Murdered.

That word sticks in the storm roiling through my brain. My vision is glassy with a scene I can't shake: Ursula's mottled face, skin taut and thin as a crepe. No spark in her eyes. No breath in her lungs. Her power fled—gone back to the night, the earth, the ley lines spidering beneath.

The great Ursula Hegemony suddenly just a weight in my arms.

I feel as if I might be sick.

We're in Ursula's third-floor study, my vision spinning. I grip the ornately carved lip of the desk. Winter is right there beside me, sniffling and shaking in a way she can't lessen despite the fact her arms are wrapped around her body as tight as they will go. The slamming of the double doors snaps me to my senses. I let go of the desk and straighten, my expression immediately impassive—the picture-perfect Hegemony.

Evander leads the Blackgate girls into the room from the now-sealed entrance. He lights the hearth with a fingertip as he directs the sisters toward the bookshelves, where they take up residence behind the high back of the reading chair Ursula loved more than any jewel in her extensive collection. The sisters gape at the study, blinking at the final trappings of Ursula—the newly wilting plants upon the massive desk, the quilt draped over the back of the chair at their elbows, the towering collection of magical tomes glittering with gold-leaf spines—the ghost tour they'd joked about coming to fruition in the worst way possible.

This room is Ursula's spirit more than any other.

The other High Families are already arranged, spread apart in clusters and facing the desk. The Cerises by the fire. The Starwoods toward the center—Luna settled in one of the two guest chairs. It would be proper for the other elder present to claim the remaining one, but Marsyas Blackgate is not in this room.

Evander sweeps toward the front of the study, charging in to direct us, like he did in the garden.

He's the oathed Hegemony heir. It's what he's supposed to do.

But Evander isn't the only one with a role.

I clamp a hand on my cousin's very solid shoulder as he rounds the corner of the desk, swiftly cataloging the cabinets and drawers for where to start searching for Ursula's final directive. "I know where it is."

My voice is purposefully low as I produce a small key on a whisper-thin chain from beneath the open button of my lavender shirt.

A muscle in Evander's jaw twitches as Winter closes the gap between us until we form a tight triangle behind the desk, every eye upon us. "You have a key?"

Every High Family has their own way of marking their chosen heir. In the Hegemony Clan, oathed heirs get keys. Evander has had his on the same type of chain since he was sixteen and Ursula made it official. But what he forgets is that though our parents died, the tradition of familial roles didn't. There is more to a family than an heir.

"I have a key because I'm the executor of Ursula's estate."

His broad back to the High Family members, Evander looks as if I've actually landed a punch. Winter's whole trembling posture stiffens, rigid enough it might shatter.

Our guests don't comment, though they can surely hear what I said. The exchange of interested glances from all three lines is enough.

This is the price for keeping secrets from each other—weakness before those who matter most.

But this secret was kept at Ursula's request. I had to lock it away.

I pull the chain over my head and insert the key into one of the many drawers within Ursula's desk. She had no need for hidden compartments or even magical protection—fear and power were enough to keep the three of us out of her things, and no one else, not even the staff, had access to this room.

The tumblers turn easily, the drawer opens without a hitch, and there, without any finery or fanfare, is the single page that is the last will and testament of Ursula Hegemony.

Evander looms over my shoulder, peering down at the contents.

A lone line, written in enchanted ink, glittering upon the page: Ursula's looping signature.

Beneath it are two thumbprints, stamped in blood. One, long and elegant, the other calloused from too much time spent with a lacrosse stick.

I stare at the mark I made more than six months ago now and my chest tightens. The goal for this meeting is the same as before. As always. Exactly as I reminded my cousins as our guests arrived.

Convey what's important.

Reaffirm Hegemony power.

Scatter to the winds for another three hundred and sixty-five days.

I hold up the will for High Family inspection. Most everyone accepts it as exactly as expected, though Hector decides to lean in as if his personal scrutiny is necessary.

"Would you like to get a better look?" I ask, mildly perturbed but not surprised.

The Cerise patriarch straightens and smooths a hand over the front of his perfectly shellacked hair. It doesn't move. "No, no. It seems legitimate."

As if I could fake what is about to come next.

I set the will back flat on the desk, right in the center, where no one's view will be blocked by Ursula's plants. The oil task lamp steadily illuminates the page's contents as I place my right palm on it, my thumb aligned to match with the print I left in Ursula's blood when she told me of my role and presented me with the key.

A warmth seeps into my hand and the letters of Ursula's name shimmer. Then, with a glint of jade light and yawning motion, the letters begin slithering like a single snake untangling to reveal it was a nest of asps all along. The mass writhes and wriggles until what was once Ursula's signature unravels into lines of text upon the page.

Hundreds of words, maybe, all in the same handwriting as before but in a much smaller scrawl. Her signature has reappeared at the bottom, my much less ornate one below it, as executor.

I remove my hand, and, for the second time tonight, Ursula's voice floods into our ears—from the grave, from the recent past.

"I, Ursula Elvire Muscatel Hegemony, High Sorcerer of the Four Lines, have produced this last will and testament while of sound mind, body, and magic."

The announcement booms around us, as if the sound waves feed off the fire-warmed air, our awed bodies, the vaulted ceiling of her favorite room in the mansion that had been her lifelong home.

The roaring in my ears subsides to an eerie calm encasing nothing but her words. A chill spreads up my neck. I notice now that this room smells of her, like the mountain wind and new rain. Soil, and verdant life, and the leather and paper of her beloved books.

I close my eyes and focus on the sound.

The words. Her instructions. The last time I will hear her voice.

"In accordance with tradition and magical law, more than one iteration of this last will and testament was written in my hand. Per the particulars of this document's spell, the executor of my estate, Auden Emerson Hughes Hegemony, will verbally confirm my cause of death as one of the following: natural, accidental, or foul play resulting in murder."

That word again.

Murder.

As painful as the first time. Perhaps worse. The horror of it grows at the drop-dead period in her pause, building to a chasm over our heads. The crushing weight of it seems to lead the assembled crowd forward, bending them toward the desk like a thread of gravitational pull has split from the earth and is contained in this single sheet of paper.

I swallow. "I confirm the cause of death as foul play resulting in murder."

The page shimmers yet again and the words grow sharper with this confirmation, each sweep and slash crisping up into focus.

"In the case of my murder, this last will and testament must be read before High Family representatives of each line. If all representatives are present, Auden Emerson Hughes Hegemony will verbally confirm their attendance."

As I draw in a breath to answer, Evander's fingers brush my elbow. I know his concern—Marsyas's absence. But it's not incorrect to state that the Blackgates have a representative. They have two, even if they're both underage.

"I confirm that High Family representatives from all four lines are in attendance. Evander Hegemony of the Elemental Line; Hector Cerise of the Blood Line; Luna Starwood of the Celestial Line; Lavinia Blackgate of the Death Line."

In my periphery, I note the Blackgates exchanging horrified glances. Lavinia is the oldest and therefore the de facto leader of the Death Line, even if she's not yet oathed as an heir. She should know this.

"With this confirmation, I require each High Family representative to stamp this page with a thumbprint in their blood to seal the magic to each of the Four Lines."

I return to the drawer that held the will and retrieve four quills, each sharpened to a razor's edge at the tip. "Representatives, please come forward and add your print to the bottom of the page."

Hector approaches first, eager as always to adhere to Ursula's instructions, even in death. He's pricked his thumb and added his print before Luna has even stood up from her chair. He skids out of the way, leaving room for the Starwood matriarch to add her thumbprint with Infinity's support.

"Can't believe I'm the one doing this for you, Ursa," Luna mutters with a sigh that wracks her entire body as she jabs her thumb as hard as she can next to Hector's print. "Should've been the other way around, you insufferable battle-ax."

A tear falls in a rolling track down Luna's weathered ebony cheek. With a sniff, she ignores it and turns away.

Lavinia hesitates as Infinity guides Luna back to her chair.

"Go ahead," Evander instructs. "It's tradition for a family member to be last."

More timid than I'd expect, Lavinia swallows hard before finally stepping forward to the desk and the will, spun around to face her instead of me. She stares down at the paper, clean save for the lines of magic inked and four thumbprints.

"Are you sure I should be doing this?" she asks me, quietly. "Nona—"

"Nona isn't here. The magic requires a signature. Oathed heir or not, it's expecting yours."

Lavinia's dark eyes widen at my tone, which is perhaps a bit harsh. But I won't snuff out the spark of anger in my belly at this break in expected protocol. I'm the one trying to survive going through the motions, the least she could do is respect them.

Point taken, Lavinia grabs the third quill, stabs her right thumb, and presses the pad next to Luna's print. She returns to her sister without another word.

Evander spins the will toward where the three of us stand in a line behind the desk. With a decisive jab, he pricks his thumb and punches it to the bottom of the page. The moment the blood seeps into paper, the warmth of the magical seal flashes through my own veins.

There's a flurry of movement as everyone in this room accepts the spell that binds us to the remainder of this last will and testament. The Starwoods hold hands, the Cerises stand at attention, the Blackgates watch each other, cheeks pale and mouths pulled taut. Winter's fingers flex beside mine, and Evander closes his eyes in tight acceptance.

When it's through, I place my hand again to the will, and Ursula's final testament plays on, magically satisfied.

"In the event of foul play in my demise," Ursula announces with the same cold precision she'd use to adjust Chef Maggie's weekly grocery list to match the season, "the contents of my last will and testament have been altered to suit the situation at hand."

A new ripple runs through the looping scroll of enchanted ink. What had been sharpened in the previous pass is darkened further, now a rich black.

We all know what's coming next. The confirmation of a penalty that predates Salem.

"The first request of my last will and testament is in accordance with Four Lines magical law. Within three days' time, you must investigate my murder and punish the responsible party. For clarification of this deadline, this spell recognizes the day of my murder as day one, ending at midnight."

The clock on the mantel has just struck nine. That gives us fifty-one hours to investigate Ursula's murder, try, and punish the witch responsible.

There's a shifting in the assembled crowd as the eleven of us remaining accept this.

The Cerises speak in low tones. Infinity adopts Luna's resigned expression. The Blackgates are bent together, wordlessly running through an entire fretful conversation built on facial expressions, hands twined yet again.

My cousins react too. Winter with a wheezing inhale, and Evander with a roll of his shoulders, one hand firmly clasping the opposing wrist in front of his body—a stance meant to be intimidating. I know Evander has likely been mentally planning the investigation since reality set in, expecting to oversee it all. That's futile too. For all the forced politeness between the families, with what's on the line, no one will let him do so without a reminder that *he* is a suspect too.

Ursula begins again. "My second request concerns the successor of my title as High Sorcerer of the Four Lines."

Evander straightens next to me, like a would-be knight waiting for the tap on the shoulder from the king's sword that makes his ascension real. "In the event of foul play in my demise," Ursula repeats, "the details of succession have changed per magical law. The Hegemony Clan and the Elemental Line forfeit the transfer of the title of High Sorcerer to an immediate family member. The Hegemony Clan cedes automatic control of the Four Lines and the power therewith to the ultimate holder of the four master relics."

All air leaves the room.

For one thick, unwieldy moment, there's nothing. Then reality floods in, Evander's voice the first coherent sound.

"That can't be right."

Evander's delivery is stiff, his whole powerful body deflating as he tries to force the words into the utter silence that's fallen in Ursula's study.

The master relics—commonly called "the masters"—are exactly what made Ursula Hegemony the most powerful witch in North America and one of the most powerful witches in the world.

What will make someone in this room one of the most powerful witches in the world.

They're the keys to the Four Lines, funneling and amplifying our magic into the type of power that secretly keeps the world running, and keeps the Four Lines rich enough to buy, break, and bully anyone or anything who would expose our secrets.

"These relics have been installed on the Hegemony Manor estate since the rule of High Sorcerer Shadrack Zebulon Gradefon Hegemony."

That means they've been in place for a hundred years at least. Perhaps more. The land was purchased by Shadrack in 1881 and added onto summarily since then until it totaled the ten thousand acres that it is at this very moment. The house was built over the next decade and then renovated time and again. Though, the master relics have been in our family much, much longer.

The consolidation of the masters and control of the lines have been under Hegemony aegis since Mercy Abigail Hegemony—neé

Hedgewidge—saved the Four Lines from both the witch hysteria of the 1690s and the power-hungry designs of Napoleon Demont Cerise, who tried and failed to destroy all types of witches but his own.

The masters are crucial to the Four Lines of magic, yet they're a mystery to which only the High Sorcerer is privy. I've never seen a master—no one here has. I don't know what they are or where they are. I only know that by holding all four we can feed each line from a central location and enforce the protections that have kept our magic—and our witches—safe.

Evander gathers himself, his feeble protest giving way to something with breath and anger and logic behind it. He's still arguing like she hasn't spoken. "There's no magical law that changes an inheritance in the event of foul play. If that were the case—"

He's cut off by Ursula's voice, continuing.

"Clues as to the master relics' locations and forms will be provided subsequently one at a time. The first clue will appear at the conclusion of this reading on this very same paper. Once the relics are gathered, the holder of the four will earn the ring signifying the title of High Sorcerer concerning the Four Lines until the event of their death. All families will retain control and representation of their individual lines of magic no matter who assumes the title of High Sorcerer."

That means Evander's inheritance as Hegemony patriarch and the head of the Elemental Line hasn't changed. Only his chance to control all Four Lines is affected.

After a pause, the paper beneath my hand shifts again.

"I am sure every family and every person present will have their own opinions about the passage of this title. I would implore this extraordinary group to avoid allowing your personal ambitions to negate the nearly four centuries of cooperation our families have in the enduring and sacred tradition of magic. Find my murderer. Find the relics. You have three days."

CHAPTER 9

AUDEN

There's a definitive point to the end of the sentence, a stern jab of a finger to the sternum, the desk, a waiting open palm.

The study is again deathly still. Something in the air has changed. A shift in pressure. Perspective. Weight.

Everyone in this room has a chance at ultimate, rare power for the first time in nearly four hundred years.

From Ursula's death don't come the twin pillars of continuity and stability, but opportunity—raw, ripe, dangerous opportunity.

To rule the Four Lines and the thousands of witches within them.

Technically, practitioners of the Four Lines are all equally skilled, simply different vessels for the magic. But with the master relics comes something impossible otherwise.

Control.

The High Sorcerer holds the masters, which means they hold the eye through which each line's powers thread.

Like a satellite signal, every single witch within the lines sends their powers to its master relic, which then amplifies and narrows the magic until each spell cast is the tip of an arrow, a blade, a bullet. Without the masters, our powers would be like the wind, always there, but unbalanced—strong at times, weak at others.

With the masters come safety and protection—as long as the High Sorcerer doesn't intend to harm the lines. Masters literally in hand could make the High Sorcerer holding them so powerful every other witch on the planet couldn't stop them.

Which is exactly why the master relics have been in one family, in one place, for so long.

I scan the three families before me, left to right, as if reading a newly turned page.

The Cerises whisper like contestants on a syndicated family game show.

The Starwoods watch each other, already in silent, closed-circuit communication.

The Blackgates are divergent. Lavinia looks like she wants to leap into the fireplace. Kaysa stares at the will as if it has more answers to give.

Flanking me, my cousins are barely breathing. That chill on my neck spreads with the new silence, plunging below my collar and down the ridge of my spine. The only audible sound is the snapping of the flames in the hearth.

"So, it's a game . . . ?" Kaysa Blackgate asks slowly, breaking the quiet like a weak jab from an ice pick.

"I wouldn't call it a game," Evander grumbles. He's bent over, meaty shoulders hunched to his ears, green eyes flicking from Kaysa to the traitorous paper still beneath my palm.

"It may not be a game but it *is* a competition," Hex counters with a foxlike grin. He's doffed his suit coat, tucking it under an arm and releasing his cuff links for a chance to literally roll up his sleeves and get to work. His tiger stripe of tattoos is bare on his left arm, magicked ink as eye-catching as the ruby ring on his right index finger. "We all heard the woman. Let's find her relics. Let's do this."

I swallow down the feeling that the Cerises are a little too eager. I'm all for compartmentalizing, but this isn't meant to be fun.

"Hold your horses, and give it a second," Luna says, settling back into the embrace of her armchair. "Parameters are a-comin', child, couldn't you feel it when we signed?"

"Parameters? You mean rules to a *game*?" Hex asks, with a cock of a dark brow.

Evander's lips flatten into a serious line. "It's not a—"

The rest of Ursula's spell hits in a skein of lightning that flashes within everyone in the room like a vein of wildfire, leaving nothing but cooling, ashen embers hardening into place. It pushes outward until it coats our skin, heavy as lead though thin as frost. The world has the cool countenance of a winter midnight filtered through that familiar emerald green of Elemental magic. Glittering, frigid, still as death.

We can't move. We can't speak.

All we can do is listen.

This time, Ursula's words aren't amplified by the page. They're conducted in our blood. My vision narrows, blotting black from the corners until the paper before me disappears and all I can see is Ursula, speaking to me in a direct manner—a group hallucination, propelled from our shared blood into our field of sight. A second spell, prepared individually not simply for the reading of the will but for each person in this room.

"Bound by my power, the following rules will be agreed upon by every one of you," Ursula intones, unblinking. "Break any of my rules, and you will be suspended in an impenetrable, air-rendered prison for twenty-four hours. You will be as immobile as a marble statue, trapped where you stand. No chance to search for the relics, no chance to hunt for the killer, no chance to clear your name of whatever the magic has deemed you did wrong."

As one the lot of us verbally answer "Yes." Ursula's secondary spell literally has us by the throats, there isn't anything else to do.

"Rule one: All of you must be present at the reading of each clue. Each of you will have the opportunity to locate any relic upon Hegemony Manor estate. All security wards surrounding the relics have been disarmed and will not harm the individual who finds them."

My heart stutters at the mention of the security wards—I'm sure Evander's and Winter's did the same or worse. Again, we verbally agree.

"Rule two: There will be no use of magic *against* each other during the search for the relics or during the murder investigation. Moreover, no relic should be *taken* from its rightful line after procurement until the group can elect a new High Sorcerer and voluntarily release the master relics to the title holder."

With as much power as is on the line, this is necessary. Everyone seems to be agreeable to working together in this game, thus far, minutes in. But it's not hard to imagine that changing as soon as the masters are in hand.

"Rule three: There will be no vigilante justice in punishing my killer. Anyone suspected is to be questioned and confirmed by all of you, a jury of peers. Do you understand?"

Again, we concur as one.

"Break any of these rules, and, to repeat, you will automatically be bound in a prison of your own making via this spell and the magic herewith. Do you understand?"

We do.

With our chanted verbal acknowledgment, Ursula recedes from our shared vision, her spell fading into our blood like an ebbing tide. It's part of us now, until the magic is satisfied.

The will and my hand sharpen back into view, my breath kicking out in a hasty exhale. In my periphery, Luna jabs a geriatric elbow at Infinity's kidney.

"This grand dame knows a few things, doesn't she? I'm two for two!"

That she does and is.

"Wait." Lavinia's voice is hollow, unsure. She swallows and tries again, visibly shaken by the deepness of Ursula's binding spell. "What about the other task? How are we to punish the murderer?"

Hex's teeth flash in a double take. "You're—she's kidding, right?"

"No, I'm not kidding," Lavinia insists.

"You're a hundred percent serious right now?" Hex prods, lips curling into a smirk as he catches eyes with the rest of us, expecting someone to break or laugh. "This isn't some joke? A lie for Blackgate shits and giggles?"

I don't think Lavinia's lying. Beside her, Kaysa's brow is knitted in confusion. And . . . it seems genuine, Blackgate genes or not.

"The crime of murder can only be punished by death," Evander answers, bluntly. "Which I can only assume is why Marsyas Blackgate is currently missing."

Both girls pale, lips dropped open, their hands scrabbling for a better grip on each other while the rest of their limbs seem to freeze up.

They truly didn't know.

Don't know.

It strikes me then that perhaps this is why Lavinia has seemed so unlike herself. It wasn't time or distance or maturity . . . something's been done to them to *make* them forget. They've been spelled to forget. What happened, why, all of it.

That's either cruel or genius—maybe both. Until the truth catches up.

"Especially," Ada cuts in, something nasty in the baby blue of her eyes, "considering what happened with Marcos."

"Our father . . . ?" Kaysa's voice trails off.

"Your father is of no consequence to this game," Sanguine answers, pointedly cuffing her daughter's wrist and forcing it to be at her side, an apology.

Ada isn't having it, and squirms away from her mother's taloned grip, crossing her arms over her chest, her pink mouth twisting into something sharper than her twin's smirk. "Unless your family *murdered* Ursula in retaliation for his fate?"

Now both Blackgate girls look like they want to leap into the fire.

"I, what, no—" Lavinia sputters.

"Of course not!" Kaysa insists, aghast.

"Where *is* your grandmother, girls?" Hector asks like a perturbed principal, and though Sanguine stepped in at the mention of Marcos, she now squares her shoulders, clearly in line with her husband on this. "Isn't it mighty suspect that Marsyas vanished right before Ursula's last breath?"

"It isn't a crime to use the loo," Kaysa claps back with a very Winter-like roll of her eyes. "Nona's lucky her bladder saved her from watching her friend die."

Hector spears Evander with an inquisitive glance. "Given your tardiness, I'm assuming you checked the restroom when you came inside." His eyes flick back to the Blackgates. "And yet you didn't locate your grandmother?"

"We haven't checked all sixteen washrooms," Kaysa snaps.

"Did she leave?" Sanguine tilts her head, both inquisitive and demanding. "Did she abandon you?"

"We don't know where she is, but we'll find her," Lavinia answers, much more measured than her younger sister, but her eyes betray her, because even at this distance, even with the fire across the room, I can read in the dark depths that she's uncertain—maybe even scared. Scared that Marsyas did it or that she met the same fate as Ursula, and we haven't found her yet.

Perhaps they can smell it in Lavinia's blood, or maybe they just have plenty of practice from leading a highly volatile line, but Hector and Sanguine seem to home in on that fear. Hector winds up to push more but Evander interjects, big, blunt hands in the air, placating.

"Perhaps," my cousin says, "so that we can answer some of those questions, it might be best to use tonight to pause on the search for the masters and instead spend the time taking statements regarding Ursula's murder. I believe the best scenario is the use of a truth spell—"

"That *you* control?" Hector scoffs, all eyebrows and surprise—his voice has its usual jovial tenor, but there's something about his delivery that's rushed, fevered. He holds up a ringed hand. "Evander, I will agree to anything to help the lines but that's a bridge too far. There's no way to control the result without an independent investigator."

The man has a point.

"Then we'll perform truth spells on each other," Evander tries again, his tightly woven edges fraying as he offers diplomacy but really wants his way. I wonder if the others can see it like I can. Like Winter must. "Given Marsyas's absence, the Blackgates will submit first, and we'll work from there."

"You want us to what?" Lavinia asks, stricken.

Hex tips his chin, eyes twinkling darkly. "How do you even *do* a truth spell with the elements? Burn flesh until they cave?"

Winter grins at him with more grit than she's had in an hour. "Depends on if we like them or not."

I clear my throat. "I think this perhaps might skirt too close to breaking the rule of using our magic against each other, unless the participant verbally submits and all of us agree it's fair."

There's a general mumbling of "fine" and "okay" before Luna primly places one gnarled hand on top of the other and tosses a metaphorical bomb onto the desk.

"Hector makes a fine point about the independent investigator. We don't have one. And while I appreciate your budding leadership acumen, Evander, what if Ursula's murderer *is* a Hegemony?"

Evander stiffens, my heart drops, and Winter gasps.

"Luna, you know I love you, but that's completely out of bounds," Winter says, voice breaking. She swallows, a shaking hand covering her mouth. "We would never. None of us would ever."

"But one of us did," Infinity points out in support of their grandmother.

"*Marsyas* did," Ada scoffs.

"We don't know that," Lavinia bites back.

"Which is why we should start questioning the Blackgates tonight," Evander states flatly.

"Wait." I hold up a hand. I can't believe I'm about to say this but . . . "You suspect *these* Blackgates? The Blackgates that are so magically cloistered—*altered?*—they didn't even know their father was punished by death by the woman who died here tonight until we *told* them?"

"Hey, we're not idiots," Lavinia snaps at me like I didn't just defend her and Kaysa. "We're just uninformed."

"Yeah, we shouldn't be punished for our childhood trauma," Kaysa adds. "Or for the fact that Nona seems to have wandered off at the worst possible time."

Luna's whole body sags in a frown. "As someone two years more senior than Marsyas, I'd like to note that she's old, not senile. Sharp as a tack and cracking the whip, that one."

Hector resets, both hands up and taking a step forward toward us as a group, placating. "I think we should read the clue. Punishing Ursula's murderer is important—*obviously*—but it's not nearly as crucial to the continuation of the Four Lines as locating the master relics. By my count we now have a little more than fifty hours to find all four of them. We need to know what type of clues we're working with, so we have an idea of how to pace ourselves to successfully locate the masters in time."

He's right. I hate it, but he's right.

Ursula was adamant that we do—that *I* do—whatever necessary to continue the Four Lines. The masters are key. Even with Ursula's murderer punished, we can't continue the lines without the relics in hand. And if Marsyas is missing because she killed Ursula . . . well, we might be spinning our wheels by spending the night taking statements.

I blot a clammy hand on my pant leg and prepare to place it again on the page to call the clue, but then Hector steps toward the desk, rubbing a thumb across his jaw. He manages to appear casual but I've seen him use this approach—the careful, thoughtful, seasoned friend—a dozen times with Ursula. He wants something.

"Before we begin—Evander, the High Sorcerer's ring, you took it off Ursula's body. I think we need to discuss a better place for it than your pocket."

"We don't need to discuss it. It's safe with me."

Hector's teeth flash gold in the firelight—he grins harder but doesn't relent. "I'm sure it is, but I was thinking perhaps it might be appropriate to have Luna hold it until the relics are found and the High Sorcerer is named, as the eldest head of family here."

"I don't want it," Luna spits without hesitation. "Should've left it on the body."

I'd have to agree except all of us expected Evander to be the next High Sorcerer. That ring was supposed to be his, as it had been for generations of Hegemony heirs before him.

And while Hector's interest in its location could simply be simpering concern that a mere teenager will mishandle something so valuable . . . I don't know. It's very *pointed*.

Evander produces Ursula's ring from his pocket. It's silver, inset with a gem for each magic line—garnet for Blood, emerald for Elemental, onyx for Death, opal for Celestial—and the symbolic key to controlling every known Four Lines witch in North America. Well, and the *actual* key, given it is spelled to be bound to each of the master relics.

For something so powerful, it sits unremarkable in Evander's wide palm.

"It should stay with the Hegemony family until the High Sorcerer is elected." Evander's fingers close around the ring, swallowing it from view.

"Fine," Hector stiffly concedes, all his attention fixed on Evander's fist as he fishes for what to say next. "However, it's blasphemy to wear the ring without rights. Punishable by ten to thirty years of censure of powers by a panel of your peers."

Evander nearly rolls his eyes at the hand-wringing. He would if he'd been alone with Hector, I'm sure. Instead, he maintains an aura of professionalism as he fishes his own chain and heir's key from beneath his snow-white button-up. Without another word, he unclasps the chain and slides the ring onto it. It sinks down the length until it clinks softly with his key. Evander's is larger than mine, and iron, not copper, with more jags on its edge and a more ornate fob at its top.

Evander returns the chain to his neck and slips the ring and key out of sight beneath his shirt. "Is that satisfactory, Hector?"

"Yes," the patriarch agrees, almost automatically. He straightens his suit jacket and backs away from the desk.

"Okay, now that we've settled that matter," Evander says in a way that makes it obvious he did not care for Hector's lapse in agreeability, "Auden, the first clue, if you would."

I press my palm into the will. My thumb is again lined up perfectly with the bloody print, but this time no magic sparks under my skin.

The paper is cold, dull, lifeless.

After a beat, there's a collective shuffle and lean.

"It hasn't yet appeared." I glance first to Winter and then to Evander, but it's obvious they see nothing but the sheet we started with—looping with Ursula's signature and marked by our bloody thumbprints. "Perhaps the clue must be read by someone of the appropriate line?"

Testing this theory, I present the single page again to the other families.

Hector and Sanguine crowd the desk, squinting—nothing.

The Starwoods don't move from their home base of the guest chair, but both shake their heads, unable to read a thing upon it.

The Blackgates—

My eyes dart around the room. The corners, the shadows.

The Blackgates are nowhere to be found.

Just like their grandmother, Lavinia and Kaysa are missing.

CHAPTER 10

RUBY

"Witches. Motherfucking witches," Wren whispers as we barrel down the most beautiful set of stairs I've ever seen. They're wide and winding, with shining marble planks and twin polished walnut banisters spiraling down to what looks like the main entrance to Hegemony Manor.

"And a kid named *Hex*! Like, what *is* that if not a dead giveaway? I suppose it's only a giveaway if you know magic is real, but Jesus Christ, talk about hiding in plain sight."

"Shhhhhh," I warn because I'm moving too fast and in too high of heels on a slippery surface to clamp a hand over her mouth.

The foyer is as sonorous as it is grand, and Wren is being too loud for the lack of distance between us and the room we just escaped from. It rises all three stories of the main house, with a massive, candle-burning chandelier hung from the ceiling, suspended from a long chain as thick as my forearm. But I don't dare linger upon the glittering extravagance of it all—I don't look anywhere but where my feet need to go.

Down, down, down.

Out, away, and into the cover of night, where we can slip off the lie that we're Lavinia and Kaysa Blackgate. Where we can hide, and forget we ever set foot in Hegemony Manor.

Because if those witches, sorcerers, mages—*whatever*—get ahold of us and realize who we are and what secrets we've seen?

"Stop talking and keep moving or we're dead. *Just go.*"

Our plan is to run straight out the front entrance toward the cars, slip through the barbed wire, and onto the road. There's a slim hope in the back of my mind that because we weren't supposed to be here, because we're not actually Lavinia and Kaysa, the magic can't hold us and we can disappear into the trees, wander long enough to get cell service, and safely call a ride.

It's a gamble, a guess, but it's all we have.

Wren beats me to the final landing, her strides stuttering, mouth dropped into an awestruck *O*. "It's so beautiful."

Instead of the stately wallpaper of the solarium, hallways, and the parts of Ursula's study that weren't covered in books, the entire foyer is painted in a massive mural of mountains and sun, wild-flowers, and wet-bottomed basins.

It's striking and completely at odds with the gothic noir of the exterior.

There's a creak from above, a sound, movement, and in a blink, I'm grabbing Wren's hand, my heart ratcheting back up to a furious pace against my sternum. "Stunning, gorgeous, amazing. Definitely haunted. *Go*."

We plow toward the front door—doors, actually, a pair of them. The way they've been painted into the mural, it's as if we're stepping onto a trail leading through an alpine grove instead of barreling out onto those gravestone steps we saw in the daylight on the drive.

I wrench down on the levered handle, expecting resistance of the locked or magical kind, only to find I'm pressing far too hard, and leaning too far in. The door falls open easily, and as we fall with it, I lunge forward. My foot catches my drooping A-line skirt—the delicate hem rips.

Shit.

I won't be able to return it now, and as much as it's gut-wrenching to know that most of my cut of Marsyas's upfront advance will now go to paying off the credit card bill for this dress, it's really the least of my problems at the moment.

I barely break a stride, hiking up my skirt with the hand that isn't holding on to Wren, my new flayed hem swinging, and rush down the front steps.

"She did ditch us. Old hag," Wren grits out as we hit the bricks.

My head snaps up.

Our SUV is missing. A bald patch of drive squats beside a sleek silver sports car.

Marsyas left us.

Before the spell took effect. She slipped out, taking those keys she weaseled away from the chauffeur, and jetted before the speech. Before Ursula's last breath.

"Oh *God,*" Wren screeches. "That's the driver."

She extends a finger toward where a pair of shiny shoes catches the gray of the moonlight.

"He's just like the rest of the staff, he's a vegetable until they fulfill Ursula's request," I remind her without a second look, my attention on the looming gate, the barbed wire obscured by brush.

"Jesus, Ruby, look at him. *That* is not the same."

There's a stiff inhale and a sob bracketing her words, and she's become completely immovable. I yank hard, but she tenses up further.

"We don't have time—"

She folds over and *vomits*. It's wet and thin, and stinks of champagne and watermelon. "Wren, what the—"

My eyes land on the man's face.

Wren's right. It's not the same at all.

The driver isn't asleep. He'll never wake again.

His face is a bloodied mess, still wet, but it's clear by the sunken lines of his features that his eyes are missing. His mouth gags open, an empty void, blood all over his teeth—tongue ripped out. His neck has collapsed in on itself, like a jack-o'-lantern left out too long after Halloween. No windpipe. No throat. No Adam's apple.

All the soft parts above his torso are just . . . gone.

Gone. Like Marsyas.

A spell. She used a spell to kill him and get away.

If Marsyas can do that, what can the others do?

My thudding heart rabbits in my chest as bile lurches toward my still-working throat. I swallow it down, a ringing in my ears now, the coppery scent of this man's blood on the Rocky Mountain wind.

I turn to look at Hegemony Manor. The specter of downward movement is in those dead-eyed windows, right where the staircase coils around the massive chandelier.

Fuck.

"Wren, we need to run, or we'll be just like him."

We race for the gate.

"Hard right." I guide us into the grass off the drive, hoping that we'll be more difficult to spot, even if it's slicker here, the fresh dew of evening clinging to each newly deadened blade.

There are footsteps behind us now. I don't know how many. I don't even try to guess, or look back, or even count them over the pounding of my blood in my ears, the rough churn of my breath, the yammering of my heart.

It doesn't matter who's following us, only that someone is, and though we haven't seen exactly what the younger ones can do, it won't be good for us.

We need to leave.

The property line is straight ahead. Fifty yards. Thirty-five. Twenty. Ten.

"It's not there," Wren says, her voice hoarse from vomiting, and laced with fear.

I squint at the barbed-wire section, obscured by the close brush, and shadows of the private road, which, like most anything that's not in the city, has no streetlights.

"It's there. We'll get close and try to slide through the strands. I'll hold it for you and then you for me and then we'll be out."

Five yards. Three. One.

We stutter-step to stop on the slick and uneven terrain, the manicured grass giving way to the natural roughness of Colorado at altitude. The barbed wire is there, black and purposefully dull. Impossible to see without being two inches from our faces. It's too tall for us to scale, so we'll indeed have to go through.

I squint to check the terrain on the other side—

Beyond the wire is literally nothing.

The same sort of nothingness of negative space and dreamless nights, and consciousness before life or after death.

Absolutely blank.

Before I can stop her, Wren reaches a probing hand between the wires.

"No—"

My hand shoots out between her fingers and the fence, preventing her from touching it . . . and grazes the nothingness in between.

With a yelp, I snatch it away as if I've touched a hot pan on a stove.

Only it's worse. Much worse.

The skin of my knuckles and the tops of my index and middle fingers on my right hand immediately frays and peels away. The fingernails are just gone, swaddled in a mass of sausage-casing skin, the ridges of flesh along tips of bone are exposed—as red and raw and throbbing as a literal beating heart.

Wren takes one look and screams.

I bite down the wail forming in my throat as the pain tears through me. My gut lurches, and I again fight the urge to lose the meager contents of my stomach along with my gumption because it's clear now that we can't go out, we can't stay in, and they'll be on us in—

"Turn around with your hands up, and relics clear."

Auden.

His words are not commanding or even mean, but they're an order. Over the searing agony of my hand, I vaguely wonder why he didn't just use whatever magic he possesses to physically stop us. There was nothing in Ursula's litany of rules that said they couldn't use magic against two would-be escapees, only against each other during the search for the masters and the murder investigation.

But Auden would know more about magic than me, who learned of its existence mere *minutes* ago.

Wren is whimpering at my side, as she cups my wrist with a furious flurry of "I'm sorry, I'm sorry." Tears are on the run down her face, her expertly applied liner bleeding into the hollows under her eyes, mascara gathering in the corners. She's white as a sheet. I have no doubt I'm much worse. My cheeks are wet, and I'm in so much pain, my teeth have started to chatter.

And so *of course* my little sister squeezes her eyes shut, opens her big mouth, and argues. "Why? You can kill us facing away just as easily as you can kill us looking at you. I'd rather not have your murderous sneer as the last thing I see."

"Kaysa, I'm not going to kill you." Auden's voice is calm and moving closer through the brush. Judging from the volume, he's only feet away now. And probably not alone. I don't know what he can do as a witch, and I don't really want to find out. "I have no interest in seeing any more dead bodies tonight."

I suck in a breath and blink at the wall of literal nothingness ahead of us. Our only other, terrible option. "So what are you going to do?"

He clears his throat. "First, if you'll let me, I'm going to heal you, Lavinia. I know you've been injured by the barrier. Next, I'm going to escort you back inside, where we're going to tell anyone who's decided you're collateral damage in Marsyas's assumed murder of Ursula that you simply left to search for her on the grounds, concerned for her safety and eager to prove her innocence."

Wren and I exchange a glance. I find it hard to believe Auden Hegemony is helping us out of the goodness of his heart with his grandmother dead and his family stripped of its power. I also doubt it's because I was such an enchanting dinner guest because literally everything about our "reintroduction" was awkward as hell.

But Auden's file claims he loves to read, and if there's anything I've learned selling books it's that most readers like to unravel a mystery. I know I do. Maybe Auden does. Maybe right now that's enough.

I didn't want to be here tonight. I don't want to be here now. I didn't want to lie. But there's no way out.

There's only through.

"Quickly, girls," Auden prompts. "They're bickering over who stays with the will, but soon enough more searchers will be out here, and they won't be as forgiving about the dead man on the drive."

I look over my shoulder but don't pivot my body. I need to gauge his expression. To search those very nice blue-brown eyes of his for any sign of malice. But they're the same as when we first met—bright and alive—and if anything's changed, it's the exhaustion ringing them.

I want to trust him. I have no other choice. And I need to make sure Wren and I get out of here in one piece.

"You'll heal me?" I confirm, finding my voice, as rough and stilted as it is. I don't even bother with my accent.

"Yes."

I swallow. "We'll turn and raise our hands. But my hands need to stay together."

There's no way my throbbing, burning right hand can manage anything right now without support.

There's a pause. "If that's the case, I must remind you that if you use your magic on me, not only will I rescind my willingness to tell the others you were innocently searching for Marsyas and not trying to escape—you'll be caught up in Ursula's spelled prison."

"Understood," I bite out.

Wren turns first, arms raised and compliant. I follow slowly, darkness spotting my vision now, and my legs are seriously unstable beneath me. My hands are cupped out before my body, almost like one of those angel statues offering water in the waiting well of her palms.

When I present myself to Auden Hegemony, his magical eyes aren't on my face—they're on my wrists.

On the rabbits' feet.

He's watching them like cowboys in old Westerns watch another man's gun. Ready to run or draw his own weapon the very second I reach for them.

That's when it hits my pain-scrambled brain. The weight of what he's said. What he asked of us.

Relics.

Our bracelets are relics—not masters but still. That's why he doesn't want us touching them. They're magical and *what*? A shield? An amplifier? Something else?

Auden Hegemony truly believes we have magic. The same Death Line magic that Marsyas wielded on our poor driver. That can dissolve a man like acid.

Considering the way he flinched in the garden when he grazed the rabbit's foot? Maybe it *is* a loaded gun in the right hands. Not mine, but Auden doesn't know that and neither do the rest of them.

The Blackgates are witches.

Which means *we* need to be ones too. At least for the next three days.

If we survive that long.

CHAPTER 11

AUDEN

Healing Lavinia Blackgate isn't as simple as I've made it out to be.

Each magical line is amplified by its preferred specialty. In my case, the elements enhance my magical abilities, and my magic is at its best when they're used in each spell cast. In this case, to heal Lavinia, I have to manipulate the fifth element, life, to do it.

Not her life—*my* life.

The price is a balance between what's been damaged and what I have to give whole. Sometimes, it's a life for a life. In her immediate grief, Winter was ready to make that exchange tonight for our grandmother—a cost Evander and I thought was too great. Here, the price is small, but will mean big things to the Blackgates.

The Blackgates don't know this—and I need an answer as to why they don't.

It's been clear since they returned to Hegemony Manor that not only have the girls been spelled to forget the execution of their father—and as someone with a dead father, I can't blame them for being completely uncurious about that particular hole in their collective memory—but they've been left completely uneducated about both the Four Lines and their inheritance within them.

I want to know why.

And I want to know who.

Who murdered Ursula? Why?

And what does missing Marsyas Blackgate have to do with it?

Death witches aren't typically a cuddly lot but still it seems too terrible to think that not only is Marsyas guilty and gone, which robs us of a chance to fulfill the necessary tasks to break Ursula's final curse, but that she'd condemn her beloved granddaughters at the same time.

"Place your hand in mine," I tell Lavinia, crosshatching my palms.

She takes a step forward and immediately sways as she tries to plant her foot, pain claiming her balance this time instead of the clumsiness I saw in the garden. On pure instinct, my left hand shoots out to steady her, cuffing her upper arm to keep her from tumbling to the grass. Her skin is cold and trembles under my touch, pain and adrenaline pulsing through her body.

Lavinia's jaw unhinges, and she seems to attempt a smile, though it comes off like a grimace, the streaking lines of tears bracketing her full mouth as she calls back to our conversation in the garden. "I guess I'm not good to walk on my own after all."

I can't look away from the mixture of panic, pain, and resolve in the glassy darkness of her eyes.

No, this is not the Lavinia Blackgate of old.

Though I suppose I'm not the same Auden Hegemony either.

The one I am now calmly assures this panicked and pained girl, "You will be in just a moment."

Then, as gently as possible, I gather her injured hand in mine. The first two fingers are so mangled by the magic I'm surprised she didn't immediately faint. I'd seen the whole thing—Kaysa reaching for the barrier and Lavinia reacting without a care for herself, putting her body between her little sister and disaster. They may have been spelled to forget and coddled to be in the dark, but that sort of fierce protection isn't something that can be stamped out.

A curl of admiration unfurls in my chest as I cup my hands over her injury.

Lavinia hisses, and a new batch of tears wells in her eyes as they flit from the verdant magic flickering between my skin and hers and my face. I hold her gaze for the barest of moments, the spell to heal her nearly as quick as the exposure to magic that ruined her flesh in the first place.

A breath, the tiniest fleck of my life element, and it's done.

The magic dies into her skin, and, steering well clear of the charged Death Line relics dangling dangerously from her wrists, I carefully let go. As they fall away, Lavinia's right hand is revealed, repaired and whole.

As good as new.

Flexing her fingers, Lavinia seems stunned to silence. Kaysa gawks beside her, wide-eyed and mouth curled into a little *O* before she exclaims, "Shiiiiite, that's amazing!"

"It's too much." Lavinia catches my wrist with her newly healed hand, her preserved rabbit's foot swaying but not touching my skin. "Thank you for healing me but—why are you doing this, Auden?"

Honestly, I don't know until I'm talking.

"Your grandmother abandoned you, and you know none of that looks good for you"—I jab a finger behind us, toward the void left by what I assume was Marsyas's chauffeured vehicle—"especially with that man very visibly mangled by Death magic."

Both girls go a little green in the waning light of the night. "And," I say, "given the obvious gaping *chasm* in your magical education, it's no wonder you tried to leave. You panicked. I would panic too—"

"Auden! Are you out here?" Hex's voice calls out.

Without hesitation, I yell back. "Stay there! I've got them!" Then, lowering my voice, I whisper to the girls, "Quickly, now. Toward the house before he leaves the steps and sees the body down the drive."

Lavinia's brow creases, even as she follows my instructions and begins swift-stepping forward, her newly repaired hand tucked into Kaysa's own. "But they're going to find it eventually—as soon as it's light. What's the point in hiding it?"

"The point is to give you more time to figure out what your grandmother has done—and why."

Lavinia frowns and gestures toward the man, now twenty paces ahead with the rate we're moving. "Doesn't that make us look even more guilty?"

Hell. She's not the same, yet still stubborn as ever when push comes to shove. And right, regrettably.

"Coming!" I shout to Hex with a wave. It does the job, and when he's looking at me and not our surroundings, I reach for the spark of my magic. When I'm sure the driver's hidden from Hex's view behind Evander's ridiculous Maserati, my magic descends in a green haze, instantly cloaking the dead man in his own corner of night.

Beside me, Lavinia's step falters anew. My hand shoots out again to steady her, but Kaysa is already on the case, holding her sister about the waist as her body's equilibrium recalibrates from the receding pain. "What . . . I . . . did you . . ."

"Did I buy you more time? Yes."

Lavinia and Kaysa again exchange a look, and I know they're as skeptical of my aid as they are scared of the truth.

I am too.

"What was that all about?" Hex asks the sisters as the chandelier light from within the manor finally reaches our faces. "Your memories flood back and chase you out the door?"

"No," Lavinia answers flatly. Her voice is still rough from pain, but she's trying to hide it.

"We were searching for Nona," Kaysa explains.

"Like, *physically* searching?" Hex squints at her. Kaysa squints right back. "Why don't you just use a hunting spell?"

"In case you haven't noticed, Athena isn't one for magical education," I reply, dryly. I try to push past him and into the house in an effort to keep his curiosity away from the driver, but Hex doesn't budge.

"Not an excuse to keep them wondering, Auden." He turns to the Blackgates, grinning a little too widely. "I can do it for you. It'll only take a sec."

The girls exchange yet another glance—they're quite possibly more in tune than even the Cerise twins when it comes to wordless communication—but before they can consent, Hex leans in and plucks something off Lavinia's shoulder strap.

"What—is . . . is that her hair?"

"I would assume so, unless you're going gray mighty early," Hex answers with a waggle of his eyebrows.

Lavinia purses her lips and, despite what she's just been through, manages to cross her arms, relics suddenly prominently displayed—an obvious threat, should he attempt to pull anything like when he tried to "help" with her nicked skin on the terrace. She may have been left in the dark by her mother and grandmother, but it's clear she knows how to use those amplifiers. "How does this work?"

"We just need a piece of Marsyas to trace," Hex tells her, the silver hair shiny in his pinched grip. "The rest is magic."

And then he goddamn winks.

"On with it, show-off. We need to get back upstairs."

Hex smirks at me and shoves the rolled-up shirtsleeve on his left arm until it bunches past the elbow. There, on the underside of his forearm, is a long set of vertical lines. They're carved in the same silver-tinged magical ink that shimmered up from the page on Ursula's will. He doesn't yet have the extra line that the Cerises use to signify an oathed heir, but he likely will soon.

Tattoos bare, Hex twists the ring on his right index finger. The ruby stone slides away to expose a small, slightly hooked metal point. It's the size and shape of the thorns on a rose stem, and far more sharp.

The inked lines aren't labeled, but Hex seems to have gotten my memo about haste and doesn't bother to dither or explain as he slices the length of the first line with the thorn point. The cut is the exact length and width of his tattoo, the blood that rises to the surface of his skin completely blotting out the black line.

Hex swipes the blood onto the opposite palm, and presses Marsyas's hair into it, holding it until it's sufficiently soaked and sparkling with the ruby red that signifies Blood magic. "Auden, a gust of wind, if you would?"

I oblige, gathering a strand in my palm and shooting it at Hex's spell.

The Blackgates gasp in tandem as the emerald-tinted Elemental wind snatches up the stained hair and foists it out into black of night, traveling north in a counterclockwise loop around the house and across the grounds with the same effect as a sonic boom.

In one delayed thrust, the gust boomerangs around the ten thousand acres in a jolt, returning Marsyas's hair on a raft of air as soft as an exhale.

The bloodied strand lands in Hex's palm. He closes it for a

moment, then opens it again. The stain of his blood remains, but the hair is gone, disintegrating to white ash that smears of crimson.

"What . . . what does that mean?" Lavinia asks, staring at Hex's result with big, dark eyes and a prettily furrowed brow.

"It means Marsyas isn't on the grounds."

Lavinia visibly swallows but Kaysa scrunches up her nose. "I really thought she was in the loo." Her eyes snap to Hex's. "Did it check the loo?"

Hex just dusts his hands. "Of course. It checked everywhere. Your grandmother isn't locked in by the spell with the rest of us."

✦ ✦ ✦

"Marsyas Blackgate is not on the premises," Hex announces as the four of us enter the study. "Magically confirmed by *moi*."

Ada squints from her brother to the girls to me. "You were looking for Marsyas? Now? When we're about to read the first clue? You decided that was the perfect time to put out a Silver Alert?"

"I'd rather not have anyone on the grounds after dark," Evander adds. "It's extremely treacherous."

"Noted. We're sorry. We're just a little overwhelmed," Lavinia replies as the sisters assume the same standing position they'd had before they left. Evander scoffs under his breath at her word choice—because yes, he, Winter, and I own the lion's share of rights to feeling overwhelmed tonight—but says nothing. Lavinia swallows and announces, "But, yes, now we don't have to wonder. Nona isn't here, and the car we came in is gone, so we know now that she left before Ursula's spell locked into place."

"So, if Marsyas *did* kill Ursula," Infinity starts, glancing at Luna, "either the magic will have to be more flexible than Ursula intended or . . . it won't."

"Meaning we're stuck." Ada frowns.

"We're not *stuck*. We just need to execute Ursula's final directive as a team, together," Evander answers. "Perhaps if we find all of the master relics, we can pool our magical talents to create a counter spell so great we can break Ursula's spell as a last resort."

It's a decent plan. Therefore Hector seems to take credit for having the same idea.

"Which is exactly why we shouldn't delay further in reading the first clue," he says, "now that *we're all here.*"

"We could've done without that last bit, Hector Cerise Senior," Luna scolds. "Especially since you're the one who was griping at those girls to know exactly where the woman went not ten minutes ago. Don't order them to sing and then complain they're too loud. It's rude. Now, let's get on with it. We don't have all night."

"Luna's right," I say, rounding the desk.

"Of course I am."

I pointedly place my hand on the page, thumb neatly aligned with the blood-marked print. Immediately, the paper warms beneath my skin, like wax over a flame. The signature swirls, sharpening into five lines.

I clear my throat. "The first clue is this . . .

"*When breath became air,*
   the mountain stood tall with forever frost.
   Though the call of the falcon
   and flick of salmon fin, did not dim the fires,
   we worship."

"Who wrote this clue?" Kaysa asks, perhaps trying a tad too hard to appear engaged after their disappearing act. She knocks her sister's arm. "What the hell does that mean?"

Lavinia frowns. "I think it sounds poetic—a bit like Dickinson, actually."

Making a left-field comparison to poetry is something *I* would do in literally any other situation. It's practically my secondary aim in life given I'd been named after a smattering of Callum Hegemony's favorite poets.

"It would if it were written by the man who built the manor," I confirm. "Shadrack Hegemony and Emily Dickinson would've been contemporaries."

No one counters my assumption that the clues are likely as old as the deed on the land itself.

"So we need to think like someone who would be more than two hundred years old at this point?" Infinity asks, slightly stricken, their meticulous brain clicking forward.

"Oh come on, it's not *that* hard," Ada sniffs. "It's *obviously* an Elemental clue. All the elements are mentioned, including life."

"What does it mean, Hegemonys?" Hex asks.

All eyes seem to find Evander's form beside me. I look to him too, our de facto leader. The would-be High Sorcerer. The Elemental patriarch.

Evander rubs a hand down his face, and admits, rather bravely, I think, "Honestly, I don't know."

There's a beat of silence and then Hector shifts on his feet. "Well, one of you must know," the Cerise patriarch urges. "Surely."

"The clue is full of signifiers," I say. "They aren't direct, but they aren't completely opaque either. They were designed to help us locate these relics, not stand around second-guessing ourselves. It's not a riddle, it's a *hint*."

"Okay, so what's it hinting at?" Hector pushes. "Surely you have an idea of what it's supposed to signify within your own home."

When we remain silent, he gapes between all three of us. Winter sighs. "I've lived here nearly my entire life, and yet I've never seen the Elemental master, let alone any of the others."

I nod, and Evander adds, "We need to think about it."

"But she wants—*wanted*—us to find the relics," Hector argues, almost to the room itself as if Ursula's ghost is listening. "She wouldn't have given us clues we couldn't decipher."

"They're Shadrack's clues, not Ursula's," Winter reminds him.

"She was High Sorcerer. She gave us a hunt worth completing. That's it." Luna begins to slowly rise from her seat, and Infinity immediately offers an arm. "If you don't know now, let's not start scrabbling for straws. It's an hour past my bedtime and if my experience is going to be of use to any of ya, I need to rest. Infinity, help your grandmama to our room."

I check the clock. It's half past ten now. Very late for Luna and her century-old bones.

"Yes, you rest up, Luna," Hector agrees, rising as well. The patriarch reaches into the interior lining of his coat, slips out a cell phone, and snaps a quick picture of the clue. Satisfied with his photograph after rotating it, he packs the phone away and tips his head. "The Cerises will begin our search immediately and report back in the morning."

Evander moves to round the desk toward them and repeats the same concern he flung at the Blackgates. "Wait—please stick to the house. As I just explained, the grounds aren't safe at night."

"Oh, if they want to break their ankles, let them, Evander. They'll learn or they won't," Luna says with a dismissive wave before disappearing into the hall, Infinity at her side.

"We have no intention of that," Sanguine says, "we'll just be putting our heads together."

With that, the Cerises file out.

Winter pivots to Lavinia and Kaysa. "I know you didn't intend to stay—Marsyas never does—but we did set aside a suite in the event that she wanted to spend the night. I'll lead you there."

The girls nod, unable to hide their weary surprise. As Winter collects them, she throws a glance over her shoulder, back at us. Her smudged face is as placid as a glass-clear lake, the broken girl she was just minutes ago stuffed down deep where no one will ever excavate her. Her bright blue eyes glow fierce and so much like Ursula's in that moment that my heart stumbles.

Then, just like our grandmother did so many times in this very room, she gives an order we're expected to obey. "Neither of you move an inch. We need to talk."

CHAPTER 12

RUBY

Auden's magic hunkers beneath my skin, nothing like the biting, terrifying chill of Ursula's binding spell. He'd only touched me for a moment, but the mark of his power is pleasant, and enduring—and I can't stop grazing my fingertips along the ridge of my repaired knuckles as we follow his cousin to the room that's been set aside for Marsyas.

Winter leads us down a flight of stairs—not the big winding ones in the foyer, but the kind of hidden corner stairwell found in hotels. From there, we pop out onto the second floor and turn down a hall that takes us in a totally different direction than the way that would lead us to the solarium—I think.

It's all very confusing, and darkly lit by sconces that do almost nothing to brighten up a hallway hung in more wallpaper that could double as a weighted blanket. The only irregularity is a long bank of windows at one side that might show some sort of green space. It's hard to make out anything but what looks like the fuzz of landscape in the moonlight.

"All the guests stay on the second floor. The Starwoods are on the other side of the courtyard. The Cerises have a double suite here." Winter gestures as we pass a pair of doors beneath twin female elk heads. "Your room is at the end of the hall."

Winter gestures and makes a beeline for a suite settled under a huge roaring mountain lion. I suppose we'll always know which door is ours. "In the morning, I'll bring you a selection from my closet upstairs that might fit you both."

We thank her profusely because this is truly generous, and Winter plasters on the same hostess smile we saw in the garden. It looks out of place on a canvas of her tear-stained makeup. "You're welcome. Good night."

She disappears down the next bend of the hall, rather than going back the way we came.

I shut the door and lock it, just as I did when we went to the bathroom earlier. Before I even have the dead bolt in place, Wren twirls into the center of the sitting room, arms wide and flailing.

"Holy shit, can you believe this?! This is insane! I totally thought we were goners back there on the drive when Auden was like, 'Turn around with your hands up,' but—"

Now, because I can, I literally clamp my repaired hand over her mouth. She bats at it, but I hold fast, scanning every corner of our suite. The richly appointed sitting room in which we're standing leads to two bedrooms, each stuffed with a massive bed, marble fireplace, fainting couch, desk, vanity, wardrobe, plus enough mirrors and lavender-stuffed flower vases to guarantee something will be broken by the end of this all—if we survive.

Satisfied, I haul Wren into one of the two en suite bathrooms. Her heels slip on the tile in muted protest as I check both linen closets, the rainwater shower, the massive tub.

Finally, I remove my hand and Wren mutters something about her ruined lipstick. Like it was in such great shape after she vomited her guts out on the drive.

She might have said more, but it doesn't register—my body is a live wire of worry that someone will overhear us.

I turn on the water—sinks, bath, shower—until it's roaring. There's no fan, but honestly, given the look of this place, I should've been pleased to have running water. I haven't spotted a single electrical outlet to go along with the lamps—which I'm beginning to suspect are actual gas lamps, not replicas—and the lack of both Wi-Fi and cell service. Everything about Hegemony Manor is a step back in time. And not in the fake "let them joust" way.

My sister watches me race around. "Is all this necessary?"

"Yes," I snap.

Wren's hands fly up. "Whoa, there. I'm on your team."

I suck in a deep breath. This room smells like they clean the tile with literal lemons. The air burns going down.

I snatch Wren's wrist to pull her close. I force her to look in my eyes as the words flood out, as furious as the water all around us.

"We're trapped on an estate with nine witches, and someone—possibly one of those nine witches—was willing to murder an old lady in her own backyard to trigger some magical Easter egg hunt. No one knows where we are. We can't contact the outside world. We need to be as careful as possible. *This* is me being careful."

By the time I'm done, spit clings to the corners of my mouth, my nostrils are flaring, and I'm sucking down this fiery, citrusy air hard. To show for it, all I get from my baby sister is a flash of her winning smile and a firm dismissal. "Oh, calm down. Just think of the story we're going to tell."

"Are you insane? We're never going to get out of here to tell anyone."

I clutch at her bare shoulders again, but when Wren yelps, I fling my hands out wide, palms bunching. "Sorry. It's just—you *are* on my team. And I need you to focus with me on how the hell we're going to survive the next three days."

Wren's lips fall into a flat, colorless line. "I am focused. Focused enough to amend your statement, *Lavinia,* with the fact that we aren't locked in with a murderer." I raise a stiff brow. "Marsyas did it. Why else would she vanish? Why else would she kill our driver?"

"If Marsyas did it and left, there's no one to punish *except for us*."

"You heard them in the meeting. They're going to find a way around that. And they're witches, surely they can."

"We don't know these people. They could've already agreed to off us if they don't come up with a better plan," I point out. Before she can protest that there's no way, I add, "They had the time while we were running away."

Wren blows out a "fine, jeez" breath, before whining, "But we didn't have anything to do with it." She motions to my newly repaired hand. "Auden will vouch for us."

"We don't know that."

"He likes you, Lavinia. He's helping us because he thinks you're hot. And lucky you, because he literally has magical hands."

Because she's Wren, she adds a dreamy sigh.

A furious heat starts to creep up my cheeks, and I attempt to swallow it down. I barely know Auden and he didn't seem to like me much at all until he saved our butts and my hand on the driveway. I'm not about to put all my eggs in that one very handsome basket with our lives on the line.

"He could be lying," I remind her. "He could've healed me to ingratiate himself to us. I mean—we don't know. Auden says he believes we weren't in on it but even if that's true, he's one of nine other people here. There's only so much he can do."

"Trust him to fight for us—he already basically magically lied or whatever for us."

He did. I don't know why but he did. My thoughts are too jumbled to make sense of any of what he did for us when he found us escaping. Still—no. This won't work.

I hook a brow at her. "Do you recall the last time we trusted one of these people when they simply seemed like they wanted to help us?"

Wren places a hand over her heart. "I take full responsibility for trusting Marsyas. Auden is different. And you know it—I can see it in the way you're totally going full tomato right now."

"Am not."

"God, look at yourself, will you?" Wren flips our grip and hauls me closer to the mirrors. Then, my sister abandons her mission altogether when she notices the toiletries lined up in antique metal-and-glass packaging on the counter. She rummages until she finds a toothbrush and a little lip-balm-sized pot of toothpaste.

"Oh, thank God, my mouth tastes like bubbly and bile."

The moment Wren's dabbing the corners of her lips with a towel, fresh and clean, I launch into her.

"The point is we could become collateral damage, which they won't figure out until we're dead and they're still locked in. They can only kill us once, and I'm pretty sure magic can't bring us back, or Ursula would've been revived and doled out punishment herself."

Wren shrugs her slim shoulders like I'm being completely melodramatic about all of this. Like she isn't the theatrical one and I am. How on earth is this still an adventure to her? We have a single white-knight moment with Auden—who may or may not be trustworthy, by the way—and she's back to floating on a cloud, being an adorable, bullheaded thrill seeker.

"So we'll just tell them."

I gape at her.

In answer, she hauls her butt onto the vanity counter—which is definitely antique and probably very breakable—and positions herself right in front of me. Wren shakes her head, voice low, amber eyes level with mine.

"We drop the accents, pull out our driver's licenses, and prove we're not Lavinia and Kaysa. We're just two innocent girls who were propositioned by an eccentric witch-lady con artist while slinging falafel."

I frown and Wren snatches up my hands, holding them tight.

"They'll take pity on us, Ruby. Protect us. Auden is already in our corner and Evander has 'overprotective grump' written across his permanently furrowed forehead. I mean, even Winter is letting us wear her clothes, so she's not totally two-faced."

I wonder if, for all her time spent on stage and mainlining movies, my sister has completely forgotten that motive isn't just something that appears in the aftershocks of a crime. It's woven into all of it. Motive compels people not just to do bad things, but to do literally everything. Why on earth would the motivation to protect two strangers be stronger than the motivation to protect their own family, and its legacy?

Wren thinks she can bat her eyelashes at our problems, and they'll solve themselves. That's never how anything works.

Finally, I punch out an exhale. "It's as hard to believe as it is to prove. Our driver's licenses won't mean anything to these people—

they probably think the only valid type of identification is a passport anyway. Can you picture Sanguine Cerise driving herself anywhere?"

I can barely envision the woman brushing her own teeth. She probably has a manservant for that. The next two days and change will be roughing it for her.

Wren's eyes begin to sparkle, and she waggles her brows in a way I should've seen coming. "I've certainly pictured Evander going a hundred miles per hour in the Maserati parked out on the drive, with me in the passenger's seat."

Exasperated, I tug myself away from her grip and run my hands through my hair—a terrible and futile idea because it's full of product carving out waves I don't truly have.

"Look," I half-sigh, walking to the end of the bathroom and pivoting on one teetering heel, "they won't believe us when we tell them who we are because they were already suspicious of us thanks to Marsyas vanishing, the dead guy in the driveway—when they find him, and I'm sure they will eventually or Auden will toss us under the bus or . . . something—and our unlikely appearance at this particular party after, what, ten years away?"

God, I'm truly pacing now, multiple laps under my belt. "And, on the extremely off chance that they do believe us, we're two regular people who now know all about their very secret, very important witch stuff. If they're willing to kill their own, they're not just going to let two party-crashing imposters walk away with a handshake promise not to tell."

I'm prepared to go off on Wren if she so much as mentions Auden "liking" me one more time, but instead she draws from her vast experience marathoning sci-fi on Dad's Netflix account. "Maybe they can magically zap our memories. You know, just clean our clocks, and leave us by the side of the road, then we'd be two hot schlubs with no recollection."

"I don't think they're 'do no harm' kind of people."

Wren's shoes fall off to the immaculate honeycomb tile with a one-two *clunk-clunk*. Her eyes lift to mine.

"Okay," she says, and the word is a relief. The giddiness has receded, my worry hammered home and nailing over the thrill of tonight—the flirting, the magic, the surprise. You'd think seeing a man with his eyeballs literally ripped out would've done it, but Wren is nothing if not a pendulum swinging her way through the most exciting points in life. "So what do we do?"

And that's when reality hits me too.

"There's nothing we can do."

"*Rubes,*" she whispers, "do you hear yourself? We're stuck in a haunted-ass house with witches, a dead body, and probably several *named* ghosts. We need to start thinking out of the box or we're dead meat."

Gambling, I haul myself onto the counter too and hold up the hand I'm very lucky looks and feels normal right now, an exhibit in what I'm about to say. "If there's a way out of here other than what Ursula announced . . . don't you think the witches would be on that?"

Her brows touch. "No, because they're all focused on the relics and power they'll win. It's robbed them of their sensibility. And even if they didn't have that distracting them, those people aren't *us.*" Wren finger-guns me. "We're resourceful."

I nearly laugh because "gullible" is more like it. I bite my lip but it doesn't cut the sarcasm. "It's our resourcefulness that got us into this mess, sis."

Wren sighs. "Bought hook, line, and sinker for a couple thousand bucks, a few compliments, and the promise of a good time for an easy lie.'"

We sit in the heavy truth of it. The running water is growing warm now, the enclosed space stifling and condensation beginning to mist on the counters. Wren's eyes narrow.

"Marsyas had to have expected us to sell her out. Right? Tell them who we are immediately and beg for mercy. And to what end? She still looks guilty—her whole family looks guilty." Wren taps her bottom lip. "So what's the play?"

"Does it matter?" I sigh. "Whatever she intended, it was for her own means. Now our job is to survive. That's it. Not play the game, just to survive it and make it out. To Dad and Karen."

To Dad and Karen, who are in Boulder for a weeklong art exhibition. It's Saturday night in midsummer and with the Ren Fest over, no one's even going to miss us until my shift at Agatha's on Wednesday afternoon. By then, we'll either be locked in here forever or free because we survived or we died. Fuck.

"How?" Wren asks, softly.

My sister knows how to act, but I know how to strategize—or, well, at least *plot,* thanks to every dog-eared mystery I've ever read. "We learn everything they expect us to know and wield it like a shield. We're going to have to *be* them to *survive* them."

"Okay, but that's just defense. Reactionary." She claps for emphasis. "We need to *do* something too. We need a sword to go with the shield."

Wren's right. A hundred percent right.

"They suspect us . . ." I start, my mind stumbling through the fog of our situation. Then, it clears, open and bright. "So we're going to have to prove them wrong and find the killer. It's either Marsyas—and we'll have to show we had nothing to do with what she did—or it's someone framing Marsyas. Either way, finding the truth will protect us from the witches' suspicions and from the actual murderer—"

"Because we'll tag their ass before they can off us." Wren grins something feral. "Okay, where do we start?"

Our fencing metaphor has a good answer. "Before we wield that sword, we need to strap on the shield. Both the informational one—the basics about the families and the magic—*and* the actual one."

I present my wrist.

Wren's face scrunches. "You think the dead bunnies are shields?"

"Auden said as much—they're relics." She blinks at me, and I throw my hands up like we were ordered to do at the fence before lowering my voice into something deeper. "Turn around with your hands up, and *relics* clear."

Wren smirks. "Was that supposed to be Auden?"

"You know it was. You just didn't get the line right when you did your impression five minutes ago." She's annoyed but doesn't argue.

"The point is the Blackgates are witches. If they're witches, *we're witches.* The kind who do eyeball-sucking, murdering magic—with these things. Relics, not master relics, just regular ones." The foot swings in exclamation, a little furry pendulum. "The more we know about what they can do and how they use them, the better we can protect ourselves with their reputation, even if we can't actually do a single thing."

Wren flicks her bracelet. "It would be cool if it weren't so utterly disgusting. Doing magic *through* dead things? I mean—ew."

"It's just an educated guess. One we need to confirm," I say, though the skunk story and the way *everyone* glanced at us before Ursula's body was covered are pretty good hints along with the "Death Line" moniker attached to the Blackgate name. "We need to know as much by morning as possible."

"Morning, when somebody might notice the magical Band-Aid covering the dead driver?"

"Yes. Exactly."

"Okay." Wren slips off the counter to the tile, stomps into her heels, and looks to me for direction, repeating her earlier question. "Where do we start?"

Ursula's office would be ideal—she probably had the most top-secret information close at hand—but it's also probably still full of Hegemonys. Judging by the way things went tonight, they had *lots* to discuss.

I raise a brow. "You think this place has a library?"

"Oh, I'm betting it has at least three." Wren straightens the waist of her dress, which has meandered. "Probably all haunted."

"As long as the ghosts don't report back to the witches what we're actually looking up, it'll appear we're doing our research for the master relic scavenger hunt."

I turn off all the faucets in succession. Without the rush of water, the silence is suddenly deafening.

I grab my sister's hand. "Let's go figure out what we're dealing with."

PART TWO

THE
MAGIC

CHAPTER 13

AUDEN

Ursula told me my role at the year's turn. The day before I was to return to school after the winter holiday. More than six months ago now.

I'd come into Ursula's study and shut the door as requested. She was speaking before I'd even completed my approach across the stately room.

"My boy," she said from behind her grand desk, and I knew then that this was a serious matter because private affection was involved. The silt-gray light of a cloudy morning streaming in the diamond-paned windows only put a point on it. It was as if she'd summoned the dreariness herself. And maybe she had.

Ursula gestured to the set of guest chairs before her. I always sat in the one to the right. That day wasn't one for trying something new. I lowered myself to the bespoke brocade cushion and the moment I was still again, Ursula began, nearly impatient.

"I will be dead and gone sooner than I would like."

My gut twisting, I nodded. There was no sense in contradicting her with platitudes and overconfident reassurance. Both were lies. My grandmother was a powerful woman closer to a hundred than most humans would ever see. Her husband had been dead as long as I'd been alive. Her children nearly ten of my seventeen years. She'd lived with death my whole life, a constant companion. One we couldn't ignore. One that wouldn't be ignored.

Ursula leaned forward, her eyes as bright as lit matches at midnight. The blaze in the hearth achieved exactly nothing except providing warmth and a low current of power to the High Sorcerer. Every room in Hegemony Manor had a flue for just that reason. Fire was a powerful and pervasive element.

"Auden, when I am gone, you will be the executor to my last will and testament."

This was where someone else would demur and plea, "Ursula, are you sure?"

I didn't. Still, she explained, as if I'd asked.

"Evander is the one most loyal to the Hegemony name. Winter is the one most loyal to the Hegemony family."

This was true. Evander would tattoo the name across his face if Ursula wouldn't behead him for being so embarrassingly brash. And Winter would do anything for her family, including ditching every responsibility we had to anyone beyond our blood.

"You, however, are loyal to who the Hegemonys *are*. That is an important distinction."

It was.

The Hegemony name literally meant power. It wasn't a mistake or a quirk of language and luck that the word "hegemony"—the prominence of one over others—described exactly who we were. It was a purposeful rebranding choice by Mercy Hegemony after saving the Four Lines from disaster. Since that moment, her descendants were Elemental witches, yes, but also so much more—supreme rulers of the Four Lines for the past four hundred years, as dictated by our hold over the powerful master relics that were key to the survival of modern magic within North America.

And my cousins and I all had very different ideas of what that power meant.

Ursula primly folded her hands atop her desk. The four gemstones of the High Sorcerer's ring she wore glinted mildly in the dull light. Her movements were always so unhurried, smooth, deliberate. Steady. Just like her voice.

"When I die," Ursula had announced without an ounce of hesitation or recoil, "our fissures will come to light."

Sixty years. That was how long Ursula Hegemony had held the title of High Sorcerer. One year after the death of her older brother, Matthias, and two years after the death of her mother, Elvire, who had been High Sorcerer for fifty years.

Ursula had been the High Sorcerer for so long that a power vacuum would be inevitable. The history books along these walls, in the library, the turret reading room, heck, in my dorm room at school, were filled with examples of the same, all over the world.

We were not the same, though our *hegemony*—so to speak—was quite different.

"We will crack and bleed, and fester until we're healed," Ursula had continued, her tourmaline eyes unwavering. There was magic in that, a thread of power that meant what she said in this here and now would never fade from my memory. "Some will see this as a game to be won. What *you* must see it as is a set of instructions. Auden, it is crucial that you do exactly as I say. Is that understood?"

"Yes, Ursula."

A stiff nod—curt, hard, decisive. "Now, here is what you must do."

✦   ✦   ✦

All those months ago, Ursula had been right.

Our fissures ruptured at the surface.

They spider-webbed every which way, the shotgun blast of ice cracking on a frozen lake before shattering and swallowing whole anything heavier than a feather.

Between the four High Families. Within our own. Within this very room.

Ursula's murder is simply the first crack visible to all of us. A sign of what's shattered beneath.

We will crack and bleed, and fester until we're healed.

I hope she's right about the end. I fear it's the first time she's ever been wrong.

The fissures have just begun, and even with Ursula's words looping through my mind, I already don't know how to repair them. I don't know if I'll get a chance. The breaks I can't see—yet—could widen to gaping chasms by the end of Ursula's final directive. I think that's more likely than our crevices healing up, our "most unusual and unbreakable family" knitting back together, stronger than ever.

Ruminating, I stare into the flames of the study hearth. There's always a fire in this room. Day or night, season after season, hour after hour. Until I'd walked into cold embers tonight, I'd thought those flames to be as endless as they were alive. Now I know they died along with Ursula, like the grass outside, like the wilting plants in this room and all along this floor. Death spilling over and tainting anything that had Ursula's magic in it. Even me. Even my cousins. Maybe everyone trapped in this estate.

Winter returns with the snick of a lock latching closed. I have my back to her, sitting cross-legged in the right-hand guest chair I always used when Ursula was alive. Evander has claimed the large leather desk chair, the fire casting a shimmer of gold on one side of his face. His expression flickers with all the things he's planning to say.

We haven't so much as exchanged a word since Winter left with the Blackgates. Just assumed our current positions and retreated to our thoughts.

"I told you not to move," she scolds with a sigh.

My gaze snaps away from the fire. "I thought I'd get comfortable. This conversation won't be short."

Winter drops into the other guest chair. She slips off her ridiculous heels and tucks her knees to her chest, the floral-print silk of her dress hugging her skin as tightly as the vise cage of her strong, tennis-player arms.

"The length of this conversation depends entirely on how quickly you want to tell the truth," Evander says, leaning on the desk. "What did you know, Auden?"

This time, because he's seated, his elbows dig into the leather blotter on either side of the page that had been the will and is now our clue, his hands cupping his biceps. His jacket is off again, just as it was in the garden. His shoulders strain against the brilliant white fabric, and his jaw works in his heavily hung head.

I know Evander's stressed. I know he's sad. I know he can't believe this any more than I can.

But I have no idea why, after what's happened tonight, his first inclination is to aim all his anger at me.

I straighten my trousers where they've creased. "I would say you'd have to be more specific, but the answer is the same whether you're referring to what happened to Ursula or to what was in the will. I didn't know."

Evander inhales a thin, angry breath. "I'll try again, and put it as plainly as possible: Did you know she was going to die?"

I did know Ursula was expecting death. I didn't know she would be murdered.

"Evander, how can you ask him that?" Winter's voice tears through my thoughts and the air, a warning shot of anger threaded into each syllable. "Our grandmother is dead—*murdered*—and your first move as patriarch to the Elemental Line is to accuse Auden of being *in on it*? What in the absolute fuck?"

Every ounce of restraint has been wrung out of Evander from this long and terrible night. A familiar sparring partner is never a reason to hold back. He doesn't.

"I'm doing what Ursula would expect from us at this moment—"

"By interrogating Auden like Ursula whispered in his ear that she planned to be offed at her own dinner party?" Winter thrusts a hand in the general direction of the belly of Hegemony Manor and the residential wings that make up the second floor. Tears spark again in her azure eyes. "By one of her guests? One of the High Families? Are you serious right now?"

"Win, I know you're upset—"

"Of course I'm upset!" Winter explodes, and the tears break free, spilling onto her reddening cheeks. "Do not try to mollify my feelings, Evander Hegemony. That's not leadership, that's dismissal. I'm not a fucking robot."

His hands raise like a white flag. "I'm sorry, that was the wrong thing to say."

"Yeah, it was." Winter sniffs and blots at the wetness on her cheeks with the backs of her hands.

Evander sighs, sinks back in Ursula's chair, and drags a hand down his face. Then, he changes his mind and leans forward, pressing his palms flat on the desk, as if grounding himself. "I'm not saying Auden was part of Ursula's murder, I'm just starting my questioning with what he knew as executor that we did not—including the information that he'd been named executor, a fact that he kept from us—"

"At Ursula's discretion." My tone is flat. Evander is digging—he'll find nothing but bare earth. "It was technically a request, but we all know that her requests were orders. I obeyed."

He narrows his eyes at me. "And you didn't think that was suspect?"

"Jesus, Evander," Winter curses. Her slim fingers fist the hair at her temples as if she's about to yank it out at the root. "The woman's vanity spells were top-tier but lest you forget, Ursula was ninety-nine years old. Of course she planned to die, she was a High Sorcerer, not immortal—don't give Ursula shit for being prepared but not wanting to worry us. Don't give Auden shit about being her executor. You were the heir, Evander, you couldn't be the executor too." She pauses. "It was going to be either of us, and he's older. It makes sense."

Evander's head tilts as he stares at me.

"But I wasn't the heir, was I?"

If he wants a wrestling match, he'll get one. He's bigger and older, but that's never mattered when it comes to words, or to actual wrestling, because I've always been quicker.

"You are the heir. To our family. To the Elemental Line and all the thousands of witches who practice within it. Patriarch." With each new word, the cords in Evander's thick neck seem to tighten. I keep going. "If you're implying that I knew Ursula's will would change in regard to the title of High Sorcerer if she was murdered, no, I did not."

Evander rubs a thumb along his jaw, the light scraping sound of the pad against stubble the undertone for his unblinking assessment of my expression. "You're the executor, how—"

"Hey, hi, over here." Winter waves a hand. "Before you dial in and cost us ten more precious minutes by interrogating Auden more, understand that I tossed you the perfect opening to ask if *I* have a role too." She pointedly fishes her own key out from behind the ribbon choker at her throat. "Liaison of the Lines."

Evander squints at her. "Liaison? Really? We haven't had one since . . ."

"Since my mother. Yes," she answers. Unlike my role as executor, the role of liaison had been absorbed into Ursula's own duties when Aunt Lana passed—a role that made the High Sorcerer's life easier but wasn't a necessity like heir or executor. Important, but a matter of delegation in the scheme of things.

And Ursula had delegated the role to Winter.

"Perhaps," I say, "we should start by asking what we all knew—"

Evander smirks, but not in the kind way he did at Kaysa when he thought no one was looking only hours ago. "Oh, so you've come up with an answer for me now?"

"No, a question. For you."

I wait to see what he'll do with that. If he'll use my own aborted questioning as a shield, or if he'll let me move forward as a means to prove he has nothing to hide.

Bulldozer in a three-piece suit, he does exactly what I think he will. Evander crosses his arms over his barrel chest, a shield disguised as outward intimidation. "Fine. Shoot."

"What happened when you left the solarium to question Ursula?"

Winter freezes. "Wait, when was this? After I went to greet the guests?"

"Yes," I answer because Evander doesn't. "When you left to greet the Blackgates, Evander announced he was instead going 'to the source.'"

Now, Winter grips both arms of her chair, stricken. "Evander Hegemony, were you the last person *alone* with our dear grandmother before her death?"

"No," he spits, curtly. "I came to her study, but she wasn't here." He lifts a thick eyebrow at me in challenge. "Happy?"

"Not entirely." I shrug. "I thought you might have something useful to say."

Evander scowls. "Are you certain? Because it very much seemed as if you were making an accusation."

"Not any worse than you were making of Auden five minutes ago," Winter reminds him.

Though I appreciate her defense, I hold up my hands—not in surrender but in exasperation. "I'm on your side, Evander. If you didn't find Ursula in her study, I believe you." He squints at me. "And beyond that, you're a terrible murder suspect."

It's true. Still, he squints harder.

Between that and his tight jaw, how he doesn't have a headache all the time is beyond me. I spell it out. "You lost both your grandmother and the guarantee of your future the moment Ursula fell. I understand why Hector doesn't want you leading the investigation, but in truth you're the least likely suspect of everyone here."

Evander plants his elbows on the desk like he's about to argue, but Winter won't allow it.

"Auden's right. You're pretty much the only one who isn't a suspect, Evander."

I clap my hands together, because, as she often does, Winter finds a way to put a finer point on my own thoughts. "Whomever killed Ursula also stands to benefit from gaining control of the masters. That's the motive—kill Ursula, trigger the change in her will, set up a hunt that can recast the holder of the master relics, and therefore the seat of power for all Four Lines witches in North America."

"Yes. Exactly," Winter agrees.

Evander, of course, is not so sure because none of this is his idea. In many ways Winter is the tactician you don't see coming because her beauty often gets in the way of people's perceptions, while Evander is the tactician who doesn't see any other way.

To wit, he literally owns up to it next, grumbling, "I don't see why you're down on me questioning the Blackgates immediately—"

"Because I don't think they did it."

This stops him cold. Winter too.

"You know I'm no fan of the Blackgates, now or ever, but Marsyas and Athena literally shipped those girls across an ocean to protect them from the Four Lines and specifically Ursula. Why on earth would Marsyas kill Ursula and leave her granddaughters trapped in this spell with us?" The ice around them cracks as they consider this. "Moreover, how the hell do they benefit from a possible change in leadership if they're both suspects and clearly magically altered to be clueless? It doesn't make sense."

Winter aimlessly rubs a finger over her bottom lip, the last of her expertly applied gloss vanishing. "So, you think it's a setup?"

"I think something's wrong here."

Evander shakes his head. "Auden, I know you had a passably friendly reacquaintance with Lavinia—"

"Oh, come on, you were working very hard not to smile in Kaysa's presence," I toss a hand in his direction. "We all saw it."

"We *did*," Winter confirms. "That sourpuss business finally worked on someone—a Blackgate, no less—and you were thrilled enough *to smirk*."

Evander doesn't acknowledge either of us.

"But," he plows forward, completely ignoring our accusations, "we can't rule out the Blackgates. They're the most obvious choice with Marsyas missing—everyone in this room just agreed to it."

"They agreed because it takes each of them off the hot seat," I point out. "Listen, if not the Blackgates in vengeance for Marcos, the Cerises have the most obvious motivation. They had control of the Four Lines in Salem—Napoleon Cerise was the first High Sorcerer, after all, before he decided to commit genocide against the other three lines. Maybe before he was executed, Napoleon passed down information that led them to believe this exact *hunt* could happen. Maybe they've been waiting more than four hundred years for the right time to put this in motion."

My reasoning isn't ironclad—the ring wasn't tethered to the High Sorcerer until Mercy saved the Four Lines from Napoleon

Cerise—but it's the best I have, and likely important if not imperfect.

"I do agree with you that Hector's enthusiasm for teamwork does seem a little . . . *manufactured*," Evander agrees. "The man's a textbook sycophant. He attaches himself to power like a tapeworm."

Winter rolls her eyes. "Or," she counters, "he's just a different type of team player than the kind who tries to decapitate people with lacrosse sticks." She takes a swing that proves she's a tennis player and has never once attended one of our lacrosse games. Which is fine. Apparently, she was busy schmoozing with the rest of the lines in her free time. "The Cerises try too hard but they mean well. Really. They're doing some amazing things in the medical field."

"You mean they're making a gold mine on blood-testing patents," I amend.

"Like the Hegemony name wasn't built on the literal California gold rush."

I smirk at her. "That money went into clean energy decades ago."

"And the Starwoods?" Evander asks, forcing things per usual. "They didn't seem interested in power, only getting out of here and moving on with their lives."

"Isn't that motivation enough?" I ask. It should be.

Evander just shrugs at me. Winter sighs. I lay it out for them the way I see it. A way that won't jump the gun but will be efficient.

"Look, I think we join the game and watch how it's played." Evander's nostrils flare at the word "game" but I continue. It's the word Ursula used all those months ago and it's the word I'm going to use now. "That's our investigation—observation only, which isn't against the rules. We need to look at the murder probe and the masters hunt through the same lens—two sides of the same coin. If someone killed Ursula specifically to get their hands on the masters, they'll reveal themselves as the masters are being found by how they react."

Evander grimaces, ready to argue. I drill him with an unblinking stare.

"And before you shoot down this idea, let me tell you that it'll simply look like you made your priority the game."

"It's *not* a game. Stop calling it that. And reclaiming our family title as High Sorcerer is my priority. I just don't want us to lose sight of punishing Ursula's murderer."

"Evander, it's something to be won. Call it what you want— hunt, quest, competition—I'm calling it a game."

Winter draws in a thin breath and nods in a way that makes me think she's on my side about this stupid terminology but then wisely goes on.

"And no one is losing sight of the fact that we have twin aims here. You were in that meeting just now, Evander, the same as Auden and me. The determination was to focus on the master relics. That's what we'll do *while* keeping an eye open for clues as to who was the killer, Marsyas or otherwise. Then, we watch, we ask questions, we keep tugging at threads. And if we get to the end and determine it is Marsyas who did it, then we focus all our energy on using those relics to break the lockdown, and then punish her for what she's done." Winter turns to our older cousin. "Which was your idea, I may remind you."

It was. Evander swallows his grimace. "Fine."

Our logic has hit the mark. But I push further.

"And just so we're on the same page, don't make it seem like you're interrogating someone," I add. "I can't believe I'm saying this, but you don't have to have *already* murdered someone to *become* a murderer. This situation is stressful enough, and keeping our emotions under wraps will go a long way to ensuring we don't have anyone else do something rash."

To my surprise, Evander bursts into a low laugh.

When we gape at him, he stabs a finger on the leather blotter, full mouth twisted and incredulous. "Auden, you don't want to cause discord between the lines. This is you trying to keep me from a confrontation."

"That's not what I'm doing."

"That's exactly what you're doing—"

"Because he doesn't want to see you hurt." Winter glares at our oldest cousin. "*I* don't want to see you hurt. Those relics are valuable and we don't know what everyone is thinking when they're not sucking up to us. You may be a bad murder suspect, but you're a good target. If someone is motivated to control the lines, you're in the way, Evander. And hurting you—hell, killing you—is a way to get you out of the way."

All mirth falls from Evander's face as he looks at her.

"Ursula's rules won't allow that."

"Her magic isn't a shield, Evander. It's a deterrent." I wish I could knock the reality of it straight through his skull. "If anyone kills you, it'll be worth a day locked in Ursula's magic because with you out of the picture, they'll win. They'll win the title, have enough power to avoid punishment, and be in charge while you'll be in a grave next to Ursula."

Evander's gaze snaps to my face. His mossy-green eyes are rimmed with red this close, from sadness or anger or exhaustion. It's impossible to tell. Maybe all those emotions, pressing against his skin, hoping for release but not getting it from the one of us who's too stubborn and determined to allow it.

"Fine. Fine. Understood. Noted. I'll be careful with my phrasing and attitude tomorrow. Happy?" We nod. He smooths his hands over the desk blotter. "But I can't just sit here and do nothing tonight. We have to do something. We have to know what Ursula was thinking."

I fish out the chain at my throat. "All three of us have keys. Maybe we need to spend time seeing how many drawers and cabinets we can open. We go through the contents, and if there's anything that won't open for us, we open it by other means."

Winter is incredulous. "You seriously want to do this right now?"

I point at the grandfather clock on the mantel above the fireplace. "It's just past eleven on Saturday night. We have until 11:59 P.M. Monday night to figure this out. We won't know unless we haven't completed the tasks and then it's too late." I yank the chain from my throat and stand up. "We're the only ones who can do this search. And I'm with Evander, I need to do something tonight."

CHAPTER 14

RUBY

Wren and I make it from our room, down the hallway lined with dark window wells overlooking the inky black courtyard and back to the foyer, which is still lit up, a guidepost in the night. While Wren stands there gawking at the mural, I wrack my exhausted brain for something close to an educated guess about the location of a library. It isn't like there are placards in a place as sprawling as Hegemony Manor, announcing the names of rooms and, if you asked Wren, their appointed ghosts.

Hegemony Manor is three stories above ground. Our quarters are on the second floor, the same floor as the solarium. It's obviously residential, with wings mashed together at right angles overlooking the courtyard in the middle. My first inclination is that a library would be on the first floor. Something mixed in next to a formal dining room or a drawing room or parlor.

But then, somewhere between looking up at the cheery blue of the sky painted into the very ceiling, and the realization that the cut and positioning of the veiny marble is part of the whole beautiful picture too, the idea hits me that even if there's a library on the first floor—and likely there is—that's not where a very powerful secret witch would keep her very powerful secret witch books.

Not out in the open where just anyone could waltz in and read about the Four Lines and secret master relics and all the ways magic can apparently shoot invisibly from people's fingers.

Ursula Hegemony would've kept that stuff close at hand, especially considering she obviously did not rely on computerized records of any sort.

Which is how we end up back on the third floor.

The faint scent of out-of-season lilac announces Ursula's floor before we finish our approach, the smooth dark planks of the staircase bleeding into a lush herringbone carpet that traps the sounds of our footsteps like secrets.

During our escape attempt, I hadn't noticed the delicate floral scent, nor its origin: two massive vases set like sentries along the landing wall, stuffed to brimming with the cuttings of lilac. They're a royal purple, and a little wilted, but fragrant and gorgeous. They frame a massive portrait in an ornate, gilded frame as thick as most windowpanes. It's not a portrait, but a painting inside. A little plate etched into the frame announces this is the man who founded the manor and likely wrote the clues and hid the relics we'll be collecting for the next three days.

Shadrack Zebulon Gradefon Hegemony (1832–1910)

His title—High Sorcerer—is missing, probably as a safety precaution. But even without it, even without anything else beyond this placement of honor pointing toward his role in procuring both this land and building this house, it's clear he's a *very important person,* with every word of that phrase italicized within an inch of its life. It's there in the cut of his jaw, the focus of his eyes, the aristocratic slash of his cheekbones and nose.

"It's Shadrack the clue scribe," Wren jokes, dismissing all the manufactured reverence with a tilt of her head. "Or maybe the secret relic Easter Bunny?"

"I know you're just trying to amuse yourself so you don't pee your pants out of fear, but please don't piss off his ghost in the process," I deadpan.

My sister's lips twist. "I *am* trying to amuse myself. Which is why I'll feed the dumbest nicknames I come up with to Hex and watch Evander eviscerate him. I disagree with Winter; sourpuss can be very sexy."

"I'm going to ignore that." I haul her to Shadrack's left. "Let's go clockwise."

Every door is locked, none of them are marked, and before we know it, we're hanging a right, down the hall that we know houses the study. It's straight ahead on our right, smack in the middle of the floor. If the courtyard weren't a donut hole in the middle of the house, Shadrack's painting would've been on the back side of it.

I mouth *study* at Wren, and point to the pair of doors, still closed.

Duh, my sister mouths back.

She rolls her eyes for good measure before pointedly pushing a lock of hair behind her ear and leaning into the door to eavesdrop.

I scramble to yank her back, but she bats at me and darts away.

No! I mouth and successfully clamp down on her wrist this time, hauling her several steps away from the double doors before lighting into her.

"What are you doing?" I snap, looking back over my shoulder, relieved to see the doors still closed. "They're going to know you're there."

"They are not. I couldn't hear a thing, which means they couldn't hear me."

"That's like assuming if you shut your eyes, they can't see you. We don't know what they're capable of, and until we know, let's assume they can hear us, see us, smell us, detect us in ways that normal people can't—"

"*Smell us?* They're witches, not vampires or werewolves. Seriously, like—"

The study doors open a crack, and Auden's head pops out, brows furrowed. He looks handsomely disheveled, suit coat doffed, the sleeves of his lavender button-up rolled up like a campaign trail politician. He blinks at us. "Can I help you?"

"Oh, um, sorry. We were trying not to bother you," I blather with a stiff smile, immediately feeling like I've used up all my get-out-of-jail-free cards with this grieving boy. I swallow and drop Wren's wrist. "The library? We don't remember where it is exactly, but we thought it was this floor?"

"The reading room is off the third-floor landing in the turret. Follow the spiral stairs."

Wren smacks me on the arm. "Told you."

Auden nods. "Good luck and good night."

He vanishes back into the study with a click of a lock.

My face flames as we shuffle back down the hallway. "I sure hope you know where these spiral stairs are after you made it sound like you did because that excuse won't work twice."

"I do, actually."

When the scent of lilacs and Shadrack's unsmiling face greets us a second time, Wren points triumphantly at an alcove beside the grand staircase landing. But from this vantage, with the nearest gas lamp flickering over my shoulder, I see it for what it really is—another set of stairs, narrow and short.

They dump us out into the open entry of a little jewelry box of a room with a single window on each of the four sides, the telltale scent of books punching us square in the face as our eyes adjust to the weak sconce light.

Window seats are tucked under each sash, a foursome of antique chairs in the same bright green of Winter's dress are spun around a small table in the middle, and every other nook and cranny is set with books. Built-in shelves line every bit of wall space, and more ring the chairs in the middle, low and perfectly aligned with the chairbacks as not to make everything claustrophobic or lose what's likely a very lovely view of both the mountains and Wood Rose in the day.

"Dear God," Wren stage-whispers into my ear, "are you sure you're not a witch? Because you might have conjured this from one of your book-nerd daydreams."

This *is* what I dream of when Agatha's is empty and I'm shelving carts of vintage paperbacks, though truth be told I've never seen a collection like this before in person. There must be at least a thousand very old, very loved tomes living on these shelves, holding new worlds between worn leather spines.

I swallow, heavily. "First objective, Death magic. Second objective, Four Lines information, like the Wikipedia overview of how it works, and—"

Wren cuts me off with a raised hand.

"Drill sergeant, a question." I roll my eyes as she lowers her arm. "This must have happened before, right? Ursula probably didn't just pull this out of her figurative magical witch hat, did she? Wait. Possibly not figurative. She probably really could rock a hat."

I don't doubt that.

"Okay, three objectives. Death magic, Four Lines information, hunt for the relics." I hold up my phone. "Take pictures of anything that might be relevant, and we'll review in our suite."

Wren does her best impression of a military salute, and, after doffing our ridiculous heels, we fan out. I claim the far wall overlooking the courtyard, while my sister opts for the shelves overlooking the front lawn.

The books are as delicate and aged as I'd inferred, with translucent pages in some parts, the covers leather-bound or moldering cloth. Most of the books are typeset but some are literally handwritten in the same strangely shiny ink of Ursula's last will and testament. And next to none have any sort of index.

I realize that perhaps I need to *think* like an ancient witch who already knows everything there is to know about witch culture and the Four Lines. If I wanted to find basic information about the Blackgate witches or the general distinctions between the Four Lines, it wouldn't be in a book any Hegemony used often. Therefore, the type of book I want wouldn't be close at hand or at eye level—in this room, Ursula's office, or any other literary repository hiding in this house.

I start hunting for big, obvious titles on the top shelves. I've loaded my arms up with five huge reference-style resources and turned toward the reading table when Wren punches out a frustrated sigh—the kind that blows her bangs up and away. "I literally just found a book of recipes. Witchy cooking stuff with cauldrons. There were unidentifiable splotches in the margins. I mean, it's cool to know that spells and cauldrons are actually a thing, but I really couldn't tell if that was blood or wine or you know, *witch juice,* on the page."

"That's quite judgmental coming from someone who vomited watermelon gazpacho with a champagne chaser an hour ago."

Wren's book slams shut. "Very funny. Now I'm both repulsed and reminded I'm doing research on an empty stomach."

"Stop complaining and help me with these thick ones. They look promising."

Wren yanks a massive one off the top. It's nearly square, as wide as it is long, and probably four inches thick. *"Ley Lines and Their Faults: A Modern Guide to Energy and the Four Lines,"* Wren recites from the cover, pulling a face. Then, she flips inside. "First printing, 1902. *Super* modern."

"Don't knock it until you read it."

Wren blows out enough air to fill a large balloon with her annoyance. Focused tasks are not exactly her jam. Which is reinforced by yet another lobbed complaint five minutes later.

"Every mention of the names we know are almost like an afterthought—like everything is already understood." Wren slumps back in her chair. "They mention the Cerises and the Hegemonys and whatever almost as a substitute for their line."

That I'd noticed too. Everything I'd come across so far seemed to have used each family name interchangeably with the type of magic. Which wasn't helpful when you were trying to figure what those were exactly and where they came from and whatever the hell else we had going on here.

"But the four families can't be the only ones with these powers," I answer, gesturing toward the books, with all their various authors. "There have to be more witches than just the ones in this building. I mean, we know their parents died, but three Hegemonys and three other people made this generation of cousins."

"You make it sound like they were grown in a lab." Wren's head snaps up from her current book, mischief gathering at the corners of her quirked mouth. "Maybe they *were* grown in a lab. I mean, did you see Winter's pores? No, you didn't, because they don't exist."

I pointedly roll my eyes in an impression of her. Wren laughs, and I expect her to just tuck back into her book, but then she pings stick straight in her chair, an idea nearly bursting out of her eye sockets as her lips drop open.

"Wait." She clambers for my wrist. "What if *we* are witches? I

mean, Marsyas picked us for a reason. What if our branch of the Four Lines got lost somehow?"

I'm about to dismiss her starry-eyed suggestion with a quip about her seeing too many movies, because Marsyas's targeting us had everything to do with our likeness to her granddaughters and our collectively gullibility, but then Wren adds, "Mom did love this place. Maybe she had latent magic and was, like, drawn to it? Like Marsyas was drawn to us?"

I don't think that's the case, but something like regret lances through me, collecting in my windpipe and weighing down my gut. I swallow and blink, doing absolutely nothing to mute the emotion.

After too long a beat, "Maybe" is all I can manage to say.

We work in silence until I flip to the firm center of the coffee-table-sized tome I'd been thumbing—*Natural and Physical: Magic in This Day and Age* (circa 1918), and a two-page spread reveals itself in full-color ink. Atop, in gorgeous calligraphy, it reads, "The Four Lines."

"*Kaysa.*" I stab the page with an exclamation point.

A drawing very much like the famous Da Vinci depiction of the *Vitruvian Man* splits the double page in perfectly drawn anatomy. In the pockets of open paper on the diagonal and wedged next to both his outstretched hands and feet are little paragraphs, each labeled with the Four Lines of magic.

I shove the book under Wren's nose, and breathless, we read the introduction.

The Four Lines

The Four Lines of magic describe the four manners of magical expression and amplification as recorded in witch clans settling North America in the 1600s. The Four Lines do not hold aegis over all magical forms and systems worldwide, in North America, or within the present-day United States. Information on types of magic outside the Four Lines can be found elsewhere. For the purposes of this text, information will solely focus on the Four Lines.

As much, the witches of the Four Lines recognize that though they all are innately magical beings, their abilities are conveyed in the way in which they are amplified. The Four Lines of witchcraft are Elemental, Celestial, Blood, and Death. The witches use available materials to enhance their magical abilities. Since the Witch Hysteria of the 1600s, the witches of the Four Lines have protected their magical amplification abilities by tying their amplification needs to a "master relic" that is protected by the designated High Sorcerer.

The purpose of this tether is to ensure each witch has continued and constant access to their amplification no matter their physical location nor external threats from non-witches. Without the tether, magic amplification is not uniform, and therefore unstable. Previous to the introduction of the master relics, some stability was provided by the ley lines, but that stability is not static and is based on location. The High Sorcerer's hold of the master relics and the High Families' maintenance of the Four Lines has provided the stability necessary to keep the sister lines safe from disruption and ensure that the continued practice of each manner of magical expression is consistent and active into the twentieth century.

"Okay, so while I'm not clear on why Ursula is making everyone work so hard, I get why the master relics are important now, I guess," Wren says.

"Yeah . . . wait, look at that."

I tap at the page, a few paragraphs down.

The first High Sorcerer to hold the master relics was Napoleon Demont Cerise in 1690, but since 1692 and the ascension of Mercy Hegemony to High Sorcerer, the title has belonged to the Hegemony family of Elemental witches.

"So, hold on." I'm trying to parse through this, pinching the bridge of my nose. "Even though everyone seemed eager to work together to find the master relics in the study . . . wouldn't someone like Hector or even Luna be interested in challenging Evander for that title if it's technically up for grabs once they're actually found?"

"Totally. This is ripe for backstabbing."

"And if Marsyas *did* kill Ursula," I continue, "wouldn't she want in on the title too? They told us they executed her son, which is motive enough, but why just bury the person when you could also steal the legacy?"

Wren's mouth pops into a little *O*. "Yeah, shit. What can we do about that? I mean, is she planning to use *us* somehow?"

"She already has. But it's true, there could be more. Not much we can do about though." I sigh. "Okay, let's keep reading. Maybe there's something else in here."

I read the descriptions, starting in the upper right by the figure's hand, and moving clockwise from there taking pictures on my phone as I go.

Elemental Magic (Green Magic)

Elemental magic bends the five elements—earth, wind, fire, water, life—to the will of the witch able to harness them. Elemental magic does not rely on overt, spoken spells, but rather the witch's personal talents to manipulate the elements.

Because, save for the element of life, the elements are limitless and always available for use, Elemental witches have often been considered the most powerful and robust of all the surviving lines of witches. Elementals have long been able to avoid detection and, thus, persecution for their magic, simply because the temperamental aspects of the natural world allow for blurring the line between magic and normal fluctuations in the elemental forces.

Traditionally, the Hegemony Clan—and families like them—oaths its heir with a key worn around the neck. Other family members within the same generation may also receive keys to designate their own roles within the family beyond the oathed heir.

"It says 'families like them,'" Wren points out. "Guess that answers the inbreeding question."

I nod. "What about the colors? Green for Elemental, and the others have them too."

"Shorthand?" Wren guesses, voice going high with a question mark.

I bite my lip. "Maybe."

Celestial Magic (White Magic)

Celestial witches like the Starwoods are bound to the night sky. Moon cycles, star cycles, the sun's rise and fall enhance their magic. These Celestial witches have power that ebbs and flows. Certain spells can gather power and bank it for use in rare cases when a large amount of magic is needed at one time.

Some Celestials, and most certainly the Starwoods, find tangential power in the sun and its solar cycles, though this magic is rare and most common in locations with the highest sun radius. The same can be said for tide cycles because of their relationship to the moon. For that reason, Celestial witches often live at or near the equator on the coasts.

Traditionally, the Starwood Clan oaths its heir with a pentagram pendant fashioned from moonstone.

"Dude, pulling power out of the stars, the sun, *and* the ocean is so badass," Wren muses.

Blood Magic (Red Magic)

The Cerise Clan is Blood magic in all its lustful force—

"Lustful? *Lustful?*" Wren crows. "A Blood witch totally authored this book."

I shush her but a grin still plays at my lips because she's probably right.

Hot to the touch, easy to stain, it leaves a mark. Blood magic drains and replenishes. It burns and heals. Rampant and unforgiving, it's impossible to escape.

"Yeah, they totally wrote this," Wren announces.

Blood witches like the Cerises use their own blood to let magic, sewing spells with a few drops, smoke to flame. But when they're given someone else's blood to use, the spells are different—instead of being let out, they're let in, which allows their magic to heal or hurt, control, or cut loose whomever has knowingly—or unwittingly—given them access. Control over another person can be achieved when a drop of the victim's blood is ingested by the Blood witch. Control then lasts up to twelve weeks.

Traditionally, the Cerise Clan oaths its heir with a horizontal line inked through the grouping of vertical lines Blood witches have tattooed on their inner forearms on the first Blood Moon of the witch's thirteenth year.

"Awww, Evander went all bananas on Hex because he didn't want us to become meat puppets for the next three months," Wren practically swoons and bats me on the arm. "What a gentleman."

Death Magic (Black Magic)

The Blackgate family is one of the lone surviving clans of Death Line witches in the world. Its proponents amplify their power and their spells through ritual sacrifice, often collecting physical relics of offerings and wearing them on their person. It is believed the historically prevalent mythology of both zombies and vampires stem from Death magic spellwork inappropriately viewed by the non-magical population.

Four Lines scholars have long tied Death magic and Blood magic in origin, offering theories of a single common magical ancestor that split a millennium ago as the two lines of magic evolved. The Blackgates and Cerises deny this connection.

Traditionally, the Blackgate Clan oaths its heir with a knife-point *X* scrawled over the heart. The *X* is made to heal without magical intervention, leaving an unmistakable scar behind.

My mind pages back to Marsyas's elaborate black pearl necklace—was there a scar beneath it? Likely. Meanwhile, the first thing Wren does when we finish reading is brandish her wrist at me, the rabbit's foot bracelet swinging in an exaggerated swoop.

"I guess you're right about these things. They're actually charged with death force or whatever and not just some sort of mage equivalent of a Scarlet Letter." Then, in a low but very enthusiastic voice, she whispers, "Like, *look over here, me in black, wearing zombie body parts! I'm a Death witch if you couldn't tell.*"

I shush her again and try to reread the section, but she's not done.

"You know when I was doing my character research one of the meanings of 'Kaysa' was 'pure torture' and I thought, huh, that's weird, surely they didn't know about that when they named her, but I bet you they fucking did it on purpose."

"Do I even want to know what Lavinia means?" I ask, flipping the page.

"You're the mother of the Roman people. Totally cool in comparison."

I scan for anything else, Wren does too. There's nothing, at least not immediately.

When we finish, Wren is quiet a long moment, one bright white incisor biting the faded ruins of her once-perfect lipstick. "I know you like to joke about me watching too much TV, but given the circumstances you can't fault me here . . ."

"Yes?" I arch an eyebrow.

Her voice drops, low and punctuated by her large amber eyes. "You don't think we—*they*—reanimate the dead or anything, right? Like, necromancers? What else would inspire zombies and vampires?"

"I mean, you heard the skunk story. Sounds like it."

"But," Wren starts, "I think if we could do that, they would've had us interrogate Ursula. Ask her if she knows her killer's name? Or who would want to kill her and why? All the answers her soul didn't spill."

She's right, except . . .

"They didn't do that because they immediately thought we were guilty. Or that Marsyas was. They wouldn't trust *us* to reanimate her, especially after her 'soul's truth' was out. They didn't want us to touch her, they probably thought that we'd manipulate her somehow."

My sister sighs. "Good point. Also: ew."

Wren plunges her head into her hands, elbows propped on the table to support the weight of it. Her fingers ruffle her bangs, scrunching them up, out of their perfection yet again. She stifles a yawn. "Now what?"

I check the time: 11:23. "We read until we drop."

CHAPTER 15

RUBY

I wake with a start. Book smell tingling my nose, my hair blotting out most of my vision. My neck aches, and my skin smarts, and it takes a few blinks and a full-on swat at my hair to realize I'm not in our suite.

I'm in the reading room.

I fell asleep doing research.

I peel the side of my face off the delicate, now smudged, page of a book the size of the seat cushions Dad brought to my track meets last year to survive hours in the bleachers, the crick in my neck audibly sighing with a snap as I make my way upright.

The indigo light of lifting dawn ambles in the windows, which I see now have no curtains. Strange because most of these books should not be in direct sunlight. Maybe magic protects them when the brightness goes from this hazy greeting to the white blaze of noon. I'm about to wonder aloud as much to Wren when my eyes adjust.

My sister isn't asleep at the table, the window seat, the floor.

I push back my chair and realize I'm still barefoot, my strappy heels crammed next to the window seat. Wren's are there too.

That can't be good.

Panic rising, I shut the grimoire that served as my pillow, tuck it against my chest, sweep up both pairs of stilettos, hurry down the stairs—

And run straight into Infinity.

I clip their shoulder as I hit the hallway carpet, barreling out of the spiral stair alcove.

But in one smooth motion, time seems to freeze along with my forward momentum. Suspended in place, I can only watch as Infinity tips me back onto an upright axis, before sweeping droplets of sloshing tea away from the front of their shirt and directly back into the mug in their hand.

Then, just as quickly as it froze, time speeds back into motion again. I'm left wobbling on tensed legs, the book pressed against my chest throwing me off-balance even with Infinity's magical adjustments.

They brace their free palm against my upper arm to keep me from falling a second time.

"Oh my gosh, I'm so sorry. I didn't see you—"

"Blind corner." Infinity shrugs, and gestures with their teacup. "Breakfast is laid out in the solarium if you're interested. You might need some caffeine to get through . . ." They trail off, tilting their head to read the spine of my colossal tome, "*The Migration of the Four Lines*. Full offense to the dryness of your chosen reading material, not to your comprehension skills."

I hug the book closer and laugh. "Yeah." Then I realize that they must be taking their tea up to the reading room, and I go for a tiny gamble to find out why—research, a hunch, an errand for Luna? It might be good information to know why. "You've got your caffeine, are you sure you don't want to take this riveting educational tome for a spin? I don't want to hog it."

"I'll pass." They slip a small book out of their pocket and wave it between us. "Sudoku in the reading room with tea is my usual go-to on the morning after the meeting dinner. Today's going to be a shit show, and so I thought, why mess with the tried and true?"

"Good idea." A little disappointing as far as sleuthing goes, but understandable. I nod, and move to disentangle myself, because I realize the longer I stand here the larger chance there is that Infinity will start asking real questions about my research. Not to mention I really need to find Wren. I paste on my Blackgate smile. "I'll leave you to it."

I make to sweep past when Infinity softly announces, "I don't think she did it, by the way."

"Um, what?"

"Your grandmother. I don't think she murdered Ursula. And before you read that the wrong way, I don't think you or your sister did it either."

"You . . . don't?"

"No." They take a sip of tea and lean against the alcove wall, one foot kicked up against the molding, as comfortable as can be while my heart dribbles against my sternum. I need to run to Wren, but as a Blackgate, I have to stay and listen. I swallow and they continue. "I know you haven't been back here in a decade, and I don't blame you. But what you need to understand that you might not remember is that Ursula was her own worst nightmare."

I blink at them. That could mean literally anything. Was Ursula cruel to the other families? Did she pit them against each other? Did she use the master relics to torture them in some way? Or play favorites? Or whatever else people in power do for fun?

I have no idea where to start, so I buy time with something so general I hope they'll fill in the blank. "You don't think . . ."

They purse their lips, dark eyes unwavering under eyebrows that are criminally perfect. "That Ursula did this to herself? It wouldn't be unheard of."

Again, the specter of all I don't know and probably should know if I were really Lavinia Blackgate whispers in my ear. I keep my expression as neutral as I can.

After a moment, Infinity shrugs and toys with their tea bag. "That's my grandmother's going theory. I'm inclined to believe that if you've known someone for ninety-seven years, you might have an idea about what they're capable of."

Ninety-seven years of friendship. It's almost unfathomable. And it ended before our eyes.

I have so many questions about that relationship, about their theory, and if anyone's shared that with the others because we're definitely in a terrible bind if it's true because Ursula can't be punished in any way that will get us out of here, as far as I know.

"But what I want to know," they say, eyes checking the shadowed corners at either end of the hallway behind me, "is why and when did Ursula put this stipulation in her will?"

"I . . . I don't know."

"I believe Evander's shock—he didn't know this was a possibility. Which leads me to surmise this wasn't something in previous High Sorcerer antiquities. Meaning it's new." Infinity pauses. "It's easy to draw a line perhaps between this stipulation and the death of Ursula's children. A mass casualty like that is a tragedy every way around."

All the breath kicks out of my lungs.

Mass casualty? God . . . so they *did* die at once.

It doesn't really matter how it happened—car wreck or magic spell, it's terrible.

And Marcos Blackgate had something to do with it. Maybe.

Infinity continues, their voice low. As they lean in, there's the hint of something floral edging their frame. Not the nearby lilac or the pretend peony smell of a dead maid, but something akin to Winter's perfume. God, do all witches smell amazing literally all the time? "Ursula was a leader, but she was also a mother, and that sort of grief may have meant that not only did she update her will to name her grandchildren as heirs, but also to add alternate stipulations should foul play occur. And . . . I know she had all the reason in the world to want to stick around and prepare them as long as possible, but what if she was thinking long-term? What if she decided that if she were killed by foul play, she'd want to make sure her only remaining family members wouldn't be offed too?"

I seriously don't have any words, so I just nod.

"If it's been like that for more than a decade, well, you'd think someone would've found out." Infinity sighs. "But Grandmama insists she didn't know. And there is very little she doesn't know."

They look to me and I can't conceivably nod in answer to that because I don't actually know either of the Starwoods. My mouth is bone dry but I manage a passable "Yeah."

Infinity kicks off the wall and takes another sip of tea. "Anyway, that took a turn. I have a tendency to talk once I get going." They smile. "Didn't mean to be a downer first thing in the morning. This day is going to be hard enough. But I thought you should know. Something to keep in mind."

"Um, yeah, thanks." I force a smile. "Enjoy your Sudoku."

Walking as slowly as I can as to not seem as if I'm completely panicked, I make it to the main stairwell and down to the second-floor landing before I start into a barefoot run across sound-sucking plush carpet. I pass the Cerises' double suite and close in on the door beneath the mountain lion's head.

It's ajar.

My heart skips.

My steps quicken.

I clamp on the massive grimoire in my arms—a blunt object if I need it—and loosen the straps of the twin pairs of heels. I'm ready to drop them or throw them or otherwise discard them in whatever way necessary to ensure Wren's safety if I walk into an interrogation or dangerous situation or something else I didn't think likely twenty-four hours ago.

As silent as possible, I nudge the door to our suite with my shoulder. It creaks out a moan—the traitor—as it yawns open.

Straight ahead, the fire is roaring. A tick to the right, I can see into one of the twin bedrooms—the sheets torn back and rumpled. Wren's ridiculously expensive dress from the night before is heaped on the floor.

But my sister isn't anywhere to be found.

Raising the book out in front of me as both a weapon and a shield, I cross the threshold. "Kaysa?"

No response. Both bathroom doors are flung open.

Something hot spikes in my pulse, and I suddenly can't draw a breath. Ursula's prone body prods at the backs of my eyelids when I blink. The driver and his mask of death.

I can't see Wren like that. I can't—

Movement from under the closed bedroom door. I drop the shoes and get both hands on the giant book, wrenching it back, ready for a baseball swing at someone's head.

The doorknob twists, the latch releases . . .

And Wren startles at the sight of me.

"Ru—*Lavinia*!" she recovers, hand flying to clutch the literal pearls at her throat—Mom's, recovered from her purse, apparently. Wren's eyes dart over my shoulder, to the open door behind me. "You're awake. Winter brought us *the most awesome* stuff."

Barefoot, she twirls in place, showing off a strapless sundress with an A-line skirt and blue pattern embroidered on the white poplin to look like waves. It must be said that while the dress is very cute, it's far more appropriate for grabbing a cappuccino and hitting the farmers' market than spending a day untangling motive in the assassination of a woman who sure sounds like she was recently the most important witch on the whole continent.

I frown. Lower the book. My heart kicks in my chest.

"Don't look so mad," my sister coos with a dismissive wave. "It's not like I'm going to wear this while looking for relics. I just *had* to try it on. There's plenty of sporty gear for us, but when else am I going to wear a Dolce & Gabbana dress? Never. If you want to try it on too, go for it, but we both know your boobs would look for an escape hatch in this bodice. It's just—"

I fumble the book into the crook of one elbow and snatch her wrist.

"I'm not mad about the dress, I'm mad because you left me! How could you?" I let go of her only long enough to kick the door closed, then I'm right back to whisper-yelling. "We *promised* to stay together! And if we have to separate, we *check in* with each other. I need to know where you are at all times. And you need to know where I am. We're all we have, and this place is dangerous. You know that! And you just left me alone, in a room with no door, in a house where at least half the people here think we're murderers or accessories to murder."

"I knew where you were. And where else would I be?"

"Dead in one of the sixteen bathrooms? Magicked into a sinkhole? Hidden in two square feet of the ten thousand acres outside this house?"

At this, Wren rolls her eyes like *I'm* the one overreacting. Then, she raises both wrists out in front of her. "I didn't take these off. Safe as safe could be with my dead animal shields." She gestures to my wrists. "And you have yours. You're good."

"I . . . am not. That's not . . . We can't *actually* use them." I punch out a frustrated breath. "A suggestion of power isn't a replacement for power."

Her mouth drops open in the most perfect, excited little *O*.

"Oh, that's a good line! I know books are your jam but when we get out of here, definitely think about screenwriting because you're a natural with dialogue." She bops me on the nose. I drop both sets of shoes.

"Our first line of defense is one another. Our second line of defense is our reputation. Including those." I wave over our entangled bunny bracelet collection. "Can you just promise that from now on you won't disappear? I need to know where you're going and who you'll be with and when you'll be back and—"

"Yes to all of that and whatever else you were going to blather about."

I frown at her. "I'm serious."

"So am I. I didn't know it was a rule. Now I know. Got it. Go take a shower. You'll feel much better." Wren flicks one of the bracelets. "These things are even waterproof."

I squeeze the thick girth of my book until the leather binding pushes back. It's all I can do to modulate my tone over the accelerating *thump-thump-thump* in my chest.

"We don't know if these people can walk through walls or appear in fireplaces, or God knows what else. Just—assume they can." It suddenly occurs to me to lock the door to the suite and deadbolt it. I do with a slamming flourish and then round on my sister. *"Please."*

Wren doesn't bat an eye.

"They're witches, they're not gods. If they could do shit like that, they'd be ruling this country, not hiding in the mountains, hosting dinner parties."

"How do we know they're not running things? Ursula mentioned threats in her speech. You don't have threats if no one knows you exist."

"And then Ursula was murdered. And the call was definitely coming from inside the house." Wren gestures to the book still in my hands. "Speaking of, did you learn anything else after I left? Perhaps by osmosis via"—she bends herself sideways—"*The Migration of the Four Lines.*" She squints at me and then her thumb is rubbing furiously at my cheek. "You've got some ink."

I crinkle my nose and jerk back. "I'll shower in a second, but first." I sigh and plop onto the couch positioned in front of the fire. "I actually did learn some things. But not from this book."

I discard the tome on the coffee table. "I literally ran into Infinity outside the reading room. They told me they thought that perhaps Ursula changed her will after her kids died."

"Well, yeah. Forget magic, anyone with the kind of moola to own an estate like this has to keep the legal stuff up-to-date."

"Yes, but the insinuation wasn't just because her children had died and she had new heirs, but *how* her children died. Wren," I whisper, girding myself for what I have to relay, "Infinity called what happened to them a 'mass casualty.'"

She gasps. "No—did they say how?"

I shake my head. "No, and I obviously couldn't ask. But they think that when Ursula rewrote her will that she was trying to protect her remaining grandkids. Basically, that if she died by foul play, then if she removed her grandkids from direct succession of the High Sorcerer title, that it would protect them from being murdered too."

"God, that's bleak."

"It is but it makes sense."

Wren shivers and immediately begins to rub furiously at fresh gooseflesh pebbling her arms. "Let me just state for the record that while this succession bullshit sounds really good in a movie or book, it blows in real life. Waiting for a loved one to die off so you can get what you want? And then putting yourself in the crosshairs because you finally got it by losing that person you loved? Bull. Shit."

"Yes, but think about it. We know Marcos Blackgate was executed as punishment for murder—"

Wren freezes. "Wait. You think Marcos Blackgate . . ." I shrug and nod as she puts two and two together. When she gets there, she squeezes her eyes closed and presses her fingers to her temples. "You're telling me *our dad* is a *mass murderer* and we came to this party and had dinner with the mother and children of his victims like it was no big thing?"

"That's exactly what I'm saying." Wren's eyes fly open and she watches me as I toss a hand in the general direction of the study a floor above. "It's part of the reason everyone is so convinced Marsyas did it. Most mothers think their kids are innocent if they commit a heinous crime, I'd imagine. She probably fought tooth and nail to protect him, or exonerate him, and they—*Ursula*—executed him anyway."

Wren runs a hand through her hair and flops bonelessly onto the couch. "First we'll have to prove your theory, but if it's true, did it take ten years for Marsyas to exact revenge, or ten years for someone to frame her?"

"Either is possible."

"God, if I weren't starving, I might vomit. This is so messed up."

I punch out a deep breath. "I have a feeling it's only going to get worse."

Chapter 16

AUDEN

I don't sleep. More precisely, I don't *remember* sleeping.

Everything from the past six hours runs through my mind like a flip-book. Just scenes adding up to a whole.

Finding nothing with my cousins.

Literally *nothing*.

Just locked drawer after locked drawer, all opening with our keys, all opening to nothing. We kept turning our keys, expecting a different result. Madness.

It's like every scrap of paper died with Ursula.

And we have no idea if it was our grandmother or her murderer who removed everything but the will from the room.

Then it's suddenly morning.

The birdsong filtering through the diamond-pane windows with the haunted blue of a new day.

I'd fallen asleep in the study. The mantel clock reads five thirty-eight.

And so I stumble down four flights of service stairs, into the basement kitchen, through the brewing of three pots of coffee, and haul my best approximation of a Chef Maggie breakfast spread into the solarium. Thank God the woman is a champ at making everything ahead of time. With her preparation skills, even a boarding school whelp like me can present top-quality sustenance while she lies in a Cinderella sleep, hopefully getting the kind of rest my grandmother never allowed her.

Then, croissant in hand, I decamp to my room, where I wash my face and trade the buttery flakiness of the lingering pastry for a toothbrush and paste.

As I rinse, it hits me.

Right there, in the last line of the clue.

We worship.

I swallow a gulp of water, pull on a clean Walton-Bridge lacrosse T-shirt and shorts, grab my running shoes, haul open the door to my third-floor suite—

And nearly flatten Winter, standing there, hand raised to knock.

"We worship?" I ask before it even computes that she's basically dressed exactly like me.

A little smile creeps at the corners of her mouth. Her skin is bare and as perfect as magic can make it, any sign of last night stripped away. "Great minds, Auden."

"Let's get Evander—"

"Already tried." Winter nods over her shoulder, reddish-blond ponytail swishing. Of course she did. His suite is between hers and mine. "He's not there."

I can't decide if I'm annoyed, frustrated, or mad. Maybe just tired. We should be doing this together. As a team. "I guess either he'll find out because we're successful or because we can cross it off the list. Let's jet."

We're stepping onto the starburst tiles of the garden walk less than a minute later.

Ursula's shroud is undisturbed to the right, as hard and smooth as the night before, the deep, reddish brown of the Colorado soil blanketing the small fall of her body.

Beyond, the table is in shambles, shards of porcelain and glass glittering in the meager light. White-jacketed waiters lie crumpled in the grass, and the magical fairy lights that edged the garden from twelve feet up litter the garden perimeter like a fallen police line. All evidence of Ursula's spells collectively failing or taking effect.

All of it detritus of our terrible night.

We don't discuss it.

Past the lawn's edge, Winter and I veer left onto the manicured beginnings of a path that will become nothing but bare earth and gravel in a mile or so. It's a trail as old as the house itself, one that leads up a steep incline to a small peak called Mercy's Point.

Normally, I'd only willingly suffer through a run like this in the name of training for lacrosse season. But this morning I plan to suffer through gasping breath and screaming quads to inspect what Shadrack Hegemony himself installed at the top of Mercy's Point more than a hundred years before I was born.

A chapel.

An outdoor chapel—with pulpits facing both east and west, for sunrise or sundown services, and general devotion. It's the only place on the grounds even remotely religious.

We worship.

We make it a mile, lungs heaving in the altitude and incline, before I catch a scrap of a red Walton-Bridge lacrosse jersey up the trail and know that it's confirmation that we're on to something.

"Evander!" I try to shout, but it comes out in a half wheeze because though I've had a month to adjust to the altitude, I am running uphill on a suspicious amount of rest after the second worst day of my life.

He doesn't even flinch at the noise.

"Either he's got his AirPods in or he's being a straight jerk," Winter grumbles, tone indignant and determined. "Coach Rose's weekly hill repeats are about to come in handy."

She puts on the jets. With a groan, I follow. My jog shifts into an all-out, mountain-climbing churn of steps. It's not a sprint—we're not super athletes, and it is a sixty-degree incline at eight thousand feet—but it most definitely is a race pace.

"Evander. Ulysses. Hegemony!" I grunt out as we close in on his broad back.

When he doesn't acknowledge that or our footsteps, Winter slams on the brakes, sticks both fingers in her mouth, and whistles so loud that every dog in Grand County probably just started barking. That fails to work also, so I pelt him with a pine cone. It bounces off the back of his head.

Evander finally turns around. He does not have his headphones in.

We gape at him, breathing hard while walking the final ten feet or so to meet him on the trail.

Though I'm not sure I slept, I'm pretty damn convinced Evander spent his entire night pacing the halls. He hasn't shaved, dark stubble lining his jaw, and somehow even the beads of sweat dotting his temples look utterly exhausted.

I elbow him in the ribs. "Jesus Christ, man, did you think we were Kaysa's ghosts?"

"Don't hand him a viable excuse for *ignoring us,* Auden."

Rather than defend himself, Evander draws a water bottle from a pack around his waist and takes a swig. As soon as he lowers it, Winter snags it for a drink of her own. "I assume you're here because you had the same thought I did."

"We worship," I confirm.

"Can't believe I didn't think of it the moment we read the clue."

With that, his single-mindedness slides back into place. He turns around to keep climbing toward the summit, which is about another mile, but Winter isn't done. She shoves the water bottle to my chest and jogs past Evander before making sideways progress so she can both move forward and eviscerate him at the same time.

"And I can't believe you thought of it and your next move wasn't *to go get us.* Because you know what our first thought was? Finding you. You, who happened to be already out here without us." She halts, and Evander nearly runs smack into her. He has to weigh at least twice as much as she does, but Winter doesn't even flinch. Not that she flinched when I did something similar mere minutes ago. "I know you're the patriarch. I know that you want to be High Sorcerer too and feel like the title is yours alone to win. But we're your family—your only family, in fact. And like Auden said last night, we're on your team. Act like it."

Evander's head drops back like it's filled with bricks.

"You're right."

"I am. And you have no excuse. I don't want to hear you're tired. Or that you thought it was your responsibility."

Evander's shoulders heave in a sigh. "Anything to add, Auden?"

"Nope, I think Win pretty much covered it, except . . . last one there's a rotten egg."

I toss the water bottle straight at Evander's face and dart past him, past Winter, and around the next switchback. Evander bobbles the bottle, which thuds to the trail, while Winter's competitive spirit churns into full speed ahead with a squeak and lunge.

In the end we hurtle ourselves to the top of Mercy's Point in a dead heat of bumping shoulders and jumbled elbows. The toe of my running shoe hits the flat head atop the mountain first—a fact my cousins both register and totally ignore—and we're there.

The sky is a brilliant, cloudless blue, and beneath it is the outdoor chapel. Five rows of pews, with a pulpit on both the eastern and western horizons. The sun has just crested the eastern pulpit, its rays caught in the moldering planks of the little wooden lectern. It's something that needs to be stained, or replaced altogether, the wood soft, split, full of holes. The one on the western end isn't much better. The outer border of the little outdoor chapel is lined with faded red brick, uprooted by time, weather, and probably global warming.

The bricks and the wooden pulpits and benches were pristine the last time I was up here—preserved by Ursula's spells, just like the garden, lawn, and the plants in her office. Another sand grain of her magic, evaporated. Something we'll need to remedy.

Evander pulls out his phone and reads the clue aloud.

"When breath became air," he recites, trailing a pair of thick fingers along the first pew. "The mountain stood tall with forever frost." He squints around hard enough that his thick brows plunge those circles under his eyes two shades deeper. "We're not high enough for any summer snowpack."

"Nowhere on the grounds is," Winter amends, stealing Evander's water bottle again and stepping onto the nearest pew—when the wood groans, she thinks better of it and hops back to the dry earth. "But maybe when Shadrack first arrived that wasn't the case? The earth has warmed about two degrees since he moved west."

Evander nods and continues. "Though the call of the falcon, and flick of salmon fin, did not dim the fires . . . we worship."

It really is gorgeous language, and despite the stress of it all, the part of me who reads *Leaves of Grass* is going to be exceedingly disappointed if Shadrack blew all his poetic talent on the first clue.

In a round, Evander tilts his exhausted face to the sky—no falcon; to the ground—no running water featuring salmon nor circle for burning.

"Maybe we have it wrong."

He sits heavily on a pew, prescient enough to put his weight on the *T* where a leg meets the bench—the most solid part of the rotted wood. "We've got the tributary out in the southwest quadrant. It has salmon but they don't leave deep water to spawn in running water until August at the earliest. And falcon eat fish, but they're more likely to steal it from a bear than from the stream. Not to mention that's a pretty low-lying area and the first section is all a mountain covered in trees."

"You are so literal."

I plunk down opposite him, straddling the bench, and swipe a bead of sweat out of my eye. He's grinding his molars and staring at the rock-strewn dirt as if it'll spit out a tea-leaf answer. Winter hovers somewhere over my shoulder, her shadow falling like a knife slash across the pair of us.

"Evander, the clue is a metaphorical description of the sweeping beauty of the Rocky Mountains," I explain. "This is the only place on the grounds where any sort of worship has taken place unless you're counting the groveling the Cerises have been known to do."

Winter coughs out a laugh.

"And, because you're the ambassador of the Hegemony Literal Society . . ." I knock his sturdy hiking boot with the toe of my running shoe. He continues to stare at the dirt between us. "I'll point out that this is the place Shadrack built to literally worship the beauty of the natural, *elemental* world. It's been magically maintained by every Hegemony after him. Which means every Hegemony, including Ursula, thought it worth their magical energy."

Her name is heavy this morning, and we sit with its weight for a good minute.

When I feel like I can, I glance to Evander ahead, to Winter behind.

"All three of us, separately, decided it would be the first place we'd look. That means something. And let's not forget these are supposed to be clues, not riddles. Shadrack, Ursula, every previous High Sorcerer wants us to find the masters."

We start with everything man-made.

The pews. The bricks lining the space. Then, the pulpits. Evander, being Evander, insists we should divide and conquer, but what he truly means is that he should handle one while Winter and I start with the other.

As expected, they're in just as bad a shape as the pews—worse even, with more nooks and crannies and joints to collect water and mold. Winter pries the railroad ties Shadrack used as nails free with magic and elbow grease as I steady the top portion of it, the soft wood twisting and splintering, even though I'm holding it with a cushion of air between my fingertips and the rotten construction.

"Without the benefit of magic or modern stain sealant, this thing is basically sawdust," Winter grumbles, using her own magic to tip up the pulpit shaft now that it's free from the base, a verdant mist engulfing it. She knocks it with a knuckle and listens hard. Her nose crinkles, sun-hewn freckles showing without her usual heavy makeup. "This one is solid—"

"*Wait.*" Evander's voice is strained, like he's holding up a parked car and not a half-balanced, mostly rotted pulpit. "There's something here—Auden, I need your help to grab it."

"What's wrong with *my* help?" Winter whines as she works with me to gently right our pulpit.

"Nothing, just—come."

I give her a hand, and to my surprise she takes it, standing and dusting her fingertips on her overpriced leggings. Across the summit, Evander has both hands above his head, a force of wind funneling through the calling power of his fingertips. Above him, the pulpit bobs steadily on the emerald updraft he's created, like a hawk playing on the breeze.

The strain on his purpling face is enough that we both break into a run. When we crash in next to him, he grits out, "It's in the recess. Nailed in." He's holding steady, fingers flexing and concentration unwavering.

I can see now why Winter can't retrieve what's inside. Though she's tall, she doesn't have enough height to reach inside the hollow pulpit where it's currently suspended. It's clear Evander's doing all he can not to destroy it, trying to keep it steady and sturdy with pressure inside and out to prevent the ancient wood from flying apart.

"Auden," Evander grumbles, impatience and strain in his voice.

"Trying not to defeat your efforts. Give me a sec."

It really just takes a moment, and then I see my opening—the right place to enter the air stream Evander has created without upsetting it. I press my hands together and enter the hollow base of the pulpit like an Olympic diver, while leaning my torso away as not to inadvertently bump the updraft, working blindly, quickly, to retrieve whatever's inside.

"You're sticking your tongue out," Winter teases.

"Concentrating." Then, a weight drops delicately into my hands. "I've got it."

Evander immediately shifts the magical air stream to whisk it straight up and off my arm. Next, he sets the altar gently on a patch of dirt beside the base, and presses forward, saying, "Let me see," at nearly the same moment Winter whispers, "What is it?"

Almost in answer, the ground beneath us begins to shake.

It's violent enough that Winter's center of gravity abandons her and she falls into Evander. He catches her, and I work on instinct, clutching the relic to my chest with one hand and throwing up a spell to surround us with the other. The moment the magic locks into place, a cushion and a shield, I curse, voice strangled, "The safety wards."

The same safety wards that Ursula promised had been disarmed for our protection.

The same safety wards that detonated ten years ago.

The perimeter of the chapel explodes in a wall of pure green fire. It rings us, hot and heavy, shooting twenty, thirty feet toward the rising sun in thick, flaring, dangerous magical power—

And then, as quickly as it came, the fire snuffs out.

Shield in place, I lift my head.

Nothing is left. Not even a thin curl of smoke.

That isn't—

That shouldn't—

This is not how it should work.

A security ward injures before any magical protections can be shown. It wasn't meant to maim us, it was meant as a sign. A remnant of the wards removed by Ursula, proof that we are touching an artifact powerful enough to demand the strongest protective spells known to the Four Lines.

I swallow and present my tightly balled fist. "I suppose that's as good a proof as the next clue that this is a master."

"She could've warned us that the wards would still discharge," Winter mutters, nervously sweeping wisps of wayward hair back into her ponytail. "Especially with . . . well . . ."

"Let me see," Evander cuts her off with a gruff repetition of the very last thing he'd said. I'm prepared to point out that no one appreciates an asshole, especially when narrowly escaping a redux of childhood trauma, when I see his face. All color leached from his brown cheeks, eyes glassy, mouth turned down at the corners. He stares at my hand as if it's the only thing keeping him tethered to the here and now.

The memories of what was are hard on him too. He doesn't want to talk about it.

Fine.

I extend my closed fist and open it. Together, we peer down in a little bent-headed circle at the item nestled in my palm.

An ornate silver ball and chain.

The bauble is reminiscent of a tea diffuser, though it doesn't appear to have any holes, just lacelike silver scrolling in looping and interlocking patterns.

"A locket . . ." Winter muses. "That was not what I was expecting, I'll be honest."

"Not all relics are finger bones and locks of hair," I tease.

"Ew, no. I was thinking, like, Excalibur or something."

I shrug and gently sweep the delicate chain to the flat of my palm and present it to my older cousin. "For the patriarch."

Evander accepts it with a curt nod, blinking away the dampness, though he can't hide the crimson rimming his lashes. He sniffs, staring down at the master.

All that power, all that pain, packed into something so small, delicate, unobtrusive.

"Wait, *says* something . . ." Winter ducks until her nose is an inch away from Evander's palm. Her fingers lift to probe the relic. Evander rips it away.

"Don't touch."

"Don't be a baby," Winter snaps back. "It's as much mine as it is yours or Auden's. Let me see it. I'll give it right back, *patriarch*."

Evander sighs but doesn't react as Winter tips the underside of the orb-shaped pendant into view. I watch her blue eyes, so much like Ursula's, read something I can't see . . . and I watch as the spark of excitement within them dims to confusion.

"No . . ." she says, almost to herself, pale brow crinkling. "No, that can't be right."

CHAPTER 17

RUBY

Once I'm showered and dressed in high-end athleisure courtesy of Winter Hegemony—and have made sure Wren trades the cocktail dress for the same—I tie on a pair of designer tennis shoes so pristinely white it feels like a crime to wear them, and go in search of food.

As Infinity promised, there's an entire spread set up in the entrance to the solarium. Laid out is a tray of delicate pastries, whipped butter to match, several bottles of Evian, three carafes of coffee and one of hot water for tea, and actual cream served with sugar cubes and wafer-thin bone china. There aren't any scones in the pastry selection—a fact I would've attributed to a joke by Auden at my expense if last night hadn't gone so terribly, horribly wrong.

Breakfast in hand, I cast about the gorgeous space—which I didn't really admire in the fevered minutes after the murder. The room's west side is completely made of glass, configured in a trio of grand double doors and windows with sashes so slim they seem but a whisper in the glass. This allows for an unfettered view of the stone veranda with the gardens, fountain, lawn, and mountains beyond.

Mercifully, the room is empty. I'd like to engage in as little small talk as possible with people who think we're cogs in a murder plot.

Wren trails her fingertips along an ancient settee more expensive than Dad's house, arranged like the others with side tables and coffee tables, and their own bevy of candle pairings in such a way that somehow makes them perfect for both small, quaint conversations, or purposeful seclusion. Take your pick.

Though we're alone, Wren has her accent pulled on, straight and tidy, when she turns to me with coffee so pale it could be straight cream and two absolutely heavenly looking croissants piled together like throw pillows atop a parchment-thin plate, and announces, "It's a lovely morning to sit on the terrace, don't you think?" She gestures dramatically with her priceless porcelain like the stage rat she is. "We can't sit in this giant room, alone, stuffing our faces with croissants. We should be outside, alone, stuffing our faces with croissants."

"Did you not just tell me half an hour ago that you wanted to throw up?"

"And *you* told *me* it's only going to get worse, so I better get serious about sustenance and hope my gut can keep it together."

Wren takes off, absolutely expecting me to follow. And I do—but not before snatching two butter knives from the arrangement, slipping them into the long pocket sewn into the hip of my tights.

Silly? Maybe.

But without actual magic, and with the multiple x factors making up the rest of the Hegemony family, a butter knife—two—seems like a reasonable weapon to keep on hand. With my flowy tank top settled over the waistband, the knives are completely camouflaged. And . . . there if I need them.

The terrace is affixed to the western part of Hegemony Manor and therefore the wrong direction to enjoy the morning sun, but I trail Wren as she drags me to a bistro table just far enough from the roofline to be positioned squarely in the rising light as it crests the turrets.

As we sit, I try not to stare at the still, shrouded form of Ursula over the lip of the terrace. The proximity tugs at my heart, especially with the abandoned hull of the dinner table, with its shattered porcelain and beached chandeliers, a still-life reminder only a few more feet to the west.

I nibble at my croissant and force myself to look at the view and work on a plan of how we're going to address today. Everything is a painter's palette shot through with the unfiltered crispness of Colorado summer. Gone is the abject perfection that came with Ursula's magic when we first arrived, and what's left in its wake is the abject perfection of nature's own hand, told in wheaten golds, soft greens, warm browns, and sapphire, cloudless sky.

And there, on a trail in the distance, is a blur of motion.

"Is that . . . Evander?" There's a figure in a red shirt and black shorts kicking up dust along a trail. The brawler's build and the warm brown skin are answer enough, but then, as I lean forward, I realize there's another person behind him. "And Auden?"

"And Winter." Wren points to someone in pastels moving against the brush toward the tree line. I squint at the moving bodies, cranking through a switchback and into a wall of netted pines.

Wren stuffs the remainder of her pastry in her mouth, dusts crumbs from her hands, and stands. After a swallow, she says, "Good call on athleisure. Let's get moving."

"Wait. You want to chase them?"

"I want to *join* them, duh." Wren's already quickstepping it toward the stairs that lead down to the garden. "They're up to something, and if that something has to do with the relics, it'll be the perfect distraction to the discovery of our friend on the drive."

I rise from my seat but hesitate. "You *do* remember that the last time we saw all three Hegemonys together, Evander wanted to interrogate us. I mean, he literally tried to stop everyone from going their own way for the evening because he wanted to drill us about Marsyas."

"I *do,* which is why I think it's best to change the narrative. We need to show them we're engaged in the magical scavenger hunt, and we're fun to hunt with, not to mention beautiful and talented." She shimmies her shoulders and winks, again pointing herself at the garden. "Nona's vanishing act really killed all of our goodwill last night, but we can build it back up."

I hold up a hand. "I have a better idea."

Wren cocks a brow at me in question.

"If they're there, that means the third floor is empty." Winter all but spelled out that the Hegemony family lived on the third floor, with guests on the second floor, and the first floor for entertaining. "Which means the study is empty."

A mischievous gleam instantly appears in Wren's eyes. "Oh my God, you want to snoop?" she whisper-squeals. When I nod, she does too. "Better idea is better. Lead the way."

✦ ✦ ✦

The third floor of Hegemony Manor is deathly quiet as we wedge open the door from the corner service stairs and peek into the convergence of two halls.

To the right, the corridor leading to our target, the study and all the books therein. To the left, a line of heavy wooden doors interspersed with plant stands, pedestals with cut-flower vases, and oil portraits.

We creep into the hall, and I hold the stairwell door until it *snicks* shut rather than slams. Despite my proclamation of an empty floor, Infinity might still be in the reading room, and—

"Oh shit," Wren curses, as the nearest door in the non-study hallway yawns open.

I fling us against the wall of the opposing corridor, until we're both obscured and pressed against the heavy wallpaper. Wren nods toward the study, obviously suggesting we make a break for it, but even on carpet pile three inches thick our footsteps will most definitely be heard by whomever is this close.

And besides, I want to know who else is up here and why.

I shake my head, a finger pressed against my lips, and pointedly shoot a glance toward the turn of the corner, where the other person is five feet away at maximum. Wren gets the picture and stops struggling against me, her own features scrunching in concentration as she listens too.

"I can't believe you," seethes a whispering voice—a female. Ada, maybe? Or Winter, and we misjudged on who was hiking up the mountain. There's the whip of something soft colliding with something much harder. "Put on your damn shirt."

"She was upset." Hex. Definitely Hex. Wren and I make eye contact. His voice goes muffled as he must pull the shirt over his head. "I was trying to help."

THE LIES WE CONJURE ✦ 147

"You were trying to help yourself to a vulnerable girl who'd rather light your balls on fire than ever date you again."

"She let me stay, didn't she?"

"On the couch. Because you weren't needed or wanted, but she's a Hegemony—"

"Says you. And how'd you even know I—"

"How could I *not*? You're really goddamn lucky I care enough to lie through my teeth about *the two of us* going to get Mama and Papa food and then marching up here to retrieve your ass." There's a tap on plastic. "We've already wasted five minutes. Come on, we need to materialize with pastries and coffee ASAP or we're both screwed."

Footfalls start echoing our way as they head to the stairs we just used. Beside me, Wren squeezes her eyes shut, her body pressed flat against the wall and still as stone. I hold my breath, but I can't look away as the twins appear in profile, still deep in conversation as Hex fixes his collar.

"Okay, yeah, I'm sorry. I didn't think about what it would mean for you—"

"Of course you didn't. You never do. And it's not just me. You know the stakes here. And stakes make *everything* worse."

Unblinking, I wait for them to notice us. Wondering just how we can explain away our eavesdropping—which we can't. But Ada storms ahead of Hex, through the door to the stairwell. He follows in a rush.

When the door crashes shut behind them, I finally exhale, snatch Wren, and jog straight for the study's double doors, the thick carpet muffling our advance. It's blessedly unlocked, and empty.

"Holy shit, Hex *dated* Winter?" Wren asks, breathlessly latching the doors before throwing herself against the jamb with a dramatic flair, like she's about to faint. "And then he snuck out and tried to get with her last night? After all that?"

"None of our business," I stonewall, making a beeline for the stuffed bookshelves.

"Are you kidding?" Wren screech-whispers, following my path.

"It's totally our business! A secret like that is exactly the sort of juicy shit we need to know."

"I highly doubt Ursula was murdered because those two used to date and Hex apparently has exactly zero self-awareness or boundaries."

"But it could be important. You heard Ada—their parents might blow a gasket if they figure it out. *Quel scandale!*"

"The *wrong* scandal. We want to learn about whatever happened ten years ago."

Wren cocks a brow, her mood swinging back to mischievously delighted with the croissant carbs hitting her bloodstream and the thrill of what she's just learned in the hall. "Turn our educated guess into a research-based reality? Or drop it on the cutting-room floor?"

Talk about mixed metaphors. "Yes. That." I gesture to the bookshelves. "Let's dive in at eye level and work from there. You start on the left; I'll start on the right. Our priority is anything that can give us insight into what happened to Marcos Blackgate, the cousins' parents, and, I don't know, any sort of ledger or record that Ursula may have kept."

Wren rolls her eyes but allows me yet another mock salute and gets to work. Though she can't do so without hearing her own voice. "You know, I'm supposed to be the trusting one and all that but maybe I've been listening to you because, well, not that they have something nefarious going on but . . . why would Infinity just offer up their theories to you in the hallway?"

This does surprise me. Both the timing of Wren's query and that she'd think of it at all. Even worse, I don't have a great answer. "I . . . uh, thought they were making conversation."

"Before seven in the morning after a night full of literal terrors?"

My breakfast flops unceremoniously in my gut. "Valid point. I thought they just wanted someone to talk to. Some people are morning people, you know."

"Well, yeah, but, like, why *you*? You're so much of a stranger that they didn't *recognize* you." I don't miss her emphasis on the fact that I'm not the person they knew all those years ago and yet they accepted me as such.

"Um . . . I guess that's something to think about."

Wren taps her temple. "Multitasking. Searching books, thinking about motive."

"You know studies show that multitasking actually makes you mediocre at everything instead of more efficient, right?"

"Only someone who fears the power of multitasking would even set out to prove that point." Wren starts combing through her side of the shelf. "Anyway, something to chew on with Infinity."

"Indeed."

It doesn't take long for me to key in on several uniform, leather-bound journals. I pull out the first one and flip through it—last year's date is prominently stamped at the top. Short entries line page after page, with longer missives taking up pages in handwritten ink. "Looks like these are dated ledgers of some kind."

Sweeping across the slim spines, I go ten years back. Ledger retrieved, I begin thumbing through, intending to find the dates in July because the yearly dinner seems like a good place to start in figuring out the timeline and circumstance of the deaths in question.

My sister frowns. "Where's the one for this year?"

"Maybe in her desk?" I guess.

Wren must agree because without a word, she scuttles around the desk and starts yanking at knobs and handles carved into the massive piece of furniture.

Within the ledger, the pages are lined, and thick with the same looping handwriting I'd seen in Ursula's signature when I bound my blood—and the two of us—to the contents of the will. Dates run in an orderly fashion throughout—each page is topped with one, and though there are often gaps of three and four days, they're sequential entries of what appears to be Four Lines business.

Funds donated against a new oil pipeline.

A record of a presentation from Horatio Cerise (Hector's father?) on new medical technologies.

Correspondence with the United States Forest Service.

But in mid-March the pages go blank with a strange gleam.

"Locked, locked, locked," Wren groans. "Maybe that key Auden has goes to these?"

"Maybe. Though Evander had a key too, remember? He put that ring on its chain."

"Oh right."

As Wren gives up on the desk, I turn back to the strange border between what appears to be bare paper and the pearlescent sheen— it's like where a frozen puddle meets its melty edges, the line of delineation a haze. Before thinking twice, I rub my thumb across it.

". . . and knew Callum was gone . . ."

I yelp and drop the book.

"Was that . . . ?" Wren gasps.

"Ursula's voice?" I confirm. She'd said those words. "Yeah."

Fingers shaking a little, I kneel to retrieve the slim ledger. I'd dropped it face down, and when I pick it up and turn it back over, two gleaming pages stare back. Bracing myself a little, I tap my forefinger on the shiny part.

Again, Ursula's voice blares up from the page.

". . . the wards were intact, something that Ulysses would've known."

Wren is kneeling now too, lower lip snagged between her teeth as her hazel eyes flare wide. "It's almost like she did a magical voice memo or something. Maybe go to the beginning?"

"Good idea."

I place the book on the thick rug between us, and thumb back carefully until I find the first page on which the strange gleam appears. On the page next to it, Ursula's entry celebrates the spring equinox.

The next date, March 21, is scribbled at the top. Below it, words are scratched out with thick, deep scratches of quill. Then the gleam begins.

Starting at the left-most edge, I touch my index finger to the shimmering page and drag it across like a new reader following sentence after sentence across a chapter book page. There's a delay, some muffled noise and settling for a second or two at the beginning, then yet again the words of High Sorcerer Ursula Hegemony rise into the room.

". . . This is the voice of Ursula Elvire Muscatel Hegemony, High Sorcerer of the Four Lines. There has been an accident. No—no, an attack."

There's a pause and Wren and I exchange a glance—though Ursula's voice is now familiar to both of us, what's not is the tone. Rather than the gravitas and confidence we'd heard in life and after her death, here she sounds exhausted. Shaken. Like she's been crying.

"I have opted to record my voice because . . . honestly, my fingers are not working properly at the moment." There's a deep swallow, a long exhalation of trembling breath. "I must regret to enter into the Four Lines records that my children, the oathed heir Ulysses, Lana, and Callum, are gone."

Gooseflesh prickles my arms.

My finger skips to the next page and Ursula's voice picks up again.

"The following is a timeline I have put together from the evidence and circumstances around the discovery of their bodies in various locations upon the grounds of the Hegemony Estate. For reasons that will become apparent, I will not go into detail about the location of where each of my children was found. I will state for the record that Ulysses, the oathed heir, was found first, followed by Callum, then Lana, and that the evidence suggests they all died in the same manner."

Ursula's voice is clipped and professional, even as it seems worn to nearly nothing. Her sense of duty hangs in the air like humidity at the beach.

"It appears," she continues, "that on the morning of March twenty-first, the three of them were . . . *coerced* into attempting to find and destroy the master relics hidden upon the grounds of the Hegemony estate. As directed by Four Lines decree, the locations of the master relics are known only to me, the High Sorcerer, and each one is guarded by lethal security wards in addition to the secrecy surrounding their locations."

Ursula had mentioned the disabling of the security wards in her last will and testament. I'd figured they just deterred theft or detection . . . not that they were *lethal*.

I truly shouldn't be surprised.

"The security wards were intact, something that Ulysses would've known as oathed heir from his years of training under my aegis. Per accordance with custom, he did not know the location of the master relics, nor their composition. However, it appears that with outside influence, Ulysses, Lana, and Callum were able to locate three of the four master relics, and performed a coordinated spell in an attempt to bypass the wards and retrieve the master relics. The spell did not work, and the security wards activated." There's a deep, tremulous inhale. "The security wards for all four master relics detonated, killing my three children instantly."

Oh. God.

My heart plummets, nausea churning in choppy waves against my sternum. Wren's chin bobs as she wipes a hand across her face, catching a fat tear before it dribbles down her cheek.

"At exactly ten A.M. this morning, the High Sorcerer's ring alerted me to a trip in the wards. First, I summoned the nanny on staff to escort my grandchildren to a predetermined safe space within the manor. Next, I summoned my children to search the grounds for intruders while I, alone, inspected the security of each master relic. My children did not answer."

Ursula's voice breaks, and now there's something hot and hard in my throat.

"I learned very quickly why they had not responded. Ulysses was nearest, found seven minutes after the trip in the wards. At first, I believed he had perhaps come across the would-be thief and was injured in a fight. But when I tried life-saving measures, I realized what had occurred. My eldest son was dead by the wards meant to keep his inheritance safe."

I swallow thickly, doing absolutely nothing to dislodge the emotion balling in my windpipe. My gut trembles; Wren sniffles.

"From there, I moved to the next closest master relic. I could see from afar the shape of a body and knew Callum was gone. Here, the master relic had been revealed to the open air, but the security wards kept it in place. I obscured the master relic and searched for the final two. The third place I tried was empty, the relic apparently undisturbed. There were footprints but not a body or signs of an injury that could have been a result of the detonation of the master relic's security ward. No telltale sign of spell use or magical signature. The fourth location was where I found Lana, gone like her brothers."

Ursula takes a moment here to collect herself with several breaths that bleed from one page to the next with my moving finger. When she picks up again, anger sparks in her tone, her words gaining speed and ferocity.

"I found no other bodies with them, but the evidence of coercion speaks for itself. My children are heirs to the title of High Sorcerer. Ulysses, Lana, Callum. They'd all taken their oaths to the Four Lines. They'd all produced an heir per the Hegemony custom of volunteerism and surrogate vacation of rights."

"Wait . . . they were *bred*? Like racehorses?" Wren hisses. We don't have time to parse *that* weird witch shit—I shush her with a shake of my head and start my finger across the page again.

"It is unfathomable to me that my children, with all they had given to the Four Lines, with all they had given to me, would abandon their ambitions and abdicate their duty to protect the Four Lines by making an attempt to steal the master relics that provide order and safety to thousands of witches who call the Four Lines home. For this reason, I believe they were spelled by powerful magic to go through with this . . . this plot, that ultimately led to their deaths."

Ursula's voice trembles and my fingers shake right along with it.

"I do not know at this time if the coercion occurred from another magical group, unmagical persons, or from *within* the Four Lines. But I will find out who did this—and I will make them pay."

The shiny page comes to an end.

"That's it?" Wren asks, craning her neck, greedy fingers tugging at the pages.

The entries afterward are one bleak day after another.

An adoption ceremony for Evander, Auden, and Winter.

A joint funeral for Ulysses, Callum, and Lana.

Meeting after meeting of heads of the High Families—Ursula, Horatio, Luna, Marsyas.

And then, thumbing ahead, we find the entry for the next annual meeting, July of that year, just like the one we'd attended.

This time, there's no stunned voice memo. There's not even a hint of emotional edge to Ursula's looping, confident script. Just one inflectionless paragraph.

> *At the annual gathering of the High Families of the Four Lines, arguments were presented, and a verdict reached concluding Marcos Blackgate of the Death Line was guilty in the coercion and ultimate deaths of Ulysses, Callum, and Lana Hegemony on March 21 of this selfsame year. Per Four Lines law established in the time of Salem, the punishment for the murder of another witch is death. I, Ursula Elvire Muscatel Hegemony, meted the appointed punishment at 11:43 P.M. on this date, July 13. It was determined that the line of succession would point from Death Line matriarch Marsyas Blackgate directly to her granddaughters—Lavinia Blackgate, age seven, and Kaysa Blackgate, age six.*

And that's it. The passing of a torch, lives changed forever.

I sit back on my haunches, completely wrung out.

The Hegemony parents died while locating and trying to remove—destroy?—the very relics their children were now tasked with finding. A fact that Evander, Auden, and Winter clearly knew—they'd been there for the murder trial and subsequent execution of Marcos Blackgate.

Truly, they all saw him punished. Executed. Every person in this house. Marcos's mother, his wife, his kids too.

How absolutely horrifying.

Wren draws in a rattling breath. Her face is pink, her eyes still leaking. "Do you think—"

A violent *pop* from the fireplace behind us cuts off Wren's question, and we both jump—but then another voice we know booms into the room.

"Hegemony Manor guests!" Evander calls from both the fireplace flue and seemingly everywhere. "Please gather in the third-floor study. A master relic has been found."

CHAPTER 18

AUDEN

"The 'Breath of *Morgana*'? That doesn't make any sense," Hector sputters, rising from the study guest chair he's claimed—the one previously reserved for Marsyas Blackgate. The patriarch takes a step toward the desk, as if inspecting the relic himself would lend a different result from what the three of us found ourselves. "Are you sure that's the inscription?"

Evander is not in a sharing mood. And, honestly, if he barely trusted Winter to touch it, he'd certainly fight tooth and nail to keep Hector's paws off it.

"Yes."

Since everyone arrived, Evander, Winter, and I explained in turns exactly how we came to have this relic in hand. It has all the markings of having been protected by a powerful spell—no erosion, no damage. It's as pristine as it likely had been the moment Shadrack spelled it and concealed it. Exactly as one would expect an invaluable magical relic to be preserved.

Yet, what it supposedly contains has been a point of contention for at least ten minutes now. Despite all the evidence, despite our assurances that the disabled security wards showed themselves.

Luna sighs from the other guest chair. "The clue is clearly Elemental in nature and breath a component in the element of life, though Morgana is a Death witch, and therefore it's quite perplexing from a historical standpoint."

The Blackgate girls simply nod along, not adding anything.

"Not just *a* Death witch," Infinity amends, their eyes slipping away from the two silent Blackgates in our midst, "*the* Death witch. The originator of the line."

"Which is why this is . . . suspect," Hector cuts in. "Merlin is the originator of the Elemental Line; why is an Elemental relic tied to his Death Line counterpart?" Hector's eyes are glassy with exhaustion invading the corners, yet he sparks with an idea, his whole body tensing beneath today's Cerise family uniform—a navy tracksuit with their individual initials monogrammed at the breast. Yeah, it's as ridiculous as it sounds. Especially given the context. But they are always aggressively coordinated. "Could it be mislabeled? Or perhaps it's not a master relic at all?"

Evander frowns at Hector's insinuation of mishandling and I decide to save both of them—and all of us—from yet another time-killing dick-measuring contest.

"Though I can assure you the three of us all saw the security wards fire and fizzle at the removal of the master relic from its hidden location, there is one way to answer that final question indefinitely. If it's a true master, Ursula's will should confirm it by providing the second clue." I pointedly gesture to the clock atop the mantle—9:07 A.M. Twelve hours since Ursula's death. Approximately thirty-nine hours left. "Now, if you please."

Thankfully, Hector dutifully returns to his chair, tracksuit nylon swishing the whole way.

I line my thumb up with my bloody print, gaze lingering on Ursula's signature, forever part of this document. It holds the last of the secrets she'd planned to share with us, and maybe it's simply the residual shock speaking, but I don't think the secrets she plans on sharing are the only ones she's left here.

The initial clue shimmers, fading out. Then, in ink as dark as night, comes the next clue. There's a collective inhale—we have our confirmation that we have collected the first master. I can nearly feel Evander's shoulders soften and his grasp tighten. I read.

> "Our blood is in the stars,
>   Streaming down from the Great Bear's paw,
>   Magic bathing magic as the moon smiles
>   With the sun, its reason, its heart, the gaping center
>   Body and soul."

No one has to say it. The clue is for the Celestial Line.

Luna holds fast to her coffee cup as all attention turns to our remaining matriarch. Infinity kneels at her elbow, their face tipped up to their grandmother. "Grandmama, where do we start?"

After rearranging the drape of the voluminous ivory fabric across her shoulders and taking another sip of coffee so heavily sugared I can smell it from ten feet away, Luna swallows and finally addresses the matter at hand.

"If I knew I'd tell you."

Infinity's brows knit. "You . . . you don't have any ideas? Nothing rings a bell?"

"Oh, plenty rings my bell about the language, but what it might be or where it might be? No." The matriarch turns her attention to me. "If these are hints—as you surmised last night, Auden—these are hints you Hegemonys recognize better than the rest of us. It would behoove all of us to learn everything we can from your successful hunt this morning."

Luna aims her wizened gaze at Evander, who's white-knuckling the master's chain. "As we've said, it was nothing more than the three of us keying in on the final line of the clue—'We worship'—and deciding to search the only place ever used for worship on these grounds and climbing Mercy's Point. We zeroed in on man-made objects first, not knowing what we were looking for. But when we saw this piece"—he opens his palm to reveal it to the light—"we knew it was put there for us to find, even if the inscription was unexpected."

Luna sucks her teeth. "Your success was completely based on your understanding of the grounds and what they contain. I have visited Hegemony Manor more times than I have years, yet even my knowledge is no rival for what is inherent to you as nearly lifelong residents."

"Is there a map?" Ada asks. "Maybe we can start with that, make some educated guesses like the one you made to get to the outdoor chapel, and go from there?"

I nod. "We can do that."

Winter is already on it, retrieving the maps from their careful storage on Ursula's office bookshelves. The desk drawers and storage may have been swept clean of paperwork by either the spell or her killer, but her bookshelves remained untouched—as far as we can tell.

Winter unfurls one on the desk so that it faces the guests. Hector and Sanguine immediately crowd in for a look. Lavinia and Kaysa edge forward. Luna and Infinity stay put.

"This would've been good to have last night," Sanguine muses.

"I didn't want you going on the grounds after dark," Evander reminds her.

"Yes, yes, broken ankles," Hector says with a laugh that seems strong enough to be forced before gesturing with a flat hand toward the depiction of Mercy's Point. "But any of us would have eventually come to the conclusion to check the chapel."

"Wait, no, look more closely," Lavinia says, and circles the top of the mountain with her own finger. "The outdoor chapel isn't designated, only the summit of Mercy's Point. Sure, any of us maybe would've gotten there eventually, but we'd work faster with Hegemony knowledge."

The elder Blackgate glances up at me as she says this, and I realize she's not wearing makeup today, no intricate styling to straight dark hair, no telltale magic spell to perfect things a la Winter, just long-lashed eyes and creamy skin. Faintly, in the back of my mind I'm suddenly in agreement with the Winter of last night—not just eye makeup but all makeup should be illegal on Lavinia Blackgate if this is what's underneath.

"She's right," Infinity says, and I blink away from Lavinia and my thoughts. "We need teams. Our next priority should be to identify likely locations and split up with a Hegemony in each group as a grounds expert."

"Yes, that's it," Luna cheers, emphatic. "My grandbaby with the methodical plan."

The rest of us agree it's the way to go. There's some shuffling, and as I snap a picture and stow away this clue, I realize something.

"Winter?" I ask. "Can you find us a map with Shadrack's original plot delineated? If he wrote the clues, I think it's best to start within the bounds of the estate he owned. The relics could've been moved by another High Sorcerer, but I think it might be the way to start."

"On it." Winter sweeps around the desk and back to the map portion of the bookshelves. As she does, Evander seems to notice I've safely removed the clue from the workplace and draws out his key, pulling it over his head and walking over to Ursula's safe.

"Evander, what are you doing?" Hector asks, in a voice a little too rushed and a little too loud. The tonal difference is enough that the whole room takes immediate notice—even his kids flinch before going stock-still.

Confused, my cousin looks up from the newly opened safe to Hector, following the man's dark eyes to the master relic held tightly in his own hand. "I'm putting the relic away."

"You can't do that."

The hollow certainty settles in my brain that another fissure in our unusual, unbreakable family has just clawed its way to the surface.

Evander narrows his eyes at Hector's rare but effusive stiff-arm. "We don't want anything to happen to it. It'll be safe here."

"You can't do that because we still haven't determined it's yours." Standing around the desk, Hector is close enough that he puts what he appears to think is a comforting palm on Lavinia's shoulder. But even I can see her stiffen from several feet away. "Morgana is the originator of the Death Line. The chance to hold these master relics is a once-in-a-lifetime opportunity—no, once in half a millennium. We need to ensure each family holds the correct one for their line. Moreover, it's one of Ursula's rules—"

"*The rule,*" Evander cuts in, "is that a master relic shouldn't be taken from the rightful line. I haven't taken it from anyone."

Hector tosses up a pair of placating palms—and Lavinia immediately rolls her shoulder away. "I understand that, but I feel it's necessary to have a discussion about the fact that the Breath of

Morgana might actually belong to the Death Line and the Black-gates."

Evander swallows a scoff, though he can't hide the way his big paw tightens around the chain.

"It's the Elemental relic. We all immediately agreed the clue was Elemental in nature, just like we all immediately recognized this clue to be Celestial." He gestures around the study, noting how all of us turned to the Starwoods like sunflowers to the dawn. "Our instincts as witches count for something."

"There's not even anything in the clue that confirms this relic is Elemental save for the word 'breath,'" Hector points out, "which might be a coincidence. I think—"

"Hector, we appreciate your concern, but this is not our master."

The entire room swivels toward Lavinia.

"How do you know?" Hector asks. "Do you know what your master is? Or where we can find it?"

"No, of course not." She gives a little shrug. "But I think Evander is right—we all believed this is the Elemental master, and despite its connection to Morgana, I'm not interested in spending any more time arguing about it. We have less than forty hours to find three more. I want to focus on that."

Honestly, though I know this isn't the Lavinia Blackgate of my childhood—the one who always had to be right, the best, the smartest, the one who would never back away from anything she decided was hers—I appreciate the focus on the bigger picture.

Yet, her mature attitude seems to embolden the Cerise patriarch further.

Hector is still smiling as he continues to argue but there's something dark about it, like the roll of thunder on a sunlit morning. "Why aren't you more concerned that a Hegemony could have your relic, Miss Blackgate? If I were you, I'd be damn suspicious that the Hegemonys were holding the seat of your powers and concerned they won't relinquish it when a more appropriate master comes to light. Isn't it worth ensuring the wrong person isn't in control of *your* relic?"

"He's not—"

"I'm not—"

Lavinia and Evander speak at once. My cousin backs down, letting Lavinia have the floor. "The master is yours, Evander. As far as the Blackgates are concerned, it's the Elemental master relic and we cede it to you."

"Yeah, ceded," Kaysa agrees with a stout nod.

"Thank you. Accepted." Evander raps his knuckles on Ursula's desk like a gavel, and my mind's eye pictures more fissures snaking through us, cracking, bleeding, and everything else Ursula warned me about. My cousin rolls back his shoulders—the cut of his jaw could etch glass. He's immovable in his glare, danger in the low tones of his voice. "It's ours. Can we move on?"

He asks it of Hector, but Luna answers. "*Please.* At this rate I'll be dead by the time I hold my master."

Infinity rubs their temples. "Grandmama, don't say such a thing."

"Why not? I'm ninety-seven, I'm being pragmatic." Luna gestures to her chair. "Scoot me up to the desk. Let's have a look at this fiddly map."

✦ ✦ ✦

It takes a solid hour, and three maps—a delicate illustration of Shadrack's original parcel, a modern-day printout, and one from the year Ursula became High Sorcerer, before we identify six likely locations based on their ties to hints within the clue, their age, and their uses.

Clockwise from the north compass arrow: Field of Stars, Shadrack's Lookout, the Bat Cave, Little Bear Den, the Pool, and Horace's Last Stand.

From there, we divide into teams, minus Luna who won't be testing her ancient bones on the treacherous grounds—a relief, honestly.

I'm assigned both Blackgate girls and Ada, and before we inspect our two locations, the Pool and Horace's Last Stand, I determine that perhaps first we should take a detour to visit Horace of the last stand himself.

Which is how the four of us end up in the first-floor tearoom, with me standing on a chair, using my magic to delicately probe inside the jaws of the massive head of a 130-year-old grizzly bear.

Horace is roaring—teeth staggeringly long, eyes fierce, ears flat with anger. He's packed with wire and cotton, but I want to make sure there isn't something relic-shaped within before we hike out onto the grounds.

Kaysa stands beside me, squinting up. She's the only one who seems interested in this actual bear. Lavinia is taking in the wall of Hegemony portraits a few feet away, and Ada is inspecting her cuticles in a chair by the door.

"So, Shadrack shot this poor bear, mounted him, named him Horace for shits and giggles, and put the location of his murder on a family map?" Kaysa asks, squinting up at both me and the enormous bear head.

"Correct." I nod to the heavy metal body of the Colt .45 revolver mounted on the wall right over his left ear. "And that's the gun he used."

"Jesus Christ. No need to wonder if Shadrack had a healthy ego," Ada mutters. "Look, this is a waste of time, Auden. There's no paw—it's just the head. The clue says, 'Streaming down from the Great Bear's *paw*.' The clue clearly refers to the Great Bear in the sky. We're not going to find the master relic here, or anywhere until the stars come out."

"There's no actual paw in the Ursa Major constellation, just a representative star," Lavinia reports, and I can nearly hear Ada roll her eyes. Lavinia's voice comes closer along with the sound of footsteps as I finish up my inspection of Horace's skull cavity. "But this *is* a bear, so I think Auden might be—"

"Lavinia and Kaysa Blackgate!"

I nearly fall off the chair as Evander's shout beats him to the doorway. He's panting, looking exactly like he's just run here. My stomach drops.

My magical gamble from last night has been discovered much sooner than expected. So soon I never got a chance to ask the sisters if they'd learned anything with the time I'd bought them.

And now time's up.

"There's a dead man on the driveway," Evander spits, livid and sweating. "Your grandmother's driver. The car's missing. Outside. *Now.*"

CHAPTER 19

RUBY

"Textbook Death magic."

Hector is squatting down next to the driver who's exactly where we left him last night. Hex is at his shoulder, like a second examiner, and they both are far too close to the man's ruined face. "God, such an *ugly* magic. Turning people into moldering fruit to kill them. Completely unnecessary."

He's not wrong. And I'd agree with him if I wasn't supposed to be so offended. The driver's worse in the daylight, and the coffee and croissant slosh violently in my gut, half-digested.

I look away and immediately find myself connecting with Auden's calm expression. His eyes only slide my way for the briefest of moments, not betraying anything we discussed last night.

"It is ugly," Evander agrees, "which is why he was very obviously covered up by an invisibility spell."

I can't tell if Evander knows Auden was the one who obscured the body, or if he assumes Marsyas did. And I don't know how to defend him if it comes out.

Wren, however, keeps to the only script we've got.

"I can't believe this. I can't believe this," she repeats, disbelief in every syllable. Her body crumples just enough, her shoulders caving, fingers curling into her palms. "I didn't hear him say a bad word toward her. Just offered us cinnamon candies and still water and kept to himself as drivers do. Had the partition up most of the way. Lavinia," she turns to me, amber eyes expertly teary, "you didn't notice anything else, did you?"

Solemn and meaning it, I shake my head.

Evander clears his throat. "Are you suggesting you were unaware

Marsyas had used her magic to murder this man and escape before Ursula's spell put Hegemony Manor into lock-down?"

Wren takes a step forward, nailing Evander with the doe-eyed innocence she used to weasel out of a speeding ticket on the last day of school while driving Dad's car.

"Evander." His name is delicate on her lips. "Don't you think we would've told you if we knew? We had no idea Nona—"

"Bullshit," Hex exclaims, rising from where he'd been squatting.

"Language, Junior!"

We all turn, and there's Luna Starwood, sour-faced as she holds fast to Infinity's arm as the pair of them navigate the driveway bricks. The front doors are thrown wide, the painted foyer of Hegemony Manor exposed and open to the real beauty rendered across its plaster.

"I apologize, Luna. I, just—you didn't notice it last night?" Hex asks us, but he's watching Auden. "When you were out *searching for Nona* and Auden marched you back inside from *this direction*?"

Aw, shit. Everyone rotates toward Auden.

Hector rises from his crouch to place an affirming hand on the back of his son's neck, while Sanguine crosses her arms over her considerable chest, and Ada smirks.

Evander and Winter are harder to gauge. The cousins don't look much alike, but their expressions are the same temperature—icy.

Luna and Infinity are silent, waiting.

Auden weathers it without a reaction that's obvious to me, but it's evident in the slight hardening of Evander's jaw that he's reading something in his cousin that the rest of us can't distinguish.

"Is that correct, Auden?" Evander prods. "You walked them up the drive, past this driver, and didn't notice? I saw this obscurement spell a mile away. Surely you would have too, even in the dark."

"We were *very* distressed." I can't cry on command like my sister, but I'm so stressed my voice helpfully frays and scatters like light refracted. "So far from home, and then suddenly Ursula's dead, and Nona's missing, and we . . . we panicked and just ran around screaming her name."

I grab Wren's hand, which she clutches tightly to her chest—a little melodramatic but probably perfect—and look Auden straight in his too-handsome face with genuine appreciation. "Auden was a gentleman and guided us back to the house. Honestly, if we'd found this man, one of us would've probably fainted."

I realize I've gone too far when Luna swipes a dismissive hand through the air. The woman could take out an eye with her sudden gestures. "Oh, none of you are the fainting type. No witch has been the fainting type since Salem. I don't care what Marsyas did to wipe your memory and knowledge banks, you're not built to be soft no matter what's happened to your minds."

Hex, though, has a much different angle of criticism.

"You were distracted and distressed, sure. But Auden wasn't." Hex pauses, letting the accusation sink over us like bonfire smoke. "Auden was observant enough to locate you both very quickly on the grounds. In fact, he was observant enough to be the first of us to realize you'd left the room."

He has a point.

"I," Sanguine says, voice like ice cracking in a cold glass, "find it hard to believe that you came out here looking for Marsyas at all. That story never made sense, and the timing was even more strange. You knew we were about to read the first clue, and you slipped out? Just to see if you could find her? Why then? Why not after the reading of the clue? You had all night. You've had all morning."

"Because they weren't looking for Marsyas," Ada answers her mother, just adding to the pile-on. "They were probably supposed to cover up her tracks. Maybe perform a spell on this poor bastard and, I don't know, supercharge their gross bracelets with his death rattle, then use that power to escape somehow because they were left behind as *part* of Marsyas's plan."

I don't know if we can "supercharge" our rabbits' feet, and therefore I don't deny it. In fact, I don't say anything at all. Wren is silent too. We're holding hands and it doesn't escape me that though she's putting on an amazing front, she's trembling beneath my grasp.

Evander sighs, hands on the hips of his workout shorts and big shoulders slumping enough to strain the seams of his Walton-Bridge jersey. I realize then that even without magic, he could haul both Wren and me off and there'd be nothing we could do about it.

"I hate to say it, but I agree with this line of questioning." Shit. "I don't think you were looking for Marsyas. I think you know where she is, what she did, and you were simply executing part of the plan."

Now I think Wren might actually cry.

"Evander, no. That's not true."

He scoffs, teeth bared and bright for the flash of a second. "My cousin here hasn't said a word, which means he knows at least some of it is true and he's not stupid enough to lie right now after being caught in one by Hex."

Evander glowers at Auden who, to his credit, doesn't look away.

He *is* in trouble. It's our fault. And now we all look guilty.

Panic catches me by the throat. This is not how we should repay the kindness of his healing magic, no matter what prompted it. I can't let Auden go down for this. I drop my sister's hand and step a step forward. "No—"

"I'll submit to a truth spell!"

I stifle a gasp and turn to Wren, who's pleading with the group at large, desperate and reckless. "We didn't know this was going to happen and we have no idea what Nona had planned or even where she went. Ask me. Ask me right now!"

I've gone as pale as one of Wren's ghosts, I can nearly feel the blood draining and there's no use in hiding it.

My sister has just offered us up like lambs to slaughter.

We're not who we say we are and the second they find out, we're goners. It doesn't matter that we're innocent, we're also knowledge-able now about something we were never supposed to know.

And that might be worse.

Still, Wren goes on, her cheeks flushed and eyes bright as she makes her case like she's under a spotlight in front of a packed house.

"I don't care which of you does it. I will prove to you that we are innocent in three questions or less," she announces, guessing the format based on what we learned last night. "Then we can stop with these games and questions and insinuations. You'll know what we know, and we can get on with finding the relics and sorting out the murderer because though we can all agree this man is Nona's handiwork, I'm not convinced she killed Ursula. And I can affirm to you that if she did, we had no idea it was going to happen nor had anything to do with it."

Wren's planting questions in their heads. Giving them topics. She's leading them like a lawyer in cross-examination. Wren is an excellent improv partner, but this won't be enough.

It's a good idea, but it's not *magic*.

And I don't know how I can reasonably help.

Though it's seventy degrees and the air is as dry as a bone, I start to sweat.

"I'll do it," Ada offers, already advancing with a twist of the ring on her index finger. Like Hex's, the hidden point within it springs out like a rose thorn of a switch blade, ready to take Wren's blood and make it dance.

"No," Winter snaps. She's still as a statue, the buttery fabric and light colors of her high-end yoga clothes at odds with the sharpness of her voice, her brow, her words. Decisive and without the ragged marks of hesitation. "Evander should do it. He found this body. He's the one who wanted to interrogate the Blackgates last night. It should be him."

"It should be Evander," Hex agrees. When his entire family turns on him, he shrugs. "What? Don't you want to see how the Elementals do it? I, for one, want to know if he's going to light her skin on fire until the truth blows out."

Winter curses. "Jesus Christ. I was being facetious when you brought that up last night."

Hex smirks. "I know."

And that's it.

As Ada frowns and stows her ring, Wren whirls on Evander. "Three questions. That's all."

I expect the eldest Hegemony to shake his head and inform

her that's not how it works. Or perhaps to haggle—going for five knowing they'll compromise at four and he'll buy himself a question for the trouble.

Instead, Evander takes my sister's slender hands in his meaty ones, mindful of her bunny bracelets, and flips both of them over, palms up. "Look at me."

Wren does as she's told, shoulders back, and chin up, expression remaining cut clean with defiance. She is the picture of calm and collected. She doesn't fidget, she doesn't even smile in that automatic way she can't seem to help when making eye contact. The air around both of them appears to still, matching Wren's demeanor.

I want to will myself to draw on it, copy it, glom on to it. But I can feel my blanched cheeks going clammy under a fresh layer of perspiration. My heart rabbits in my chest against my immobile lungs. I try to force myself to take a steadying breath, but my body only does that little under protest, preferring to be as stagnant as possible beyond my heart. Like I'm watching a careening car and waiting for the crash.

Everyone around me has gone fuzzy in my periphery, and it's just Wren and Evander in focus. Dark hair and hazel eyes and a sliver of blue sky between them. Their eye contact is as tangible as Evander's grip on the backs of Wren's hands.

Slowly, deliberately, Evander places Wren's right-hand knuckles to the palm of her left, forming a gentle basket. He cradles it from below, and continues to look Wren straight in the eye.

"The Elemental truth spell works like this. I'll create a flare of energy between us. I'll ask you three questions. If the flare turns green, it detects truth. If it turns black, it detects an equal amount of truth and lie and the question is recast. If it turns red, it detects a lie."

My stomach knots. I can't believe our lives hang in the balance of what sounds exactly like the magical equivalent of a mood ring.

"Kaysa, do you understand?" She nods. "Are you ready?"

"Yes." The sound is still confident but small and controlled.

"Watch your hands."

The moment Wren's eyes narrow on her own palms, Evander whispers under his breath. As the final word falls from his lips, Evander snaps his fingers.

A ball of fire appears *in* Wren's hand.

Smokeless, orange, and completely spherical.

My sister doesn't cry out in pain, she doesn't react at all except the tiniest flare of her eyes as she hooks onto the light, unblinking.

Under its spell.

"Did Marsyas Blackgate kill Ursula Hegemony?"

"I don't know."

Immediately, the ball shivers from where the base touches Wren's hand, flaring green as an emerald.

I try to swallow, but now my throat doesn't work along with my burning lungs, traffic-jam gut, and my eyes, which don't leave my sister's hands. I suppose I should be thankful I can actually see this color change, if not whatever magic is behind it. Just like with Hex's hunt spell and Auden's disguise of the driver last night, I can see the effects, if not the actual work going into it.

Evander asks his second question, his concentration sharp under the heavy furrow of his brows.

"Did Marsyas Blackgate tell you or your sister about her plans to disappear, or instruct you about what to do after she left?"

"No."

The fire flares back to orange and my knees lock. It's possible Marsyas pulled Wren aside. It's possible the old woman put a spell on my sister and drew her into her plan. It's possible she's lying without knowing.

All those possibilities pound in my ears as I watch the light as if under compulsion myself, unable to look away.

But then, the ball flares green.

A muscle in Evander's jaw twitches.

"Ask if they killed Ursula," Hector stage-whispers.

"Or if they know who did," Sanguine adds.

"And use her first name to preface the question, it's much more accurate," Ada sniffs.

Winter, Auden, and Infinity all turn to shush them. But I can't break my gaze from the concentration of my sister's eyes on the fire ball, and Evander watching her.

Finally, he asks his third question. "Where is Marsyas Blackgate right now?"

There's a groan from the direction of the Cerises at Evander's choice not even to consider their advice, as spelled Wren answers again, in a strong voice. "I don't know."

Three of the four Cerises toss their tracksuited arms up in frustration as, again, the ball shifts from green to orange to green.

Evander nods at the final color change, whispers, and again snaps his fingers. The ball disappears. He's left holding Wren's hands as she blinks herself awake—at him, at me, at all our faces.

She clasps both Evander's hands in hers. "I passed?!"

"You passed."

All the air in my lungs leaves me in a slow leak, my chest burning as I smother a sigh of relief.

"I mean, obviously. Because I'm telling you the truth." Wren hugs my arm and yanks me to her. "We're both telling the truth."

"Perhaps, but we know nothing new about Ursula's death," Hector argues. "We have no definitive answer about if Marsyas murdered Ursula, only that the Blackgates don't know if Marsyas murdered her."

"We know that we can trust them," Auden says, "and that's valuable to them and to us. We know the Blackgates aren't planning anything nefarious with Marsyas. If anything, they're pawns and victims like the rest of us. That's what we learned."

"Thank you," Wren says, pointedly to Auden. "Now can you all stop looking at both of us like we're walking landmines with excellent hair?"

She squeezes me one more time before freeing me to stand on my own. But I feel like my knees are about to give out.

Hector scowls. "I wouldn't go that far. These two could've cooked up plans to kill Ursula as revenge for their father's death, and Kaysa's answers would've pulled the same results from those close-ended questions."

"No," Evander says, definitive. "If they were involved in Ursula's murder, the answer wouldn't have come out so clear. We all know there are shades of truth, and every answer was definitive. I felt Kaysa's intent in each answer. She and Lavinia are not involved in Ursula's death."

That declaration is a small relief as my nerves jump with the thought that he could feel Wren's intent through their connection. Could he feel her lack of magic too? Her lie? Our lies?

We're threading the needle here with a margin of error so small I can't believe we've made it out with all our blood on the inside. My anger flares at Wren. This was too close.

It wasn't worth it.

"Then it was Marsyas," Luna concludes. "You saw her—she walked to the table with Ursula. Had plenty of time and opportunity to spell her with something during that stroll. It took near a millennium for them to approach the table—Marsyas is nearly as slow as me and she has her original knees!" There's some nodding— Hector and Sanguine bobbing like marionettes on the same string, the twins a half step behind; Evander, Winter, even Auden. "Then she killed this man for his car and drove off."

I meet Wren's eyes because it all makes sense . . . except for the fact that Marsyas already had the man's keys. We'd both seen her drop them in that wretched raven's-body clutch. *Jangle, thud, zip.*

But to everyone else, it adds up.

It should.

Neither of us says a word about Marsyas's key possession. I can't explain why, but I want to keep that bit to myself. I don't trust them with it. Not yet.

"Now, hold on. Wait." Hex's features are scrunched up like he's eaten too much ice cream too fast.

"Get that thought out or your face'll stay that way," Winter mutters under her breath.

Hex's eyes shoot to the youngest Hegemony, but not with disdain, that flirty smirk back for a ghost of a second before he asks, "What if this is a diversion?"

"It's a mess is what it is. A hurried, panicked mess of a murderer."

"But what if it's on purpose?" he asks, gesturing indulgently at the man on the ground. "We all know talented witches, like, say, members of the High Families, can all disguise our magic to *look* like another line's."

My gut twists—that's why my instinct was to hold back about the keys. If someone imitated Marsyas to set her up for the driver's murder, they both don't know about it and they're likely standing right here.

"Yes, and the best comp to Death magic is Blood magic, genius," Ada seethes, punctuated with an elbow to her twin's kidney. They've confirmed what we learned in the reading room last night—a fact I'm sure these other witches know. "Are you saying me, or Mama and Papa did it? Or you?"

"What? No. But I am saying we can check the magical signature."

"Oh," Winter exclaims. And it's a surprise when she clarifies Hex's thought for him. "You mean, glean the magic and see if the person who cast the spell on this man is still on the grounds?"

"Yes?"

"Why can't we do that to Ursula?" I ask slowly, trying to sound as magically incompetent as they expect me to be. "Wouldn't that be the best way to make sure Nona did it?"

"Because of the victim's shroud," Infinity answers, not unkindly. "That sort of magic is considered tampering when it comes to another witch. But a normal old dead guy? Should be fine."

That does not make sense to me, but I don't probe more. What I've broached is already dangerous enough.

"Go ahead, son, let's see what you've got," Hector says. Sanguine gives an encouraging nod, while Ada stews silently next to her. I'm getting the idea that chances for both compliments and opportunities are few and far between in that household.

"No—it should be someone who can't mimic the magic so easily," Auden suggests. Hex's mouth drops open to argue, but Sanguine grips his wrist and he immediately steps back into line with the rest of his family. "Luna? Infinity?"

Luna dislodges herself from Infinity and stands on her own. "Go ahead, child."

As Infinity steps forward and kneels to the man, I find Wren's pinky and twine it with mine. I don't know what this magic will do or how it will work, but this is the best I can do for the pendulum to swing the other way after her success with the truth spell.

On their knees, Infinity draws up their hands to the sky, letting the bare sunlight soak into their palms. Then, with the precision of a piano player, all that gathered power and magic sluices into the tongueless mouth, to the vacant eye sockets, to the maw of the driver's throat.

The body immediately seizes.

Infinity presses both hands down, pinning the man and his spinal column convulsing wildly against the brick. All the while, they bend and whisper in the dead man's ear.

The driver shudders in one, two, three more huge flailing movements before he jerks to a sitting position, throws his head back, and spews black smoke from gaping lips.

At first it's a plume, then it spreads out *horizontally*.

The gaseous horizon begins to dip and swirl but stays parallel. It doubles back on itself and straightens in places, and then it stops.

And . . . it's readable.

Not a symbol, calling card, code. An actual, literal signature, straight from the victim's mouth to the rest of us.

Marsyas Lavinia Blackgate.

"Well, that's definitive," Luna concludes. "Good job, child."

Infinity smiles weakly at their grandmother and looks up at the rest of us from their spot, still kneeling at the man's side. "Should we bury him? Or perhaps give him a shroud? It seems so uncivilized to leave him to rot on the driveway."

"I can give him a shroud," Auden volunteers. "Just like Ursula's—nonpermanent but private. It's the least we can do. Murdered over a set of car keys."

"No." Luna's tone is completely inflexible, her usual orneriness evaporated. "He's not a witch. Shrouds are not for non-witches, no matter how unfortunate or magical their end. Cold storage. Safely inside. Away from here."

PART THREE

THE
LIES

Chapter 20

AUDEN

The search for more dead bodies goes quickly.

The magic does its work easily between the three of us, as we toil in silence. Within minutes, we not only know there aren't any more, but that every other person who entered the property through the gates is accounted for.

The five permanent employees, ten contractors, and the single remaining driver—the Starwoods' chauffeur because Hector always insists on driving the Cerises—are all accounted for. All sleeping soundly under Ursula's spell.

The magic is definitive. It is the eleven of us, alive and moving about. No one else.

And so, as soon as we get the Blackgates' former driver into the house's root cellar and spell the body to an appropriate temperature, my cousins seal the exits to the cook's kitchen in which we're standing, seeming intent on murdering *me*.

Not with magic, but with pent-up accusations and withering glares of disappointment.

Evander is the first to speak, of course. He crosses his arms and leans against the central island, still dusted with flour from Chef Maggie's toiling before our guests' arrival. The hearth fire in the old kitchen throws shade on the profile of his face, already bruised with sleep deprivation and he's silently simmering with a level of perceived betrayal he's been holding in since the driveway.

"You knew about that body, and not only did you not tell us about it, you *covered it up*."

I should've figured out something to say by now, but instead I fumble. "I—"

"Auden," Winter cuts me off, grimace as sharp as the tilt of her clavicles above her aggressively folded arms. "Don't deny it. We'd know your magic anywhere, and even if you hadn't been stupid enough to cover it up, even *I* believe Hex's account of you walking right past it."

I lean against the pantry door as leisurely as possible and pretend to be unbothered, inspecting my nails but wishing I had a book to feign reading. "Congratulations. You've caught me with something I finally *do* know."

My sarcasm might as well bounce straight off Evander, his body language and expression as hard as stone. "Something you purposefully kept from us."

"Something you *lied* about," Winter adds, more to the point. Like Sanguine, she has a habit of drawing blood with her admonitions. "Why?"

"We know the Blackgate girls don't know of their grandmother's plans, but *do you*?" Evander goes further, for blood. "Are you working with Marsyas?"

"What—no. Of course not."

Frustration sharpens the edges of my voice. I'm so sick of him questioning me, but this time I deserve it. Looking Evander right in the eye, I swallow down the frustration and speak as plainly, as directly as I can. Nothing to hide behind, all of it in the open.

"I covered up the body. Yes. Honestly, I'm not even sure why I did it."

That's the truth of it.

I took one look at the dead man, read the panic on Lavinia's face, and I just did it. Her fearful eyes and pale cheeks rise in my vision now and I have to shake them away. Doing such a thing for this version of Lavinia that I barely know makes even less sense than doing it for the version of ten years ago I knew well enough to loathe.

I don't understand it. I can't defend it.

"But," I continue, drawing in a deep breath, "I didn't tell you because I simply recognized that we had enough going on last night and chose not to say anything."

Even to my own ears the answer is both vague and weak.

Evander bares his teeth. "Last night you told us not to put all of our attention on Marsyas. You literally argued for us to look at everyone else while knowing there was a man dead by Marsyas's hand on *our* property." He's no longer stoic, he's shouting. "Knowing about the murdered driver could've changed things last night—"

"What would it have changed, Evander?" I shout right back.

Even I'm surprised when there's the heavy bludgeon of anger in my words instead of simply my hot, festering annoyance that they've managed to tack this indiscretion onto a fight we had when Ursula was alive. I try to swallow it down, to soften my voice like I'd managed to do mere moments ago, but my next words still come out edged like a razor.

"It would've given you more leverage to interrogate the Blackgate girls, yes, but it wouldn't have changed the outcome. Kaysa would've submitted to that truth spell just as she did this morning, she would've passed, and she would've shoved your sniper's target off their backs. That's it."

"Auden's right."

We both turn to stare at Winter. She's hauled herself onto the counter by the fridge, sagged sideways against it, pinching the bridge of her nose.

"While I'm not pleased he *chose to keep this information to himself* when he had *ample opportunity* both last night and this morning to share news of the dead driver with us *and* the group at large," she continues, adding stress to each word aimed at my indiscretion, "the outcome wouldn't have changed."

Evander looks like he might blow a literal gasket.

"Between us? *Everything* has changed. Auden, I believed you yester—"

"Right, which is exactly why you're bringing it up again. Asking me if I'm in on it. Again. Third time's the charm, Evander. It's totally when I'm going to cave and blurt, 'Yep, you've caught me, I murdered Ursula for your title!'" I explode back. "Is that what you're hoping to hear? That I'm the villain?"

Evander scrubs a hand down his face, worrying the fresh dark stubble lining his jaw. He pins me with his heavy-browed stare, the clear green of his irises the only pinprick of light. His exhaustion is different now, somehow. Older, deeper.

"Before we lost Ursula, I thought *she* was keeping something from *me,* not you. But now? You didn't tell us about the body. You didn't tell us about your title—"

"Our titles are not anything to be guilty about," Winter snaps, slamming the side of the fridge with a thump that rattles the mixing bowls on a nearby shelf. "Let's not re-litigate this shit, it's just dick measuring by another name. No thank you, boys."

Evander throws up his hands. "The point is . . . I'm going to be wondering what you're keeping from me."

I pin him with a glare of my own. "I'm not keeping anything from you."

Evander stabs a blunt finger into the flat of his palm. His tone hardens into the one he's been using to try to prove his authority to us, to the other High Families. "No more secrets from here on out. No matter how small."

His strong-man act is not appreciated.

"What about you?" Winter challenges. "Can you honestly tell us you have no secrets, *patriarch*?"

"None," Evander insists—a slammed door.

Winter's lips draw back, ready to attack him on both his answer and his attitude.

I don't let her. "Okay, look. What we all know now is that Marsyas killed that man and left. Though, I do agree that Hex could be right about her being set up, I think we need to recognize that if Marsyas murdered Ursula and vanished before the deed was done, then she has a *second part* of her plan."

That gets their attention.

Winter stiffens as she unravels what I've said. "If Marsyas murdered Ursula because she *knew* it would trigger the clause in the will to make the High Sorcerer's title up for grabs but then left before she could be entrapped on the grounds, she has a phase two coming so that she can obtain the relics and the title."

"Yes, exactly."

There's a little spark in Evander's eyes in the millisecond before he narrows them and scoffs, "And you seriously think the Blackgate girls *aren't* in on that?"

"I truly think they aren't *knowingly* in on that. And after that truth spell of Kaysa, I believe deep down you think so too."

Evander glances away. That's enough to tell me I'm right. He could feel Kaysa's innocence in that magic the same way I could read it in Lavinia's panicked eyes last night as she stood, bravely holding her damaged hand.

And . . . shit.

"I just realized I've kept something else from you."

They pivot my way, and I wince.

"I didn't do it purposefully—I just, look, take this for what you will," I sputter, flashing my palms, placating. "I'm so dead set on the Blackgate girls not being in on it because they tried to escape."

"They *what*?"

"They tried to escape," I repeat as Evander's eyes narrow. "They weren't looking for Marsyas. I think they knew she'd ditched them. When I spotted them, they were approaching the barbed-wire fence. I could see they were negotiating what to do about the spell and Kaysa put a probing hand—"

Winter gasps. "Oh no."

"Oh *yes*. Only, it wasn't Kaysa who got injured—Lavinia wedged her herself between Kaysa's fingers and the spell at the last second. When I got there, I ordered them to turn around and told them if they would stand down with their relics clear that I'd heal her. They knew they were in a bind and agreed." I shake my head. "They were truly panicked and frightened. I don't think it was an act."

When I glance up, Winter presses the backs of her hands to her eyes, letting her head thud dully against the kitchen wall. Evander, of course, looks like he's ready to gore me at full speed.

"You *forgot* to tell us they tried to escape *and* that you healed them?"

"I'm telling you now. Don't make me sorry for it. Just take the information and use all your macho patriarch energy to solve this instead of sending me on some self-serving guilt trip."

"She left them to take the fall." Winter drags both hands down her face, the clarity of it hitting her now. She blinks at us, head shaking ever so slightly. "Or she simply didn't tell them so they wouldn't know. If they don't know, they can't reasonably be accomplices."

"Shitty either way," I agree. "If Marsyas has plans to use Lavinia and Kaysa somehow to obtain the masters and the High Sorcerer title with them, that means she has to hold all four master relics by the end of tomorrow. We need to consider how she plans to do that if she's not on the property—I was there when Hex performed the hunt spell. She's not here. And we just checked ourselves for any other people on the property and came up empty. Even if they'd obscured themselves, we would've found them with that spell. We're locked in and it's just us."

For all our magical knowledge, for all we studied at the knee of the great Ursula Hegemony, for all that we are probably some of the best educated witches on the planet—I've never once heard of a spell that can transport someone *into* the kind of powerful magical lock-down that is currently imprisoning us.

Winter slips off the counter and starts pacing the length of the kitchen. "If Marsyas killed Ursula, she'd be insane to come back here. Marsyas knows the punishment for murder is death whether she was here for the will's stipulations or not."

"Which is exactly why she ran," Evander grumbles. "*And* killed that man in the process."

Winter hits the end of the room by the fire and makes an about-face, pinching the bridge of her nose as if this is giving her a headache. It certainly might. "I'm going in circles—*we're* going in circles."

"You're going in a straight line, actually."

"Shut up, Auden," they both bark at once.

I don't, but I do change the subject.

"Look, we need to get out there. Last night's plan is still in effect. We need to talk to who we can and figure out if even with the evidence on the drive—someone else had motive. Or perhaps *shares* in Marsyas's motive. It's possible she could be working with someone else. If not her granddaughters, another party with a joint goal. It could've just been Marsyas's role to leave, and someone else is still inside fulfilling their piece."

Evander checks his Rolex—a graduation gift from our grandmother.

"Thirty-six hours." Noon now, then. "Win, you hook up with Infinity and use that Liaison of the Lines relationship to check for Starwood motive." She scoffs at the idea that either Celestial witch would have anything to do with this, but he ignores her. "Auden, you're with me."

A drop of relief swells in my gut. We're on the same page. He's making a plan and agrees with me.

"The Cerises or the Blackgates?" I ask.

"Whomever we run into first—the Blackgates might not be as clueless as they appear to be, and the Cerises have generations of motive. Win, if you see either group out there when you're with Infinity, join forces. They'll appreciate a knowledgeable Hegemony, and we'll work both sides of this thing as much as we can."

CHAPTER 21

RUBY

"Your impulsivity is going to get us killed, *Kaysa.*"

Wren scrunches up her nose. "Or *exonerated,* which is what just happened, may I remind you. Impulsivity isn't the same thing as stupidity."

As the Hegemonys dealt with the body and Infinity settled Luna back inside, the Cerises announced that we shouldn't waste time and split up to search for the master relics. To wit, they'd piled into a tank of a black SUV and hit the two locations available via the single access road marked on the north side of the grounds: the Field of Stars and Shadrack's Lookout.

They probably had room for us in that massive thing, but we told them we'll hit the two locations we'd been assigned as part of Auden's group before everything went south—the Pool and Horace's Last Stand.

We're alone now—which means I have a chance to lay into Wren about her apparent *death wish.*

I sigh, words loading on my tongue as we navigate the artfully crafted flat stones that curl down the drop from the manicured garden and lawn of Hegemony Manor to the unkempt wilds of the land beyond. Wren has skipped ahead, fingers trailing along the delicate ivory skin of an Aspen when she pauses in her descent long enough to lob one more preemptive strike before I deepen my attack.

"I knew what I was doing."

My sister's tone is fierce and the look in her eyes purposefully cutting. This is how it goes with us—I try to protect her, to teach her, and am summarily rewarded when her shame lashes out, going for the bone in an effort to avoid any unfair correction from her big sister who can do no wrong.

"Wren," I whisper, "I know you think you're the best actress in the county, but you can't out-act the truth. What if they'd asked you point-blank if you were really Kaysa Blackgate? We've all seen those lie-detector scenes on TV. They start with known facts to set a baseline. What if they'd done that and simply asked your name like the Cerises suggested? You would've *failed*."

And failing in this case means punishment at the hands of people who hold their own investigations, trials, and executions without an ounce of constitutional oversight.

Wren seems to have chosen to give me the silent treatment in answer, skipping down the last three steps to a patch of dirt that has three thin ribbons of trail snaking off into the scrub and columbine. Right in the middle, there's a wooden sign with a list of destinations on it, very much like the more official-looking ones in Rocky Mountain National Park.

Three of the six locations we need to search—the Pool, Horace's Last Stand, Little Bear Den—are listed among a jumble of other destinations, along with various mileage. Wren checks the trail against the grounds map on her phone—we all took pictures instead of opting to carry a full map—and heads down the middle path, stomping footsteps kicking up puffs of dry dirt, pine needles, and navigating pellets of deer poop. When I catch up, she's finally decided to answer me.

"Ruby, they're witches, not cops. They wouldn't have done that because they think their magic is infallible."

"For all we know it *is* infallible."

I snag her wrist and tug her to a halt. Wren doesn't fight me, though she brazenly pretends I'm not right in front of her, annoyed expression pointed toward the crests and crevices beyond. I shove my own frustrations down—she won't look me in the eye? Fine. I'll force her to listen.

"Your impulsivity is a *pattern*. A dangerous pattern. One you've had from the beginning. You said yes to Marsyas and got us in this mess. You abandoned me in the reading room instead of thinking it through. And now you played Russian roulette with a type of magic that could've . . ." I lower my voice as much as possible, "outed both of us."

Wren is as still as stone. Somehow that hurts more than if she'd flinched. Her lips thin as her gaze flicks to my face, hazel eyes hard as amber.

"But I *didn't.*" She's emphatic. "And now they won't try to truth-spell us again. I saved our asses, and nobody thinks we did anything. You're welcome."

"The cost was too great! Not just the potential outing, which we're lucky we avoided—"

"*I* avoided for us."

"You avoided, yes, but if Marsyas *didn't do it,* now that we're not scapegoats, we've blown the artificial cover of the real killer. That could make us *targets.* We could've just enraged the real killer."

Wren tosses her head back in exasperation. "I'll take rage over the magical punishment for a murder we didn't do. There's no 'I told you so' in the afterlife." She throws herself forward, leaning in now, arms wide and bangs swinging. "We need to do all we can to make sure that no one thinks we murdered Ursula by the end of the next, what, thirty-eight hours? What I did just now went a loooooong way toward opening a window and airing out that stupid cloud of suspicion over us after Marsyas jetted. You can't argue with that."

"I can't," I admit. "But the punishment for Ursula's death isn't the only danger here, and we need to respect that. I know there's the X factor of Marsyas being the killer, but we have to ignore that. It's best to assume that one of these people is the murderer and that they'd do it again in a heartbeat to keep punishment off the radar."

"Of course we do! Of course they will! We're in danger! I heard you the first time this morning when you completely overreacted." She launches herself toward me, jabbing me in the ribs. "But what *I* think is that you don't get that *everyone* is in danger. Heck, Ursula wrote it right into the rules—they're not supposed to use magic against each other. She knew things would get ugly."

God, she's right.

Wren's full mouth twists, knowing she's managed to touch on something I haven't considered. "I'm not an idiot, Ruby. I know what I did was a gamble. Yes, the killer might want a scapegoat or two, but you know what they want more than that? The title. Don't forget that either."

There's triumph in her voice and carriage.

"You're treating this too much like a game, Wren."

"It *is* a game. A screwed-up game, but *I* was right, and with apologies to grumpy, hot Evander, it is one. The prize is the title. The murder of Ursula was a means to an end, a starting gun."

I snag her wrists again, the metal pieces of our bracelets clacking while the rabbits' feet bump. It's stupid but at this point I feel I can only get her to listen by grounding her as much as possible in the here and now with actual, physical me, standing before her. "Yeah, but we're *not* players. We were never players."

"That's not true. Marsyas brought us in."

"As decoys, as pawns, as two replaceable targets to sub in for her granddaughters who are *so irreplaceable,* they're hidden away on another continent!"

My sister grins at the frustration in my voice.

"And we need to know *why*." Wren wriggles completely out of my grip. "And before you suggest sneaking back into the house and paging through books, let me point out even you know deep down that actually *talking* to these people is far more efficient." She points down the trail. "Let's get out there and see who wants to win."

My heart quivers, tips, plummets.

"Fine." I bite my lip. "But if we're going to do that, we should follow the Cerises. They're the only ones we know for sure are out here already, and therefore the ones we can learn from. Who knows when the Hegemonys and Infinity will start searching."

Wren slaps a hand against her thigh, triumphant. She's so excited in fact that she doesn't complain about how it would've been nice if I'd come to this conclusion when we could've hitched a ride. Instead, she sweeps past me, crunching over rocks and hopscotching over thick tufts of scrub to off-road to the trail leading to the Field of Stars and Shadrack's Lookout. "There you go. Thank you for seeing it my way."

I follow and when we're shoulder to shoulder on the trail and angling to the northern corner of the estate, I reiterate, "But we're not just talking to them—if the conditions are right, we need to observe these people in a situation where they don't think they're being watched or overheard. It's not so much what they will tell us as what they will tell each other when we're not around."

Wren's light attitude has returned, quick as a pendulum swing. She elbows me and winks. "I think you're underestimating what someone will tell me, sis."

Oh, for heaven's sake.

"Please tell me you're not going to flirt with anyone upright and breathing. You're going to give them the wrong idea."

Her face breaks into the picture of exasperation. "Who said I'm giving them the wrong idea? I genuinely like some of them. And do you not recall that I rated everyone a nine and above on my own personal attractiveness scale before we even set foot beyond these gates?"

"I can't forget that."

"And *I* can't help that flirting is my superpower. I'll get us some good info." She raises a finger and boops me on the nose. *Jesus Christ.* "*And* the more these people like me and feel that I like them, the safer it makes me—and you."

"Not if one of them has a jealous streak."

"There's not enough time to get jealous, Rubes. I'm the least of their worries."

"Yes, but you're the *most* of my worries." I twine our pinkies together—reckless because I'm skating too close to using our sister promise code too often this weekend. But with all that's on the line, it's just . . . I can't not do it. "Wren—"

"I'm trying to make sure in my own way that we aren't murder material. Okay. Please, just—you're older, and you're less impulsive and whatever." It's a whisper—not exasperated, not bratty, but full-throated, pointed, sincere, if not quiet. And though she jabs me in jest at herself, her eyes are serious and maybe a little sad. "But I have my strengths too."

I kick a small rock and it skitters off the trail and into the underbrush. "I know."

"Let me use them. Without second-guessing or mom-ing me. I might not be doing things the way *you* would do them, but that doesn't mean they don't work. It doesn't mean we aren't a team if we do things our own way."

She's right. She is.

Still, I slip my hand into my tights pocket. I present the butter knives I retrieved this morning. "Look, just before you do anything else your way, take one of these."

The polished silver glints in the high morning light and Wren skids to a halt, incredulous. "Are you kidding me?"

"You're the one who just pointed out that everyone is in danger. They have magic. It's not unreasonable for us to have something too."

Wren smooths a lock of hair behind her ear. "I could make a joke about bringing a knife to a gunfight but I won't because technically they can't use their magic against Lavinia and Kaysa Blackgate."

Now I'm the one rolling my eyes. I snatch her hand, open it, and press the metal into her palm. "Take the knife."

"It doesn't go with my outfit."

"Wren—"

"Kidding. Kidding. There's a hidden pocket."

✦ ✦ ✦

A half hour after we descend into a thick tangle of firs knitted together along a stream bed, I check the map on my phone, zooming in to gauge the distance from the house to where we are now. Based on what I gathered in the discussion of potential locales in the study, the Field of Stars is a sort of moraine park carved between mountains by a glacier ages ago. What's left is a low-lying oasis of knee-high grasses; soft, loamy soil; and a stiff swath of stream shallow enough for fly fishing.

I point to the flat red girth of a large boulder about thirty feet ahead. "The trees should end on the other side of that big fella."

"Good. I was worried we were going to miss them."

"Still might. There are four of them searching, and they had a head start."

"And a car."

"And a car." I echo and pick up the pace, shutting off my phone in the process to conserve battery.

We skirt the boulder and, indeed, the trees begin to thin, a brightness rising in the distance—the promise of a wide-open destination. I can just make out the rolling golden green of wild grass when there's the unmistakable sound of a door slamming shut and an engine revving, drowning out an exchange of words.

"Aw, shit," Wren mutters, and we both start jogging.

But as we hit the trail's end, I'm sure I hear anger in the nearing voices and my gut pings. I skid to a stop, cuffing Wren's arm and pressing a finger to my lips before tucking us both behind a knot of spiny trunks. Her brow furrows, but she gets the hint and doesn't say a word.

In the clearing is the black SUV. Hector is at the wheel, window rolled down. Clad in their matching tracksuits, the twins stand side by side and empty-handed. A small backpack is dumped at Ada's feet. If Sanguine's there, I don't see her. Hector glares down at Hex with a look so cold I nearly shiver.

"You will, and that's final, my son. End of discussion."

"But Papa—"

Hex's voice dies as Hector raises a hand. If there weren't several feet between them, he might have slapped his son across the face. Even at their current distance, though, it's clearly a threat.

This is not the debonair family man we've seen.

"That's what I thought," the patriarch growls at Hex, before turning the stern set of his jaw to his daughter. "Ada, I trust you will keep your brother on task for me, yes?" As he speaks he makes a point to tap his forearm—right in the location of the tattoos we saw Hex use for last night's spell.

Ada's fingers graze her own sleeve.

"Yes, Papa."

Hector pats the car's doorframe with a hollow clang, slips on a pair of aviator sunglasses, and the blacked-out window rolls up. The engine revs again, and the twins must take this as a sign. Hex shoulders the pack that had been at Ada's feet, and she blinks at her phone before pointing at a trail that disappears into the trees away from the Field of Stars, and in a completely different direction from the other site the Cerises had planned to check first—Shadrack's Lookout.

Hector reverses in an arc, turning the massive car around, and disappears down the service road in a cloud of beige dust and the creak of tires on packed-down ruts.

When they're gone, Wren whispers, "I knew Hector's father-of-the-year act was as fake as Sanguine's dye job, but what a turd. How can you be that aggressively asshole-ish to your kids while wearing ridiculous matching outfits?"

"We can hardly judge anyone here for acting differently in private than in public," I say, accent stripped away, leaving my flat, Midwestern pronunciation unabashed. "But I'm more interested in what he said. What does he want Hex to do?"

Wren bites her lip. "What is 'Hex isn't to be lugged out of Winter's room for a second time' for three hundred, Alex?"

"It's a possibility," I say slowly. "But I don't think that's it."

I click on my phone, pull up the map, and tuck the display between us. With a finger, I pinpoint where we are now, and what's around us. Whatever path Hex and Ada are on is unmarked, but much of the land is now. My finger stubs along the webbing of marked lines. "Look, if we head back up the trail, we can take this connector and we'll be parallel to them. Maybe we can come across them farther down and pretend we ran into them by accident?"

Wren socks me on the shoulder and beams. "Aw, sis, look at you, setting up the exact scenario where I can use my strengths. How supportive."

Chapter 22

AUDEN

"You have a secret."

The words have been lodged in my throat for more than an hour. I'd kept them at bay for the entirety of my hike with Evander to the Pool. The entirety of our fruitless search of the waters and surrounding area. No master relic.

But now, as we point ourselves toward a site that was on my group's list, I can't hold back anymore. It's very clear that we're not going to get to interrogate the others, so I choose to interrogate my cousin. I may have been relieved when he turned the spotlight of his suspicion off me in the kitchen, but that doesn't give him a pass to hold on to lies of his own.

If we're a team, his omissions need to be out in the open just as much as mine do.

Evander lowers his water bottle and turns, hiking boots scrapping pebbles out of the dirt. His expression is immediately a brick wall, as is his body language. Hands on hips, legs planted, chin raised. Even the straps of his waist pack full of supplies seem braced and tense. "Excuse me?"

His tone invites nothing but an apology. He won't get it.

I cross my arms over my chest. "What did you do last night?"

Evander's brows shoot up.

I tilt my head. "I was in the office, you were somewhere else. Winter checked your room, you weren't there—and your bed was made, which you don't ever do yourself at home. The maids are quarantined, which means your bed was last made yesterday." That muscle in his jaw twitches. "I knew the second I saw you on the trail this morning that sleep wasn't how you occupied your time.

And you didn't hit Mercy's Point until daylight. So, what did you do?"

A snatch of mountain breeze rushes between us, rustling pines and lifting the hems of our shirts, both Walton-Bridge lacrosse gear—his is an actual jersey, mine is a T-shirt—that prove in more ways than one that we know how to be on the same team. Something I hope he remembers after insinuating several times that I'd forgotten.

I stare him down with the same medicine he's given me. Closed expression, unwavering gaze, posture like a steel beam pounded deep into the dusty earth.

I expect him to walk away from me. To start hiking and toss some bullshit excuse back my way.

I don't expect the truth.

"I searched Ursula's suite."

I cover my surprise with a question. "For?"

"A diary, a letter, something with a lock. Anything that could be a hint or a clue to what happened to her." The knot in his throat bobs. "I . . . I just couldn't believe this could happen without a paper trail."

He gestures in the general direction of Hegemony Manor, referencing the empty drawers. The rows of books without even a scrap of loose paper, an unexplained margin note, not even her ledger for the present year. Nothing. Evander shakes his head. All of it gone—either by Ursula's hand or her killer's.

"Someone," he says, "knew about the stipulation in that will. Someone had known long enough to plan the murder and remove any shred of physical evidence from Ursula's personal effects."

"Or the spell removed everything but the will," I say. It's possible. With a spell as strong and encompassing as the one tied to Ursula's murder, nearly anything is possible.

"She wouldn't have done that."

I raise a brow in question, but otherwise wait him out. Evander will tell me—this is his opportunity to brag about being the oathed heir to the favorite grandchild.

He doesn't disappoint.

"That woman wrote every single thing down. Not just for herself, but for me."

There it is.

He starts walking again, and I don't comment, just speed up so that we're smushed, side by side, in the thin ribbon of trail playing hide-and-seek with the afternoon sun.

"My training was always underscored in written examples, journal entries, maps, documents, ledgers. Ursula had a mind like a steel trap but kept notes that were set in stone. She felt it was her duty to the lines to keep meticulous records, draft copies of her correspondence and the original replies from other High Families and clans of note. I know she left me something. Nothing makes sense otherwise, unless all her paperwork was stolen by her murderer, and even that doesn't make sense because access is impossible without her key or ours." We both know her key dissolved the moment she died. "So, I did the only thing that made sense to me, and opened up her suite, searching for something the killer may have missed."

It's a long monologue for him. Which means it's not fully true.

"You thought she left you instructions, didn't you?"

Evander is pointedly watching the uneven trail. He doesn't look at me. "Instructions?"

Stealing from the playbook Winter used hours ago, I take a long step right in his path, cutting him off. His head pops up as he nearly runs into me. We're toe-to-toe, a large rock shelf behind me, a step up, a natural barrier. "Oh, don't play dumb. You thought she left you a cheat sheet. If she wasn't murdered, she still would've had to transfer her knowledge of the master relics' locations to you as part the final step in your inheritance of her title. You knew she wouldn't leave that in her office, and checked her suite."

With every word, color rises from the neck of his red jersey up his throat.

"Fine. Yes. I was looking for that too. Happy? I don't see why you have to be so smug about me trying to do something to help all of us get out of here and keep our family's legacy intact."

The undertone is unmistakable. Considering my error with the Blackgates, I have no leg on which to stand to criticize him.

I smile in the face of his stony admission. "And I don't see why you felt the need to keep that to yourself. You could've told us this morning; you could've told us when Winter asked you directly if you had a secret. You had the past hour to tell me of your search, and, I'm assuming, failure, because you're not lording your discovery over the rest of us in a bid to prove your worthiness."

Evander looks like he wants to run through a brick wall. Instead, he has me to go through.

"I didn't find anything, so it wasn't worth sharing."

He pointedly shoves around me, up the stair-step rock.

"I think that's worth sharing in and of itself. What if someone took whatever High Sorcerer's manual she had prepared for you?" His pace speeds up. I speed up with him. "That seems pretty noteworthy to me."

"It is, but it didn't happen."

"How—"

Now he's the one who stops, whirling on me and blocking the rest of the trail, pines leaning close on both sides. Evander's voice pitches low, and he taps the collar of his jersey, the chain below. "Auden, it's in the ring."

I gape at him.

"The knowledge?"

"Yes. I'm sure of it. I . . . I don't know what I was thinking—it was probably exhaustion or shock, or all of it. But I realized after we found the first one this morning that it wouldn't be safe to write down instructions to the next High Sorcerer. And there's one thing that ties every High Sorcerer together, whether they've been properly trained or whether they were called upon late, a younger heir—"

"Like Ursula."

He nods. "Like Ursula. She wasn't the oathed heir. Her brother was. Matthias went through the training, took the ring from their mother when her time as High Sorcerer was done. He didn't yet have children of his own and died two years into service. Her mother was dead by then, her brother was dead, the only way to pass along knowledge was through written correspondence—which we didn't find; which I didn't find—or the one thing they have in common."

He pats his chest again. The tangle of ring and key bump out from the sweat-wicking material.

"Okay, that's a fair assumption." I draw a deep breath—pine and sunshine and rustling mountain air filling my senses as well as my lungs. "Are you thinking that whoever cleared out Ursula's office—and perhaps her suite—didn't know that?"

"Either they think there's something in her paperwork that's useful, or they assumed—correctly—that we would also search the office, and then freak out when we didn't find anything."

"Also correct," I agree, my frustration lifting now that we're getting somewhere. I'm still pissed I had to drag it out of him, but perhaps he'll see enough value in talking it through to not avoid doing so next time. "And if they were trying to get a rise out of us, perhaps they assumed you didn't know about any magic within the ring to relay information." Wait. "Didn't Hector suggest Luna should hold the ring rather than you?"

"He sure did." Evander's hand drops from his chest. "It was Mercy Hegemony who first bound the masters to the ring, but that doesn't mean the other High Families don't know its secrets beyond being tethered to—"

The snap of a twig shuts his mouth.

Magic sparks in my fingertips, a shield spell gathering there, at the ready. I have no doubt Evander has done the same. We can't use magic against each other, but we can use it to defend ourselves. We turn.

And there, twenty feet away, are Lavinia and Kaysa Blackgate.

"Um, sorry to interrupt," Lavinia says, an apologetic grimace softening. She's got a firm grip on her sister's wrist, her body planted between Kaysa and the pair of us, awkward and leaning, a hurried posture she's trying to make look natural. The Death magic relics at her wrists sway, a marker of the sudden movement we didn't see.

Kaysa shoots us a more convincing grin. "We weren't eavesdropping, I swear."

Lavinia shuts her eyes with a sigh. If she weren't holding so tightly to her sister, I'm fairly certain she'd pinch the bridge of her nose. Instead, she says, "We finished searching Horace's Last Stand, and thought we'd search the Pool. But it looks as if you might have already done so?"

"We did, and found nothing," I confirm.

"Are you sure you searched Horace's Last Stand thoroughly?" Evander asks.

Now I'm the one who wants to pinch the bridge of my nose.

Fantastic opening gambit to starting a much-needed conversation with them.

Kaysa Blackgate has lost exactly none of her gumption, though. She skewers my cousin right in the eye and smiles sweetly. "You can trust us now, or you're welcome to waste the next two hours of your life to prove us right."

I break into a laugh, and I swear I see Evander's lips twitch in a smile. This girl, so silent and dour as a small child, has somehow grown into a match for the gruff, stoic Evander Hegemony.

"Well, that answer is good enough for me," I reply, and clap my cousin on his thick shoulder. Lavinia's eyes widen in surprise. "Don't you think, Ev—"

"Watch out!" Lavinia screams.

She's running—not away, but instead chugging straight for us like a freight train in yoga tights. I blink, tracking her gaze to something over my shoulder.

But I'm already too late.

With a single, sick thud, all the breath in Evander's lungs leaves in one stout wheeze.

A knife is buried in his back.

That shield, on the edge of my fingertips only moments earlier, sparks to life, a shimmering emerald mist. It flares out around us as two things happen.

Evander slumps into me, his legs giving out.

A second knife whizzes past Evander's ear.

It would've hit him if he'd been upright. Instead, because he's moved and the shield with him, it grazes Lavinia before burying itself in a tree on the side of the trail. Lavinia hisses as a slash of crimson blooms on the exposed skin of her upper arm. Kaysa is feet behind her, eyes the size of dinner plates.

"Two more incoming!" she shouts, and dives at Lavinia, effectively pressing both her and her sister against the wall created by Evander and myself.

The points of both knives dig and drop, one, two, off the shield.

"Is that it? Please tell me that's it," Kaysa whimpers as the blades skitter over the rocks embedded in the trail to the soft cushion of mountain daisies beyond.

I swallow, gaze stuck on the knife buried in the pine feet away. I recognize the black handle, three metal rivets catching the sun. These aren't throwing knives. They're chef's knives.

"Three more. Seven in Maggie's knife block."

Evander wheezes. His fingers scrabble for purchase at my waist, trying to stay upright. Kaysa wraps an arm around him, her other around her sister. Lavinia's blood cuts a looping swath down her arm, seeping into the thin, flowy fabric of her shirt. Seeping into mine too, warm and wet as her heart rabbits so hard, it flutters against my own ribs.

"Extend," Evander grits out. "The . . . shield. Pause too . . ."

I do exactly what he says, encasing us all, realizing in that moment what he's getting at.

They're trying for a better shot.

Just as I manage to wrap the shield entirely around the vertical column made by the four of us, the final three knives fly in from the opposite direction of the first four—*THWACK, THWACK, TWHACK*—right off the newest portion of the shield. Perfectly aimed to hit Lavinia directly in the back. Both girls scream, as if they didn't realize the shield was there, stiffening into our chests, a jumble of lavender soap and sweat, fear, and blood.

And then it's over.

All four of us clamber together, in our huddle, breathing hard, eyes wild and searching.

No color, no shadows, no footsteps over the thundering of our collective breath and heartbeats. Nothing at all.

Evander's head lolls and drops heavily on my shoulder. "Go . . . after . . . them."

"I hate to break it to you, but that's not a cat scratch. I'm not going after them because I need to heal you." I turn to Lavinia. "You can manage while I help him, yeah?"

Lavinia lifts her head from where it had been pressed against my breastbone, eyes dark wells. "Yes, yes, of course. We can go after them."

"Yeah. We can search," Kaysa says, peeling herself from the huddle and brandishing her wrist relic a little too hard.

But I don't even flinch because I'm not seeing anything but Evander's blood. It's saturated his jersey, the crimson now a heavy black. My wrist and forearm are slick with it from where I anchor him about the waist, grasping both his pack and his failing body.

I can't waste any time.

"That won't be necessary," I say. "Are you able to provide a shield?"

I know the answer before the question is out of my mouth, but I need to ask it. The Blackgates shake their heads. I hold up a hand. "Fine—I'm going to need both of you to watch for another attack while I divert my magic to heal Evander."

"Let them go," my cousin says, his voice sliding from gritted effort to slippery whisper. "I can wait."

He finishes with a wheeze and a rattle now. The knife isn't just bleeding him dry, it's buried in a lung. Maybe two. My eyes meet Lavinia's. She pales and I know she can read the panic in them as surely as I read her own last night. She nods. "We've got this."

I lower the shield and she grabs the largest knife left at her feet with her uninjured arm. Kaysa collects the other two. The sisters face out, shielding us as best they can from the woods at all sides. Something itches the back of my mind—they're Blackgates with knives.

No, I can't question it. I can't split focus. Evander needs all my attention on the immediate threat to him, not ghosts of years past and reputations earned.

I get Evander to the dirt and remove his waist pack, lying him on his side so I can probe his wound. I don't miss that he's trembling. That beneath his scruff, his lips are growing blue with each labored inhale.

The blade is an eight-inch chef's knife, razor sharp and plunged straight through to the hilt. It missed his spine by mere millimeters. Definitely hit a lung. I run my fingers along the front of his shirt. The tip nicks my skin. I swallow away the panic.

"I've got to pull it out," I inform him, forcing myself to look him in his paling face. His eyes are squeezed shut. "The magic will staunch the blood and heal. Ready?"

I'm already in position before I pretend to accept an answer to that question, one hand over the knife's exit wound, the other wrapped around the knife's handle. I clench my teeth, prepared to pull when Evander touches a cold hand to my own. His eyes are open now, fierce.

"If it's too much, don't."

Forcing a smile, I hit him with his favorite dismissal of my pompous ass. "Shut up, Evander."

I pull.

The knife releases with a slick tearing and Evander wails. Then my magic is pressing into him, life element fizzing from my body into his, knitting his wound, refilling his veins, inflating his lung. My own breath catches at the weight of it, my vision blurring in an emerald haze, my mind fuzzing, furring. I sway where I kneel, seasick. I clamp my eyes closed, but the feeling doesn't dissipate. Still, I hold tight, every muscle in my body willed to hold myself steady, upright. Nausea crashes like lightning in the darkness of my mind as my life element flows out into the wound still spewing viscous, deep blood.

There's a hand on my shoulder. "Auden?" Lavinia. "Are you okay?"

I feel my head droop and she catches it. Something clatters beside us. The knife.

"Evander?" Kaysa's voice now. There's some shuffling. "Oh, for goodness' sake, you were just knifed. Take my hand to stand. It won't tank your manliness quotient."

Beneath me, Evander shifts. I slump from my kneeling crouch to sitting, guided by Lavinia's hands. She puts an arm around my shoulders, her relics somehow not touching my bare skin. "Auden?" she whispers. But no answer lines my tongue. Not yet. When a life element is drained like this, so quickly, so forcefully, it takes the body time to recalibrate to what's left.

There's some shuffling, and then the unmistakable surge of power surrounds us. A shield.

"You left us unguarded," Evander grumbles, his voice raspy but there.

"And you almost left us entirely," Kaysa shoots back.

Even though I feel like literal shit, my heart swells and I want to laugh—the youngest Blackgate is on to his shit and won't let him get away with it.

That little spike of emotion seems to be the last step my life element needs to get rebalanced within my body enough that I feel as if I can open my eyes. I blink. Lavinia's face is the first I see, only inches away, watching me intently for some sort of sign that I went too far, pushed it too hard. It doesn't do to think of what I've just lost. I need to focus on survival—which means knowing our attacker. "Check the knife. Magical signature?"

Kaysa gets the picture and immediately shoves the ones she's collected—a paring knife and a longer utility blade—at Evander. The moment they're tight in his grip, he frowns.

"No magic here, nothing to check. They were thrown."

I comb through the cotton in my mind, trying to recall if I'd seen the knives this morning when I made breakfast, or at noon when we'd had our aside after putting the dead driver in the root cellar. I can't remember.

"Who the hell throws knives?" Kaysa asks.

"Someone who wanted to hit me straight in the heart," my cousin answers.

"Not just Evander. He went after Lavinia too," the younger Blackgate points out. "Didn't try to hit me even once."

She's right. The final three throws weren't just from the opposite direction, they were for a new target. The way we were situated, if the attacker wanted to hit Evander from another angle, the knives would've bounced off Lavinia's portion of the shield.

Evander and Lavinia as targets.

My cousin gets there before I do, his mind churning forward as his body completes its renewal with my life element.

"Heirs," Evander says. "Someone's going after the heirs."

I look to Lavinia then. She cups my shoulder, her face farther from mine now and pale. Blood covers her opposite arm as it lies limply in her lap. I press my fingers to the wound, fully expecting her to shrug me off, to tell me not to, with what I've just done. Evander beats her to it.

"No, you don't, I can heal her. Lavinia, don't let him," Evander barks. "Lavinia?"

"The heart."

That's all she says. Quietly, almost to herself.

She blinks up, her lips falling open. We're all staring at her now.

"Straight in the heart. The gaping center."

I nod at her. "The clue—yes. With the sun, its reason, its heart, the gaping center."

"The master's not inside me, I can assure you," Evander responds in what I think is a joke? Thoughts churn across Lavinia's fine features, and I watch the white kiss of teeth as she bites her full lower lip. As a sudden light appears in her dark gaze.

"The gaping center—could the master relic be in the courtyard?" Her voice is breathless. "Is there something with a bear on it? The moon? The sun?"

Her attention flies from my face to Evander's, and another surge of wooziness slows my guess, my mind spinning forward at a pace my body can't keep.

"Plenty of somethings. Sundial, gargoyles that could be bears—oh shit." My mouth goes dry as the muscles in my legs fire and I try to get them under me to stand. My body won't move properly, and I knock into Lavinia. She steadies me just as the answer finally falls out of my mouth.

"Shadrack's mural."

The Blackgates stare at us with twin pinched expressions of confusion.

"Speak in non-Hegemony, please," Kaysa begs.

Evander is already refitting his waist pack, ignoring the question in favor of getting a move-on. I swallow, my parched throat catching.

"Shadrack painted four murals in Hegemony Manor." Though I'm exhausted, a smile tugs at the corners of my mouth. "One in the foyer, one in the dining room, one on the boulder marking the cemetery, and one in the courtyard—a map of the night sky."

CHAPTER 23

AUDEN

Evander looks like a dead man walking. The entire back of his lacrosse jersey sticks to his skin, the blood heavy and stinking of iron and earth, pasting the fabric to his skin.

Yet it's me who receives a cautious prod about my well-being.

"Are you sure you're okay?"

Lavinia whispers it as the four of us traverse the narrow trail back to the house in a slow, tight slog. Our bodies are packed together under a shield created by Evander, his healing body able to manage the spell and forward movement, and not much more.

I, however, am having a very hard time masking my utter exhaustion.

Though my life element has rebalanced enough that I'm no longer catatonic, it hasn't refilled. I'm drained in every sense of the word. Dehydrated, nauseous, shaky. My vision blurs at the edges, plummy spots casting through the center. Any thought I have of gaining information from the Blackgates has gone out the window as I struggle to stay upright.

Altogether my symptoms have manifested to produce a stumbling, weaving performance on this hike no matter how much I focus. The toes of my running shoes snag every rock and root, stumbling through smashed pine cones and brittle leaves crunching over the trail, and as a result, I weave here and there, palming the sturdy firs as I pass.

"I'm fine."

"You literally just bounced off that tree."

She gestures with a little laugh, and I glance at her.

Lavinia's whole left arm is streaked in blood, the fine hairs dark and matted. Evander's fingerprints had buffed away some of the stain around the original cut, healed by his renewed magic so quickly it would be an afterthought if not for all the evidence.

"But really—I know you're *fine,* but healing him took a lot out of you. Literally, it seems." She's watching me now, and I have to look away as I bump another rock with my toe and stagger to the side. Lavinia makes to catch me, but I toss my arms out, balance firing at the last moment.

Thank God we're almost to the manor.

"Come on, keep up," Evander shouts from up ahead, feeling the tug on the shield as we fall behind, his pace increasing steadily with the stark onyx visage of the house looming ahead on its elevated perch. Like the world's most gothic, inedible cake on a stand.

When we've resumed our huddled march, Lavinia places a hand on my elbow, her relic angled down and away. It's the hand I healed—just a gentle reminder that she's close enough to steady me. When I don't move away, she grimaces at the ground and asks, quietly, "What if you have to do it again?"

"Let's hope I don't."

I need water and food—and rest that I'm even less likely to get.

"Are we going to talk about who threw them?"

"Not many choices."

"No," she agrees, quietly.

The Cerises. Infinity. Winter. Maybe even Luna—nothing seems impossible or easy to dismiss since Ursula left us.

I nod to my cousin, driving fast and determined up front, Kaysa on his heels as we knot tightly—woozily—behind. "Let's just see if we're right and move from there. It's much easier to confront everyone if we have another master."

We march straight into the courtyard from the most direct route, the tearoom, which straddles the back of the house and the courtyard on the first floor. A relief, because I can put eyes on the only other possible weapon I know that exists in this manor—Shadrack's Horace-killing Colt .45.

It's still there. On the wall, next to the bear's roaring final protest.

I don't know if the antique revolver is loaded, or if it would work if it was, but it's a relief that it hasn't disappeared.

"Courtyard, straight ahead," Evander directs, picking up speed.

We step through the glass doors leading to the courtyard.

The gaping center.

Unlike the outside of the black-as-night exterior of the house, the siding here is whitewashed brick, a canvas for climbing ivy reaching for the sky, gargoyles growling down from above. There are enough fountains to dry the Colorado River, and vegetation is packed into every inch except for the thin, star-tile walkways crisscrossing to various points of interest like so many veins, an echo of the design in the garden behind the manor.

Squat and square, the courtyard was designed as an outdoor space that could guarantee privacy in a world that was becoming increasingly less private, more prying eyes and population, even in the wilds of the Rockies.

But in the time since Shadrack envisioned it as a place of contemplation, it'd evolved like everything else. Not in a technological way—everything here is frozen in the time of Ursula's childhood, her preference as matriarch and distrustful modern citizen. No, in that over the generations, bare soil and magical talent were augmented with love, time, care.

Like the rest of the grounds, the plants here are dying now. Drooping, drying, petals falling, and stems withered brown.

There are cracks in the whitewash too, ones that weren't there days ago. Not superficial like Lavinia's wound, but deep enough to touch the next layer, bricks dislodged and falling to the courtyard, cracked, broken, pebbled. The decay is from magic withdrawal. A spell from Ursula or some other source, I don't know.

My bleary vision zeroes in on the eastern wall, where the ivy runs in thick ropes, as dense as yarn taut in a loom. The leaves overlap into a patchwork, feathers by another name. A single slash of sun nails the bare spot between swaths of ivy, revealing a smattering of black dots that freckle the whitewash. I point. "It's there—the mural."

Lavinia gasps—the most delighted noise I've heard in at least a day—as a smile lights her dirt-smudged face. "It's a negative. Black stars on a white sky."

"Exactly." I nudge the ivy apart. Evander doesn't help, holding the shield. "But I have no idea where the Great Bear might be. Nothing is labeled and with all this ivy, it's hard to know what we're looking at."

We're quiet for a moment, surveying the massive space before us. The sky above us has gone indigo, the clouds from this afternoon ambling on east, an intrepid slash of sunlight lasering onto the ivy, cut with precision by the western roof line.

"Wait, I have an idea." Lavinia produces her phone and turns it on. Marsyas didn't give her the memo about bringing an external battery, I see. After a moment, she unlocks it, swipes, and taps. "I have Radical Stars. My da—I, um, thought this app might be neat to use while we were in the mountains."

Pinking with excitement perhaps at the fact that she can contribute, Lavinia flips the phone around so I can see. "You hold it up to the sky and it shows you what you're looking at."

"I have it too," Kaysa adds. "It's totally cool. Doesn't need Wi-Fi or cell data, so you can really use it in the middle of nowhere."

Evander leans in to inspect and Lavinia gestures to it, maybe a little sheepish. Over the fact that she hoped she might enjoy this trip enough to stargaze or that as a Blackgate she'd even think of doing something so *romantic,* I'm not sure. Now that I'm really looking at it, I notice the phone is nearly obsolete, which is odd, but who am I to judge someone who likes old things when I grew up within the halls of Hegemony Manor?

"It might be too bright now, but it could be worth a shot because I bet you Shadrack painted the sky how he saw it," Lavinia explains, before looking up. "So, if we comb the night sky above, we can transfer the location of the Great Bear and go from there?"

I nod. "Genius."

Lavinia smiles tightly, and her cheeks pink further. Without hesitation she points the phone straight up, her brows furrowed in the reflection of her shiny screen as the gyroscope within the phone syncs to the app's features.

"Please work," she whispers to it.

It sounds a bit like a spell spoken aloud, and maybe it is, because the second it's out of her mouth and into the air, the app springs to life, and the darkening sky above is overlaid with the names of the constellations and stars of note above.

Ursa Major does not appear.

Lavinia slowly moves the app up and around. "Okay, there's Ursa Minor . . . with the North Star, soooo . . . Ursa Major would be over there."

She's turned toward the western wall now, almost exactly opposite from where she was when we began.

"Wait," Kaysa pipes up, with a little note of triumph right where she's standing. "It's a mirror. Ursa Major is in the northwest sky, but the mural is on the east wall and facing west."

"You're right," Evander agrees.

And then we're all nodding as Lavinia takes a screenshot of the location of Ursa Major and spins around. She holds it up to the ivy-draped mural, brows furrowed to touching and lips bitten in thought. "So, if we go southeast on the wall . . ."

And that's when I see it. Right where the last fingers of daylight touch the ivy. It's as if the sun itself is giving us a clue with the pointed direction of a penlight.

With Lavinia manning the app and Evander holding our shield, I turn to the youngest Blackgate. "Kaysa, do you think you can kill the ivy here?"

"What?" she gasps. "I can't do that—that would be horrible!"

It would, but—

"Dehydrate it, Auden," Evander suggests, gruffly.

I don't argue, I just press my hands to the ivy and draw every ounce of water from the stems and leaves. The vines shrivel and peel back. The dried plants fall away, too brittle to put up a fight. Lavinia is on her tiptoes helping me reveal the constellation.

"You're going to rehydrate the ivy, right?" Kaysa asks, voice small.

"Of course. I'm not a monster."

The Blackgates of old would've taken my attempt at humor and flipped it back at me, barbed and well-aimed—I'd asked them to kill it outright, after all. The sisters don't. Focused on the task, and perhaps truly changed.

Together, we scramble and pull and twine the dried pieces together and . . .

There it is, the Great Bear, Ursa Major.

Unlabeled, but just as Lavinia's screenshot promised—hundreds of stars forming the larger of the two bear constellations. And there, literally highlighted by that final falling strip of sun, is the beast's representative paw.

"Is that a niche?" Lavinia asks, fingertips brushing the paint.

I smooth my hands over the brick. There is most definitely a piece that doesn't fit. I knock it and a hollow thrum sounds back. "It is."

"Open it," Evander urges, still holding fast to our shield enclosure. He knows if we're right, the security wards will detonate, and we'll need it. There's no use in changing places now, though I would if he asked. I'm surprised he hasn't ordered me to do so yet. That he'd demand to hold it first. Maybe that's progress.

Kaysa inspects it, nose scrunched. "How *do* we open it?"

The entry has to be hidden, but well-made if it's lasted this long, blending in with the side of the house. Brick isn't an element, but it is made of *pieces* of the elements. That, I can work with.

"Stand back." I press both my hands to the hollow piece.

Moisture floods from the brick into my fingers until the paint and mortar flake and crust just enough that the brick dislodges with a satisfying little sigh, dehydrated, not unlike the ivy.

I wedge it free, and there, behind the hollowed brick, is a dark vial—magically preserved, completely without dust, mold, age. I fish it out and turn to our little group and the fraying, narrow light.

The vial is cobalt blue and ringed with protective iron and a stopper set in wax, and more iron crosshatched over the top and neck like a spiderweb. We peer at it, foreheads bent and nearly touching as I rotate it slowly in my palms. A liquid roils within, sloshing against the sides, and leaving a film that darkens the vial to near black with every revolution.

And there, on the side that had been pressed into my palm, is the thickest piece of iron in all its protective trappings, letters etched in a hand that is blocky and efficient.

The Blood of Nostradamus.

"Wait, like, the prophet?" Kaysa asks, voice thunderstruck and eyes nearly cartoonish. "The guy with the long beard who predicted the rise of Hitler? *That* Nostradamus?"

In answer, the security wards detonate.

The Blackgates yelp and cover each other, while Evander and I track the wards as they ring us in a ten-foot diameter. This time, instead of a wall of fire, it's pyrotechnics—gun smoke and magic exploding in a string of light and sound, all beginnings and fizzled endings. Again, the security wards just show their hand, they don't do anything near the lethal capability they once had.

"I suppose that means this is the right one." Kaysa gives a relieved little laugh once the wards dissipate and the smoke clears. "Good job, sis."

She tags Lavinia on her healed arm, but then yelps when her fingers come away sponged pink with her sister's tacky blood. "Ugh, gross. Maybe we've earned you a shower. You too, Evander. Might be time to throw away that shirt."

His lips kick up in something of a smirk. "It's not a shirt, it's a jersey, and for your inf—"

Whatever pithy, flirty, grumpy response Evander had at the ready goes unheard, cut off by the long, desperate howl of a scream from inside Hegemony Manor.

CHAPTER 24

AUDEN

The stench of blood coats the back of my throat as we climb the stairs.

It's as sharp and fresh as the scream we heard, new and distinctly different from what happened in the woods, hours ago now. The recovered knives clink heavily in Evander's waist pack as we hustle, the wail ebbing into sobbing by the time Lavinia, Kaysa, Evander, and I trace the noise to the second floor and then the solarium.

Inside, Infinity and Winter are huddled beside the Victorian settee closest to the hearth on the south wall, the dying day weakly illuminating the space through the massive windows. The fire has snuffed out yet again, and as I light it the terrible scene adopts a golden hue.

Infinity is on their knees, hands pressed to their face. Winter's tears sparkle in diamond streaks down her cheeks as she cups their shaking shoulders.

I already know exactly what we'll see as the entire Cerise family bursts in from the terrace door.

Luna, dead on the antique cushions.

What I don't expect is the fresh golden sunlight wrapped taut and shimmering over her still form.

A victim's shroud.

We've got more on our hands than a tragedy—we've got another murder.

One that we can't assign to Marsyas Blackgate.

One orchestrated by someone in this room.

There's a noise like a collective gasp and a shuffle of involuntary movement—hands flying to lips, knuckles squeezed, steps hitched, and in the case of Evander, completely stopped dead—as we take in the scene.

A teacup lays in shards on the rug, a half-eaten croissant growing stale on a plate atop the side table. Upon closer inspection, a book of large-print crosswords is abandoned next to Luna's shrouded form, the stub of a pencil still clasped in her gnarled fingers. Her sable lips are tinged blue, but it's impossible otherwise to tell how she died. Given our recent encounter, I anticipate a knife slash—a murdered witch receives a victim's shroud whether or not it was magic that did the deed. But I don't see it.

We're too late for a soul's truth. The phenomena appears once—there's no automatic replay. It's there and gone. I wish we'd seen it; I feel lucky that we'd seen Ursula's, though it meant witnessing her end too.

"Infinity," Evander nudges, more gently than I've ever heard from him, "what happened?"

In answer, they look to Winter. "We came in from the terrace and she was just here and . . . can we have this conversation away from here?"

It's a question but their voice frays and they stand, backing away. The Cerise twins and Blackgates part to let them through as Sanguine puts a motherly hand to their shoulder. Infinity doesn't acknowledge Sanguine's attempt at placating them, just slips away from the woman's hand.

We follow their lead.

At first, I expect them to seek fresh air on the terrace, but instead they lead us into the hall and to the suite they shared with Luna. We file in silently as they sway on their feet, buffered by Winter.

"Do you need to sit?" Lavinia asks, hands reaching out as if to help.

Infinity shakes their head fiercely, their brown cheeks slick with tears under eyes rimmed crimson. Their gaze snags on her bloodied arm. "What happened to you?"

Lavinia shrugs it off, clearly not wanting to pull focus from Luna. "Just a cut that bled too much."

Winter rounds on her, suspicion in her eyes. "A cut? Or a defensive wound, because we all know Luna wouldn't have gone without a fight. Let me see that—"

"She got it with me, Win," Evander barges in, twisting enough to show the coated back of his jersey. All four Cerises have noticed, called like a shark to the mess, but they stand apart, across the room. Evander makes eye contact with each and every one of them, the message clear—*don't you dare*. Then, he says to the group at large, "Unrelated. And unimportant right now. Infinity?"

Infinity nods, effectively calling off Winter, whose nostrils flare as she watches the four of us, questions loading on her lips. The youngest Starwood—the only Starwood—slips from Winter's steadying hand and begins pacing in short bursts in front of the darkened hearth. I snap my fingers to light this one too.

We spread ourselves around the sitting room, waiting as they walk in a tight line before the flue, the rising fire casting their dark skin in burnished light with each step and turn. They seem steadier now, somehow. Gaining balance with each footfall.

"Let's start at the beginning," Winter suggests, sounding much calmer than I feel. "What happened when you left the driveway this morning?"

The question settles into the air, and I shake my head when my older cousin glances my way. Now isn't the time for Evander—or Hector, for that matter—to show off their leadership skills. Winter and Infinity have always been as close as far as the High Families go. Best that she asks the questions.

Infinity blinks at her, throat bobbing, and pauses at the turn of their next round of pacing. They lean into the far wall and gaze down into the middle distance of the flames as the rest of us watch and wait.

It takes a moment, but Infinity's voice comes in stops and starts, then, their tone worn.

"Grandmama was hungry, so we went to the solarium. She picked out two croissants, I made her a second cup of coffee, and walked her over to her favorite place to sit." Their face breaks into something of a sad smile as a new jag of tears spills down and they press a trembling hand to sop them up. They lean harder into the wall. "It's the right height for her knees."

Winter nods, gently. She doesn't goad, she just waits, and it's both a relief and a testament to how much everyone here respects Luna that no one prods them further, letting the story unravel at its needed pace.

"Then she kissed me on the cheek, told me to keep my wits about me, and reiterated for at least the third time that she wanted to have supper in our room so that I could brief her about the day's search if no master had been found."

No-nonsense matriarch Luna, finding her preferred spot and sticking to it until her grandchild arrived with a field report—that was exactly what would be expected from her.

"I confirmed and . . . and then you walked into the room." Infinity looks up, finding Winter. They seem to sink into the wall at their back as they press a palm right over their heart. "We left for the grounds. We were gone . . . what . . . five hours? Six? And then we walked in and . . . and she was . . ."

Their voice trails off into a series of panicked, shallow gasps. Winter steps forward and places both hands on their shoulders. "Take deep breaths. Infinity. Look at me—"

"I . . . just . . . no." Infinity gapes at all of us, shrugging themself loose of Winter. Their dark eyes land on each and every one of us, tears smearing out the lined corners. "Why is no one imprisoned by Ursula's magic?"

My stomach clenches.

Ursula's spell should mean her murderer is trapped in a pressurized prison. It should've been automatic, day or night.

And yet we're all accounted for. Every last one of us.

We were all out on the grounds when this murder likely occurred. In pairs, and in the case of the Cerises, a whole family unit. It's possible every single person in this room did it, and it's possible every single person in this room has an alibi.

"Why—who *did* this to her? Why? *Why would any of you do this? Who did this?*"

Infinity's soft accusation is now a shouting one, and the answers are incomplete and braided together as what they're saying hits like a tidal wave.

"*I—*"

"*No—*"

"*We—*"

Hector is the first person to get out a full answer, cutting and accusatory in the air. "Are you saying one of us is the culprit? Because we're not."

Lavinia shakes her head. "We can't blame this on Nona Marsyas. What if someone else is inside? On the grounds?"

"We checked for others after the driver was found," I answer, gesturing to my cousins. "There's no one else but the people in this room."

Still, Hector scoffs, teeth flashing in an imperious smile. "Are you suggesting someone in this room is the culprit? Check your ma—"

"The *culprit*? The *killer*. The *murderer* of my grandmother!" Infinity pounds both fists on the wall behind them so forcefully sparks of brilliantly white Celestial magic flare into the air before retreating, falling away like snowflakes hitting wet pavement. "I . . . I don't want any of you in here right now. I want you to leave."

Infinity has never been a loud person. Ever. But in their eyes is a wild emotion I recognize—the same one I tamped down deep last night. The one my cousins locked away too. The one we're not supposed to show.

Rage.

The one the Blackgates chose to bury with their girls' memories of the reason for it. The one Infinity is brave enough to reveal in the face of immediate, terrible pain.

Reflected back, my own rage rouses and unfurls. I'm angry for them. For us. I want this over. I want to move past, even though I know it won't hurt less. The victory of minutes ago seems hollow now. But it's a way forward, as weak in the face of this new horror as everything else.

"We'll leave, but first, I have something for you." I reach into my pocket and pull out the vial. "We found the Celestial relic."

In the firelight, the vial glows crimson and bold, like noon through vermilion stained glass.

Infinity draws in a sharp breath, their eyes growing big. "It— you did?"

Their fingers stretch to accept it, but Hector is suddenly in motion and between us. "It's blood—that can't be the Celestial master."

I draw it away so that he can't snatch it. "It's the Blood of *Nostradamus*. He's a noted Celestial witch."

Infinity is nodding, but Hector is not assuaged, digging deeper, despite how petty it may seem as we stand here in the echo of Infinity's loss. The patriarch has the audacity to smile, as if that will suffice in muting his single-mindedness.

"The first master relic was literally breath—the elements of air and life wound into one—and this is blood. The first relic was harvested from a Death witch, and this from a Celestial witch." He waves a hand in the general direction of the sisters. "Therefore, we have immediate precedent that the Celestial witches should cede to the Blood witches—"

"Are you kidding me?" Winter challenges, stepping in to block Infinity from view. "You want to fight Infinity for this vial right now? In this moment? With what they've just lost? Just so you can hold something that's not even yours? Fuck no."

"Perhaps—"

"Papa—" Hex jumps in, but Hector shakes him off, barely pausing to swallow before he appeals to the person he suddenly sees as his closest equal and someone who might agree: Evander.

"*Perhaps* we should check the next clue. It could point to—"

"I don't fucking care about the next clue!" Infinity explodes, pushing off the wall and toward Hector. Winter steps into them, hooking an arm around their middle. They don't go around or shake it off, but yell at him from over the frame of Winter's shoulder. "I don't care about any of it! I care about my grandmother." They thrust out their hand, past Winter, toward me. "Auden, give me the vial."

I don't hesitate. They snatch it away. "Now *leave*. All of you!"

I turn to exit but Hector blocks the door. Gone is the sycophant, the team player, the noble patriarch. In his place is something disgusting, greedy, repugnant.

"No, we'll read that clue right now." Hector crosses his arms over his chest and stands as still as a tracksuited statue. "If it points to the Celestial Line, I want my chance to hold that vial of *blood*. The Cerise Clan has worked for years to atone for the crimes of Napoleon Cerise, and we have earned the right and the credit to hold our master relic."

"Jesus Christ—" Evander moans, cut off by Winter whirling around, eyes blazing.

"Fuck you, asshole!"

Hector doesn't blink. "It's our right just as much as it's theirs."

"Holy shit," Hex breathes, and for once in his goddamn life the boy looks completely embarrassed. Next to him, Ada is so horrified she's nearly purple. She's stopped tugging at her father's arm. Sanguine, of course, stands next to Hector, with him, a front.

"Unbelievable," Infinity bites out, shoulders quaking as they hang their head. Then, "Auden, do it. Read it."

I produce the will and place it on the coffee table, kneeling down. When my hand makes contact with my thumbprint, the second clue begins to fade and swirl, shift and rearrange, warm to the touch.

Then, the third clue fades in. Five lines and poetic, just like the other two.

I draw in a deep breath and read.

> "*Out damn spot, blood will never go*
> *It paces, hot and urgent, then goes cold*
> *The heart moves it, Princess*

Until it succumbs to the elements, shriveled, hard, alone
But never gone, stained with what was."

I'm not even to my feet when the silence is broken, and when it is, it's somewhat of a shock because it comes in the form of Hex turning to his father and saying, steel in his voice and color in his cheeks, "It mentions blood and the elements—not a hint of anything Celestial, Papa. This one's ours." He glances back at Infinity, an apology hanging in the void. "Let's leave them be, please."

Ada must agree, because she shoves open the door and holds it for the rest of her family. Sanguine grabs Hector's hand and announces, "We'll be in the study for a proper regroup."

They don't shut the door, and as I'm closest to it, I resume the position Ada has vacated, holding it open for the rest of my family and the Blackgate girls, who've already risen from where they'd planted themselves on the settee.

"I'm out of the game."

There's a pause, and then a shuffling turn of all of us to where Infinity stands, clutching the vial in both hands before them like it's something to be prayed over.

Winter whispers from close range, "What?"

"The Celestial Line is out." Infinity swallows, their shattered voice repairing with each word. "This master relic stays with us— with me. That's what Grandmama wanted."

"What . . . Luna wanted?" Evander tries to clarify, more gently than I'd expect but everything Infinity deserves.

"What she wanted, and she speaks—spoke—for the line. Last night after we left the will reading, she told me we would accept our master relic and cease participation—in the game, in the competition for control of the lines, and with the Four Lines themselves."

There's a commotion at the door and Hector tries to lean past me. "The Celestial Line can't just leave—"

"Why can't we? This is our master!" Infinity holds the vial above their head like a championship trophy and shakes it, making it impossible for Hector to miss, even with me blocking his path into

222 + SARAH HENNING

the suite and his own children hanging on him, trying to drag him back into the hallway. "Our power is tethered to it. Our line's power. And my grandmama was adamant that she didn't want us tethered to any of *you* after we leave this place."

"What—why?" Winter asks, quietly.

"Does it matter? It is what we wish. It is what she wished, and what I wish. And honestly, I don't want to see any of you again until the master relics are found, the murderer is punished, and the spell is broken." They meet Winter's eyes, and the meaning is clear—you too. "I have food and water here. I'll put up wards against all of you if I have to. Do not come into this suite again."

With that, Winter nods but doesn't dare to touch her friend. "We understand."

The Cerises drag Hector down the hall as he protests with words and fighting steps on the plush carpet. I again hold the door and as the Blackgates approach, Lavinia turns before exiting. "I'm so sorry for your loss, Infinity."

"Yes. We're so sorry," Kaysa adds, splotches of color high in her cheeks, eyes wet.

Again I'm struck that the Blackgates seem to be the only people acknowledging those of us who've lost someone. The rest of us echo the sentiment, but if I'm being honest, without their immediate example, I'm not sure any of the rest of us would've taken the explicit time to give our condolences to who—what—Infinity, their father, Erasmus, their line, just lost.

Infinity doesn't walk to the door to close it, so I do. And then, the lock immediately *snicks* shut, followed by the *shink* of the deadbolt right behind it.

I've just turned around when Hector Cerise has escaped his family and looms in my face. "I need to see that clue."

"Not here," Evander growls, and then uses every ounce of his weight-room strength to muscle Hector away from Infinity's door. He's taller and heavier than the Cerise patriarch, and the older man fights aimlessly as he's bodily dragged down the hall.

"Well, I'm not going back up to the study. We have a master to find, and I want to confirm it is the Blood Line relic before I lose access to that vial."

"Your priorities are dismal," Winter spits.

Both kids protesting, Hector pulls out his phone. I'm not sure who this man is—pushy, petty, entitled. But I'm starting to believe this is who Hector always was beneath his sheen of agreeability. "Just let me snap the clue and I'll haul my priorities away from you."

"I wish you'd haul them off the side of Mercy's Point," Winter mutters.

Evander nods to the hallway that leads to the grand staircase in the foyer. "We can use the tearoom."

"That's no better than the study," Hector argues. "I'm not leaving this floor—"

"We can't just dissect this clue like that didn't just happen," Winter argues, running ahead and then wheeling around so she can bar the lot of us from moving forward down the hallway. She stops in a square of light from the courtyard, eyes blazing, her whole body rigid with exasperation. "Luna was murdered. *Murdered.* And we're not going to discuss it?"

"Winter's right," Lavinia agrees without hesitation. "How can we just meet about the clue like that didn't just happen?" She and Kaysa are twined together, holding hands. The younger sister's face still blotchy from tears shed at Luna's expense, though the girl hardly knew the woman, her empathy's been run ragged, astonishing for anyone and unheard of for a Blackgate. "I'm all for compartmentalizing but Nona Marsyas did not kill Luna."

"Which means someone here did," Winter snaps. "And only one of us is pushing forward with their dismal-ass priorities."

She glares at Hector Cerise.

"If that look is to insinuate that I had anything to do with Luna's death, I will not tolerate it, Winter."

"I don't give a shit what you'll tolerate, Hector."

"Papa, Winter's right," Hex says. "It's pretty messed up that you want to hunt for that master tonight."

"*Messed up?* I have my eye on the prize, Junior. Finding the masters is the way out of here. I'm not going to let what happened to Luna distract me from getting my family home safe."

"And gaining control of the Four Lines?" Evander challenges.

"I will hear no such thing from *you*."

"Then hear it from me, Senior." Hex steps toe-to-toe with Hector. He's actually taller. "If someone murdered Luna, what's to keep them from murdering any of us?"

"They *did* try to murder us." I step in. All four Cerises turn as one—Winter too.

"Auden, what? Evander said it was unimportant . . ." A hand flies to Winter's stomach as if she's going to be sick. Her eyes read my face, Evander's—looking for a hint. She rounds on Lavinia. "I thought you said it was just a cut."

When I speak, it's as much to her as to Hector. "Someone threw several knives at us in the woods today. Grazed Lavinia but got Evander in the back and nearly killed him. A fact I'm sure you guessed from the sheer amount of blood coating his jersey—you know what a lethal wound might spill, don't you?"

Hector rears away, gesturing to my cousin. "He seems fine other than the ruined jersey for a school he no longer attends."

"Because I healed him. If I hadn't been with him, he would've died. And the attacker took aim at Lavinia too—three knives straight to her back that I repelled."

All color drains from Winter's face as Hector simply blinks at us, as if any reaction will lead to an accusation. As if he can avoid it.

"Both of us are currently leaders of our families. People who might be in line for High Sorcerer if it's truly a competition—same as Luna," Evander says, his baritone flat. "Where were you today, Hector?"

Anger flares Evander's nostrils, leaving his shoulders heaving in a way that would make a normal man back away.

Hector, though, doesn't move.

"The stress of what's happening here is making you entertain ideas that are completely out of line and unreasonable, Evander. I refuse to answer this nonsense—"

"If you want to take a picture of this clue, you'll answer where you were," I say, brandishing Ursula's magical paper. "Answer the question."

"This is a waste of time!" Hector explodes, barely missing Sanguine with his arms thrown wide. She flinches. "We're all dead if we're locked in here. Don't you see? We'll die here. The lines will be in shambles. If I must find the remaining two relics by myself in the next twenty-seven hours, I will. Because I want out of here."

"You want control more," Evander accuses.

"I want both!" Hector roars. He stabs a finger at Evander. "I have dedicated my life to leading the Blood Line and that's what I plan to do until the day I die. And if I find the next two relics by myself while the rest of you hide out, I should be given control of the Four Lines as High Sorcerer!"

"If you want to be High Sorcerer," I reiterate, "you can answer the simple question of where you were today."

Hector's nostrils flare and he runs a hand through his pomaded hair. Sanguine places a hand on his elbow. "This is so childish. He was with me." She gestures at her children. Still matching, the four of them. A unit. "He was with all of us. Looking for the masters at the Field of Stars and Shadrack's Lookout. We were together all day. There. Are you happy? My God."

Hector tosses out a hand, like *there you go*. The twins remain silent.

"They're lying."

Lavinia's voice is soft but clear, determined. We all turn to her, and she looks Hector dead in the eye. "They weren't together all day. Kaysa and I saw them—"

Hector's head is shaking, jaw unhinged before she can even finish.

"Lies. Lies. Tossing out lies to divert from what *her nona* did." Hector whirls on his family. "Enough of this. Let's go."

Sanguine jumps to join him, though there's a note of hesitation in her expression. "But, darling, the picture—"

"I don't need a picture," Hector snaps. "This is our master, our clue. It lives in my blood."

So much for fighting for Infinity's vial. The patriarch bodily spins his wife toward their suite. Still, Hex and Ada hesitate—and Hector smacks the wall so hard the plaster splits and sags beneath the wallpaper. *"Come on."*

This time, it's not a direction, it's an order.

This time, the twins follow.

"When push comes to shove it turns out *someone* is an asshole," Kaysa mutters when they're out of sight.

"Honestly, seeing this side of him makes me feel sorry for Hex, and that's saying something," Winter admits before literally seeming to shake the thought away. Whether or not it works, she rounds on Lavinia. "Is that true? Did you see them separate?"

"Yes," both sisters confirm at once.

"Why didn't you mention this earlier?" I ask. "After the knife attack?"

"Yeah, I need to hear way more about this knife attack," Winter cuts in.

"I—" Lavinia begins.

Evander quickly hushes her. "We're not talking here in the open. Not about this, not about Luna. We need a closed door. And a lock."

"Where do you propose we go? The solarium is a crypt, the library and the tearoom don't have locking doors, and Ursula's study doesn't have enough seating if we're going to hunker down." Winter ticks off every ill-fitting space on her fingers.

"I have an idea," Evander says. "Follow me."

We head for the wide, open safety of the grand staircase, following him upstairs at a healthy clip. Suddenly I know where we're going. We turn left, past the alcove to the reading room, and then right, into a long hallway with a single door on the courtyard side.

Evander pauses, the key around his neck clinking with Ursula's ring as he removes it. The Blackgate girls stand behind him, shoulders smashed together and hands still twined. They're so consistent about it that I try to recall the Blackgates doing the same as kids but

I come up blank. More proof, I suppose, that my memory is biased toward keeping my *animus* relationship intact.

"Do you truly trust them?" Winter leans into my ear.

In her voice is years' worth of knowing. Six is not too young to remember the before as well as you recognize the after. I only have a few months on her; our memories are siblings, not cousins.

Lavinia's dark eyes find mine as she steps over the threshold.

The past lives with me and though this present is both new and nearly unimaginable on all sides, after last night, after this morning and afternoon, I can be certain of one thing in this moment.

"Yes. I trust them."

CHAPTER 25

RUBY

"Do you think one of them killed her?" Wren whispers in the plush confines of the en suite bathroom that once belonged to the great Ursula Hegemony.

Evander's great idea seemed to be locking ourselves in the High Sorcerer's suite of rooms. Now my sister and I are huddled together in a dead woman's bathroom, hoping that we haven't made a terrible mistake. I've cleaned my arm and changed out my shirt for another of Winter's donations.

"I don't know."

It's the truth. Logically, we're getting mixed messages. The magic says there's no one else on the grounds. But the magic also should've trapped Luna's murderer before the victim's shroud even materialized. Unless non-magical murder—like the kind attempted with the knives—is a loophole . . . which means one of these nine people . . .

"Well, I mean, *somebody* killed her," Wren cuts in. "And it's possible the same person tried to knife you and Evander."

Who *did* knife me. Who nearly killed Evander.

"I wasn't taking this seriously enough—God, you're right." Wren presses the heels of her hands to her eyes, like a hard reset on a computer. "I . . . I can't believe we're locked in here with a killer. I was so sure it was Marsyas and all we had to do was survive the circumstances she left us." Her hands fly away and she snatches my elbow. "Do you think everyone else is having this exact same conversation?"

"A hundred percent, yes."

Winter and Auden used a hidden stairwell built into Ursula's sprawling suite to retrieve food from the kitchen. Evander absconded to the secondary bath to clean up his bloodied mess of a torso, insisting that myself—and, therefore, Wren—use the larger bathroom to wash off the blood and change. And though all three of them aren't together, motive and opportunity are likely the topic of choice. For them, for the Cerises, and for Evander and Infinity too, even if they're just talking it through with themselves.

"I don't see how they couldn't." I smooth down my newest top in the same flowy, aggressively pastel style as the first. It's far too soft and pristine for the sharpness of today's blood. "Unless the one who did it told the others and they're all talking about how to look innocent for the next day."

Wren splashes water on her face, bangs damp. She sweeps them to the side, blue smudges darkening her eyes underneath. "But, like, why? Why kill her? She was a little old lady. She didn't hold a relic, and there's no way she killed Ursula—they were friends since diapers."

I sink to the floor, my back to the ornate claw-foot tub, the tiles cold against the thin fabric of my tights and tank top. I hug my thighs into my chest and set my chin against the tops of my knees. My previously pristine shoes are now a muddy mosaic of trail grit caked onto brilliant white leather, more than one fat drop of blood staring back.

I glance away from the reminder of the attack and force a deep inhale, only to be hit with the mingling scent of old-fashioned cold cream and dying roses, weeping from a vase on the vanity. A visceral reminder that we're in a space that once belonged to a woman who wasn't just a matriarch, a High Sorcerer, but a human being.

Gone now.

"If someone thought Luna killed Ursula," I start, "they would've fessed up because then that would be one less thing for all of us to worry about, *or* they would be on magical lock-down because Ursula's spell said no vigilante shit." I take a deep breath. "It's probably more likely that someone killed her because they knew she knew they had killed Ursula, or, using Evander's logic for our knife attack, that she made too good a competition for High Sorcerer."

Nodding, Wren slides to the floor across from me, long legs

splayed out in front, a light sunburn from our hike pinking the skin on her forearms. "I'm so glad you weren't seriously hurt."

Her pinky twines in mine, and maybe it's the exhaustion, or the stress, or a delayed reaction to being grazed by a knife and targeted by three more, but a knot of emotion gathers hard and hot in my throat. I draw in a shaky breath and nod.

It's all I can do.

"Okay . . . so looking at everyone . . . it's got to be Hector, right? I mean, he literally drove away from his kids and lied about it, so, opportunity. And then after Luna's death, the real him crawled out like that scene in *Alien,* just straight out of his gut, into the light." Wren tears at the front of her shirt, mimicking a creature emerging from her belly. She sighs dramatically, arms flopping into the air and then back to the tile, pink nail polish a flash in the sconce light. "He made it clear he didn't care about Luna, or Infinity's anguish, he only cared about the relics. Maybe that's all he's ever cared about. Regaining control lost four hundred years ago by that relative of his."

Emotions rolling in the pit of my gut, I page back to the beginning in my mind. To the last time Ursula was alive, the dinner that feels like a lifetime ago, with the flirting, the awkwardness, the ghosts and gazpacho.

"He was seated next to her at the table. To her right. Marsyas was to her left." My voice is rough, and I try to clear my throat. "Meaning it could still be Marsyas who murdered Ursula, and whoever did this to Luna and whomever attacked us in the woods could be someone else."

We're silent for a few seconds before Wren stiffens.

"Could . . ." she starts. "Bear with me, I don't know how magic stuff works, but do you think maybe she was magically poisoned or spelled or whatever in the same way Ursula was? Not at the same time, because whatever it was seemed to work quickly within the small window of opportunity everyone had with her, but . . . maybe the killer had extra? Got Luna alone, or she threatened them, and they acted while we were all spread to the wind."

Her eyes narrow as she talks through it.

"I mean," she continues, "if it was a fast poison or spell—potion?—it could've been very quick."

"True." Then my stomach bottoms out and I scoot across the tiles to whisper as low as possible to Wren. "I hate to say it, but the Hegemonys were also in the building longer than the rest of us. The three of them had opportunity, *and* they'd probably know how to get around the spell logistics."

Wren's face sours into a grimace.

"You don't think one of them took out their grandma and then murdered a second grandma, and maybe orchestrated a fake attack on us in the woods . . . do you?" When she puts it like that, it seems more than farfetched. It seems ludicrous. "I mean, why not just murder Hector? He's the one who wants their special title. Apparently, Luna never did."

"But that's not something everyone knew until just now. Infinity clearly didn't mention it and neither did Luna as far as we know."

"God. Ugh. True." Wren sighs with her entire body. "Are all the mysteries you read like this? With questions and no answers and motives and *blergh,* I have a headache. I need more visuals. What is going on here? I want off this ride."

"You and me both, kid."

Wren balls herself up and drops her head between her knees. "So how do we survive this new murderer who is not our missing nona? Just abscond to our suite and slurp from the tap? Maybe open a window, hope a crow flies in, and roast it over the ever-present fire?"

"God, that got bleak fast."

"I'm hungry. And I just realized it. It's been that kind of day."

I sit up. "Okay. They'll be back soon and this aside of ours might seem suspect. So, our plan: we keep doing what we're doing—proving we're good partners, and not suspicious in any way despite our grandmother's apparent tyrannical designs, our amnesia regarding our father's death, and our obvious complete lack of magical knowledge."

"Seems tenuous considering there's a whole new dead body in the mix. I think we're going to need more than that."

I release a heavy sigh. "I'll think of something."

"Or maybe I will," Wren counters with an arch of her eyebrow.

I shove myself to standing. "You can't flirt your way out of this."

Her eyes narrow to slits. "It's my superpower but it's not my only power. I have other skills and you know it."

"I do. But I do not need your impulsivity to mess this up right now."

As soon as it's out of my mouth, I regret it.

Wren shoots to her feet. It's not just an indignant reaction—actual anger curls her lips and kicks up her tone. "Hey, that's not fair."

Maybe not. But I don't care. I—*we*—do not have time for this shit. I roll my eyes in the same way she does so very often. "Take it up with me when we survive this. Until then, follow my lead."

"Don't be a dick—"

"Please tell me you still have your knife."

Wren matches my eye roll with an annoyed little scowl before hiking up her tank top and patting the slim outline of the butter knife. "What does that have to do with anything? It's not like it can hold a candle to a meat cleaver or magic. We're basically sitting ducks—"

"Lavinia?" Evander's voice. I clamp my hand over Wren's mouth. "Kaysa? Are you doing okay?"

"Yes! One sec!" I shout as Wren rips at my hand—tired of this move of mine, but apparently still in need of knowing when to shut up because if he heard what she just said, our cover is probably blown. "Just tidying *up*."

The last word comes out nearly a yelp as Wren *bites* my fingers.

My hand flies away, tears immediately springing to my eyes at the pain.

"What the fuck?" I hiss, holding my throbbing hand, angry skin marked with white indentations from her teeth. Pinpricks of blood well to the surface.

Wren's eyes are fierce and furious. "I love you and I'm glad you weren't hurt today but you aren't the only capable one. I got us into this, I can get us out."

Then, Wren wipes her mouth with the back of her hand, pastes on her best grin, bodily sweeps my shocked form aside, and un-latches the lock.

I suck at my fingers, blood metallic on my tongue, and shove my throbbing hand into my pocket—and the knife pressing coolly into my aching skin.

CHAPTER 26

AUDEN

"Tell us about the Cerises," Evander prompts, fork and knife sawing through the wagyu steak that had been on the menu last night. He's washed away the blood, tossed the jersey, and has basically—appropriately?—gone full John McClane from *Die Hard,* wearing one of his favorite white undershirts, biceps and shoulders free to the night and from the constriction he abhors. Maybe this is dressing for the job he wants now more than the suit was before.

We're seated around the round, marble-topped table in Ursula's sitting room. Lavinia swallows her own bite under his gaze and presses a napkin to her lips. "We hiked toward the Field of Stars to join up with the Cerises, witnessed them separating, and then hiked toward our original locations as a group—the Pool and Horace's Last Stand. We met up with Evander and Auden between the two."

"What time did you see the Cerises split up?" I ask.

"Maybe an hour after we all left the driveway?" Kaysa responds. "Hey, can I get some chips?" She nods at the sideboard, which holds not only Ursula's preferred scotch but also an assortment of junk food we picked up from the kitchen too, including Evander's favorite salt-and-vinegar splurge.

"Protein first," Evander barks in a way that makes me believe they aren't totally off-limits to her. "And you made no contact with them?"

"No," Lavinia answers. "We planned to, maybe to work together, but when we arrived Hector and I'm assuming Sanguine, though we didn't see her, were in the SUV, and the twins were at the rolled-down, driver's-side window. Hector was angrily telling Hex to do something, and enlisting Ada to make sure it would happen."

Winter narrows her eyes. "What kind of something?"

Lavinia glances at Kaysa. "We're not sure. Hector just told Hex, 'You will, and that's final, my son. End of discussion.' Hex pushed back again, Hector raised a hand like he was going to slap him, and Hex immediately shut up. Then he turned to Ada and directed her to keep him on task. She agreed. Hector seemed satisfied and drove away, back down the access road. Then the twins grabbed a pack they were sharing and hiked into the woods on an unmarked trail."

Unmarked? If only we'd been there—the offshoots from the Field of Stars were numerous.

"Did you follow them?" Evander asks.

"We took the marked trail that went toward Horace's Last Stand because it looked like it might be parallel to the twins," Kaysa explains. "But they must have gone another way, because we lost track of them pretty quickly and they weren't at Horace's Last Stand."

"Okay, wait, hold on." Winter massages her temples, food all but forgotten. "How do we know any of this is true? Can you prove that the Cerises separated? Did you take photos? Video?"

"No."

"So all we know is this story about the Cerises and the fact that you weren't with my cousins all day, and when you were with them, they were suddenly so viciously attacked that our patriarch nearly bled out and Auden spent so much of his life element to heal him that he could barely walk straight?"

Lavinia pales.

My mouth pops open to defend her—but then Evander pointedly sets down his fork, his steak already inhaled. "Look, Win, you know me. I would not agree to be barricaded in here with the Blackgates if I had any doubts. I trust them. They didn't throw those knives at themselves today. No magic was involved. They didn't trick us. I trust them—and I trust you if you trust Infinity."

"Wait. *If* I trust Infinity? If you're suggesting they had a hand in any of today's violence, that's preposterous. They're the least violent person in the history of the Four Lines. Practically a Quaker."

Evander doesn't budge. "The Blackgates aren't the only ones who weren't with us all day."

Winter narrows her eyes. "*Both* of you are suspicious? Jesus Christ. Look, I saw Luna alive with them before we left to the grounds. We never separated on the grounds. Left together, returned together, discovered Luna together." She wheels back to Evander. "And before you start asking me if I have any interest in being High Sorcerer, I don't. I never wanted it, and now I'm not even sure I want *any* of this. Maybe I should be like Infinity and peace out."

Evander cracks a smile, a throaty laugh escaping as his eyes dance. "You can't 'peace out' as long as I'm patriarch. The Elemental Line will always be connected, whether we go from four lines to three in the next twenty-something hours or not."

Winter's nostrils flare in a way that mimics Evander, her jaw as tight as the fists balled atop the table. She glares at him. "I know. I know exactly what you want, Evander." Winter whirls on the Blackgates. "What I don't know is what *you two* want."

Lavinia raises her hands, placating. "We just want to go home. We don't want to be High Sorcerer; we don't want anything except to survive and leave."

"Which leaves the Cerises," I rush in to say. Evander nods, Winter frowns, I continue. "But if they could kill someone as powerful as Luna and not invoke Ursula's magic, they would do it again to anyone challenging Hector, wouldn't they? Why even mess around with it? They could've magically murdered all of us in Infinity's room an hour ago, cut off my hand to invoke the clues, and finished out the relic search alone. But they didn't."

Evander looks up, his green eyes locking with each of us. "What are we missing?"

"The threats," Lavinia answers, immediately. "I'm sure you all have already addressed this on your own time because it's obvious, but what do you make of Ursula mentioning threats when she greeted us? You don't think it was . . ."

"That she expected someone in the High Families to be capable of murder?" I finish.

"Well, yeah."

I shake my head. "To Ursula, threats were—are—things like invasive technology, modern distaste for social secrecy, environmental changes that affect each line of magic, and outside magical rebels. I don't think she would've taken any hints at discord so casually."

"I agree," Evander says. "Though we must take into account the way she was acting. She made sure the two of you were here. She told us she had a plan for the evening but didn't elaborate. Then she not only mentioned threats to set the night's tone, but she stood to give her speech during the first course instead of when the meal was over." His eyes rise to the Blackgate girls. "And the last time Ursula did that was the night of your father's trial and punishment."

He's right.

That's exactly how that night went.

It was the first meeting after our parents' funeral. It was supposed to be a cathartic night of dinner and discussion and hearts bared raw. Those of us at the kiddie table coping in our own ways—Evander in overt mourning; Winter with a happy, put-on face; and myself, with a misguided attempt at distraction by leaving a dead skunk in the bushes for a certain brunette guest to stumble upon.

Then Ursula rose from her seat, an accusation on her lips. The night instantly became an interrogation and a punishment, ending with the death of Marcos Blackgate before all of us.

In the silence, Lavinia draws in a deep breath, lifts her dark eyes to mine, shiny with all she's lost and perhaps the memory of it too, and asks, "But what if it wasn't a threat on her life? What if it was a threat on the way things have been?"

"What do you mean?" I hear myself say as something frays within me.

"Perhaps that's what the threat was—maybe Luna told Ursula she was cutting the Celestial Line loose." Lavinia nods to herself, pieces locking into place as the words come. "Luna saw it as something necessary for the way her line was going, but Ursula saw it as a defection—a threat."

That thought nearly stops my brain straight in the tracks.

"I—you know, yes," I stumble, my brain whirring forward. "That's possible."

Winter snags my fumbling answer. "Those two were as close as sisters and if anyone would have had the balls to broach defection with Ursula, it was Luna."

She's right.

"But then why would she have come at all to the meeting?" Evander asks. "We know dropping a bombshell like that into Ursula's lap wouldn't have made business as usual plausible."

Winter sighs. "Infinity could shed some light but I'm not about to barge in on them."

After a long, silent moment, Lavinia begins to fiddle with her napkin. "I'm not saying it means anything, but Infinity went out of their way to tell me that she thought Ursula did this to herself. They could've been planting seeds to drive the investigation away from their grandmother if for some reason we figured out Marsyas was set up."

"And then what? Someone murdered Luna rather than have her submit to interrogation? Or to the potential embarrassment it would cause their line?" Winter asks. "If you're back to implying Infinity could've done that to their grandmother, I know you don't know them, but no."

Lavinia holds up her hands. "I didn't say that."

Winter stands, shoves her chair back, and gets a bar of chocolate we stole from the kitchen stash from where it's piled between Evander's chips and the scotch glasses. "This is just such bullshit. None of this is worth it—what happened to Ursula and Luna is not worth it. Not for any of these moldy relics or for the Four Lines."

Kaysa clears her throat and enters the conversation with a much more serious tone than she's used before.

"Perhaps we put a pin in that and look at the idea of threats in a more immediate sense," Kaysa says in a way that's stiff—almost like she's reading from a script. Lavinia's brows knit. For all their closed-circuit nonverbal understanding, it's clear she's not sure where her sister is headed with this. Maybe it's not as rehearsed as I imagine, then. "A murder is a threat completed—we have two of those. The knife incident is a threat in itself."

"Yeah, a threat that almost made it four murders." Winter tosses the remaining chocolate bar onto the sideboard so hard it slides and skids off onto the rug. "Someone killed Luna, and it wasn't Ursula's fucking ghost. Evander and Auden, I swear to God, I'll kill you a second time if either of you manages to get murdered over a meaningless title."

Evander stands too now, his chair nearly tipping. "The title isn't meaningless; it keeps thousands of witches safe in this country—"

"It didn't keep Ursula safe!" Winter shouts. "It didn't keep Luna safe! It didn't keep our parents safe! In fact, it put them six feet under! Can you believe—"

A loud knock snuffs Winter's anguished voice.

We all turn to the door. This isn't a hotel, there's no peephole.

Evander shouts, "Who is it?"

There's a pause, whispering between the wall and us. Not Infinity then. Which leaves—

"We have information you need to know."

Hex's voice is as clear as a bell.

"Unless it's the third master, it can wait until morning," Evander answers.

Magic sparks at my fingertips. Magical defense is allowed, not offense—despite the evidence of Luna's murder, I have no interest in testing Ursula's rules about using magic against each other and spending twenty-four of our remaining hours frozen like a statue.

Rising, I grab the nearest blunt object—a massive decorative rose quartz bookend on the sideboard. It's sized like a bowling ball and just as heavy. I cock it, prepared for a quick-release lob if the Cerises force their way in.

Finally, Hex's voice comes again, quietly but plainly, "Our parents weren't with us the whole day."

We all go collectively still.

"Are you confirming they were unaccounted for?" Evander calls.

"Are you confirming you lied?" Winter yells too before they can address Evander.

"Yes and yes," Hex answers without hesitation but wielding more of an edge than before.

"When did you separate and where?" Lavinia shouts. A good idea—a confirmation of what the Blackgates saw would prove both the Cerises' intentions to tell the truth are real, and also back the sisters' alibi.

"At the Field of Stars. They drove away, leaving us to hike," Hex answers.

When he finishes, Ada crowds in with another plea. "Let us in, please."

I put down my blunt object. "Evander, two truths. We need to hear what they have to say."

"I don't like it," Evander growls.

"There are five of us and two of them. It's a more dangerous situation for them," I point out. "We should let them in, hear what they have to say, and go from there."

Still, Evander hesitates. Winter, though, charges toward the door. "They sound terrified. Have a heart, patriarch. If you won't open it, I will."

"Fine," Evander relents, sliding in front of Winter at the last second. He calls fire in his palm—basically the Elemental equivalent of raising a gun with the safety off and the chamber cocked—and unlocks the deadbolt, the regular lock, and cracks the door.

Though his broad back fills the frame, from where I'm standing, fingers wrapped around the bludgeon I've chosen, I can see the twins standing there together, Ada under Hex's arm, cheeks shiny beneath crimson-tinged eyes. Her brother is sallow and rumpled, his hair an unmitigated mess, bruises beneath his eyes.

"Do your parents know you're here?" Evander asks.

"Of course not," Hex snaps, frustration surfacing. "And they'd ring our necks if they knew we were. And the longer we stand out here, the more chance we have of getting caught. Let us in."

With a curse, Winter bodily shoves Evander aside, the flame in his palm shivering as she uses his own stumbling, surprised weight to crack the door open farther. Hex seizes the opportunity and slips through the gap, hauling Ada by her wrist.

Evander leans into the hall, and seeing nothing, seals the door with deadbolts in place and stands in front of it. The fire in his palm has dimmed, and he crosses his arms, staring down at our new guests like judge and executioner.

"It's not enough to tell us your parents weren't with you all day. I want to hear you say it."

Hex and Ada drop onto the couch, putting space between themselves and the table I stand at with the Blackgate girls, and between where Evander guards the door. Winter hovers in the negative space between our three points of contact.

Hex scrapes a hand across his jaw. "I know you can put two and two together, Evander—"

"Say they killed Luna," Winter prompts. "Hex, we need to hear it. There's no room for misunderstanding why you're here or what information you have."

Hex's head falls back, eyes scrunched closed. Beside him, Ada stares at the bejeweled familial ring on her own finger, chords of her neck straining beneath her drape of blond hair. Hex lifts his head, looks Evander straight in the eye, and when he speaks his words are sharp enough to draw blood. "Our parents weren't with us, but they didn't kill Luna."

My jaw drops, Winter's eyes narrow, and Evander pushes off the doorframe, emerald flames flickering dangerously in both hands. "I'm not interested in a spoon-fed alibi right now, so you can just—"

"Our parents didn't kill Luna," Hex cuts him off, voice climbing high and loud, "because she was *already dead* when they returned to the mansion to get the knives *we* used to *attack you*."

Chapter 27

AUDEN

In the next second, every one of us is in motion.

Lavinia hauls Kaysa to the floor, using the table as a shield.

I throw up an *actual* shield, covering the three of us as Evander launches twin fireballs straight at the Cerises. While Winter . . . sprays water directly at Evander's fireballs before the magic collides with the Cerises' cover.

In the silence of the flames hissing out, my eyes dart between the twins, shielded behind a glittering vermilion wall of magic, and Evander, who spits, "You admit to attacking us?" at the same time Winter whispers, "Hex, you *what*?"

Hex draws his phone and waves it behind the magical protection.

"Would you like to see the video? Because I documented it."

"I'd rather not watch myself nearly bleed out, thank you," Evander retorts. "You've had your time to gloat. Now give me one reason I shouldn't march you straight out of here."

Hex bares his teeth. "Look, we're not gloating. And we don't have much time."

I give an exasperated laugh. "None of us have much time. We're coming up on twenty-five hours, to be exact—"

"Not that," Ada snaps. "We don't have much time because you don't know how *he* is. You don't understand . . ."

"Stop speaking in riddles, and we *will* understand," Winter hisses. Her eyes shoot to Hex. "What the hell are you talking about? Tell us *clearly,* tell us now, or leave."

The Blood witch draws in a deep, shaggy breath, and pushes his hair out of his eyes, his carefully gelled coif now ragged. He makes eye contact with his sister and they both drop their shields.

It's an olive branch—unguarded physically, to lend credibility to an unguarded truth.

"Blood Line families have a secret—one that even Ursula did not know," Hex says. "We can control others with a single drop of blood, yes, for a short time. What isn't something that's documented or discussed is that in Blood Line families, parents can control their children *indefinitely*."

The Blackgates pop up from beneath the table, eyes wide and watching as silence descends upon us, his admission sinking in.

If this is true, the twins have never truly had bodily autonomy. Their parents may coerce them into doing things without their consent. At any time.

Again, I lower the bookend.

"They can force us to do anything because *our* blood is *their* blood. As long as it's in their veins and ours, they can control us until that connection is permanently severed." Ada is still staring at her familial ring, head bowed, as her brother finishes. "And today they forced us to hurl knives at people we call friends."

There's a beat of silence.

"That's what you told Hector you wouldn't do at the Field of Stars," Lavinia surmises quietly from where she rises to her full height. She looks from Hex to his sister, eyes narrowing. "And he told Ada to keep you on task."

"They can *make* us, but being absolute controlling assholes in every sense of the word, they'd rather we just do what they say. Less painful for all involved." Hex swallows. "If I resist, it affects Ada too. And I don't want to see her get hurt."

"We both try to resist but . . ." Ada adds, sullen, "in the end it's too difficult and too painful to outlast their coercion."

Hex's coal-dark eyes lift to Evander's face. "I'm sorry, man." Evander is a brick wall, per usual, but there's not a trace of anger on Lavinia's face. Something about the juxtaposition makes Hex's throat bob. "I'm sorry, Lavinia."

"Because they're competition?" Winter asks.

This time, it's Ada who answers, her face grim. "Originally, it was supposed to be just something to scare whomever we came upon. A way to turn the players against Evander as the best candidate for High Sorcerer. But when our parents found Luna murdered in the house, they changed tactics. Papa decided we should go after all of the heirs, and make it look coordinated with what happened to Luna. He was going to 'survive' a knife attack too—we just didn't get time to properly stage it before you found Luna."

Hex's gaze shifts around the room. "He didn't want to hear our concerns about how two different methods would make no sense, or that his survival would make him look guilty, not powerful and innocent like he hoped."

"How do we know you're not under their control right now?" I ask.

"They're asleep."

I nearly do a double take. "Wait—after that big show about how he needed the clue and someone had to get us out of here or we're all dead, your parents are asleep?"

Hex shrugs and for the first time, a little smile crosses his face. "They travel with sleeping pills."

Kaysa *does* do a double take. "You drugged them so you could come here and tell us you tried to knife Evander and Lavinia today while under the influence of your parents?"

"Yes. But also that they didn't murder Luna. And if they didn't, who did?" Hex tosses his arms wide. "A person in this room? Infinity? Or is there someone else on the grounds that we don't know about? Someone not bound by the rules we are?"

"We've been down this road," Evander argues. "It's a dead end."

"You know what's not? The information we brought you." Hex swipes at his phone and again turns it toward Evander, who still stands several feet away, a coffee table dotted with Ursula's knitting magazines between them. "Papa changed his plans and arrived two days before the rest of us. And I'll give you one guess as to the two individuals I found in his incoming calls the day he altered his schedule."

"Marsyas and Luna," Evander answers, resolute, eyes pinned on the small screen several feet away.

The twins nod in unison. "We don't know that Papa murdered Ursula, but we think he knew she was *going to be* murdered. Maybe Marsyas, Luna, and our father had a plan. Maybe everything changed when control of the Four Lines came up as a possibility. We don't know. But what we do know is they didn't just call each other, they met up."

He swipes at his screen again and shoves the device bravely in Evander's air space. Winter carefully accepts it.

"A private room at Le Sur in Denver," she says, squinting at what looks to me from over her shoulder to be an emailed receipt, "a day before the annual meeting."

"Papa paid for three meals and a bottle of *very nice* cava during a four-hour lunch," Ada says. "The three heads of family met together the day before Ursula was murdered. Now Ursula is dead, and her title is on the line."

Hex taps the phone in Winter's hand. "And of the three people in that meeting, only Papa is still standing here."

"Are you sure your parents didn't somehow murder Luna and avoid Ursula's punishment?" Lavinia asks.

The twins exchange a glance.

"We don't know," Hex says. "But what we do know is that they will do anything for the prize because the power's the point."

The power's the point—the line kicks me straight in the chest.

Was that always the truth? From Napoleon to Mercy to Ursula to us?

"Being seen as the redeemer of the Cerise name?" Ada's voice is no longer weak but as thorny as ever. "The one who finally avenged the power lost by Napoleon Cerise? The one who returned rightful power to the Blood Line after four hundred years on the sidelines? It's what they dream of. And after what they made us do today? Nearly killing Evander? They'll use us in any way necessary to make this happen for them. I'm sure of it. Whether it kills someone or kills us, honestly, I'm not sure they care."

"Kill you two?" Lavinia clarifies as Kaysa gasps.

Hex spears them with a stoic glare. "My sister said what she said and I agree."

The room spins as his admission and confirmation ring in our ears.

"I need a drink," Evander announces and turns for Ursula's sideboard.

"We all do," Hex agrees.

Evander unstoppers the scotch and splashes it into two glasses. An olive branch of his own, I suppose.

"I want to know what you expect us to do with this information," I say as evenly as I can, though my heart rate is increasing at the same clip it did while chasing Evander up the Mercy's Point trail. "Confront them? Given what you just told us, it won't be a peaceful meeting. We could try to plan but—"

"Look, I don't think there's a point to a plan," Hex responds, accepting the second glass from Evander. "We wanted to warn you guys. After what happened tonight, I'm not sure we can talk to you publicly in any way that's not antagonistic. If we're not plainly your enemies, we're not contributing to the family cause."

"Bullshit," Evander snarls over the lip of his glass.

And honestly, I agree with him.

"You came here. You know what's right," I say. "If your dad is who you say he is, we need to make sure he doesn't gain control of the Four Lines, no matter his actual role in whatever those three may have planned."

Ada's expression gathers like a thunderstorm. "I don't care who's in charge after all of this, but I'm telling you right now the only way my father is going to allow someone other than himself to have control of the Four Lines at the end of all this is if he's six feet under."

"Yep," Hex agrees, nearly glib, before downing the entirety of the scotch, grimacing as the burn hits. He immediately moves to pour another.

There's a long silence and then—"Why don't we just give it to him?"

Winter's voice is quiet but sharp.

"What?" at least three of us ask.

"Hector," she says, louder, braver.

"You—you want to give my father the title?" Hex asks with a wincing cough as he pounds his sternum, willing his most recent drink down his throat. "After all we just said?"

"A title is not worth any more lives," Winter tells him, steel in her voice and edging every syllable. Her blue eyes, shiny with new tears, scan the room now, pleading. "Let's just give it to him if he wants it so badly."

"Win," I start, pressing my fingertips to my temples because I can't believe I have to say this out loud, "he actively tried to kill Evander and Lavinia today. He could've murdered Ursula and maybe Luna. We can't just give in to that."

"Why not? Why don't we give in? What does it matter anyway?" Her entire carriage from her pleading eyes to the tips of her dirt-scuffed shoes is hopeless.

"Because that's like giving in to terrorists," Lavinia bites out, joining my fight.

Winter doubles down. "If we give in, we're alive."

"And he's in control of our magic," I point out. "To control the lines is to control all of us."

"So? Why is that so bad?" Winter practically shouts, gaining steam as the rest of us go still. It's like watching a car crash in slow motion, my cousin actually arguing for surrender. "He's trying to avenge a perceived wrong. Why on earth would he accept that power and then try to be anything but a good leader? He's trying to undo the damage Napoleon did. The way he's going about it is wrong but maybe the end result is both inevitable and not that bad."

"Win, did you not hear anything I've said?" Hex scoffs and blinks at all of us with incredulous eyes. "I'm the fucking heir to the Cerise name, I wouldn't be sitting here if I wasn't scared shitless for what *he* will do—in the context of the game, in the context of power. This is the man who turned in Marcos Blackgate," Hex re-iterates with a grand sweeping gesture in the direction of the man's daughters. "He will say and do anything, no matter what happens to anyone else involved. Family or not. Friend or not. Everyone is disposable to Hector Cerise."

Lavinia gasps and her voice is so raw her accent flattens into nothing at all. "He . . . Hector turned in . . ."

She doesn't finish but she doesn't have to. The horror of it all crawls across her face, perhaps a memory locked tightly away washing forward in a tide of blood. Ursula did the deed, but Hector pulled the trigger.

"Ursula wanted someone to punish," Ada confirms before drawing the final dagger and stabbing the Blackgates in the heart, "Papa made it happen."

Kaysa shoots to her feet, stop-sign hand in the air. "Hold up. Wait. You're saying that your dad is the reason our dad was . . ."

"Convicted of magically influencing the Hegemony scions and compelling them to attempt to bypass master relic security only to blow themselves up in the process?" Hex asks, steadying himself against the sideboard, *another* pour of scotch in one hand as he finger-guns her with the other. "Yeeeeep."

"But . . . how . . . why?"

Hex's cheeks immediately darken.

"They all knew about it. Everyone of that generation was in on it. Our parents, Erasmus and Sorcha, Marcos and Athena. Every last one of them. They wanted to bust up the lines and decentralize control of the masters. They thought no person should have so much power. But rather than overthrow Ursula, they tried to go around her. Ran into the security curses put upon the masters and blew themselves sky high. *BOOM.*"

Evander plunks his glass too hard on the sideboard. "Everyone was in on it? That's just a rumor."

Hex's grin gets sadder and meaner with each new variation.

"Nah, it's the truth. Ursula was mad enough to take out the rest of that generation and she would've done it too if Papa hadn't served up Marcos on a platter. Death magic was always the black sheep. And it was better him than anyone else."

"His daughters disagree with you," Kaysa says, coldly.

"I know." Hex shrugs. "Blood on our hands, even if it's not as visible as the blood on Ursula's. Can't blame her for wanting closure after losing her kids like that."

Next to me, Lavinia is trembling. She's trying to hide it, hands jammed into a double grip of the marble table edge, but both arms are shivering up to her shoulders.

I swallow thickly. "We don't need to talk about this anymore."

"Why not?"

Hex takes a step and wobbles like he's got a low-grade concussion. He thinks better of it and thunks back against the sideboard, sending Evander's chip bag slumping into the baubles and glasses. He ignores it. "Look, everything changed that night. Everything. Not when your parents died. No, when punishment was doled out. Everything changed."

"You girls left." Hex tosses a hand at the trembling Blackgates beside me. "Our parents and Infinity's parents walked away scotfree. But it just as easily could've been us. You don't think Luna didn't think that? That it could've been Erasmus instead? And Marsyas—she kept showing up with a fucking smile on her face to make small talk with the woman who killed her son because if she didn't, it wouldn't just be the end of her but the end of her family." He waves at the Blackgate girls like they've boarded a train and are leaving the station. "This was ten years coming. And if Ursula didn't see the signs, she was blind as a bat."

Winter has had enough. Arms crossed and palms wrapped round her elbows, she approaches him.

"Hex, I think you need to go back to your room."

"When we're just clearing the air? That's unfair, Win."

He pushes off the sideboard again, body too loose, steps a slide. She catches him under the arms and sweeps him into her vacated chair at the table. Hex blinks at the table as Winter hands him her fork.

"You just shotgunned a couple of ounces of straight liquor and clearly haven't eaten anything." She points at her own barely touched plate of wagyu. "Finish this for me. Now."

Slowly, he nods, and obediently takes a bite, swallows, and says, "I love you."

"That's your problem," she barks back. "Eat."

I clear my throat. "I still maintain we need a plan. We have the element of surprise, thanks to the twins. What if we go down there right now, wake them, and calmly reveal what we know?"

It's as good an idea as I've got that shouldn't get violent. Won't get us any closer to finding the relics and getting out of here, but perhaps it will keep us alive long enough from Hector Cerise's apparent lethal greed to do so.

"Maybe Hector will just be dying to tell us his whole intricate plan?" Kaysa agrees. "He does have 'villain itching for a big monologue' written all over his face. No offense, Cerises."

"None taken," Hex confirms, raising his mostly empty scotch glass. Winter snatches it away and gestures again to the beef.

"Wait!" Lavinia calls, eyes suddenly bright. "'Out damn spot'!"

"Lavinia," Kaysa tuts, "we all recognized the Lady Macbeth reference in the clue. It's not like it's obscure. It was literally a callout to one of the most famous lines ever written."

"Gah—no! Hex said Ursula had literal blood on her hands." Lavinia looks down and away. "I know I have a block, that I don't remember, but—was there blood when Dad died? Was it on Ursula's hands?"

I raise myself to standing and meet her eyes. "Yeah."

The line is immediate, burned into my memory. On the paper set aside. *"Out damn spot, blood will never go . . ."*

Lavinia meets my eyes and speaks the clue's finale. *"But never gone, stained with what was."*

"I think—" Lavinia draws a deep breath and tries again, "I think the clue might be pointing to where Ursula punished our father. I mean, I know Shadrack wrote the clue, but, like . . ."

"Everything Ursula did, Shadrack did first," I tell her. "In the same place."

Several iterations of curse words fly through the air between all of us. Evander disappears down the hallway and returns with a set of old-timey lanterns that he lights with a magical snap of his fingers.

"Phones as flashlights if needed; let's use these first to protect battery life," Evander barks, passing them out, his warnings about the grounds' treachery after dark forgotten. "Cerises, are you staying with us or returning to your rooms?"

Swallowing the last of Winter's dinner, Hex pushes away from the table. "And let you have all the fun? Not on your life."

"Are you people insane?" Winter cries. "You just spent the wee hours of this morning explaining in intricate detail how deranged Hector Cerise is, and now you're going out in the pitch dark to free the relic tethering his power to the title he wants most in the world?"

"Yes," Evander says.

"He's asleep," I point out.

Winter's hands ball at her sides, color rising in her cheeks, her eyes bare fury. "No, no, no. You two need to stay right here. Until dawn. Until we can lay down the olive branch, tell Hector where we think the master is, and go together, in a sign of solidarity, so he doesn't just pick us off for *fun*." She stabs one fist at each twin. "And use our friends to do it."

"That's a chance we have to take. Let's move."

Winter curses and twines her arms around herself.

I agree with Evander, and yet I pause, Lavinia standing back, watching the movement as if from behind a two-way mirror. Kaysa is the one who immediately steps forward, collecting a lamp from Evander. "If you don't want to go to where it happened, I'll stay with you."

And I will.

I know what's at stake—we have less than twenty-four hours, another clue to decipher, another relic to find, and the increasingly complicated question of who killed Ursula to unravel.

Yet, it hits me like a falling rock that I'd stay with Lavinia. Door locked, silence descending, waiting for word.

Lavinia sighs with her whole body and when her eyes meet mine, there's sorrow as deep as the ocean. "I want to be there. If what Hex said is true, he died because he helped the Hegemonys find these master relics. And then he lost his life because of it, within spitting distance of one. I need to pay my respects."

With that, we head for the door. Leaving only Winter.

I hover in the doorway, Lavinia on one side, Hex on the other. He holds the jamb, the footsteps of his twin, Evander, and Kaysa growing softer as they move down the hall.

"Are you coming, Win?" he asks, beating me to it.

There's a long pause before the answer comes in the form of her stomping over, palming a chocolate bar and Evander's bag of chips—a bold choice indeed because he hasn't had any—and shoving the salt-and-vinegar snack with a great crinkling sigh into Hex's chest.

"Keep eating. Fall on a rock, and we're leaving you there to heal yourself and sober up. Say a word to me edgewise about what I'm about to do, and I'll shove you down myself."

Hex grins sloppily. "I wasn't kidding earlier when I said I love you."

"That's your cross to bear—you know my heart's taken." Winter shoves him ahead. "Now walk."

CHAPTER 28

RUBY

The bobbing of lanterns feels like a step back in time. And maybe it is.

We're not the first to walk this path in the dead of night, flames flickering, doing little to keep the shadows at bay as they're as much inside the mind as they are in the encroaching blackness.

Clouds have swept in, fat and low, swallowing the surrounding peaks. A stiff breeze rustles the trees loud enough to muffle the crunch of our footsteps and the low moan of conversation.

Twice, Evander's lantern blows out from the leader's position, and twice, I assume, he rekindles it with a spate of near instantaneous magic. It doesn't escape my notice that he keeps his right hand unencumbered at his side, the set of it supple but engaged, like the hand of a cinema knight sitting atop the pommel of his sheathed longsword.

Wren is next to Evander, stride for stride, chin bowed nearly to her chest, both her head and her heart taking very seriously her role and what we're about to see. I appreciate this in her even as I wish it hadn't taken so long. Winter is knotted with the Cerise twins. I don't miss how Hex keeps glancing at her.

Auden has stayed beside me in the rear, as alert and on guard as Evander, though his attention is on the twins as much as it is his footing. And with those threats accounted for, he worries over me—over Lavinia.

I worry about her too.

How would it change a person to come to a dinner party as a family and leave without your dad? Standing under a summer sky like this one, losing him forever in the blink of an eye? That's a bitter pill I know well from my mom's death, but still Lavinia had it worse, I think. The shock and searing pain heightened by the run-up of humiliation among people deemed family.

Watching helplessly as he's tried. Sentenced. Executed.

It isn't any wonder no one has questioned our scattered memories.

It isn't surprising that *everyone* was shocked to see the Blackgate girls again in the flesh.

To me it's almost more stunning that Marsyas *kept* arriving to the annual dinner. Kept slapping on a Blackgate smile and her familiar relics, returning to the scene of her greatest heartache, over and over.

"Did Nona ever come here when she visited over the years?" I ask Auden as we wind past a gated cemetery full of Hegemonys. Two dozen graves at least, maybe more. It's impossible not to notice that at the front are three identical graves so new their stones have not darkened or softened with age, the marble pristine obelisks reaching for the sky. Ulysses. Callum. Lana.

"Not to my knowledge. Marsyas was very consistent—drinks, dinner, disappeared by midnight. She never stayed until morning or explored the grounds."

"And she didn't visit any other time during the year?" Then I add, truthfully, "We never talked about Ursula."

"Not to my knowledge."

There's no sign announcing the official execution site of the Hegemony estate. It's surprisingly close to the house, separated by a massive boulder, covered completely with paint—one of Shadrack's murals from the courtyard. Facing the cemetery and the manor—though a steep drop obscures it from easy view—is what appears to be a depiction of dawn or dusk. It's fuzzy around the edges and ghostlike in the faded, inconsistent illumination of our lamps and phone flashlights, and the reflection of the earth upon the low-hanging silver of the clouds. Though, on the side where Evander halts our procession, the boulder is swathed in rich black, like the endless depths of death.

It smells of blood.

Auden and I are the last ones to arrive. He's so close, the sides of our hands brush.

And though I'm not Lavinia Blackgate, though this isn't the killing ground that took my dead parent, though this isn't my pain, the sharp realness of what happened here ten years ago drives into my chest—I find myself grabbing for the safety of Auden's hand.

He stiffens at the contact. Then the surprise fades as quickly as it came, and his hand shifts until he has me cloistered in his own grip.

"Lanterns around the platform," Evander says, an order and a direction.

It's a relief Auden doesn't let go as he obeys.

Before us, a platform and an adjoined post are awash in overlapping lamplight. The post is iron and shackles are attached to it, too short for comfort or struggle. The length of them won't reach the black expanse of the painted boulder, which almost serves as a backdrop as much as a void. The platform is wooden and low enough that there are no steps—it's perhaps no more substantial than a few shipping pallets laced together. There are wide slats built in. Drains.

Bile rises in my throat. I swallow hard, nose stinging with a flush of heat that makes my eyes water.

Beside me, Auden retrieves the clue, and I realize now he must use some sort of magic to store the paper away but keep it on his person. He reads, voice quiet and reverent, his grip on my hand never wavering.

> "Out damn spot, blood will never go
> It paces, hot and urgent, then goes cold
> The heart moves it, Princess
> Until it succumbs to the elements, shriveled, hard, alone
> But never gone, stained with what was."

"It's either in the base of the post or buried under it," Hex suggests, his voice, like his posture and stride, sturdier than it had been.

Auden and his mind for poetry has a more dramatic line of thinking. "The blood drains through the slats to the earth, where it stays, staining the layers all the way down."

Evander agrees with a stout, "Let's remove the platform."

There's a flurry of movement, and I want this over with almost as bad as I want to keep holding Auden's hand. I nudge us both forward, to help in the destruction of the platform. Wren notices and joins in, and no one questions that we're standing where our father died. I suppose it could be cast off as catharsis—physically destroying a space that took so much from us.

When the platform is removed and the lantern light reaches what's underneath, my breath catches in my throat.

It's not soft, absorbent silt, but a broad, flat tablet of amethyst. The sides are rimmed black, and after everything it's hard not to believe it's some sort of years-old, magical blood. Marcos Blackgate's blood.

And in the very center is a wooden box.

It's stained red with time, placement, tragedy.

Evander and Hex bend together to it, Wren cuffing the eldest Hegemony's shoulder as he sinks to the earth. Winter and Ada lean in, holding their breath. Again, my fingers snake into Auden's. He squeezes me back.

"You do the honors," Evander tells Hex.

Hex rubs a forefinger over the same precise lettering we'd seen marking the other two. The lamplight flares with the weight of it and he reads.

"The Heart of Cleopatra."

Wren gasps and I know her little Elizabeth Taylor–worshiping brain just short-circuited. "*The* Cleopatra?!"

"Elemental witch, princess come queen," Winter replies. "Iconic in our line."

"Iconic outside the line too," Wren agrees.

Yet another master relic that mixes lines. An Elemental witch, but the item preserved is that heart of hers, so famous for loving Mark Antony.

Auden grapples to apply the logic we've used on the other two. "Iconic, yes. But it's the motor of the circulatory system . . . so it's the Blood Line relic."

I open my mouth to agree—

"That's right. Therefore, it's *mine*."

We all know that voice, even without the unhinged joy smothering the final word.

Stepping out of the shadows beyond the reach of the lanterns is Hector Cerise.

One sleeve is rolled up, glistening, fat lines of crimson weeping from his vertical tattoos, the single horizontal stripe denoting him as an oathed heir and patriarch, a pearlescent black. The cut means he's primed to call his magic. Against us—or at least to threaten us. Maybe Ursula's prison punishment spell didn't make a mistake in Luna's death. Maybe it never worked at all. Maybe he knows this. Maybe he murdered Luna and lied to his twins.

As my mind puzzles that, I realize Sanguine is not with Hector. We haven't seen them apart this weekend—curious as it only adds to the unpleasantness of his sudden appearance.

"How interesting," Hector says dryly, "as I was informed multiple times how very unsafe the grounds were after dark, and yet here you all are, holding *my* master."

Hex and Ada freeze, the boy in a crouch, his sister bent over our find, her body roughly facing her father. Color flushes high in their cheeks in the lantern light, rushing to the surface as if it's answered a call—and maybe it has. I picture their blood drumming in their veins, at attention for their father.

"Hex, bring the box to me."

The Cerise boy stiffens but doesn't move. Doesn't even blink. "I can hold it. As your heir."

At this, his father smiles. "You're my son, but you're not the oathed heir."

Hex's mouth drops. "Not yet, but I will be, and I can hold it—"

"Your sister has already been oathed."

We all turn to Ada, who swallows thickly.

"Is this true?" Hex asks, voice a rasp, his face paling as he stares at her, his big frame suddenly seeming smaller as he remains crouched.

In response, his sister pulls up her sleeve, revealing her tattoos. They look just like Hex's, a series of vertical lines. But then, the skin there begins to blur at the edges, and a horizontal sweep of ink just like Hector's reveals itself.

Hex's face contorts as he glares as his twin. "You hid it from me? You lied to me?"

"Oh, don't be so sour, Junior," Hector crows, stepping closer. Blood twines down his arm in ruby ringlets. "We figured your girlfriend would've told you. The Liaison of the Lines is notified after each heir is oathed."

Beside me, Auden inhales sharply, surprise in it. Evander goes still as stone, still bent with Hex by the box.

And Winter—Winter is furious. *"Ex."*

Hector just smiles broader. "All the more reason for you to keep Ada's oath from him."

Winter stiffens but doesn't deny it. She knew that Ada had become the Cerise heir.

"Everyone will let you down except your blood, son," Hector says, self-satisfied. "Everyone." Then. "Hex, bring me the box."

This time it's not a question, it's an order. A spell.

What the twins described their parents to be capable of.

Hex jerks into motion like a marionette, vise grip on the box, prying it free. With a cry, he wrenches his fingers open and drops the box onto the amethyst. The relic doesn't break on impact, but tips over onto its side and slides down the stone to the blood-soaked dirt.

Hex's eyes spring open, glassy against the strain of every capillary and vein in his face puffing up, the blood within him compelled to comply with the magic of his father's words and spell. Still, he manages to lift his head and stare his father in the eye across the distance, defiance etched in his coal-dark glare as much as his will to resist.

"You are such a disappointment." Hector's mouth curls into a mean smile. Too much time has passed—somehow Hector's use of magic on, or perhaps against, his own child is a loophole within the rules. He's not afraid to use it against them, or apparently in front of us. One more secret worth revealing in the sake of the power in play. Hector aims that smile and his attention on his daughter. "Ada, my heir, the box."

A small whimper escapes her lips as her father's spell seizes hold, her body moving under his command. Ada stiff-arms Hex away and snatches the box, rising awkwardly to her feet.

"Good girl," Hector coos. "Bring it here."

Ada moves to do so, poorly navigating a step between Evander and Kaysa—

The security wards detonate.

The ground beneath the platform rumbles and then explodes in a curtain of light, encircling the seven of us on the platform. My fingers clutch Auden as I realize we have no protective shield this time. I duck my head and squeeze my eyes closed, and then it's over.

I blink back into the strange reality of Hector's cruelty—and see Evander has plucked the relic from Ada's grip. "We agreed every master stays with the Hegemonys until the clue is confirmed."

Hector closes the distance, stabbing a furious hand at Evander, spittle flying. "You just determined it was the Blood relic. You may not have invited me for your little druid hike onto these *unsafe* grounds at two in the morning, but I heard you. It's mine."

There's a terrible glint in his eye and both twins seize, magic gripping them harder.

Ada jerks and jumps, claws out as she attacks Evander under Hector's direction. On the ground, a wail of pain lances through Hex as his body fights to rise and help his sister obtain the box, as his mind fights the compulsion of his father within his blood. His whole body is vibrating with effort though his movements are infinitesimal. Like a deadlocked arm-wrestling match. Winter is cupping his straining shoulder.

Auden tenses next to me, and the ground begins to shake, a

seam opening up from the tip of his shoes and slithering toward Hector. Earth—an element. My breath hitches. "Auden," I whisper, "you can't use your magic against him or—"

"Stop compelling them and we'll let him hold the box!" Winter doesn't look to Auden or Evander. Doesn't ask permission. Just announces it, a Hegemony family decree. "You have my word."

Auden grips me tighter, and to my relief, he's heeded my warning. The gash in the earth between us and Hector fading to nothing, two yards from swallowing him whole. Hector doesn't notice the crack, his gaze snapping to Winter above a sneer. "I'm not compelling them. I'm willing them to listen, as good children should."

"However you want to justify it to yourself doesn't excuse that it's sick," Winter shouts. "There's a reason it's been a Blood Line secret, because it's deplorable."

Auden clears his throat and says, "I stand by Winter's compromise. We'll let them hold it, just *stop*."

Everyone turns to Evander, who holds the relic over his head. Ada tears long, shallow slashes on the exposed skin of his arms, his neck, his face, as he stiff-arms her. "Fine. Agreed."

"My oathed heir will hold it."

Hector doesn't look at Hex as he twists his knife. Doesn't look at his daughter either. He only has eyes for his master relic. For his chance to be the first Cerise patriarch to hold it since the man whose mistakes his family has spent four centuries attempting to atone.

What an absolute asshole.

Evander holds Ada's clawing hands at arm's length. "Call off your magic, and I will give the master relic to Ada."

The answer is immediate.

Ada droops and sways, a marionette with cut strings as Hector's magic abates. Auden catches her with an arm across her upper back as she navigates control of her limp legs stumbling into careful standing. Meanwhile, Hex slumps hard into the blood-soaked dirt. Winter sinks to his side and tries to help him up—and it's a surprise when Evander, still palming the relic in one hand above his head, reaches down and uses his strength to help Hex upright.

Hector tenses, watching carefully, fingers flexing.

But Evander is true to his word.

He presents the Heart of Cleopatra to Ada, who cradles it close, and leaves our circle under her own volition to stand by her father. When Ada arrives at his side, she looks as if she might split into two right there, as her father cuffs her into place, squeezing her wrist so hard the edges of her skin are as white as bone in the lantern light. Her eyes are downcast—unable, it appears, to look her twin in the eye with the truth she'd kept from him exposed.

"Hex, you belong over here." Hector's voice is even and stern. "Do not fight me again."

The Cerise boy nods, and without even a glance back at Winter, follows his sister to his father's side, head bent and body shivering from the pain and effort.

Nausea sweeps over me at the thought of all these two have endured under the facade of the perfect family. Handsome, rich, in good standing. And yet, the levels of control and loss are nearly unimaginable.

I believe every word of what the twins shared in confidence.

These people are monsters.

To their children, and likely to anyone else standing in their way.

And the next clue will be the Death Line one, which means Wren, myself, and the Blackgate relic is all that's standing between Hector Cerise, his accessory wife, and the last step toward what they seem to want most in the world: control of the Four Lines.

I'm not even a real witch, and that thought truly terrifies me.

If Hector would kill other witches and hurt his children with his magic—which somehow doesn't seem to trigger Ursula's parameters . . . perhaps because it's always this way with them?—what would he do to those outside the lines with power like that?

"We will read the final clue right here, right now," Hector announces, the Heart of Cleopatra now tucked against his own chest and whatever beats beneath. "Auden, I saw you read from the clue. I know you have the will on your person."

Auden lets go of my hand, leaving the night's cool fingers against my skin, and retrieves the will. "I do indeed. But as we don't have all our members in attendance, perhaps we should go into the house, and take a moment to—"

"That won't be necessary, Auden."

My head snaps up at the syrupy-sweet voice of Sanguine Cerise. She steps out from behind the large boulder looking as fresh as the new swipe of blood-red lipstick across her mouth.

In one hand, she holds the gun that once hung next to Horace's roaring bear head in the tearoom. In the other, she grips Infinity, their dark skin wan and body trembling.

The barrel of the gun is pressed deep into Infinity's side.

Winter gasps, her fingers immediately flexing as if magic might shoot at them faster than a bullet. That gun—revolver?—looks old enough that she could beat it. Winter tries to lunge forward but Evander holds her back. Sanguine smiles. "We're all here now. Please, don't delay."

Something cold pools in my gut, my anger at the way Hector treated his children hardening into a block of ice so hard it burns at the sight of Sanguine treating Infinity this way. All the pain they've felt in the past few hours now coupled with the paralyzing fear of implied violence.

"Sanguine, please put the gun down," Evander urges, placating.

"They've been through enough, you monster!" Winter's voice breaks, tears in her eyes as she meets Infinity's terrified expression. The grin widens and brightens on Sanguine's face. "I'm sure it's not necessary and Infinity will stay with us now that you have them here."

Bracing, Infinity squeezes their eyes shut. "Yes, please." Their voice is soft, lips and lungs barely moving in making the sound.

"Oh, I think I'll keep the gun right where it is, as incentive to make sure no funny business happens," Sanguine responds, blue eyes hard, even as she still gives that Dolly Parton smile. "Read the clue, Auden."

Auden nods before stepping forward and squatting to use the amethyst slab as a hard surface, so that he can properly align his thumb with the print he left in blood as executor. As he does so, I catch Wren's eye—we won't get caught in magical crossfire in the next two minutes, at least. Though the real test, and the last big hurdle to determining the heir, is about to land squarely at our feet.

The magic awakens under Auden's palm, the ink shimmering and twisting into the final clue.

From where I stand, I can see Shadrack's final hint is again five lines. I squeeze my eyes shut as Auden reads, praying to anyone who will listen that whatever it details isn't something only a *real* Blackgate would know.

Auden's voice is calm in the dark night.

> *"Ashes to ashes always meant dust to dust*
> *For us*
> *We burn bright, we burn together*
> *Magic is a shroud of its own*
> *Before the lines, one for all."*

I open my eyes as the silence deepens. There's no immediate outburst. No sighs or whispers. Perhaps we've wrung ourselves dry as we receive yet another riddle for a clue.

Then, as if the last few terrible minutes didn't happen, Hector steps forward, snaps a picture of the clue, and all four Cerises turn for the house.

CHAPTER 29

AUDEN

It seems as if Hegemony Manor is crumbling before our eyes.

When we return to the house from the killing grounds, huddled together, my cousins, the Blackgates, and Infinity, the star tiles of the garden are worn and shapeless, weeds crumbling their corners into the dry earth. Fissures spangle the terrace in the bobbing illumination of our lanterns.

Within, all the fires have gone out again.

The solarium is pitch black and cold, Luna's shroud a lump of shadow.

The cold embers in the fireplaces have been a pattern. The flames snuffed out when Ursula died, which made sense with her magic leaving elsewhere—the plants, the trappings of the outdoor chapel—but as we maneuver our way back to her private apartment, I realize there's more to it than that.

There are fractures in the walls now. Cracks, spiderwebbing out, fine in some places, gaping in others. The more pronounced crevices score the heavy damask wallpaper in large, harrowing gashes.

The magic is giving out without the masters on the grounds.

Maybe this house will crumble around us, burying the lines before we ever have a chance to get out.

Up ahead, Evander throws open the wards and physical locks to Ursula's suite, and announces, "We need to talk."

"I'm not apologizing for Hex," Winter immediately counters, the words bursting from her lips as if she's held them in since the killing grounds. Her gaze finds Infinity's. "We haven't been anything for almost two years. It's not my fault he seems to think otherwise."

Infinity's brow furrows. "Noted."

Meanwhile, Evander strides straight over to the sideboard, pours himself some scotch, and downs it in a single gulp. He squeezes his eyes shut, the back of his hand pressed to his lips, and leans heavily into the sideboard, glass clinking as his weight throws the whole thing off-balance. "We need to talk about me—I need to talk about me. Just. Sit please, now."

My heart kicks in my chest at his broken, near-breathless request.

He's spooked.

This isn't about what just happened at the killing grounds. It isn't about the Cerises, or the relic found, or the final clue. This is something else entirely. My cousin looks like he might jump out a window if he can't release whatever he needs to say.

I immediately take my seat.

"We're here. We're listening," I assure him. "What is it?"

"It's just—" Evander rakes a hand through his hair, eyes snapped shut. "I'm not ready. I'm not prepared to be the patriarch or the High Sorcerer and . . ."

"And that's not true," Winter insists. "Evander, stop. You—"

"No—it is true. It's true." His eyes open and pin on me. "Ursula never planned for me to be the Hegemony heir. She wanted you, Auden."

There's a collective sharp intake of breath but I'm already waving off this nonsense.

"No, she didn't," I scoff, ignoring the spike of hot surprise in my gut. "You've taken the oath, visited her every weekend from school—"

"And had a gap year planned for next year before excelling in the major of her choice." His green eyes flash, his teeth flash, everything about him is like a tripped fire alarm. "Yeah, I know. But I was also there two years ago when she told me that *she wanted you*."

My mouth is suddenly desert dry.

Two years ago was when Evander started his training. At sixteen.

"She never mentioned it to me," I push back. "Not two years ago, not in January when she named me executor, never."

Evander's gaze drops.

"That's because I blackmailed her."

All the air leaves my lungs.

I gape at him, inert, as if swaddled in Ursula's spelled punishment.

"You *what*?" Winter asks in a rasp.

Our cousin pointedly digs his key out from beneath the collar of his tank top. It clinks against the High Sorcerer's ring as he yanks the chain forward, bringing it into the illumination provided by the pendant above our heads.

"I stole this ring from you, Auden. You're the person Ursula chose as her heir."

I won't have him do this. Not now. None of the words he's saying are making sense. "You didn't steal—"

"Yes, I *did*." Evander drops the necklace and the twin pendants thud against his chest. "Shut up, Auden, and listen to me for once in your goddamn life."

The building excuses shrivel on my tongue. I press my lips into a line, cross my arms over my chest, and shut up.

"Thank you," Evander says, jaw muscle flickering as he carefully folds his meaty hands before him, and proceeds to close his eyes and tell the story.

I listen.

"When I turned sixteen, Ursula summoned me to her study. I nearly skipped in and sat down, ready to hear that I had been named oathed heir just as my father had."

Here he pauses, eyes flashing open. He nods at Winter, who has both elbows planted on the tabletop, hands cupped around the sides of her neck as she watches him with unreadable eyes; Infinity in the shadows; the Blackgate girls, who wear dinner-plate eyes and parted lips; and, finally, to me. When he speaks again, he doesn't drop his gaze from mine.

"She knew I expected to be named because I was the oldest, and that's how these things work. Which was exactly why she made it a point to call me in as expected and tell me that I was ill-suited to be her heir because I was too loyal to the Hegemony name."

Recognition cracks across Winter's face like a jag of lightning splitting a tree. We'd all heard it then, when receiving our keys. The same succinct discussion of our loyalties.

Evander—loyal to the Hegemony name.

Winter—loyal to the Hegemony family.

Me—loyal to who the Hegemonys are.

"My loyalty wasn't a good quality in this instance, she said, because the Four Lines expected my faithfulness to be to them, not only to my line." Evander sucks in a steadying breath. "It was her concern that as a candidate, this quality could, under the right conditions, create a myopia within me that may invite a similar reign to Napoleon Cerise."

A flat buzzing blooms in my ears. Static. Confusion.

"Wait," Winter calls out, blanched. "Ursula suggested you would want to *end* the other lines?"

Evander shakes his head. "No, she just said that being a High Sorcerer with choices for an heir, she was being judicious. And given the three of us, Auden and his loyalty to the Hegemony position within the Four Lines made him the best candidate."

My lungs expand, but the air doesn't seem to reach my brain. "What did you tell her to change her mind?"

Evander swallows. Resets.

"I told her that if she didn't make me her oathed heir, I would tell everyone that she executed Marcos Blackgate to cover up what really happened to our parents. Hex was telling the truth. That entire generation was working together to retrieve the master relics and release the lines."

I exhale, stilted. "How do you know this rumor is true?"

For a quiet beat, Evander examines his hands, folded tightly atop the marble. Then, he raises his gaze to mine.

"I watched my father die."

A sob rips out of Winter a moment before her hands fly to her mouth. The Blackgates are smooshed together, nearly clinging to each other in surprise. In my periphery, Infinity silently backs into the nearest wall.

"You what?" I choke.

Evander's whole face is so red it's nearly purple. "I saw them finalize their plan the night before. They were going to retrieve the relics at once and disband them from the High Sorcerer's ring. It was a coordinated act of rebellion—one they miscalculated. Instead of successfully untethering the lines from the master relics and Ursula and all the baggage that comes with this whole unusual, unbreakable family, they died."

Tears prick in Evander's green eyes. Still, he lowers his shoulders and plows on with the unbelievable.

"I told Ursula that I saw my father die. Watched the security wards explode around him, burn his flesh." His hands are shaking now, twined together and trembling. "That I had eavesdropped on their meetings. That I knew it was being led by my father and aunt and uncle, not the other heirs. They were part of it, they had all agreed, but our parents, her children, were doing the dirty work because they thought that was the best thing to do to make things better for all of us going forward. They didn't believe someone should hold so much power. And they suffered for it."

Evander pivots to the Blackgate girls, shrinking in on themselves like dying irises. "I think Ursula knew it; I think she knew exactly what happened but she couldn't let that stand. And she had to punish someone, to avenge their death, to maintain her iron fist, to send a message to the generation of heirs who coordinated this."

"And Hector Cerise handed her Marcos Blackgate on a platter . . ." I finish, quietly.

Evander nods, and my own thought, our own Hegemony edict, echoes in my brain.

All rumors are assumed to be lies until proven true.

"Hector knew if he put forward another name, Ursula would run with it," Evander says, still nodding, as if it'll make the words land hard enough that we won't question them. "And she did."

Winter swipes at the tears that have spilled, fury pinching her features as burnished patches, raw and wet, pebble atop her cheekbones. "Instead of interrogating herself about why an entire generation of heirs would want to dismantle the lines, she shut them up by killing a man before his daughters' eyes—that's what you're saying?"

Evander draws in a shaky breath but rather than saying more, he simply nods.

Winter's shoulders quake as she scrambles to wrap herself in a hug, and falls heavily against her seatback, the whole chair shuddering and tipping for a precarious moment.

"Why is this worth protecting? *Why?* Why are we protecting it?" Her voice breaks and her arms fly out, air quotes wrapped around the next words along with her rage. "This *unusual, unbreakable family* is nothing but an excuse. To chain human beings to a tradition that would rather kill its own than see it questioned."

Winter's looking at me, the one who is loyal to who we are. To the Four Lines. And I don't have a single thing to say. My heart feels hollow as I process what she's arguing, the fury, the truth.

Ursula used her power and position to kill a man who'd watched his friends die. A man who'd had a role identical to his friends who weren't accused. All of them grieving, one of them made scapegoat. All to keep the Four Lines going in the face of the fact that an entire generation gambled and lost trying to rip our *unusual, unbreakable* family apart.

"I met with Ursula."

My head snaps up to the new voice—Infinity.

"What?" Winter asks, hoarsely.

"I'm the one who wanted the Celestial Line to leave the Four Lines. It was my idea. Grandmama went along with it because she knew she didn't have much time left, and wanted to leave me in a happy place. So she set up a meeting for us with Ursula. We went . . . and it did not go well."

Their eyes drop and my stomach does too. "When was this?"

"December. When I was home from school."

I catch my cousins' eyes. Lavinia was right. The threat Ursula meant to address was to how things had always been. Yet another generation straying from tradition.

"I don't know how, I don't know why, but . . . I'm sure Grandmama is dead because of that choice." Infinity covers their face. "I know it."

Winter crosses to them, tugging their hands away from their face and holding them tightly. "It's not your fault. I know you think it is, but it isn't."

"Did you know Luna met with Hector and Marsyas before the meeting?" I ask as gently as possible, feeling like an asshole. "The twins had proof that Hector had a private lunch with two people, and based on his text messages we think it was the two matriarchs."

Infinity allows Winter to wrap a comforting arm around their shoulders now. "We typically travel together, but she came here early. I didn't ask why." Infinity's eyes flash up, wide and sorrowful. "Do you think they were up to something? Together? Wanting to leave the lines or . . . or . . . to assassinate Ursula?"

"We don't know," I answer, honestly. "And given Hector's behavior, we won't be getting any answers from him."

The Blackgates are downcast, their shoulders slumped. No answers from Marsyas, no answers from Luna, no answers from either woman's grandchildren, kept in the dark. And so we are too.

Infinity's head shakes and Winter rubs their forearm. They turn to her, new tears forming. "I'm sorry, I don't know more. If I'd only asked, maybe . . ."

"There's so much all of us should've asked. Don't put this secret on yourself. It was theirs to keep and . . . we have to navigate it together."

There's a long pause, and then Kaysa clears her throat. "Does anyone else have any more secrets to share? If so, I can't take much more so just yell it out, chips on the table." She taps the center of the marble, astride our half-finished plates and utensils, as if gesturing to where our secrets could go, plopped into the open, trying to lighten the mood.

I stare at my hands. My gut can't take much more.

Lavinia bites her lip. Winter and Infinity lean into the wall, silent save for ragged, teary breaths.

Evander holds up a hand.

"There's one more thing. And then we can rest. We're going to need it. But, please, you need to hear this too."

His voice is rough, drained, pleading. I lift my gaze, watching as his head hangs in the blunt hammock of his hands, his brow scrunching violently, and he pulls in yet another deep breath. When Evander speaks, the words come easier now, it seems, the weight of the rest of it out in the open.

"Auden, I lied to you when you asked where I went after we searched the study the night of Ursula's murder."

My lips drop open as I try to read his face for the answer, even as it comes.

I realize in that moment that I can't read him. I don't have any idea what he'll say. This man is like a brother to me, but the past few minutes have put so much distance between the Evander I know and the one who lived the things he's telling me . . . that he's now a stranger, fuzzy and unknown, a blip, a mile away from where I sit.

"I didn't come here to search her rooms first. That came second," he admits.

No one else here knows that this conversation happened between us, but that doesn't matter. It's easy enough to follow. The lie ripped away and the truth exposed with each passing admission.

"The first thing I did when I was alone," Evander says heavily, "was go to the place where I saw my father die. I knew there was a master relic there. He hadn't been successful in completely extracting it before the security wards triggered. I went to the niche where I knew it was, opened it—and found it empty."

My gut roils.

Of course—if Evander saw his father die, he saw him attempt to remove a master.

And we only have one master left.

Lavinia speaks first. "Are you saying there's no Death Line relic? That someone already has it?"

"I don't know. It could've been moved to another location by Ursula. Given how vague our clue is, who knows. All I know is that I didn't find it. And I lied. Again." Evander's gaze meets mine, then skips to Winter across the room. "I'm sorry. I should've told you right away."

Another piece of crucial information saved back, shoved behind two bigger, more painful secrets. Still, I mean it when I say, "I forgive you."

Winter echoes. And then we're left with a vast and stretching silence until Kaysa's subdued voice fills it. "But if we can't find the fourth one, if it doesn't exist . . . we can't leave."

Evander sighs. "Correct."

The horror of that truth ripples around the room.

There's a possibility we can't punish Ursula's murderer. There's a possibility we can't collect all four masters.

There's a possibility that no matter what we do, we're stuck here forever.

"Maybe she never meant for us to complete the tasks," Lavinia says, the blush of her cheeks fading to stone white. "Maybe it was never possible all along."

Infinity goes further. "Maybe it was punishment all along." They lift their head to Winter. "Would she do that?"

"Honestly, now? I don't know."

I don't know either.

Evander reads his watch. "We have twenty hours left to find out."

In the silence that follows, Evander hoists himself up from his seat. Then, without a word, he removes the chain from his neck, flips my hand up to the light, and drops his heir's key and the High Sorcerer's ring into my palm. Both his hands then cup mine, forcing my fingers to close over the metal.

"Wear it, Auden."

I shove it back. "Earn it, Evander."

I fling my hands away, forcing him to hold on to the key he's earned and the ring he wants. Dare him to drop it, toss it, or otherwise discard it.

But he can't.

I knew it.

Evander's big fist closes around the chain and pendants, then he backs away from the table and to the first door on the right—Ursula's bedroom. He unlatches it and steps inside, but before he shuts himself away from us, he says one final thing, lobbed at us with barely any power left in his voice.

"I'm sorry."

CHAPTER 30

RUBY

None of us has any idea what will happen when light comes on this final day—the relic is found, or it isn't, and night comes with a new set of terrors.

We agree to rest, but I don't know how any of us can sleep with these thoughts, scenarios, threats, probabilities piling up in a levee around us, and we're already neck-deep in water.

I'm not a witch, but I'm not safe. Not even remotely close.

If these people who can do magic aren't sure how to get out now, I'm not sure how Wren or I have a shot of survival either.

I've sunk into the corner of the sofa in Ursula's front room, my sister and everyone else all gone to rest until daylight, when all I seem to be able to do is stare at the ceiling until the tiles blur. Maybe if I do finally shut my eyes, I'll wake, all of it a bad dream, staining my thoughts and soaking my sheets with sweat.

I force my eyes closed—and that's exactly when the scent of mint and lavender invades my presence along with a steady voice. "Take a walk with me?"

Skin, warm and clean, cradles my elbow—not a dream, then.

There's Auden, apparently fresh from the shower with wet hair and scrubbed skin and eyes too bright for the hour. My heart catches in my chest, my cheeks go hot, and I swear he must be watching them pink in real time because his lips kick up.

"I'll take that as a yes."

We haven't talked about how I claimed his hand on our way to the killing grounds. And yet now, his fingers slip into mine. Perhaps there's something in the past I'm not reading in *their* shared, prickly history. Still, this is *my* present. My stomach flips, unsure of what happened between my choice to reach out and now. Unsure of the distance between where we were upon the old ghosts of our "reintroduction" and now.

He's healed me.

Lied for me.

Weathered a knife attack with me.

Found relics with me.

And now, we've built to this. Whomever we were before is not who we are now, navigating this space and time, the cold, dark hour before the dawn of the day when we must complete Ursula's tasks or accept that forever for us is within these grounds, within these crumbling walls.

Auden winds us down the hall and to the right, down another hall. And maybe it's the movement, but my brain finally unsticks and jogs up to meet us, words forming on my tongue as I realize he's taking me deeper into Ursula's maze of rooms.

"Are you planning to show me a way out of this mess? A secret portal, perhaps? Because, if so, that probably would best be shared with the group."

He arches a brow toward his soft brown hair, shiny and curling at the ends. "And shared much earlier. But no. What I'm about to share is just for you, Lavinia Blackgate."

I force myself to smile at the name. "What—"

His hand on the small of my back ends my question. Auden maneuvers us left, and through a door that had been previously closed.

The walls in here are the same muted burgundy of a dried rose petal, cracks running like marble veins beneath the plaster as gas sconces reflect moodily off its dark complexion. Chaise lounges in various gilded configurations run a rough rectangle around the room, a large, handwoven rug at the center, atop the plush carpeting. It smells of ink, flame, and steeped Earl Grey.

And there, in stacks and baskets along the floor, are dozens— hundreds—of paperback mysteries, overflowing like bushels of apples in autumn. I recognize at least a dozen titles from my bookseller life in the stacks at Agatha's.

"You . . . were going to share this room with me?" I ask, a little sheepish and very confused.

My thoughts don't clear as Auden leaves my side to retrieve something from a small table by the door. A jar . . . of peanut butter? Two silver spoons peek out over the top like bunny ears.

"The peanut butter. I find it to be restorative late at night." He smirks, but gestures to our surroundings and meets me in the middle of the rug. "Though you're welcome to share the room too. It's technically the sewing room, but I'm fairly certain Ursula never actually sewed a day in her life. My best educated guess is she hid away in here with her tea and read paperbacks when no one was looking."

This woman, who orchestrated the death of Marcos Blackgate out of grief for her children's choices, who put us in the impossible position we're in now, who was so very powerful . . . and yet still human. With stories, a warm mug, and a need to get away from it all.

A knot of anguish balls in my throat.

I accept a spoon, sit on the floor, back to a chaise, and inspect one of the paperbacks on top of the nearest pile—Agatha Christie's *And Then There Were None*.

I hope that's not the way our story ends tomorrow—all dead, save the killer.

Auden joins me on the floor, unscrews the cap, rips off the safety seal, and offers me the first glorious spoonful of creamy, perfectly smooth peanut butter.

I blink at him. Falling back into my role of Lavinia, spelled to forget. "Did we—is this something we've done before?"

A smile plays at his mouth. It's a good mouth. Hard to deny no matter who you are. "No, I didn't learn the beauty of eating peanut butter straight from the jar until boarding school."

With that, Auden serves himself his own heaping spoonful. We're quiet for a few minutes. His shoulder nudges mine, the skin warm and more inviting than I'd like to admit for how stressful this night has been. How can this feel so comfortable when the walls are literally crumbling around us?

It occurs to me that the lavender and mint I'm smelling must be the shampoo his grandmother used, yet Auden wears it like his own skin, his fine features, his strong body, and poetic mind.

Mostly to stop thinking about his nearness, I muse, "I don't know how we're supposed to sleep. I don't think I can."

Auden presses a thumb to his full bottom lip, and I find a frayed thread in the chaise across from us to accept all of my scattered attention so I don't stare at his mouth. "What is the thing you're worried most about?"

The uncertainty. What Hector will do. What Marsyas has planned.

Being found out as imposters.

Losing my sister.

Losing you.

Throat bobbing, I ask him a question instead. "How do you feel about what Evander had to say?"

"The lies?"

"Yes."

Everything that's come to light lines up in my mind, in neat little rows among the disaster of this weekend.

His parents' deaths. Marcos Blackgate's role. Hector's deception, his counterparts' silence. Ursula's punishment. Evander's blackmail. Infinity's meeting. Ada's title. Hex holding a candle for Winter. Winter's feelings for someone else—who is looking more and more like Infinity. Infinity, who smelled of Winter's perfume first thing this morning.

The remaining hidden secrets belong to Auden, my sister, and me.

I wonder if this is apparent to him too. That we're the only ones left on the table with our cards unturned.

Auden brushes the curling ends of his wet hair off his face. His elbows land on his knees, bare in yet another pair of athletic shorts, the points of them slotting perfectly into the little dips where his quads attach to the tops of his knees. It's so distracting that if anything is going to calm my mind enough to induce sleep, it might be the surprises he's been hiding in plain sight.

"Everyone lies, Lavinia, even if they call them secrets instead."

His eyelashes brush his cheeks as he responds. So many of the mystery books I've read, so many of the ones in this room, posit that a person is lying if they look away.

Feeling brave, and perhaps a bit intoxicated about the nearness of Auden in a private room with our terrible reality pressing in and coming closer by the minute, I reach out and crook a finger beneath his chin.

I tilt his face up. And hope that by asking him, he won't ask me. Honestly, as our secrets scratch the surface, I don't know if I can hold mine back anymore.

My secret is a lie, and the lie is a secret.

It may not have started as mine, but it is now, and it might be mine to my grave.

"Is yours a secret or a lie, Auden?"

He watches me, his blue-brown eyes sparkling even in the dim, pupils blown wide. This time, he doesn't look away.

"Depends on your point of view."

Suddenly, he's so close that I feel his breath on my cheek, warm and sweet. Now I'm the one compelled to look away, overwhelmed by his nearness.

I dip my spoon into the peanut butter again. This bite sticks to the roof of my mouth as much as my bones, but Auden doesn't hurry me into more tit for tat. He just sits there, calmly watching the fire crackle in yet another white-marble hearth, his skin still touching mine at the shoulder and now at the place where my cross-legged stance meets the swell of his calf.

After a moment, I make up my mind, gut clenching. My gaze firmly set on the flames, I say, "You aren't going to ask me if I have a secret? A lie?"

"No."

My heart stutters. "Why?"

To my surprise, Auden laughs. Low and soft. "Lies and secrets, that's how the Four Lines have survived. It's how we'll keep surviving if we get past this. As much as they hurt and destroy, at their heart many lies, and certainly secrets, are held close to keep a person and those they love safe."

Auden screws the lid back on the peanut butter, and when he balances his spoon atop it, I add mine to form a little *X*. When I've got it set and pull back, I'm surprised when he softly snatches my hand for himself.

Again. Purposefully.

He turns toward me, though his attention is on our fingers, laced. Unquestionably, two made one. He's become very good at avoiding my bunny bracelets.

Somehow, what he says next feels even more intimate.

"I'll keep you safe, Lavinia."

Auden looks to me then, with those beautiful eyes, the refined features, the curling wet hair, and my throat catches. I swear he's closer than before. His breath warming my cheeks.

When I'd first met Auden, I thought his smile was dangerous— that he was the kind of boy who'd wreck you.

But I was wrong.

He's the one who is already crashed and smoldering.

Scar tissue and burn marks from losing his parents, his innocence. Now, his grandmother is gone, his sense of community, family, order.

I'm not the one who can give any of it back.

But I'm the one who's here.

Auden's hands are in my hair, as warm and wonderful as the rest of him. Up close, those eyes are a starburst, dark lashes crowding round, his lips pink on that very nice mouth. One thumb grazes the apple of my cheek.

His lashes flutter, my eyes fall closed, and Auden Hegemony kisses me.

It's tentative and sweet. He tastes of mint and, yes, peanut butter, but it's the lavender in his hair and on his skin that seeps into me as I touch his neck, the fine ridge of a clavicle, biceps and forearms and a back made from hard work and time on the lacrosse pitch.

With each new breath, the hesitation evaporates.

For Auden. For me.

His mouth presses hard, more insistent. One of his hands cups the back of my head, the other bracing beside me, on the expensive weave of his grandmother's rug. The peanut butter jar tips and rolls, the spoons skidding away under one of the chaises, and I laugh a little against his lips, but he doesn't stop kissing me.

He doesn't stop until much later, until we peel apart, gasping for air in a room now overly warm. Heat in our blood, flames in the hearth. Still, even now, Auden holds me as if I might disappear, though I'm flush to his side, temples to ankles.

I'm not my sister—I love to write, but I don't have words for what it's like kissing a boy who thinks I'm so much more than I am. And so, instead of words, I press my lips to his cheek.

In answer, when I pull away, Auden's thumb traces my swollen bottom lip, the divot of the dimple I have on one side. "Despite the way the rest of this turned out, I'm glad you came back, Lavinia."

For a moment—until he says the name that doesn't belong to me—I think I could be Lavinia.

I could be her and we could share memories, and he could truly love me.

He's glad for the presence of the girl he thinks I am.

And I don't know what it says about me, but that feeling that hasn't been earned by the person I am still wraps me up, tight and warm. Safe.

I tuck my head against the side of his chest and whisper, "Me too."

Auden's fingers in the ends of my hair, his strong arm curled around my shoulders, the soft rhythm of his heart give me refuge and I fall into a deep, beautiful sleep.

CHAPTER 31

AUDEN

It's a scream that wakes me.

I push up on one elbow, my other arm buried beneath Lavinia, her hair unfurling like spilled ink over my skin, pale in the gray-blue of the new morning and curtained windows.

I'm gasping as if I've been underwater, and though I haven't wedged myself free, Lavinia stirs at the loss of my body completely and totally next to hers. I blink at the sight of her, and there's the tiniest of thoughts in the back of my head that perhaps this is a dream. Lavinia Blackgate, here with me, like this.

Then it comes again.

Muffled. Distinct. Anguished. Different from last night's, but still definitely a scream.

Lavinia's entire form goes rigid now, her eyes springing open. Panic washes across her beautiful, firelit features and she gets to her elbows, releasing me.

"Was that—"

She's cut off by a slam; running footsteps on carpet.

We untangle and rush for the door. Wrenching it open, the sound of people on the move floods in, full force—jostling and snippets of exclamations, and bodies plunging forward in a frantic rhythm.

I curse under my breath, and grab Lavinia's hand.

We burst down the hall and into the sitting room. It's empty, and the door to Ursula's suite is ajar, the ghost of footsteps down the lush carpet.

Another scream. Worse than before somehow. Like it's in stereo, doubling over itself, the pain having nowhere else to go.

Even in the hall there's a distance to it. Not in the house, then. Outside.

We race through to the grand staircase, thundering down to the second-floor landing. The sound here is a jumble of voices, knotted together at a fever pitch, humming from the back of the house.

The terrace, beyond.

Lavinia and I careen into the solarium, whipping into the morning bar cart, pastry crumbs and empty coffee carafes skittering sideways, the wheels moaning aside. The wide back doors are flung open; no one on the terrace, hurried steps on the stairs.

That redoubled cry is now a sob, low and heavy.

We hit the terrace and go straight for the iron railing. The one that framed Ursula for her last welcome to Hegemony Manor. I cuff the metal and gape over the side, Lavinia gasping beside me.

Down below, Evander and Infinity follow Winter in a feverish sprint on the crumbling garden tiles. The destination: Hex and Ada, in a shaking, keening tangle of sleep clothes and anguish.

One final wail comes, from Ada, her whole heart in it as she shouts at the static, stunning sight played out before them against the placid gurgling of the garden fountain.

There, wrapped in iridescent emerald, frozen like an ice sculpture in pure green Elemental magic, is Kaysa Blackgate.

Dead at her feet, Hector and Sanguine Cerise.

PART FOUR

THE TRUTH

CHAPTER 32

RUBY

At first, I don't understand what I'm seeing. It's like a Renaissance painting, and there's too much going on all at once to comprehend at a glance.

Wren, wrapped in shiny, solid air. She's partially twisted, as if she was trying to bolt when Ursula's spell registered what she'd done and caught her in a blinding flash and immediate stillness.

Hector and Sanguine are on the ground a body length away. They lie in a collective victim's shroud, blood like stained glass seeping out from under them, saturating the terra-cotta star-shaped tiles to wet, shiny black.

Hex and Ada are crumpled together, as pinned to the sight as they are to each other's arms. Distantly, I wish I could hold Wren like that as my mind muddles through the reality of this. Instead, it's Auden on the other end of my grip as I clamp down with all my fear at what this means.

What this looks like.

It *looks* like Wren killed them and was caught by Ursula's spell.

All impossible, except it's right there.

"Breathe" is all Auden says as he leads me away from the railing and to the stairs.

I realize then that I'm not actually drawing in air, or blinking, my vision going blurry through sudden tears. The muscles in my legs fire reluctantly, stuttering, jerky movements carrying me down to garden level only with the direction and support of Auden's steady hand.

This close, the method of murder is obvious.

Unlike with Luna, we can see it all. Hector's throat is slit vertically, from the well between his clavicles all the way through the palate, and around the corner of his chin to his lips, fish-mouthed and gaping, his tongue and windpipe no longer there.

Sanguine is harder to parse, given that she lies behind him, but her head has lolled away awkwardly, and it's easy to imagine her wounds are the same. Thick, viscous blood stains her beautiful face from the bridge of her nose down to the sharp curve of her chin, as if she feasted on a heart and fell asleep satisfied.

Death magic.

Blackgate magic.

The weight of attention pulls me away from the stunning sight. I lift my head to accusations bare on the twins' faces. Shades of the same painted on the faces of Evander, Infinity, Winter. I fear what I might see in Auden's expression.

The summer air goes down ice cold as I try to draw in enough breath to defend Wren.

"She wouldn't. She couldn't. We're not—" I fumble.

But there's no way to explain what's before me without sharing a secret that might make things a hundred times worse.

No, I can't say that now.

The truth of my predicament makes the panic rise faster in my gut. I tighten my grip on Auden, a lifeline in this madness that is the only thing keeping me from sinking in this terrible moment, but it won't save me. I know that.

Hex is flush with anger, his cheeks as warmly red as his tone is frigid. "It very much looks like she did. Do you see their faces?" Bald anguish swells in every word. "God, look at them! Just look! Look what *she* did to them!"

I *am* looking. I'm just not understanding.

There is no one here who can do this.

Except a Blackgate.

My throat is dry, though my words sound as if they've been pulled from a soggy river bottom. "She didn't do this—I didn't do this . . ."

"Look in her hands," Ada charges in a wail, her whole body taut as a bow. When I met Ada, I thought she was the epitome of soft and feminine. Now, every sharp point of hers is aimed at me. "What does that look like to you?"

I didn't notice it before.

Wren is turning to run, but only her feet look prepared for a mad dash because her hands are cupped together. Not clasped, but nearly touching, as if she was trying to pass something from one to the other. Squatting down and peering up, the drip of a silver chain dangles from her left hand, the fingers above it opening. Even with inches of magical static between her palm and the rest of us on the outside, it's clear what it is.

"The Elemental master?" Evander asks. "It should be in the study safe—"

"Well, it's *not*!" Ada shouts. "The Blood master is in my papa's right hand."

Ada's pin-straight body collapses into the strength of her brother's at the drop of "my papa's," her blue eyes waves in a hurricane. "She was collecting all of the relics so that when the Death master was found, she would have control of all four and claim the title of High Sorcerer."

That's not how it would work. She'd need Ursula's ring, I think dully. But it doesn't matter. Anything I say will only make it worse.

Hex rubs Ada's back as she heaves in huge gulps of air. Infinity stares at the bodies, ramrod straight. Winter wraps herself in her own strong arms like she did when her grandmother died, her whole body shaking. Auden's breathing is shallow, his grip turning cold around mine. Evander is deathly still.

They wait for me as I stumble for something acceptable to say and fail.

"What? No. No, she wouldn't. She'd never . . ."

"She *did*." Hex looms closer, his sister holding tight. "There's no other explanation. Your sister murdered my parents in cold blood when they fought back. And the spell had enough juice left to trap her before she could take the Blood relic."

The hurt in Hex's voice slices through my heart. We'd just witnessed his parents' cruelty and the lengths they'd go regarding their children, their peers, to get what they want. But his parents were still his parents.

And now they're gone.

It means nothing that I know that pain intimately, dulls nothing. It doesn't take away from what they believe my sister has done.

Auden is still cradling my hand, but I'm the one with all the grip, his softening as reality sets in. I'm the one clinging. I wonder how long he'll let me.

Wren's terrified face is the whole of my vision.

I have to fight for her. I can't rely on denial. I need a defense.

"No, look, she's turning away from them. If she wanted the Blood relic, she would be reaching down to get it—"

"Down from where they fell after she *killed* them?" Hex seethes. *Killed*.

The metallic stench of blood coats the back of my throat.

"Or," Ada argues, eyes narrowing, "she finally did something so heinous that it triggered Ursula's spell, she felt the magic rising, and bolted, knowing she was finally caught, hours after murdering Luna."

"No, no, she would never—"

"How do you *know*?" Hex demands. "Were you with her the whole time?"

"I—we were asleep."

Auden and me. Not Wren and me.

But Hex reads that "we" as sisters, together.

"No, *you* were asleep." Hex's features sharpen to a knifepoint. He's still looming, his entire body tilted toward mine, his shadow a shroud of its own. "Or so you say—how do we know you weren't here with her when this happened? Just like a Blackgate to sleep tight after watching two people die."

"Or by producing the spell that killed them," Ada spits, her blond hair wild, a lion's mane, as she bares her teeth. "Did you do it, Lavinia? Did you do it and let your sister take the fall?"

"No. No—"

"The spell doesn't work like that," Infinity cuts in, to my surprise and relief. "But it *did* work. Which means it wasn't Kaysa who killed them, or it would have frozen her before she stole the master. Both would have activated the spell. They're equal offenses."

"Stealing a master and killing our parents are not equal!" Ada explodes, shouting at the sky. The mountains echo back her anguish.

Auden signals with the hand that isn't my anchor, placating and pleading. "And we don't know that it works like that. If Kaysa used her magic against them and stole the master in sequence, it's possible she performed both offenses before Ursula's spell kicked in. It's unclear."

I should be offended that he's not on my side, that he thinks my sister could and would do such a thing. But he's trying to be logical, to think things through. Buying time like he did with the magic on his driveway, making space between passionate response and reason.

But she can't have killed him.

My panicked brain grasps for answers. Nothing crystallizes in my mind but more questions.

Why does Wren have the Elemental master? The Blood master would make more sense in this situation where absolutely everything is upside down.

I grip Auden's hand harder, but it's like clutching a piece of ice, as if it's disappearing with each passing moment. He's slipping through my fingertips.

"No, no, please, you have this all wrong." My stupid accent wobbles. A sob rises in my chest and wheezes into this impossible morning. "We want nothing to do with the relics, with the title, with power. We just want to go home."

Though I've insisted this before, now it's the wrong thing to say.

Hex advances with intent and rage now, barely restrained violence in the cut of his shoulders, his stride, the sneer carved on his trembling mouth. Ada isn't an anchor, weighing him down, but a twin engine, dangerous and cutting beside him. "You know who can't go home? Our parents!"

His anguish cracks something in Infinity, who turns to me too,

292 ♦ SARAH HENNING

their previous defense of my sister vanishing as a new wave of heart-break crashes over their elegant features. "My grandmama."

Winter places a hand on Infinity's elbow, her whole face a shadow, stern as stone as her blue eyes flicker like flame. "Ursula. And the goddamn driver."

None of them can go home.

My heart stops beating. I'm sure of it. Panic icing it out, suspending it the same way Wren is held, still and stoic. The blood within me slows to a standstill, my lungs clench like a fist. A surge of numbness spreads up my legs. I tilt and vaguely realize I might pass out.

And then . . . Auden's grip returns, and his fingers encircle my own.

He's there. He's here.

"Perhaps it's possible to break the spell?" Auden's voice is measured and calm, gentle with its request. "We could question Kaysa about what happened. A day from now, when the spell would lift, is too late. We need to know what happened now."

God. Yes. "A truth spell, if we have to." My voice is a desperate rasp. "She'll submit."

The twins take another collective lunging step forward. This time, its Ada's anguish cracking like a whip in the air. "We don't need a fucking truth spell! We can all plainly see what happened here!"

"I know what it looks like, but we won't truly know *with certainty* what happened unless we ask her. You said it yourself that your father would do anything to be High Sorcerer; what if he tried to kill her and it was self-defense?" I angle at Infinity, but they shirk away. I don't blame them, wild desperation is the worst kind. "We'll figure this out. It can't be what it looks like. We'll find out what really happened—"

"If we free her, we can punish her," Ada cuts me off, her fury coiling into serpentine coolness.

My frozen heart seizes.

Then the threat gets worse.

"I bet I could execute her through Ursula's magical barrier," Hex announces, venom in every word as he stares at Wren like she truly is an ice sculpture and if he strikes in just the right place, she'll shatter into a million pieces that he'll crunch under his feet. "I have all day to figure out how."

Tears cloud my eyes now, my dry throat catching as I scream at the pair of them. "You will not kill my sister!"

Hex rounds on me, his large, athletic body suddenly part of this equation. Marsyas's file flashes in my mind—a football linebacker. He has plenty of practice plowing humans much larger than me into the ground. "I will *personally* kill your sister if she murdered my parents! She took them from us, and I will not hesitate to take her from you in return, Lavinia."

And suddenly I see another path, dark and dangerous but the only option to shift us away. Treacherous as it is, I can't have Hex thinking of murdering my sister for one more moment. The longer that idea sits with him, the more likely it is to happen.

"Submit me to a truth spell! Hex, Ada, you do it—ask me whatever the hell you want. As many questions as you want. Please."

Ada bares her teeth—that last word was a mistake.

"That's a waste of time," Ada growls.

Evander steps forward, hands waving like a white flag. "No, no, we need answers. I'll do it."

Hex scoffs. "*Your* test again? Obviously, because Kaysa passed your stupid fireball yesterday, it's no good."

Evander rakes a hand through his short dark hair. "Then you do it. Lavinia is willing. Yes, this looks like Death Line magic. But Kaysa also has *my* relic in her hands, and that does not compute to me. I need to know where she got it, and how she managed to kill them too. And Hector is holding the Blood relic. What was happening here?" He turns to Infinity. "Do you know where the Celestial master is?"

They don't hesitate. "In my suite's safe."

"What do you want to bet it's actually missing?" Ada quirks a delicate brow. "Look at that shape against the outline of her tights. It could definitely be a vial."

It's more likely the butter knife I foisted upon her for self-defense. But, honestly, given the evidence happening here, all I know is that Wren didn't kill Hector and Sanguine. The rest? . . . I truly have no clue what my sister was doing, thinking, trying to achieve.

Her impulsivity is on display. Again. And I'm left as her only defense.

My heart heaves.

God, Wren.

"We should check for it, after we do the truth spell," Evander says. "Auden, bring Lavinia to me."

"No—no. I'll do it." Hex jumps into motion. "We can't have another failure."

Evander scowls. "If you're up to it."

"Of course I'm up to it," Hex snaps. His ring already removed from his finger, Hex twists the blade so that it shines like a rose thorn, short and sharp. He's wearing a white T-shirt with his track-suit pants, tiger-stripe tattoos exposed. "Lavinia, your palm."

"Three questions," Auden says, directing me toward Hex.

"She said as many as I want."

"We both know truth spells are better with a concentrated effort," Auden answers. "Too broad or too many answers and the results aren't reliable. No matter what line of magic is doing the spell. Five would be more than enough."

Hex bares his teeth. "Six."

Auden glances at me. "Fine."

Then, with a small squeeze, he lets go of my hand.

Stepping forward, I focus on Wren, on her panicked expression, the startled wideness to her eyes. My sister, who treats every inter-action like a moment on stage, something not totally real and with consequences finally catching up to her as she literally tried to run away.

You aren't the only capable one, I remember her saying. *I got us into this, I can get us out.*

She tried. I feel in my bones that's what this is. And now I'm the one who has to make sure she can walk away.

I reveal my palm.

Ada, Winter, Evander, Infinity, and Auden crowd in around the pair of us. Wren is my guidepost in the sliver of space between Hex and Auden.

Hex slices a two-inch gash down the second tattoo from his elbow, the seam of skin beading crimson. He drags it across my palm, leaving a smeared stain fresh and wet. Then, cupping the underside of my hand in his own palm, Hex runs the knifepoint of his ring down the line in my palm that arcs between the thumb and forefinger.

The life line, my brain supplies.

My blood wells up, seeps into the plane of his, and a sudden, fuzzy warmth flushes throughout my whole body.

It's as if every drop in my veins has been lit like crude oil atop saltwater, burning and burning despite the inhospitable environment. I can't move, I can't blink, all energy in my body seems to pool on my tongue. I instantly know it will move upon its own volition through the next six questions.

And when Hex asks the first question, panic sets in as, too late, I remember something specific about Blood Line truth spells.

"Lavinia, what happened to Hector and Sanguine Cerise?"

They start every open-ended question with a name. Because it's a measure of the truth.

But it's not with me.

Still, there's no stopping the magic, and my mouth forms words I don't recognize until they tumble into the crisp air of a mountain morning. "I don't know."

The blood in my palm curdles to ash.

Hex's expression goes cold. Ada gasps. The Hegemonys are still. Infinity gnaws a thumbnail.

The types of results weren't explained in detail, but they don't need to be. I answered truthfully, but because my name is not Lavinia, I failed the first question.

I want to draw myself out. To wipe away the ashen blood and go another route, any other route.

But I can't pull away. I'm committed to this spell, under its influence until it's finished.

Hex asks his second question. "Lavinia, where were you when your sister killed the Cerises?"

"Nowhere."

It's the truth—because she didn't murder them. She couldn't have. Even an answer of "in the sewing room with Auden, asleep" would've been a lie.

She did not kill them. She could not kill them. Because we're not Death witches.

I will the blood to run crimson, to omit the first part of the question and stick to the truth. Instead, shivers from the seam in my hand and mounds into more black, the ash duplicating, featherlight in my palm.

Fuck.

Hex's fingers flex around my knuckles, where he cups my palm.

"Lavinia, are you, your sister, or your grandmother responsible for killing Luna?"

It's a yes-or-no question rather than an open-ended one.

Yet my "no" results in ashes. I'm not Lavinia. That lie continues to skew the results. And it will, as long as it's part of the question.

Infinity sinks to a squat, head buried against the tops of their knees and bracketed by their arms. Winter places a soft palm on their shoulders as they begin to quake.

I'm truly panicking now.

My mind races in a way my body can't, plunging through the lines of this deadly maze, looking for a way out, daylight, any way to stop this. I want to yell that I'm not lying, that I never would've hurt Luna, that my sister wouldn't have. But I can only stand here, braced for the next question.

"Lavinia, are you, your sister, or your grandmother responsible for killing Ursula?"

"No."

The ashes mound higher, now the size of a juicy black plum, the color of sleep and full to bursting in my palm.

Auden shifts, his shoulders giving me more of a view of Wren's helpless form. Winter continues to comfort Infinity. Evander's whole presence is solid, hard, unforgiving on my right side.

"Lavinia, what are your instructions from Marsyas in regard to obtaining all four master relics?"

"I wasn't instructed to do so."

The ashes tower now, threatening to overtake my hand, larger than both my fists combined. Around me, everything has gone still.

One final question.

"Lavinia, why are you lying to us?"

Tears escape my unblinking eyes now, rolling down my cheeks as I answer in an unerring, unfeeling voice.

"I'm not lying."

The ashes grow so tall they spill over. Rather than falling to the ground, they cling to my wrist, slide down the back of my hand, stopping where Hex's skin meets mine.

I'm stained black. Guilty.

Hex releases my hand, and I hold it there, proof of my misdeeds obsidian in the shiplap light, the roof line of Hegemony Manor painted with the white light of this new day.

The final day we needed to survive.

The day they know we lied.

My voice comes back to me, my own.

"No, please. *No.* There's been a misunderstanding." I round on Auden. "Give me a different one. Give me yours. I—please, I need another chance."

Evander steps in front of Auden, blocking him from my pleas. "You don't get another chance. Don't ask him. Don't ask me. Don't ask any of us, Lavinia."

His words are a door slammed in my face. Every single one of them is closed off and distant. I nearly feel as if I'm under Ursula's statue spell, and yet I'm alive and blinking. Begging.

"I'll do it." At first I don't know what Winter means, but then she flexes her fingers. "It's worth imprisoning her while we find the final master."

"Imprison her?" Ada bares her teeth, and cuffs Winter's shoulder. "We should just *punish* her outright. Kaysa too. They killed Ursula. Luna. Our parents. Clear as day. We make them pay penance, then we find that relic and get out of here."

I throw my hands up, and my words come out cracked and broken, weak and uneven. "Wait, no, please. Please, I can explain!"

"We don't want an explanation for your lies," Hex snaps. "You lied, your sister lied, and you're fucking murderers. Part of some sort of Death Line initiation. Killing people for fun, making relics out of their bones? That sounds about right."

This is it. I've made it to the last resort. I have everything to lose now and nothing to gain except the slimmest hope of survival. Wren's words from our first night echo in my mind. No longer out of the question.

So we'll just tell them.

I squeeze my eyes closed and shout the truth at the top of my lungs.

"We *are* liars!"

As the echo dies to no response, my eyes flash open.

"We *are*. That's the truth."

I'm pleading, all my panic and fear and shame flooding forth. I grasp for Auden's attention and sympathy and find it blank in the shadow of Evander's bulky frame. I sink to my knees before them. Draw in a deep breath. When I speak, my voice is a fraying rasp.

"*We are liars.* But we aren't lying about what you think we're lying about."

The faces before me are closed off. Dead.

Hex scoffs first.

"Oh, give me a break." Every inch of him is mean and uninterested in any word coming out of my mouth. "There is literally nothing you can say that I would believe with my parents under that shroud, dead of Death magic—"

"We're not the Blackgate girls! We're imposters!"

Chapter 33

AUDEN

"What?" A gasp barely hisses out of my lips, entirely engulfed by Evander's fierce, *"Excuse me?"*

The girl I'd known as Lavinia draws in a stiff breath, her whole body shivering on the inhale.

"I'm not Lavinia Blackgate, and she's not Kaysa Blackgate."

I stare as she begs us to understand, voice brimming with pleading, hope—and bald shame. There's not a trace of that mildly British accent we've come to know—that I've come to very much like—the past two days.

"We're not Blackgates at all. Not even witches."

There's a long beat of silence.

I hear her words, her new voice, but I'm searching her face for signs that it can't be true. The dark hair, the dark eyes—fathomlessly deep and sparkling with tears. The delicate swoop of her nose, the pinking of her cheeks, and the swift way she initiates a smile. The dimple that appears like a shooting star. It's all there.

I took the suggestion and saw exactly what I'd wanted the moment she arrived.

I never second-guessed. Not about this.

"Give me a break." Winter skewers her with a certain expression of righteous disdain honed and perfected as tennis team captain, head prefect, Hegemony. Human beings want to be in her good graces—it's a survival technique as much as it is the path of least resistance. Winter Hegemony is never someone you want to disappoint. "This isn't a soap opera. You weren't switched at birth."

The girl who is not Lavinia presses the heels of her hands into her eyes. When they come away, her right one is smudged with the ashen proof of her lies.

"My name is Ruby—that's why I failed the test just now. Every truth I told registered as a lie because I was addressed as Lavinia."

Her tone is calm, direct, and shaking with fear. She gestures with a shaking, ash-stained hand at the girl encased in Ursula's magic.

"This is Wren. We're a pair of local sisters that Marsyas recruited to pretend to be her granddaughters for this party. She paid us—two thousand up front, and she promised another two thousand afterward—for what we thought was four hours of pretending to be Lavinia and Kaysa. It . . . obviously turned into more than that."

Evander sighs heavily. We would have learned this yesterday if he'd used Kaysa's name in his truth spell. Or if either girl had felt they could trust us enough to tell us.

Hex is so indignant with rage that his movements are unmoored, even as he stays rooted to the ground before her—Ruby. His hands flex, the point of his Cerise family ring still exposed and winking. He's absorbed her blood, which means, at least temporarily, he has control of her if he wants it.

"Are you kidding me?"

"No! Check my room. Look in our purses. It's all right there—our driver's licenses and debit cards have our real names on them."

"You know what? I'm going to do that," Winter announces. Then she grabs Infinity's hand. "And you're going to come with me and check for your master."

They leave, up the stairs to the terrace without so much as a look back.

"Wait." Hex fixes Ruby with a sneer. "So let me get this straight. You were paid a couple thousand dollars to pretend to be witches at a dinner party?"

Ruby's beautiful face is now mottled with bloody ash and tears, her despair and desperation as palpable as the ley line beneath our feet. I don't know how anyone here can question this story. Every ounce of it is true. My gut twists tighter with each word.

I believe it. I believe her. And it fucking sucks.

"We didn't know Lavinia and Kaysa were witches—that any of you were!" Her fear-streaked gaze ping-pongs between our faces, but her round of pleading expressions starts with me and ends with me. "We had no idea. *None.* We were instructed to make small talk, deflect any direct questions we couldn't answer, and stay close to Marsyas with our fake accents on as tightly as possible. That's it."

She nods to the trashed table and my grandmother's earthen shroud.

"And then Ursula keeled over, Marsyas disappeared, and magic— *literal magic*—happened right in front of our faces." She shakes her head, brows crashing together. "And, and—so you know— Marsyas obtained the driver's keys from him *before* we walked into the party. They took forever and we thought she was being weirdly territorial about them, but she probably killed him right there with magic while we were gawking at the mansion."

Evander sounds like I'd imagine Horace the bear did after taking the first of the three bullets it took to kill him, all bite and bile. "All that and you didn't think to say anything? You had ample time to tell us."

"We were shocked—*stunned.* What the hell could we have said that would've made a difference?"

Evander scoffs. "The so-called truth you're telling us now."

Ruby laughs, dark eyes shining beyond the mess of tears, smudge of ashen blood, and the flood of blush in her cheeks. "You're telling me that any of you were in the frame of mind to *accept* that two non-magical people had not only gained entry to what seems to be the most exclusive witch event of the year, but that we'd also seen your leader murdered in cold blood? That we witnessed a potential shake-up in the balance of secret Four Lines witch power? You guys would've been *okay* with our being here for any of that?"

A glacier of heaviness settles in my gut. She's right.

Hex laughs back, cruel. Like the true visage of his father exposed in this game. "I'm still stuck on the fact that you took money to impersonate people at a dinner party. Like, who does that?"

"People who need the money!"

"But a couple grand?"

"We need it!" Ruby insists. She runs her hands through her hair now, grimy ash smearing on her temples and the soft curve of her neck as she finishes one exasperated swoop. "A couple grand is a lot of money to *normal* people. Not everyone can afford boarding school or has the generational wealth for a sixteen-bathroom manor on ten thousand acres in one of the most expensive states in this whole damn country!"

"She's telling the truth."

Winter's voice cuts across the dead grass and cracked tiles. Two wristlets dangle from her arm, and she's holding a wallet in each hand. "Ruby Jourdain, seventeen, of Grand Lake; Wren Jourdain, sixteen, of Grand Lake."

Beside her, Infinity is empty-handed. For a moment, everyone's eyes skip to Wren's dress pocket. Ruby scrunches her eyes shut and draws in a thin breath, steadying herself—she didn't know what her sister was up to. She truly didn't.

Winter passes the wallets around. "Do you have correspondence with Marsyas?"

She swallows, relief in the set of her shoulders. "Yeah. Including a file she sent us to study on all of you." Ruby produces a phone. "Here."

"Open it," Winter orders, as I'm stunned enough to ask, "She sent you a file?"

Ruby addresses me but she's looking down and away—embarrassed, then, not lying.

"Yes, with pictures and basics—family, hobbies, interests. It didn't say anything about the fact that you were witches." Ruby unlocks the phone, and this time Winter accepts it. "We googled you but couldn't find any information online, so what you see there is exactly what we knew before we walked in."

"Ursula keeps—kept—all High Families and initiated witches completely scrubbed from the web." I don't know why I'm explaining this, but it seems like a bookend to this corresponding thought. One truth met with another.

Winter dismisses the app we'd used to find the Celestial master, scrolls, taps, scrolls again. Mutters a curse and tosses the phone at

Evander. He catches it easily. I lean over to view the screen, and there I am:

Auden Hegemony, age 17
Student at Walton-Bridge Academy; rising senior
Hobbies: varsity lacrosse, poetry club, running, hiking, fishing
Family: Callum Hegemony, father, deceased; Ursula Hegemony,
   Evander Hegemony, Winter Hegemony

My most recent school picture from Walton-Bridge is paired with the simple bio, and a half dozen photos—candids, sports action shots, a group picture from the last dinner party with Ursula and my cousins—tail it before the next section, aka "Winter Hegemony, age 16," begins.

When I'm done, Ruby is watching me, her dark eyes a storm, lips still rosy from my own trembling. "I'm so sorry."

I back away from the phone. From her. Ruby takes a step forward, imploring. Her words are for us as a whole, but she refuses to look anywhere but at me.

Her perfect target.

"I'm sorry that we lied to you. I'm sorry that we're here. I'm sorry about your families. Wren and I . . . we're not your killers. We never were." Then, because maybe the real Ruby appreciates a good callback, she uses my wording from yesterday after the truth spell. "We were pawns."

"You weren't pawns, you were willing participants." Ada stabs an accusing finger at the pair of them. "You're *con artists*."

Ruby's chin begins to wobble as she finds the words to respond to that, and a new tear spills over. She doesn't even bother to bat it away.

"Not intentionally," she rasps, voice brittle. Her whole body is shaking now, and she does nothing to soothe it away. Just stands there and lets the trembling take her. Like she deserves it. "We would never have said yes if we knew what Marsyas had planned. Never in a million years. We didn't know we'd hurt you; we didn't *want* to hurt you."

The girl looks absolutely miserable and wrung out.

And that's when Winter explodes.

"You pretended to be *real people*! For days! As people died! Knowing that it would matter if you told us, 'Hey, Marsyas hired us to sub for her granddaughters.' You don't think we needed that information? We needed it two days ago!"

Evander snatches the phone from Winter and stares down Ruby with that serious, stoic face.

"That information is just as important as the dead driver—Marsyas planned to murder Ursula and get out of here, and she confounded us by trapping her magically inept granddaughters here, whom she claimed to love. This same information from you days ago might have allowed us to figure out her plan and taken precautions."

Evander scrubs a hand through his short hair.

"*Now* we're behind the eight ball and all we've confirmed is that there is a second part of the plan—something Auden pointed out a day ago . . . but I failed to fully investigate."

He glances over his shoulder to me. I nod. "At first, I thought either Marsyas wanted to trap us in here forever and wreak havoc on the Four Lines from outside our bubble, or she was going to come back. Not for either of you—she's probably hoping that we dispose of your lying asses for her—but for the relics. But with what we know now—"

"She's already here," Ruby says at the same time I do.

"But she can't be!" Ada argues. "That's not possible—the spell we did was definitive. Marsyas isn't on the grounds."

"But what if she is *now*?" Ruby shoots right back. "I'm not a witch, but I understand enough to know that if Death magic is to blame for the murder of your parents, how can there not be a Death witch on the grounds with us in this very moment? Or at least when it happened?"

She isn't Lavinia Blackgate, but it strikes me that her outsider's perspective is still intact. And Ruby has just as much need to break the spell now as she did before her truth was revealed.

"The spell locks us in as well as it locks Marsyas out," Ada answers,

306 ✦ SARAH HENNING

flatly. She looks to her brother but for once Hex doesn't help. "No one can come in and no one has been here this whole time, unless they've been standing outside the gates since they locked, waiting to take us out the minute we solve this."

"So what do we do?" Infinity cuts in, ignoring Ada's ruminations. "Do we try to run the hunt spell again? See if we can find Marsyas this time?"

Evander shakes his head. "Something she's doing is clearly tampering with the hunt spell."

"Should we look for her?" Winter asks. "Like, spread out?"

"A waste of time."

"So what do we do?" a frustrated Infinity repeats.

"We find the Death master, that's what we do," Evander confirms. Sorrow is etched into the hull of his brow, pulled low—if only that master was something he'd found that first night. "We have no choice. It's just now nine o'clock. We have fifteen hours until we're locked in. And if she's already here? She's looking for it. We need to find it first. Or fight her in the process. There is no other choice but forward."

"And what about these two?" Hex asks, arms crossed and jaw tight as he tips his chin toward Ruby and Wren. "Fake Lavinia is right. We can't just let them go—they're a liability. For all we know, Marsyas may be using them somehow to control us from within or to spy on us further."

It's possible. And I let it happen, right under my nose. Just like Ursula's murder. Just like everything else that went wrong the past two days. I was supposed to look out for the Four Lines and protect them, and I couldn't even build a wall around my own weak spots.

"They're both compromised," Evander agrees, and I feel the weight of his attention on me again as my world cycles through a spectrum of purples under the weight of my hands. "We can't leave Ruby loose on the grounds. And we should remove anything Marsyas gave them in case she's using it somehow to beat Ursula's spell. What else do you have?"

"In my purse there's a card she gave us with the money."

Winter riffles through the sisters' wristlets on her arm and fishes out a small card on thick stock.

"*Saturday night. Formal. Wear solid black. I'll be in touch.*" She flips it over. "*Tell no one.*" Her eyes flash to Ruby's. "You seriously accepted this and were like, 'Yep, sounds good. *Not fishy at all*'?"

Ruby immediately blushes. Even though it's ridiculous, my body reacts with a surge of warmth. She's still exquisite. No denying that despite the circumstances. "I—no. Just. I wasn't the one to say yes. But I went along with it." Then, "The bracelets. You can't get Wren's, but you can have mine. Here, let me—"

"Don't touch them. We'll remove them." Evander nods. "Auden?"

It's posed as a question but it's an order and an atonement.

I'm the one who trusted this person so completely. I'm the one who opened my cousins up to trusting them too. My gut knew they were out of sorts, and yet it failed me, just as my heart had, finding solace in this person who was no longer my childhood opponent. This person who had over the past day or more become a friend. A new and surprising light in this terrible darkness.

You aren't going to ask me if I have a secret? A lie?

What would Ruby have told me if I had asked? Did she want me to know before this terrible moment? To place her truth alongside the rest we'd learned, another piece of ugliness bared to the light after Ursula's death.

It doesn't matter now.

That warmth in my chest snuffs out as I bow my head and approach. Ruby's still watching me, sorrow heavy in her sable eyes, and I force myself to greet her back. To look at this person who is not the person I know at all. Her kindness and beauty need to mean exactly nothing to me. That's what I tell myself.

"Hold out your hands."

Without a word, she obeys, raising them in front of her body. This close, her pale cheeks aren't rosy, but splotched with color, the wells under her eyes damp and tinged lavender, color bitten into her lips. Her wrists are delicate and bare save for the bracelets, which sway heavily beneath her pulse points.

I can't touch them, not directly, without shocking my system with the power of death. It's been said long-term contact with a Death Line relic can render the life element useless in an Elemental witch like me. The chain and clasps are, like most things in our Four Lines world, rendered of pure silver, and therefore highly conductive of not only electricity, but magic. Meaning the metal is just as destructive as the charged rabbit's foot itself.

"I can't remove these bracelets in a normal way," I say, describing like I did that first night when I healed her injured hand exactly what to expect from my magic. It's something Ursula taught us to do, a kindness and a way to inform consent, and I can't stop myself from doing it again for Ruby now. "I'm going to burn them off."

"You're going to light my wrists on fire?"

"Yes. Don't flinch and I won't burn you." My fingers brush hers. "May I?"

Ruby nods. I arrange her arm so that it's angled away from her body and parallel to the ground, the top of her wrist presented for me to work with. Then, bringing my right hand in close, I focus my powers to a hot pinprick, a thin spout of flame cutting the metal chain in a burst and blink. The bracelet *thunks* to the garden tiles.

I check her wrist for auxiliary burns. The pale skin is pristine.

She presents her other wrist in a mirror image to how I arranged the first.

When the second relic drops to the ground, and her skin is again untouched, Ruby catches my fingers in hers.

"Auden, thank you and I'm sorry."

I swallow and drop her hand. "I'm sorry too."

I step away from her, and though I don't turn my back on Ruby, I firmly align myself, shoulder to shoulder, with my cousins, Infinity, the Cerises. My unusual, unbreakable family. As one, we assess what must be done now.

"As I see it," Evander starts, and everyone is listening now, our priorities straightforward, "first we contain our guests—"

"Contain them *how*?" He might be the de facto leader, but hell if

I won't challenge him to be as thoughtful as possible. The sisters are liars, yes, but human beings in a terrible situation too. "Wren isn't going anywhere for at least a day, which is past the deadline for Ursula's tasks. Both sisters lied but it is our duty to protect them, which means if we're 'containing' Ruby, it needs to be in a way that keeps her safe."

"Sod cell." Winter gestures to the dew-slick, dead grass, matter of fact. "Open up the earth, drop her in, wrap her tightly. We can even maneuver it so she can keep an eye on Wren."

"And exposed to the elements, and perhaps Marsyas, if she attacks when the spell lifts," I point out. "Not to mention it's completely claustrophobic to have your chest cavity corseted by actual, unmoving earth. It isn't a weighted blanket, it's hundreds—thousands—of possible pounds of pressure if you do it wrong. She might hyperventilate while she fries in the sun."

For the first time, Ruby fidgets, shifting her weight. Awaiting her punishment.

Evander blows out a deep breath. "Okay, too harsh. We could lock her in a room within the manor? Create a guard rotation, and reunite Ruby with Wren after Ursula's spell wears off?"

I'm surprised he's posed these musings as questions—Evander's unsure.

Good, because it's a terrible idea.

"It's cruel to keep Ruby from seeing Wren while her sister is trapped and vulnerable. Not to mention, do we really want to sacrifice someone on the relic retrieval crew to play guard? Especially if, again, Marsyas is somewhere inside. Dangerous for the sisters and dangerous for the guard to be alone."

"Okay, wait, stop." Evander waves his arms. "We're not doing this right now. We have fifteen hours. The sun's up. We need to go." He turns to Infinity. "Is there a spell you can use to keep Ruby safe but still? Like Kaysa's—Wren's—situation but something we can easily remove?"

"Sunlight would work," Hex points out.

"I don't like this—"

"And I don't care, Auden," Evander snaps. "It's the best we have. It won't hurt her; in fact it might protect her."

"By taking away her free will. Making her a statue? That's what you plan to do?"

Evander turns the full force of his anger on me. "Any way you spin it, I'm the bad guy and it's the wrong choice. Add it to my tab, Auden, I don't care. If we get out of this alive, every choice we made up until that moment of freedom, including the wrong ones, will have been the right choice in my book. Infinity, do it."

"But—" I begin, but Infinity is quick, decisive, and clearly in agreement with Evander.

Before I know it, they've drawn a measure of sunlight in their palms, and with a quick flick of both wrists, Ruby is draped in a prison of pure, impenetrable sunlight.

CHAPTER 34

RUBY

My prison is pure gold and shimmering like water on my skin. It's a thin layer, as smooth and complete as ice, yet as warm as a freshly drawn bath.

It's the strangest feeling—and that's saying something, considering the last several days.

It's like I'm underwater with the sound turned on. The pressure of it doesn't miss a single inch of me, encased as I am, yet I'm able to breathe, blink, listen.

I hear the witches as they determine and divide up their targets.

I'm able to catalog every unsaid word telegraphed on exhausted features.

Auden's frustration overtaking the hurt in his poet's heart at my betrayal.

Evander's single-minded authority, ready to end this hell by any means necessary.

Winter's resentment at this process, this task, her rage over who's been lost and the reason why.

Infinity's resignation, their internal struggle to disengage warring with the need to see this through.

Hex and Ada's double helix of hurt, shock, horror, and the will to force an outcome that both honors and defies the blood in their veins.

I watch as they make plans, and turn their backs on us to execute them, wondering if they'll be successful in finding the Death master relic. If I'm truly safe or a sitting duck. If Wren is catching everything in the same way I am, or if the magic of her spell has her completely neutralized—a bee displayed in amber, no synapses firing, a true state of physical and mental suspension.

Then, they're gone.

All around the garden, the dying topiaries and hedges rustle with a wind I can't feel but know by heart after a lifetime of living in the Rocky Mountains.

Wren and I are alone.

Until we're not.

"I thought they'd never leave."

It's a curse as much as it is a sigh of relief, meant for the speaker and no one else. A low, raspy voice, one I haven't heard in two days. One I hadn't expected to hear again.

Marsyas.

My periphery isn't enough, only giving me the barest hint of movement over my shoulder, a person materializing from beyond the kitchen service entrance below the terrace. Moving, swathed in endless black, checking all the corners and edges for the six remaining witches.

There's more movement—someone with her. My vision blurs so much it seems as if there are four of them, not three, but I know it is because I know exactly who it is by her side.

Her real granddaughters.

I crane myself and push the edges of my vision to lay eyes on them. I need to see these girls in the flesh, to see them for what they are—monsters like their grandmother. I don't know how they're here, but I know why they are.

Revenge.

Pure and plain, and always the motivation from the start.

"You think they look like us? Really? These were the ones you picked? Seriously, Nona?"

They come into view, and it's the taller of the pair asking these questions. They're delivered in an accented scoff, a nimble quirk to her lips as she ribs Marsyas.

Lavinia Blackgate—the real one, in the flesh.

Like Marsyas, she's dressed in body-skimming black and a variety of Death magic relics. Like me, she has sable hair that cascades, dark eyes with long, heavy lashes that probably made her look like a doll as a child. Still, she's paler in that English rose sort of way, taller by at least an inch that's *all* leg, and apparently kind of a jackass.

"My nose looks nothing like that."

It's true—her features are refined and delicate where mine are, well, not.

"And that one's fringe is criminally excessive—is her forehead atrocious under all that hair?" Lavinia clucks her tongue and bites her lip, flummoxed. "I can't believe they didn't call them out as imposters on the spot."

"Memory is a wild beast," Marsyas answers with a dismissive wave, bracelets swinging. "Hard to chase, hard to tame, and never what you're expecting when you pin it down. As long as there's some distance to it, a memory is exactly what a good suggestion says it is."

At this, Lavinia sheds her feigned outrage and replaces it with a little smirk of endearment. "Honestly, Nona, convincing them these girls were us is a masterful achievement in itself. Don't you agree, Kay?"

"Oh yeah," the younger one insists.

That's all she says, end of story. Wren certainly did not nail this girl's personality. Furthermore, the true "Kay" has long layers that are more auburn in person than in the picture Marsyas showed us. To be fair, her eyes *are* a similar shade of hazel to Wren's, but rounder in a way that makes her look younger than sixteen. And though they're the same height, she's built more like Marsyas, soft around the edges of her hairpin curves.

In that moment, with all three Blackgates ogling at me, lips curved in matching expressions equally joyous and terrible, I realize it's true what Marsyas said.

Blackgates always smile.

And it's terrifying in this context.

They're here to finish what they started with Ursula's death.

Marsyas is finished with this subject. "How much time?" she asks without further direction or address.

"Hex and Ada are two hundred meters from the main house and working slowly. Evander and Auden are too busy arguing to work quickly," Lavinia answers, then she pointedly looks to her sister, handing off the verbal baton of this report.

"Winter and Infinity are installed at the cemetery. It's half a kilometer from this location."

Marsyas accepts this information with a small frown. "Not a lot of buffer room, but enough." She waves at the girls, shooing them. "Go. We must move quickly and silently. Stick to the plan."

Then she sends them off with a phrase that I know in my gut is the way the Blackgates truly see themselves and their reputation. It's not about the "Blackgate smile"—it's about what's underneath. "Be ready, be careful, be ruthless."

There's more movement, and I'm trying so hard to watch that my skin goes clammy with concentration.

What are they doing? Where are they going? What *is* the plan?

In answer, all I get are near-silent footsteps and then Marsyas solidifies from the edges of my vision.

The Blackgate matriarch is both the same as ever and not at all.

Midnight fabric from head to toe, but rather than whimsical, every inch is tactical—she came for a fight. Marsyas's silver hair is coiled into a tight bun now instead of a stately chignon. But that's where she begins to veer into the version who abandoned us—her vanity clawing its way in.

She's wearing the plum lipstick she wore to dinner Saturday night, her face made up in another round of heavy foundation and powders so fragrant I can nearly taste them, though my senses are obscured by my golden cage. Her jewelry has been replaced with relics matching the energy of the rabbits' feet bracelets she still wears. Taxidermic white cat paws (with claws extended) hug her earlobes, and a choker fashioned from a string of tiny skulls—birds, maybe?—wraps the crepe-like skin of her throat. The knife slash of an *X* marking her as an oathed heir peeks over the neckline of her shirt, the scar silvered, puckered, unmistakable if you know where to look.

Seemingly satisfied with the state of things, she veers in my direction and rounds upon me. Her Blackgate smile is in place, wide and terrible, the mischievousness in her dark eyes teetering away from ornery and toward vicious.

"I suppose though I am a witch, I am not a clairvoyant, I see." Birdlike, Marsyas tilts her head at me, examining. "I was sure you'd both be dead by now."

A pointer finger prods at the sunlight encasement over my body. I can feel the pressure as well as I can hear her—it's really a barrier more than a blanket. Stiff as a cast against my skin, but slim as a coat of shortening greasing a cake pan. Marsyas smiles when she sees the flinch in my eyes as her fingertips make contact—she must know I can feel it as much as she knows I can hear it.

The old witch seems pleased about both.

"Sunlight for you, pressurized air for her," she muses. "Why would that be?"

Marsyas inspects Wren's face, prods at her prison. She doesn't miss the item in her hands, her turning body, the expression of panic, and fear frozen in her eyes. She catalogs all of it and tucks it away in an expression that conveys both annoyance and respect.

And that's when I realize . . . while this is Marsyas's first time seeing Wren like this up close, it's not her first encounter.

No, she *triggered* it.

Marsyas is being more than facetious, she's being cruel—because she knows exactly what happened and I don't.

"Yes, I know you can hear me. Infinity is a talented witch, but a young one, and while this is a solid effort, it's not quite as secure as what Luna could've cooked up. Too bad, that one."

Marsyas rounds Wren and approaches me like a piece of art in a museum. Then, as if she knows it's off-limits and doesn't care, she reaches out and brushes two plump fingertips down the side of my face.

"It's truly extraordinary. You're immobile, yes, but I can see every thought in that pretty head of yours scrolling across your eyes like goddamn closed-captioning. You hold nothing back, Ruby."

Something sharper than pure delight brightens her expression. "I don't know how they didn't see it before you flat-out told them what you'd done."

Whatever she sees now—my disgust at her touch, my surprise at what she's suggested as far as her front-row seat to my truth spell, and my terror at what she did to the witches who've died in the last day—induces that smile of hers she wielded when convincing us of her plight more than a week ago. The deep, cavernous expression that feels like falling to my death. Pitching over the edge and into the black beyond.

Marsyas's obvious pleasure only grows.

She pats me on the cheek now, like I'm a small child.

The veil of sunlight does absolutely nothing to keep my skin from crawling.

"Yes, Ruby, I killed Hector and Sanguine. And I would've killed Wren here too if she hadn't snatched the Elemental master straight out of Sanguine's hands and triggered what I gather is a spell of Ursula's design."

This woman was going to kill my sister.

She certainly would have without Ursula's spell. Without the opportunity to break it so clearly and quickly by holding a master without permission.

I don't know how the Elemental master came into the equation of what happened here—if Hector or Sanguine had stolen it, they would be alive in imprisoning air instead of dead in shrouds.

All the unknowns and ifs and buts add up to my sister, my impulsive, bullheaded, big-hearted sister being alive.

This should be a relief. Wren is safe from the designs of this woman, who would discard both of us. Instead, pure, icy panic hardens around every organ in my body. My head throbs, my lungs shudder, my heart slows to frozen, my gut is a stone.

That smile flickers—it remains, but for the barest of moments, a frown flashed across her thin, plum-painted lips.

"Well, I should tell you I would've appreciated a heads-up from

Luna when we last saw each other." Her gaze skirts the solarium. "But given the circumstances, I'm sure she wasn't keen on warning me that there would be a side of confusion with the paranoia I hoped to stoke with her death, because the murderer should've been ensnared in this selfsame spell. The old bird knew exactly what she was doing until it was the last thing she did."

Luna was leaving us a hint.

She knew we'd be baffled by a victim's shroud but no trapped murderer. And yet it wasn't until *much* later that we realized we'd been infiltrated.

Marsyas sighs.

"And then this little one—I knew she was clever," the Blackgate matriarch says, with an almost appreciative expression on her face as she examines my sister. "It's my failure that I didn't anticipate what was coming when, instead of running from me, she stole the Elemental master out of Sanguine's hands. She called Ursula's magic by breaking a set rule, and created a shield for herself. Ingenious, really. Kept her alive. But, if what I just witnessed is any indication, she also nearly knocked you girls off the board. A little later than I'd anticipated, but both of you have most certainly exceeded my expectations."

It doesn't sound like a compliment.

"How long will she be this way? Twelve hours? A day?" If Marsyas can read the answer in my eyes, she still waves it off. "Doesn't matter, I suppose, because all of this will be over very soon."

She manages to make the last part sound both ominous and like a promise.

I wonder how long I can keep her talking. I'm not truly an active participant, but talking at me seems to be enjoyable for her ego, to say the least. If I can distract her long enough, it's possible Auden or Evander will take a break from their work inside the mansion to catch the extra figure on the lawn. Or perhaps the twins will work their way across the ley line and back here, to where it runs beneath the table, thrumming with an energy I can't feel.

I want them to be here, but at the same time, it's obvious this woman is a powder keg. And unless they come in ready to defuse her, they're walking into an explosion.

And then, Marsyas moves away from me and rocks the thin foundation I've built about the truths of magic.

She retrieves something from within the stretchy confines of her clothes, and crouches over Ursula's shroud with intention, purpose. The girls had their orders. This one was hers.

There's a sound like the back of a spoon striking a boiled egg. A muted shattering.

At the edge of my vision, Marsyas's form blurs in motion and I can just make out a large divot in Ursula's earthen shroud where her hands came to rest. More clear is the wrathful expression on Marsyas's face.

She strides over to stand in front of me, lips locked in a perturbed line, brows drawn together, fury in her dark eyes as color rises in her cheeks beside flaring nostrils.

"Who has the ring, my dear?"

This is one thing I do know. And if Marsyas can actually read me like a book, it's a dangerous truth for both Evander as the holder of the ring and Auden, who's currently at his side, somewhere inside Hegemony Manor.

I draw in a thin breath and put every molecule of my being into a blankness to my eyes. To my mind.

The Blackgate matriarch watches me, darkening.

After what feels like an eternity, Marsyas runs a lazy hand across the rabbit's foot relic at her wrist.

"You know what, Ruby? I don't need you to tell me, I don't need you to attempt a lie. All I need is to summon my *unbreakable, unusual family*. I don't even need you for that." Marsyas winks. "But I have more work to do before I'm ready to pick a fight."

A fight. An inevitability and yet . . . I'm suddenly unmoored.

No, no, no.

The witches—the kids—left have lost so much, they shouldn't have to fight anymore. Not with their magic, their words, their wills.

Marsyas retrieves something—a small drawstring bag with the same neat lettering I've seen three times before. My eyes water as I try to read the silver imprinted upon the side, but I know exactly what it is.

The final master relic.

CHAPTER 35

AUDEN

When I step away from Ruby, it's as if I've crossed over a threshold—through one door and into another world.

Perhaps I've returned from an alternate universe to the present, reality squeezing my bones like air pressure, gravity sealing my physical body back down to earth.

The situation is dire, the numbers spelling it out in stark black and white of what has happened the last thirty-six hours and what we must do in the next fifteen.

Four dead bodies.

Two non-witches who have tangible knowledge about the inner workings of the most secretive magic society in North America.

One final relic to find.

One witch to elevate to High Sorcerer.

One murderer (if not more) to punish for the four dead bodies.

Evander gives us orders and honestly, I follow them because I want to be done.

Rip the Band-Aid off and slam the doors open, leaving this spell, the last three days behind. This is my home, where I was raised, but I may never come back.

I can serve my family and my line from somewhere that isn't here.

Here, where my grandmother died. Where my father died. Where my aunt and uncle died. Where this whole ten-year travesty was built, crested, broke.

Six months ago, Ursula told me what I must do.

That keeping the lines together was worth any cost. Together we can survive, apart we begin to weather, fray, snap.

I'm not sure she knew the true price. Her life. Luna's. Hector's and Sanguine's. The driver. The particular threat and test posed by Ruby and Wren.

Though, Ursula always knew everything. Maybe she knew this too.

And still she thought it was worth it.

It's cost too much. It will cost us more before it's over.

I didn't object as Evander divided us up. Gave us marching orders. Signals to call each other—for masters and for sightings of Marsyas. Deadlines and strategies.

I didn't say a word.

And now I'm being babysat by Evander himself.

The locations for the Death master relic are . . . sparse, to say the least.

The clue doesn't seem to give us any indication of what form the relic might be in, nor is it very directive on location or even any specifics, honestly. Therefore, we've divided it into plausible hints: ashes, shroud, line.

Accordingly, our priority of search sites includes anywhere items are burned or buried, plus the location of the ley lines.

Winter and Infinity are casing the cemetery, searching for anything that might tie into the pointed dust-to-dust and shroud statements within the clue.

Meanwhile, the twins are searching the length of the large ley line that bisects the property, following it from the front gate until the mountains ruin the path, hoping to spot anything that fits in with the final words of the clue because just as every line hooks into the High Sorcerer's ring via their master relics, every line draws power from the ley lines that crisscross the earth.

That leaves Evander and me with the house, addressing the hints regarding ashes and burning—tasked with searching every fireplace flue within Hegemony Manor.

Every living space has at least one, sometimes multiple. All of them are original to the house, which means all of them need to be searched.

It truly is a two-man job, but because of the still-cooling bodies upon the grounds, we've decided to stay within view of each other. No splitting up for efficiency's sake.

Which means I'm using my time wisely to tell him precisely what I think.

We're on room number seven—the formal dining room on the first floor of the manor. The long, rectangular table is large enough to be seaworthy, the chandelier above sized to double as a temporary prison for a grown man. The walls are accented by Shadrack's mural of waves, lit on one side by floor-to-ceiling windows overlooking the interior courtyard. The fireplace is adjacent to the courtyard views, and Ursula always sat so that her back was to the fire, the element charging her through every bite and sip at the head of the table.

Evander is bent over the cooling hearth, sifting through the ashes and prodding the stones beneath. Meanwhile, I'm standing on a chair that's seen sturdier days, examining every Victorian curl of marble for a niche.

"Ursula was the High Sorcerer for more than half a century," I start, rather casually, as I finish inspecting the mantel and surrounding woodwork with the same result as all six rooms before this one—nada. "Evander, you know better than anyone—the will is the first thing a High Sorcerer does, correct? Even before a celebration or ceremony. Wear the ring, write the will, then party."

I step off the chair and haul it back to the table—even now Ursula's insistence that we protect the original parquet is so ingrained it's automatic. As I reposition the chair at the table, I've noticed Evander's movements have slowed.

He's listening. Good.

I wait, watching the wheels turn silently in Evander's brain—he bows his head, hands braced on his sweatpants, as he sits back on his haunches. Another flue, another cold lead.

"If Marsyas knew what spell within Ursula's will would be triggered early enough that she killed the driver and stole his keys before Ursula's murder and made her exit, could we assume she took other precautions?"

Evander sighs and stands—the second floor will be next. I push on.

"So, she planned and accounted for the fact that she would have to leave to avoid the punishment for murdering Ursula. But she knew that either she needed back in or she needed to have people on the inside. Not Ruby and Wren. They—"

"You know what I think?" Evander asks suddenly, though it's not a true question. His tone is low and aimed at the ashes. "I think Marsyas thought we'd eliminate those poor girls in her stead, believe we'd appeased Ursula's need for punishment, and then be shocked out of our gourds when we found all the masters and the gates didn't magically open. She wanted us to think we did it only to find out we'd murdered two innocent girls and would have to live with the guilt in our magical tomb for the rest of our days."

Dark and twisted in a way someone like Marsyas Blackgate would appreciate. Sure.

"Maybe that was the plan at first. One doesn't have to hold the power to destroy it. It can be snuffed out."

"It most certainly can be."

Turning around, Evander opens his mouth to say more but withdraws.

"What?" I prod.

He sucks in a deep breath and raises his exhausted eyes to mine. The green is faded like the morning light in this room, a shadow over the hour that can't be stowed away. The anger in his voice hardens into something else. Fear? Resignation?

It's far more terrifying than Evander in a rage.

"If we're trapped here for good," he starts, voice downshifted to a disheartened rasp, "I suppose that means we don't have to address what our guests know."

Address. As in wipe their memories or neutralize them—hurt them—in another way. Maybe even eliminate them. Two more dead in the name of the Four Lines.

"Say their names, Evander."

His big, burly body deflates until I can see the little boy Evander was ten years ago staring back at me—chubby and round-faced, spitting nails in a preemptive strike against the softest parts of him, buried down deep. "Ruby and Wren . . . That will take some getting used to."

A pang of guilt spreads, silken ice, smothering my gut. Evander truly is scared—for Ruby and Wren, for himself, for all of us.

A lump materializes in my throat and when I swallow, it lodges in my windpipe. I give Evander my best smile, knowing full well my voice will crack. "Well, we might have eternity to get it down pat."

We haven't discussed this enough, the elephant in the room. That this crumbling house will be our tomb, the grounds our final resting place. If we can't get this right. If we don't get this right.

This has never been an option for Evander.

With the barest hint of rising mirth, my cousin deadpans like a goddamn Hollywood action star, "Not if I have anything to do with it."

"And that's why we need you leading the Four Lines when this is over."

I mean every word of it, and the way his face softens, I think he believes it.

"I—" Evander holds up a hand, his eyes lifting to the stamped gold-foil panels of the ceiling above. That cold slither of discontent flashes in my stomach before he even says it. "Do you hear that?"

CHAPTER 36

RUBY

"Yes, that's right, my dear. I had the Death master relic all along."

If I could physically gape, I would.

"Since the night my Marcos was murdered, I've searched for it. Two years ago, I located it. Last year, I short-circuited the security wards—the same ones that killed Ursula's children—and gained control of *my* master."

A year. A whole year.

"The first Blackgate to hold it since Salem." A smile streaks across Marsyas's lips, fast and furious. Her dark eyes twinkle with mischievousness familiar from the day I met her but missing in every interaction since. "But not the only Blackgate to hold it."

At first, I'm confused—she's sent her granddaughters off, yet the relic is right here. But then Marsyas opens the bag, and to my shock, retrieves the contents with her bare hands.

Her small fist is closed as she withdraws it, rotating her balled fingers until they open and reveal the Death Line master in her palm.

No, not a relic—*relics*. A handful of bone shards, weak as white smoke and brittle.

They look like chalk gone damp and dried. Like nothing useful. Yet Marsyas marvels at the pieces as if they're the keys to the universe itself.

"These are the Bones of Ribe, my dear Ruby," Marsyas announces in a soft voice, gently prodding at a larger piece, turning it over before moving on to the next, inspecting them all. "They're what's left of witches burned at the stake for simply existing. For being too loud, too talented, too much. They are us and we are them, and they will be the end of the Four Lines."

Her eyes flash up and they're the sun, burning and bright and deadly to anyone brash enough to approach.

"Death magic already benefits from amplification by relics. A dead body is best, fresh death amplifies our abilities like solar power, but it's quite *uncouth* to leave a trail of corpses wherever we go. Not too good for our reputation, I'm afraid." She waggles her silver eyebrows. "But even with a lifetime of knowing that relics are like a live wire to my power, I was still shocked at what my master allows me to do. Would you like to see?"

Marsyas holds a piece of bone up, pearlescent.

"I don't know why I'm even asking—of course you do. Not that you could say no anyway, of course. A bug, stuck in amber, you are. I'll have to fix that for you, but not yet."

The last thing I want her to do is free me. That will make it all the easier for her to destroy me.

"This little bone shard has amplified my powers in ways I'm still learning a year later. Perhaps you wondered how I arrived here with my granddaughters? Did you guess through the relic? It was so kind of Luna to ensure our driver stayed without a shroud, and even better that the Hegemony brats happened to squirrel him away in a private, secluded location within the manor. The root cellar truly was a perfect place for my needs."

She'd always planned to murder the driver.

Bile sloshes in my immobile gut.

"Yes, my dear. If you wondered why I killed him, though I had the keys, why I left him in such a state without even trying to cover up my tracks, well, the reasoning was threefold. First, he wouldn't try to stop me when I left; second, it would squarely put the blame for Ursula's death on my shoulders, which would be a problem, given my nonexistent state; and third, and this is the most important, he could let me in."

Let her in? How? Magic, of course, but what? She used his spirit somehow? His body? Wait—I don't want to know. All that matters is that she's here and that is a huge problem.

Pleased with herself, she holds up the relic, absolutely beaming.

"If this one magical amplifier can allow me to do magic beyond my wildest dreams, it must truly be something what all four masters held as one can do." Marsyas shakes her head. "Ursula, it turns out, was just the latest in a line of misers squatting on a treasure trove of power and never using it. I plan to use it."

I try and fail to swallow away the fear balling in my throat at the determination in her words, her face, even the air around her, shimmering and shifting like it can no longer hold her on this plane. Instead of dissipating, the fear within balloons in my chest, my heart kicking up, my lungs smashed out of usefulness, as I watch Marsyas carefully return all but one thumb-sized piece to the little bag.

After cinching the others carefully away, Marsyas holds the shard of relic reverently in her palm, as if presenting it to the sky.

Then, with a flash of tea-stained teeth and a viper-quick grip, the old witch clasps the bone in one tight fist, and charges it in the air. That vibration of magic I swear I saw when she held the master shimmers out from her palm, magic itself so powerful it can be seen by the naked, *normal* eye. Black as a starless, fathomless night.

And it's aimed at Wren.

Panic claws out of my body and into the morning, my voice shouting uselessly behind my shroud. I toss myself against my prison, trying to bust free, stop her, shout at her, do anything at all beyond standing here like a fucking statue as Marsyas aims the full weight of master-amplified Death magic at my little sister.

The obsidian mass arcs up, up, up, ready to rain down on Wren. To pour over her head like acid rain made of shimmering, shivering mountain air leaden with Death magic and spite.

I don't know if Marsyas can break Ursula's spell with that extra power—battering ram, ice pick, chemical reaction that dissolves the starlight and leaves Wren raw and vulnerable. I don't—

The glittering spell drops like a lead balloon, smacking not into Wren, but the Cerises at her feet.

It explodes, and their shrouded bodies are instantly covered in a buffering, blurry haze.

I watch in my periphery, horrified, as the shrouds dissolve into dust and debris, littering the star-shaped tiles.

The Blackgate matriarch steps forward, steals the Blood relic from Hector's stiff hands, and tucks the box with Cleopatra's heart into the same hidden pocket holding the Bones of Ribe.

Marsyas has another master relic now. Two by my count, but perhaps three by hers. She killed Luna. She is already itching to hold the ring. It's not much of a stretch to believe that the Celestial relic went missing because this woman stole it.

And if that is true, that means the Elemental master in Wren's grasp is the last one Marsyas needs to gain control of the Four Lines.

Add the ring and it's over.

Endgame unlocked in two easy steps.

I expect Marsyas to approach Wren. To use her magic the same way now, and I brace for what will happen when she breaks the magical prison and gets her hands on Wren—right in front of me as I stand here, frozen and helpless to stop her.

Instead, Marsyas crouches closer to the bodies, and places a palm on Sanguine's forehead, as if checking her for a fever. Before I can even guess what she's doing, the impossible happens.

Sanguine awakens.

I silently gasp as the woman blinks a few times, and then, as if directed, pushes herself up and braces against the ground on extended arms. Sanguine's blue eyes are glazed over under heavy lashes, her face pale and mottled with gore, gaping wounds fully revealed as she moves to clutch her husband's arm.

"Yes, my dear, of course," Marsyas says. "You're always better together."

Then, Marsyas places a hand beneath his fall of hair, and Hector's eyes open too.

He springs up, faster than his wife, uncoordinated but enthusiastic. Sanguine meets Hector with a calming grip and a kiss to the temple.

Then, supporting each other, they stand.

And Marsyas greets them like she's the one hosting a party now in crumbling, isolated Hegemony Manor.

"Welcome to the team."

I can't look away, even as Marsyas exits my line of sight. The Cerises stretch, examining their arms and legs, scratched and bruised and mottled as they are. Hector and Sanguine don't say a word, and how could they, with their throats gone? But they're dead and standing and there's only one thing I can make of that.

They're zombies. Literal zombies.

A day ago, maybe two, I would've immediately thought *this can't be real*. Now, after all we've seen? My fatigued mind doesn't even allow the beginnings of that thought to fire. Of all the things I've witnessed since Saturday night, the walking dead might be the most unreal of all. Still true. Still more than plausible as a magical possibility.

These are Death witches.

They wield magic gained through the dead. Why couldn't they *move* the dead? Reanimate them at will? Use them for gain?

My heart freezes as my mind halts upon *why* Hector and Sanguine are standing tall.

Marsyas doesn't even attempt to hide her intent—*Welcome to the team*.

The Death witch hasn't given new life to the Cerises.

She's made them into soldiers.

As if he can hear my thoughts, Hector drags a long, elegant finger across the gaping maw of his ruined throat. Crimson blood coats his fingertip, still wet under the cover of the shroud, even after at least an hour, maybe two since he first died. He draws his hand up to eye level, flexing the fingers, a small smile gathering on his ruined mouth.

Testing his power.

I can't see his magic, but a spark of something shivers deep within my own veins. The seed of Hex's blood within mine. One drop is all it takes for Hex to control me like a marionette, and his father can control him.

Blood upon blood.

The call is distant, ferried through Hex to his father, dead and gone, and I hope beyond hope that Hex can feel that spark too and know his parents have been awakened from death.

That they've been called to fight.

And if the elder Cerises can fight, then . . .

Movement comes in my periphery, and Marsyas returns into view.

That wide smile of hers is sharp enough to breach the skin. At her side is another soldier.

High Sorcerer Ursula Hegemony herself.

CHAPTER 37

AUDEN

Hunched down and moving fast, Evander and I arrive in the tea-room, following the direction of the footsteps one floor above.

We melt into the shadows, feeling our way along new fissures in the old walls, spidering out like veins from the parquet to the stamped gold tiles of the ceiling. The portraits of dead Hegemonys, including our fathers, watch wordlessly as we arrive in a crouch beneath the bay windows that bracket the doors looking out onto the garden.

They're paned in a diamond pattern, and leaden—the dominant style within the manor. With any luck, the repeating shapes and the natural shadows from the ceiling created by the terrace above will provide us enough cover for a good view.

Gripping the sill, I slowly rise until only the top of my head and my eyes are exposed to the glass. Evander and his giant-ass shoulders are wedged in next to me.

To my far right, the long dinner table and debris therein. To the left of the table is Ursula's shroud . . . which doesn't look right. It's misshapen, anemic somehow. Like it was dropped and damaged.

Scanning farther left, I see why.

My breath catches in a gasp at the exact same moment Evander hisses, "Fuck."

There, standing as tall and imposing as she did every day of her life, is Ursula Hegemony.

The woman who was our grandmother is facing away from us, hands open at her sides—loose, supple, ready to draw her magic. From this angle the blood staining her temple, matting her hair, splattered down her neck and onto her dress is unmistakable. It wasn't the blow that ended her life, but it was the last chance she had to shed blood as a living being.

Next to her, Hector and Sanguine Cerise huddle, as inseparable as they were in life, basically overlapped. From behind, their kill-shot wounds aren't obvious, but big, bold arterial blood stains every one of their fingers, a threat, a sign.

Death magic.

I didn't know it could do this. Amplify their magic through a corpse? Yes. Manipulate a body? Yes. Animate it? Okay, why not? But if these particular people are animated it's for one reason only . . .

To use their magic.

Magic dies with the witch, yes. But if a living witch is powerful enough to wake them from the dead, she's powerful enough to wake their magic with her own. Marsyas isn't just animating three corpses, she's going to conduct her magic *through* them.

They're marionettes with all the powers each had in life.

As if waiting at attention for orders from their general, all three corpses stare ahead.

Ruby and Wren are still magically imprisoned, and at the apex between them, hands thrown wide like an orchestra conductor and face split with a knife's-edge smile, is Marsyas Blackgate, in the flesh.

Movement from the left.

A figure steps beyond the staircase banister and into view.

I should've guessed. I should've known. Maybe deep down I did—because this time I don't gasp when I see a dead woman *walking* toward Marsyas.

Luna Starwood.

Free of her shroud and trailing white linen, Luna is gaining ground much faster than I'd ever seen in life. Her usual careful advance isn't supported by another human, and it's been sped to a run. She ambles forward like a touched-down tornado, bobbing and weaving with such uncontrolled care that I expect her to fall into a shattered heap, wheels still spinning like a car overturned.

She hurtles toward Marsyas as if called.

From behind her comes a laugh—the second set of running footsteps, this one the amused jog of a kid playing keep-away with a puppy in the park. Trailing, but not helping. Not in the way Infinity always had. The shadow moves with a fluid confidence I don't recognize until the figure casting it comes into view.

Dark hair, pale skin, long lines, and a stiff sort of self-indulgent pride reflected outward in a pout.

"Lavinia," I breathe.

Evander curses softly. "Where's Kaysa?"

It's a crucial question. Where there's one Blackgate, there's another. Evander wasn't wrong, these girls have been kept like offshore funds for the past decade, but they've also always, *always* been kept together.

I scan the garden, scrutinize every ragged topiary, the fountain and its stagnant water, the measure of the walled hedges on either side, paper-thin and yellowing at the edges. No one else.

Two Blackgates, two imposters, four dead witches.

Marsyas greets her true firstborn granddaughter not with praise for the magic she's wielded to break Luna's shroud and animate the woman, but with criticism.

"What took you so long? She was right upstairs."

Lavinia raises a brow; though the movement is subtle, she truly seems surprised by the swift admonishment. She schools her expression. "Looking for Auden. I can't wait to play."

A chill runs up my spine.

The real Lavinia Blackgate hasn't forgotten our *animus* childhood relationship.

Marsyas is completely nonplussed. "You'll have your turn with him soon enough—with all of them soon enough."

This is the second part of the plan.

Six on three. But the Blackgates have our dead on their side.

"Will four be enough?" Lavinia asks, gesturing to the corpses standing at attention. "Shall I retrieve the driver to give us an extra body?"

Marsyas is fussing over Luna, getting her situated with the three other zombies she's raised—there's no other way to put it. Fear spikes in my veins as Lavinia huffs out a deep sigh of annoyance at the lack of immediate answer. She turns on her heel for our exact location—on a mission to head straight through the tearoom, down the stairs to the kitchen and attached root cellar.

Fuck.

Evander hits the tile, flattening himself as best as he can. I, meanwhile, press myself against the wall, knees drawn to my chest. My heart pounds, sure Lavinia saw the ghost of our retreat in the glass as she turned to approach.

Over the pounding of my heart, I count her footsteps—futile in that I don't know how many it takes to get to the door, only that she's taken ten steps in our direction . . . when they stop.

"No, no, we need to keep our door open." I frown. *Door?* "If we need a non-magical body, there are two waiters in the grass. You can make them fresh. Hurry, hurry, there's not much time."

Immediately, the pitter-patter of Lavinia's return taps itself out against the tiles. I count twelve steps this time before there's a pause on the tile. I motion to Evander, who follows along only to whisper, "Portal. Driver."

A bolt of horror rips through me.

The driver *is* the door.

Marsyas didn't kill him for the keys. She killed him for convenience. They used the driver's body as a pass-through—a trapped door into, and potentially out of, Ursula's lock-down spell.

Evander nods, disgust pooling in his own eyes at the recognition on my face.

Together we slowly return to our previous positions, peeking over the edge of the sill.

Lavinia is beside her grandmother now. She clutches something in her grip, and Marsyas's hands are full. I can't see the contents, but knowing what I do about Death magic, they likely have relics within their palms to amplify their power.

They've used the dead as a door.

They've shattered the victim's shrouds.

They're waking dead witches and using their power.

None of those things is normal, and yet they've done all of them at the same time.

A stone of fear drops in my gut. My mouth goes dry. Evander's secret and the scale of what they can do crash into me at once.

"They have the Death master."

Evander inhales sharply.

"That's it, that's how they can do these things," I whisper.

Evander gives the slightest of nods but touches a hand to my wrist. A signal to quiet. A signal to watch.

I do.

As Lavinia arrives at Marsyas's side, the old woman flashes the contents of her hands.

Bones, white as chalk. The box containing Cleopatra's heart. The vile of Nostradamus's blood.

The don't just have the Death master. They have *all* the masters, save one.

"Ursula, my dear," Marsyas addresses my grandmother's body, "let's rid Wren of her relic, shall we?"

"Which one's Wren?" Lavinia asks, as Marsyas calls my grandmother to her like a fish on a line. Marsyas gestures to the turning, running form of Wren.

Lavinia pins her attention to Ruby, and her sunlight prison. "And what's this one? Robin? Kestrel? Peregrine?"

"Ruby."

"Well, that's disappointing."

"Not everyone has a vision," Marsyas tuts, as if she wasn't named after a flute player who got himself flayed alive by Apollo. "Come help me with dear Wren."

The final relic—*our* relic—is still cupped in Wren's hands.

If they can magically coerce Ursula into breaking that spell, they'll hold all the master relics. All they'll need is the ring around Evander's neck and that will be that. The Blackgates will control the Four Lines.

And all we've fought for, all every Hegemony before us has fought for, will be over.

Evander's hand on my wrist tightens. His eyes darken under heavy brows.

He doesn't have to say anything to give this order, this direction. Time to make our move.

But before we do, Evander does something I don't expect.

He removes the chain. Holding the two pendants tight in his grip so they won't clink, he drapes the necklace over my head in one smooth motion. I gape at him, but he mouths, *Misdirection.*

The Blackgates will expect Evander to have it. Either by pure educated deduction, or by magical means in manipulating bodies that once were people who *saw* Evander put the ring on the chain he wears around his neck.

Something gathers in my throat.

This is everything he's ever wanted. And yet here and now Evander is entrusting me to keep it safe. To keep the Four Lines safe.

I want to hug him, but I can't. So, with a minuscule nod I slip the ring, key, and chain beneath the collar of my T-shirt.

He drops to a crawl, and I follow him, moving under the window to the double doors. They're diamond-paned like all the rest, and what I wouldn't give for some solid wood in this very moment. Still, Evander and I have plenty of practice in conducting wordless conversations on the lacrosse pitch. We know exactly how to create an offensive attack the other side won't see coming.

They've raised the dead, but we'll defend the living if it's the last thing we do.

He places a hand on the lever, ready to open the door as silently as possible. But before he does, he motions with a fingertip. *Left.* Again, I blink in recognition.

When he wants to be, Evander is as loud as a freight train, stomping and smashing and acting out everything he doesn't tend to say with words. But when he needs to be, he's as silent as a shadow. Two sides of the coin, Evander Hegemony.

One eye on the Blackgates as they turn their attention to Wren, I slip into motion behind him.

Evander pulls the lever, smooth and slow, and the catch releases from the doorjamb. With a second hand bracing the movement of the door, he opens it slowly, pauses, and peeks into the night.

I wait, my heart hammering in my ears as my body presses into the floor.

Evander shuffles into a silent, crouched walk, and I follow, slipping behind him and to the left as planned. We're completely in the open, with only the shadows from the terrace above as cover, for about two yards until we make it to the destination Evander had planned: the wet bar erected for the dinner party.

He gets behind it safely, but the moment I arrive, I'm in trouble—there's not enough room. There *should be* enough space for both of us to safely crouch unseen, but the Saturday night's bartender is flat on his back beneath the bar, passed out in the same vegetative "quarantine" as every other member of the staff. There's a pillar behind the bar and we can't simply nudge him out of the way. Worse, his feet are sticking out beyond the bar, and will most certainly draw notice if we try to roll him.

Good thing we have a magical solution for that.

Reaching for my magic, I layer the bartender in the same spell I used on the dead driver that first night to keep Hex from noticing the body as I approached with the girls I now know as Ruby and Wren. It isn't perfect, and the daylight will make it more easy to detect if anyone is looking, but it's what I have. The moment the man is covered, I roll him, giving myself enough room to wiggle under the bar sideways.

Obscured and, it seems, unnoticed, my heart begins to slow, and my ears again rejoin the action happening only feet away.

The dead risen.

Three of the four relics in Marsyas's hands.

And where the hell is the final Blackgate?

Or is it final *Blackgates*? What if the girls' mother, Athena, is here too? Four women looking for revenge upon, and control of, the very organization that took their shared love. Father, husband, son, heir—Marcos Blackgate.

I can't make out anything from where I'm at, but I think Evander can, pressed against the opposite corner. I funnel all my attention on what I can pick up with my ears.

The merry tinkle of the fountain.

The rustle of wind in the trees in the rising day, pine, and bird-call deep within.

Then, something I don't expect.

"Papa! Mama!"

Hex. Ada.

Running feet chase their panicked screams on that wind. Again, they yell.

"Where are you?" Hex's words are desperate, breathless—spoken with lungs fueling a full-on sprint.

"Are you there?" Ada this time.

Running feet. Steps skidding to a tripping halt. "Papa—"

The word dies on Hex's lips.

I don't need to see it to know what's happening—Blood magic from beyond the grave.

Evander curses so quietly only the ghosts and I can hear it.

Now we don't just have a fight, we have a rescue mission.

CHAPTER 38

RUBY

I'm panicking.

Truly, wholly panicking in my magical cage—heart pounding a wild clip, jaw so tense it might crack.

From my frozen vantage, I have a perfect view of the moment Hex and Ada crash up the path from the cemetery, my very wish that they would feel their parents' magic sparking in their blood. Which means I also see the very moment zombie Hector and Sanguine capture them like flies in a web.

The twins cry out in a wail of surprise and pain, left to hang mid-step as the warring hope and confusion slip away, melding into solid horror as reality kicks them in the teeth.

They've been snatched by a Death witch controlling their zombie parents.

"A little harsh, Nona," the real Lavinia purrs. "You don't have to hurt them. The twins have been so helpful in reacquainting us to the lines."

My wild heartbeat fades to nothing. *Helpful?* Something cold drops in my gut as Hex's repeated assurances to his own mother in the moment we were "reintroduced" replay in my mind.

We know each other, Mama.

"Oh, I didn't mean to hurt your pen pals, Lavinia." Marsyas plays innocent with a tacked-on smile that returns me to the here and now. "I simply asked their magic to hold you in place. Whoops. Don't know my own strength."

Marsyas pauses in her work with Ursula and turns the force of her attention to the twins. "I'll make this quick—I *will* be the next High Sorcerer. Commit to me now, pledge to neutralize any of the remaining witches, should they fight back, and I shall remove your parents' compulsion over you."

Hex's charcoal eyes flash, every cord in his neck tensed as he yells across the lawn, "You want us to fight *with* you? You killed them! We know it was you!"

Marsyas laughs. "Yes, and now they have no choice but to see things my way. Isn't that lovely?"

"Fuck. You," Ada grits out.

Marsyas turns to unseeing Hector and Sanguine. "Such spirited children."

Her eyes slide back to the twins, and she winks hard enough that even I can register it, which means they most certainly can across the distance.

"Well, a *funny* thing about Blood witches is that if your parents want you to do something, they can do more than ground you to make it happen."

She knew their secret.

Unlike the black cloud before, this magic is as invisible to me as the rest, waking in their blood. I know it is, and yet in that moment, I swear *I can see it work* as Marsyas sends a bolt of instruction to the elder Cerises. Both of them widen their stance, flex their fingers, and, with dead-eyed precision, they turn up the volume on the blood spell they have racing across the distance to their children.

"No, Papa. Mama, please—"

Hex's words die as his whole body splays starfish-wide. The whites of his eyes shine, big and wet and open more than they should be even at this distance.

Ada's twin reaction is so violent she's bent over backward like a palm tree in a hurricane, the ends of her long blond hair snagging in the dying carpet of lawn.

Despite the undead state of their parents, the scene is eerily similar to hours earlier. The twins are literally compelled to step forward, reeling in like fish on a line.

Hitting the brakes as best he can, Hex puts all his weight on his heels, pulling back with every bit of the strength he earned on the football field. Eyes now screwed shut, teeth gnashed, hands thrown up together and yanking backward as if he's playing tug-of-war with an invisible line. Beside him, Ada has bent into a bear-crawl position, and is using the lower center of gravity to latch onto a small ornamental tree.

Marsyas tuts. "Children, you just bolted up that hill, racing back to see your parents. Now they call to you and yet you resist? I must say, that is both fickle and rude."

"How . . . ? What . . . ? Why?" Each of Hex's words are spit out between labored inhales.

"Do you want to toss in 'when' and 'where' too, just to be thorough?" Marsyas asks, snide and smiling. She chuckles at her little zinger and, presumably, the twins' terrible predicament. "Kidding, kidding. I'm aware that you're under *some* strain from all that fickle, rude resistance. Perhaps if you come nicely you'll be able to be a little more pointed in your questions, and therefore get better answers."

"Murderers . . . aren't . . . funny!" Ada shrieks.

"And children who don't obey aren't clever."

The mirth in Marsyas's eyes flashes cold. "Hector and Sanguine, I believe your children need some heavier encouragement."

Marsyas's arms swim through the air like a conductor's, small hands flexing and collapsing with each spelled thought, directives aimed at the zombie bodies of the elder Cerises.

The husband and wife lurch into motion in my periphery, going from standing at the ready to a flat-out sprint at their children, all the while reeling them in with the power they still have over their blood.

With every step closer to their marks, the parents' hold on the twins seems to grow. More compelling, more painful—until the result is just too much.

Ada cries out first, yanked toward her parents like a magnet. She can't stop it, her speed accelerating with every lost inch.

"Here's the thing, you insolent children," Marsyas announces, her voice raising to nearly a shout. "The *how*—how can I control your parents? How have I brought them back and gained control of their magical abilities? I am the world's most powerful Death witch amplifying my powers through *my* master relic, that's how. Even better, I have the Blood master in my possession, which means your magic is my magic, their magic is my magic."

Marsyas lets that settle in, the box tight in her palm and up-lifted, unmistakable in the late morning light, even under the cover of clouds.

"*What* will I have them do?" she bellows, clearly enjoying this. A woman who has waited a decade to say her piece. "Fight at my side, of course. And because you don't seem interested in surrendering to me as High Sorcerer, well, the *why* is simple. Because they can control you. And because they are no longer your parents, simply my very fancy puppets, they don't have any *inconvenient attachments* to either of you anymore."

"So you'll have them kill us?" Blood dribbles from one nostril, staining Hex's lips and teeth.

My heart leaps, willing him to open his eyes.

Hex doesn't know Ada is nearly captured. I can't tell him. And Marsyas and Lavinia most certainly won't warn him.

"If you won't join my team in life, then you certainly will in death."

Frozen and horrified, I watch as the moment Marsyas's declaration drops, Ada's unbroken path collides with Hector and Sanguine. They converge upon her, and the girl disappears from my view into the roiling movement of their animated corpses with a raw, high-pitched wail.

Hex's eyes snap open. "Ada!?"

He falters in shock at whatever he can see. Panic flaring in his features, Hex rights himself, resistance renewed, before something hard clamps over his expression—determination. And he purposefully gives in, letting his parents' magic draw him in as he attacks right back, flying toward them at the speed they want with the fight they aren't expecting.

They blow apart as he crashes into them like a bowling ball into a cache of three pins, the screams of the dead now ringing out among Ada's keening and Hex's battle cry.

"What are you doing to them? Stop!"

A new voice enters the fray. Bodies flash in my periphery. I can't see, but I know exactly who it is.

Winter with the demands. Infinity confirms their presence a moment later with a shocked "Grandmama?!"

"Nice of you two to join us. You remember Lavinia? Yes?"

"Hello." Lavinia smiles from beside Ursula's body. "And your grandmothers, I'm assuming you haven't forgotten them?"

Neither of them are tricked by their personal emotions. They see this situation for what it is.

"You—you broke into their shrouds?" Infinity asks, voice shattered with horror.

Winter is more blunt, less horrified than disgusted. "You turned them into fucking zombies?"

Marsyas dismisses her with a flick of her hand. "I tire of questions you know the answers to, and honestly, we're busy right now."

Winter only digs in deeper. "I know what you're doing but I don't know how you can do it. The manipulation of several corpses at once has been unheard of since Morgana's time."

Marsyas absolutely beams. "Oh, 'unheard of' isn't the same as 'doesn't happen,' baby Hegemony."

"You have the Death master."

"*We* have the Death master," Lavinia corrects, presenting a clenched fist.

"But—" Winter's protest dies as the Blackgate matriarch begins to laugh.

"But nothing, sweetheart," Marsyas crows, one hand still directed at the Cerises, scrounging with their children on the tiles around the fountain, the other now cuffing the knobby, ashen shoulder of Ursula. "Proximity to the Elemental relic made generations of Hegemonys the most powerful witches on earth, all while they claimed they were just like us, and mere shepherds for the power of the Four

Lines." She squeezes Ursula's shoulder so hard the decaying flesh compresses under the pressure like rotting fruit, the skin splitting, blood and viscera oozing. *"Lies!"*

Winter gasps audibly as she blinks at her grandmother.

"Here's the thing your Hegemony ancestors never wanted anyone to know. Holding the master relic of one's line makes them infinitely more powerful than they would be alone. And the Death relic happens to be in a form that allows more than one person to hold it at once." Marsyas smiles. "Luna, please collect your grandbaby and their new special friend."

"No!" Winter and Infinity protest together.

"Yes," Marsyas insists, wheeling around to the Starwood matriarch and drawing her forward, with a hand holding the Celestial master. "Lavinia, be a dear and break Ursula's spell. I have you covered."

The real Lavinia smiles her Blackgate grin and takes Ursula's limp arm in her own, wheeling on Wren and the final master relic in her hand.

Luna jolts forward, sunlight ropes shooting from her hands in an effort to lasso Winter and Infinity who run toward her, dodging her efforts. But they look past their attack—and that's when I realize: they're going for Ursula. They've just joined this situation and prioritized the most important piece of the puzzle.

The final relic.

Luna's magic lasso loops around Infinity's wrist and yanks them away. Winter dodges and shoots ice from her own palms, turning the ropes into a sizzling steam. But the magic reforms into briar-like vines, coming at both of them in a wave. I realize then that I can truly see exactly what they're doing. Maybe it's their ingredients, like in the truth spell. Maybe it's the prism of my prison. Either way, I'm grateful.

They fight it off with spells and grunts, but the vines crawl and grow, multiplying faster than either can burn them away.

"It's the master," Infinity wheezes.

"That's right, child," Marsyas coos. "I hold Luna's magic, and

I hold Luna's master. She's more powerful than either of you, and she's a literal sack of bones."

There's a shout and Hex breaks free from the scrum with his parents bleeding and holding Ada, limp in his arms. But then Hector staggers to his feet, one arm hanging at a sick angle at his side, and launches himself onto his son's back.

"I would tell the twins that too, but I fear they wouldn't hear me over their own yelling. So *loud*." Marsyas tosses her grinning visage over her shoulder. "Now, Lavinia!"

And there's my doppelgänger, just feet from Wren, wielding Ursula's limp arm, the corpse's fingertips aimed directly at Wren.

But before the magic can burst through, a fireball shoots in from the direction of Hegemony Manor.

A body comes next.

Lavinia dodges the fireball but not the person.

Auden.

He plows into Lavinia's side with all the skill of the lacrosse player he is. The trajectory of the magic arcs with Ursula's guided arm, swinging wide, away from Wren's frozen form.

The three of them crash to the garden tiles, falling in such a way that Ursula's arm is still forward, a jutted sword of magic.

Pointed straight at me.

CHAPTER 39

AUDEN

A sick thud sets my teeth on edge as I crash to the garden tiles, the real Lavinia Blackgate and the reanimated body of my grandmother tangled together in a crushing slide. The terra-cotta shatters on impact, road rash pebbling our skin in a searing sting.

Over my head, a jagged shard of Elemental power shoots from Ursula's outstretched arm on impact. I can't follow the trajectory, but if it's hit its mark and freed Wren, I only hope I've given Evander enough time to make a difference.

Our momentum fragments as Lavinia cuts Ursula loose. The body of my grandmother skates to the side, a puppet discarded, right into the base of a browning topiary. With full control of her limbs, Lavinia wedges herself on top of me, pinning my thrashing legs with her weight and leverage. She jams my hands together in a pinpoint over my head, her own charged rabbit's foot relic smashed between her palm and mine, burning my skin like an iron left on high and steaming.

Trying not to scream, I bite down so hard I taste the copper and salt of blood on my tongue.

Lavinia looms over me, a small sound of appreciation at the pain she sees on my face, and my stubborn—albeit useless—determination to hide it. A necklace strung with what appears to be an actual human eyeball swings wildly over the hollow of my throat, the blurry proof of her heir's *X* scar visible, red, raw, and angry in the background. The real Lavinia's face presses in, ropes of dark hair shading it in a frame of shadow as her pale features contort into a vicious grin. She stinks of damp—mold, decay. Death.

"Auden Hegemony, I've missed that smug face of yours."

I unhinge my jaw and form the best smile of my own that I

can under the circumstances, trying to keep my pride intact. "You could've seen it whenever you liked. I'm always available for tea and polite conversation."

"There's the problem. I will never have anything polite to say to you." That grin widens. "And I'm going to make sure you never have anything to say to me ever again."

I can't have her making declarations like that.

I buck and writhe beneath her, trying to slide her weight to no avail. Worse, Lavinia lowers her center of gravity, her torso folding into mine, upper body shifting so that one forearm and rabbit's foot relic pin both my wrists now. To leverage it, her face is so close that the velvet swell of her cheekbone slides against mine, her breath hot on my neck. For a heartbeat, I think she might kiss me—or bite me, perhaps—but instead, she cuffs her freed hand against my throat.

Death magic surges through me, a smoldering, fetid tide, amplified by a pea-shaped talisman smashed between her palm and my skin. A feral shout tears from my throat as her magic dissolves the skin surrounding my windpipe like ash-black acid—

A screaming force plows into Lavinia.

Her hands lose purchase on my throat and wrists as she's rolled roughly to the side in a blur of movement and cracking of tile. Gasping, I push myself onto my elbows, trying to skitter away, gain purchase, *move*.

Before me, already upright, is Lavinia with both hands windmilling forward at a figure holding her roughly by the hair.

Ruby.

Lavinia claws blindly, unable to right herself to see Ruby, let alone manage a direct hit. Ruby dislodges the hand stained black from where it had been tangled in the girl's hair. A glint of metal flashes in that freed grip and then she's stabbing at the closed fist of Lavinia Blackgate.

In the same moment I realize Ruby is slashing out with a butter knife, I understand why.

Ruby hits her mark, Lavinia's balled grip flies open and a marble-sized bone fragment plinks onto the garden tile and rolls away.

"Auden!" Ruby yells, just as Lavinia kicks out, clubbing Ruby in the knees and sending them both rolling into the dinner table.

I scramble to my feet and dive for the bone shard. It wedges itself into a weedy gap that's formed between the edge of the tiles and the fountain. I scrape my fingers in the crevice and pick it up. As soon as it's between my thumb and forefinger, I glance up to see Lavinia barreling toward me, blood streaking like rainwater from shallow cuts spotting her hand.

Thinking fast, I call the murky water from the fountain's basin and funnel it into a jet stream straight for Lavinia.

The high-powered spray blasts her back, and the Death witch lands in a heap, her skull dashing against the stone tiles with a crack. She moans but doesn't rise as I tear my gaze away, wedge the shard beneath my heel, and stomp.

The bone fragment shatters to dust, a jet-black plume of magic rising from the snow-white powder like shimmering smoke.

"You *asshole*!" Lavinia shrieks, trying to sit up, blood streaming from a cut above her brow and into an eye. "That was my master!"

Lungs heaving, throat burning, and fear stinging my veins, a smile touches my lips.

My victory is short-lived.

"Auden! Watch out!" Winter shrieks.

My head snaps up.

At first I find Winter, struggling with Infinity to offload Luna, attacking them with the full force of two relics through Marsyas's machinations. I can't see Evander, but I hope he's shielding Wren and attacking Marsyas at the same time. The Cerises are off the board to my left, the four of them in a wrestling match on the grass.

And that's when I realize Winter's eyes are drilled past me, toward the Cerises.

I shift my gaze to the other end of the garden battlefield and—

Kaysa Blackgate has finally appeared.

Charging in from the direction of the estate cemetery, a feverish grin splashed under wild eyes and flying hair.

Athena Blackgate is nowhere in sight—but the girl is not alone.

Instead of her mother, Kaysa is joined by a literal army of the dead.

Spilling over the crest of the hill to the manicured lawn are at least two dozen skeletons under her control. My father, aunt, and uncle are there, I'm sure of it. Probably Shadrack too.

Worse, Kaysa also somehow hooked a few spirits. A handful of ghosts lead the charge high above her head, soaring against the cloud-dark sky, lightning-fast bodies marked by gaping, black-hole mouths.

"Oh shit."

The ghosts zoom ahead, diving like birds of prey.

They swarm the Cerises, directed by Kaysa or perhaps a sense of the living, to surround Hex and Ada, skipping their parents altogether. Hex is shielding his sister, who is dangerously still, his hands a blur of alternating protective shields and offensive countermoves as he fights them alone.

And then they find me.

Kaysa sends the closest pair plummeting straight at me. I toss up a shield—

The ghosts go straight through.

They flank and circle beneath my useless shield. I will my feet to run. If they're going to follow me, they're going to pay a visit to the woman who orchestrated this mess.

I toss back a bolt of fire, my aim haphazard as I barrel toward Marsyas—

Marsyas, who is short, but standing tall. Evander is at her feet, turning blue and kicking beneath a spell. Before her is Ursula, her long fingers cupping Wren's shoulder. With one blitzing second, the magic prison around Wren evaporates.

My heart drops, as the girl blinks into consciousness, eyes wide and confusion twisting her features. Wren's attention solidifies on the ghosts first, her lips dropping open as she shouts triumphantly, "I *knew* it!"

"Wren!" Ruby yells, hopping up from where she'd apparently been hiding behind the dinner table. She waves her hands like she's calling down a plane. "Throw it!"

Wren snaps to her sister's voice, her arm jutting back automatically at the order.

Marsyas lunges for Wren's hands, but the girl is quick, dodging away. Her frozen feet stumble, numb, and she lists to the side, but not before she flings the Elemental relic over Marsyas's silver head and toward Ruby. There's a burst of movement as Lavinia rounds the table, bloodstained hands outstretched, angling for a fumble.

The chain and pendant with Morgana's breath loops through the air, awkward and losing velocity with each second airborne. I aim a gust of wind at it but I'm too late, and it drops to the tiles in front of Ruby, instead of anywhere near her waiting hands.

The round ball at the end of the chain slides between the table and chair legs. Ruby shoots herself between the gap.

Then, it's as if everything skids to a halt.

The swooping ghosts, the zombie witches, the movement of wind, and sun, and heart.

All of it is shrunken to the pinpoint of action as Ruby's ash-stained hand closes around the final relic, and the silver ball disappears into her fist.

And then it's in motion again.

Lavinia tackles Ruby's ankles.

The unmistakable sizzle and stink of Death magic plumes acrid in the air as Lavinia hauls Ruby bodily out from beneath the table. Ruby bucks, slaps, fights, until Lavinia roughly dashes Ruby's head against a chair so hard it falls over.

Triumphant, Lavinia hoists up the girl. Disoriented and weak on legs charred by Death magic, the skin festering with welts beneath shredded leggings, Ruby lists, a crimson stain blooming at her temple.

Yet the relic stays firmly in Ruby's grip.

The real Lavinia Blackgate clamps a forearm around her captive's middle, effectively pinning both arms and her torso against her own taller body. Her other hand cuffs Ruby's throat. The girl's eyes flutter open, immediately panicked, knowing, terrified.

Lavinia's hand constricts around Ruby's windpipe, and she gives a victorious Blackgate smile.

"Any of you move, and she's dead."

CHAPTER 40

AUDEN

My own throat burns with Lavinia's magic, the throbbing pain of it the only part of me moving. I'm not even sure I'm breathing.

Evander has pushed up on one arm now, fighting for consciousness from his spot on the ground, Wren at his side.

Winter and Infinity are back-to-back and stock-still. Hex, with an unmoving Ada draped in his arms, is being escorted by Kaysa's ghosts and their disheveled corpse parents, the skeletons fanning out behind them.

They're circling us. Closing us in.

"Look at them, obeying. They must like you much more than they ever did my Lavinia," Marsyas muses to Ruby, approaching. "None of these brats ever would've been so kind to my girls. Playing pranks on them, provoking them, doing anything they could to get them in trouble. Turns out the adults were of the same mindset."

Something twists in my gut.

Marcos Blackgate, the scapegoat.

The penance for what Ursula lost. For keeping the Four Lines together.

Marsyas crosses to Ruby and takes her closed fist in her wizened palm. "Give it to me, girl."

A muscle in Ruby's jaw ticks, her mouth drawn thin and hard. Her hand is swallowed in Marsyas's own, but the tendons in her forearm tense and flash, her grip tightening impossibly over the relic.

"Silly girl," Marsyas tuts, that Blackgate grin spreading across her face as dangerous as a knifepoint. "Just because they like you doesn't mean they will save you. Loyalty means nothing to these people.

Power, though, that is everything." She leans in close. "And in this moment, their power is *mine*."

Death magic, smoking and acrid, bolts out of Marsyas, branding Ruby's hand. She shrieks, her ashen fingers fly open, and the final master relic falls into Marsyas's palm. Wren cries out from her kneeling spot next to Evander, as tears squeeze out of eyes pinned upon her sister. "Don't you dare!"

The matriarch chuckles at the outburst, as if Wren has performed a trick instead of admonished her cruelty.

"Too late and too ill-informed, young one. What I do is never a dare." Marsyas pats Ruby's cheek. She can't so much as wince away, ensnared in Lavinia's ferocious grip. "It wasn't worth it. It would've been mine anyway."

With that, Marsyas whirls around, hands raised triumphantly over her head and toward the ominous, silver-clouded sky.

In them, the four master relics once hidden upon these grounds.

"The masters are mine, despite certain stubborn, *stupid* setbacks. Which means I'm one acquisition away from everything I've wanted since the day you cruel idiots took my son away from me. Power over you, power over every Four Lines witch in North America, the power to do with all of you as I wish. And I wish for you to pay."

Marsyas slips all the relics except for her own bone shard away into the stretchy confines of her black clothing and turns her attention to Evander and Wren, huddled not six feet away from her.

"Evander, I could've killed you five minutes ago, but I thought keeping you alive would be worth it just for the look on your face when you became the last Hegemony to hold the High Sorcerer's ring, and the first Hegemony to acknowledge Blackgate control over the Four Lines."

Evander tries to right himself to something of a sitting position, Wren supporting his arm as he shifts from a lean to a slouch. He wets his cracked lips still tinged blue from her spell and glares at her with all the intensity Evander Ulysses Hegemony has ever mustered.

"I don't have it."

His voice is hoarse but determined.

"Dear boy, I know your play is to be gruff, stern, *manly*. It's not in your nature or at least in your act to give in, especially to a soft, little old woman. Yes, I know." Marsyas flings her arms out wide. "But, Evander, look around you. You've been conquered by your moldering elders. You are literally pinned in by the ghosts of Hegemonys past. Auden's poet of a father would've loved the metaphors abounding here—thank you, sweet Kaysa, for the perfect motif."

The youngest Blackgate beams from her place among her undead army.

"Evander, just do it." Winter's voice breaks as her plea lands flat at his feet.

Marsyas's lips twitch at this turn of events, a Hegemony begging, but her granddaughters don't even try to hide their widening smiles. The matriarch shakes her head at him. "The Death Line has you at bay with our very power, and holds the master relics. Evander, you are beat. You have my ring. Either you die and I pull it off your corpse, or you look me in the eye and transfer power like the man you're trying to be."

She's right. We're surrounded on all sides by the dead. She has every relic, and they're amplifying her power with each and every use. We're outnumbered, outgunned. Too fragile.

But Marsyas Blackgate is wrong.

Not just about who holds the ring. But about who holds the power.

I drag my gaze from Ruby to Ursula. My grandmother's corpse hovers, inert, like a fetid store mannequin, her rotting flesh and animated bones waiting for instruction, lifeless cerulean eyes focused on her master, Marsyas.

When Ursula gave me my key and told me of my role, she gave me a set of instructions too.

Now, here is what you must do.

Slowly, as not to draw attention, I fish the chain out from beneath my collar. I watch Marsyas challenge Evander wordlessly. I've got it fully in my grasp as her expression wavers, frustration seeping into the set of her shoulders. "Lavinia, kill the girl."

"No!" I shout.

All three Blackgates turn my way.

I brandish the ring, unmistakable. Silver band, slim cut, the four gems flashing in the daylight.

"He can't give you the ring because I'm holding it." I pin my gaze on Lavinia. "Let Ruby go and it's yours."

Marsyas tilts herself toward me, a bull finding its target. "A trade?"

"An exchange. You let Ruby go. Let her live. And I will give you this ring."

"At the same time."

Magic flickers beneath my skin, but I tamp it down and focus solely on Marsyas Blackgate. "No—you first. I need to see that Ruby's safe and out of Lavinia's hands. She's innocent."

Marsyas's lips part and her teeth flash.

"I wouldn't call her that, she's lied to you for two days. But that's beside the point. The point is I refuse to trust a Hegemony."

Her eyes narrow, color rising in her throat, magic sparking in her palm around the Death master pinched between her fingers.

"How could I after what Ursula did to my Marcos?" she sneers. "Trust is a seed that will never grow between us again. And, frankly, it's not one I need. Shall I remind you that you're surrounded, you're outnumbered, and, though I think it's top of mind to you, my dear, sweet Lavinia, a girl you *bullied* for years, has hold of your little girlfriend. So, no—"

The magic beneath my skin flares into a fireball, engulfing my hand.

Devouring the ring.

Marsyas screeches at the sight of the metal at the heart of the flame, takes a step, hand outreached, a pitch-black twist of magic gathering—

And trips over Wren's leg, kicked out across her path.

The old woman stumbles forward, hands flying open to catch

herself before she face-plants on the ground. The bone shard in her hand skitters away. Lavinia shoves Ruby aside, depositing her roughly into the table, as she tracks the relic, pinging across the tiles and into the grass.

"Nona!" Kaysa shrieks, rushing forward as her sister falls away.

Her army of the dead advance too.

I spin, and, with everything I have left, shoot out a shield as wide and thin as I can make it. It won't keep out the ghosts, but it can slow Kaysa and her skeletons.

"I've got this side, Evander," Infinity yells. I look over my shoulder and they've thrown up a shield covering the rest of the gaps as Kaysa rushes forth. The dead rattle the shields so hard, I think they might shatter.

"And I've got the ghosts," Winter announces—and, with a defense I missed, she harnesses enough wind to blow the ghosts up and away. It's a shield of a different kind. Genius.

Between us, Evander and Wren incapacitate Marsyas. The girl sits on her back, while Evander grabs hold of her wrists and his power. The earth opens right beneath her hands, the tile cracking, two gaping holes sucking her arms in up to her armpits and clamping her in place. Marsyas is left face down, dangerous hands and rabbits' feet relics trapped.

Evander wastes no time working with Wren to fish out all four master relics from the matriarch's pockets as a hurricane of bones batters the magic Winter, Infinity, and I hold tight. I breathe a quick sigh of relief that Ursula's spell isn't triggered by their forcible taking of the Death relic. The magic didn't trap Marsyas when she stole the others because she wasn't under that spell, and now that loophole works in reverse for us.

A scream breaks from the direction of Kaysa.

I turn just quick enough to see the bodies of Hector and Sanguine Cerise bowl into the skeletons like wolverines, ripping apart the bones and flinging the skeletons aside as the younger Blackgate holds up her hands, trying to direct soldiers who are shattering one after one.

"What—"

"Blood will have blood, you asshole Death witches!" Hex screams, Ada slumped to his side—no shroud, so hopefully not dead—the picture of vengeance in his expression and posture, his anger standing on end.

With a flick of Hex's wrist, his mother's corpse hurtles straight at Kaysa.

I gasp—without a Blackgate in control, Hex's magic can move his parents, just as they once were able to compel him. No master needed.

Sanguine rips the bone shard out of the girl's hand and crushes it in her otherworldly zombie grip. Kaysa screams and tries to pitch away but is caught by Hector under Hex's control.

From behind there's a screech. I turn in time to see Ruby twisting her heel to crush the bone-shard fragment on the tile, Lavinia on her knees, hands in a panic. "Oh, you *bitch*!"

Ruby takes off in a run, Lavinia clawing at the ruined skin of her ankles. I race toward the Death witch, cuff her hand, throw up a shield, and—

There's a bolt of green magic that whizzes past my ear. I turn to follow it, and in that moment, Lavinia is suddenly frozen in the same forced-air magical prison Ursula created as punishment. I track the magic back, and there Evander stands, our Elemental relic slipped around his neck, amplifying his power. Kaysa is next, frozen in a heartbeat.

And then, suddenly, everything stops.

The skeletons drop where they stand. The ghosts evaporate. The attack is over.

All is quiet except the pounding of my heart, the heave and exhale of my breath, and Ruby appearing beside me, her hand slipping into mine as she slumps into my side. Weak but warm—alive. "Is it over?"

I swallow and answer truthfully.

"Almost."

CHAPTER 41

RUBY

With two out of three Blackgates frozen on the lawn, we converge on the final one.

I hold tight to Auden, my side pressed into his as the weight of his arm drapes over my shoulders. Though my body trembles with bruising magic—the skin around my ankles as black as ash, my throat raw, my head throbbing—I feel warm and safe, if not okay.

Cool relief swells through me at the sight of Wren, standing whole without a scratch on her, the butter knife tight in her grip. My sister watches Marsyas as if the woman isn't incapacitated, as if she'll burst free from her improvised bindings. Not likely, given the Death witch is face down on the garden tiles, her arms sucked into the earth all the way up to her shoulders, her head tilted awkwardly to one side.

Evander has squatted to Marsyas's level, all four master relics bulging in his sweatpants pockets.

He doesn't say anything until we're all assembled.

The Cerises—Ada alive but barely, as pale as a sheet and silently propped against her brother, who's smudged in a tapestry of blood and dirt, and grinning something ferocious. Infinity and Winter bracket the other side, grass staining their clothing, twigs lodged in Winter's long hair as Infinity pats their short, wiry curls, dirt raining onto their broad shoulders.

We stare down at Marsyas. Waiting. Watching.

Finally, Evander presses a hand to a mélange of pebbled dirt and cracked stone tiles in front of her.

"I want to hear your plan from the very beginning. Don't leave any part out. And don't excuse any of the elders. We know you met with Luna and Hector. We know you killed them both. I want confirmation about which one of you killed Ursula. If I have to, I will use a truth spell on you." Evander pauses, and gestures to the group at large, even Wren and me. "If we use a truth spell and are still unsure, you will die before midnight to ensure we satisfy Ursula's spell, so I would be honest with us, even if it implicates yourself. We are the future of the Four Lines, and we need to hear every word of your betrayal so that we may never allow something like it again."

Marsyas seems to consider this with a thin inhale and the purse of her expressive mouth. It's clear she doesn't appreciate being lectured at by someone barely older than her granddaughters.

"The story is long and tedious. Therefore, I do think it would be a much more pleasant experience for both myself and you as listeners if you were able to secure me in a different manner before I begin."

In answer, Evander stands from his crouch and hauls a dining chair from the table to the most level set of tiles near Marsyas. Again, he squats down to look her in the eye.

"I will release you and escort you to this chair. When you are seated, I will freeze your limbs to guarantee you do not run and you do not use your magic as you tell the story."

Marsyas's answer is to fire back with her own set of demands. "Before I tell my tale, I want you to promise me that my granddaughters are safe. They had no hand in any of these murders and do not deserve the ultimate punishment. Do not make examples out of them, Evander Hegemony. Their father's life became forfeit, and I need you to promise me you will not punish them for something they did not do."

Evander looks her in the eye. "I promise you they will live."

Marsyas's mouth sets in a grim line and she nods.

Evander presses a hand to the earth. It immediately shudders, releasing her. He gets her upright, his grasp unyielding as he carefully spins her toward the chair, checking his watch. "We have mere hours left. Tell your story accurately and fully. Do not leave anything out."

The woman waves him off and *cackles*.

"I'm old but you don't have to repeat yourself. My mind's as sharp as a knife."

Before the fall of the last word, Marsyas's hand whips out and snatches the butter knife from Wren's grasp.

"*No!*" I cry in the same moment Evander flings an arm out, an unseen shield shooting out to cover my sister's shocked form.

But when the knife comes down, it isn't aimed at Wren.

Or Evander.

Or anyone else in our group.

Marsyas aims the knife at herself.

With one violent slash, she drags the weak serrations of the blade across the width of her throat.

Despite the dull tool, the awkward angle, the slim opportunity, Marsyas hits her mark.

A wave of gasps, averted eyes, and pivoting bodies ripples through us as blood spurts from the wound in a jittering spray. Marsyas flops backward too fast, too heavy for Evander's hold on her single arm. Hex lunges forward, blood streaking down his own makeshift shield as he casts it aside to latch onto her opposite side and get her into a more controlled fall to the terra-cotta.

When Marsyas is on the ground, her eyes are wide, dark, glassy. Unseeing. Her body shudders violently as Hex wrenches the knife from her grasp and sends it skidding away, under the table. Then, she goes still. Evander and Hex sit back on their heels. Hands drop away from shocked mouths.

In a blink it becomes clear that the time to save Marsyas from herself has passed.

In that quiet, there's a *pop,* like air releasing under pressure.

Then a lightning bolt of magic crackles in the air around us. I may not be able to see magic, not like the witches, but I can register the aftereffects.

The tiles beneath our feet reshape, reform, smooth and whole.

Verdant green zips through the garden grounds, from the topiary to the lawn, to the dead rose bushes and hedges lining the edges, each plant and blade and bloom acting as a brush, soaking up a fresh coat of paint.

There's a groan and sigh as every crack and fissure in the foundation, floors, and walls of Hegemony Manor seal and smooth.

A rustle as two waiters stir from their quarantined sleep; the murmur of a man pulling himself up from behind the bar beside the tearoom entrance.

The creak and sweep of the gates of Hegemony Manor yawn open.

Ursula's final tasks, her last spell, fulfilled.

The murderer has been punished. All the relics collected.

Wren backs up and slots in beside me, her hand slipping into mine. I squeeze my own sister's pinky as a new stillness settles over us like a blanket. Just one moment of calm. There is no assembled army of Death witches outside, waiting to pounce.

There's nothing but the spell lifting. Totally. Fully. Comple— we're going to make it out.

But not before the magic has its way with Marsyas Blackgate.

Like Ursula, she ages rapidly, her corpse shriveling as the years pile on. She didn't enchant herself to look as young as Ursula, but still, the effect is stunning. Like watching a caterpillar emerge as a butterfly at warp speed.

Then, when the last of her true age is etched into mottled skin, Marsyas's soul's truth shimmers into place.

It's the same ghostly brilliance of Ursula's, the same dour expression on the smoky bust of Marsyas's face despite the perennial upturn to the corners of her mouth that made it always look like she was smiling even when at her most furious.

I've witnessed this before, yet I still fear some sort of magical trick, some sort of illusion made to appear like the soul's truth to deceive us into a momentary lapse of complacency.

But when it speaks in that wry, raspy voice, I know Marsyas Blackgate is truly dead.

"I, Marsyas Lavinia Blackgate, matriarch of the Death Line,

commit that this is my soul's truth, bare for any and all living creatures to witness."

The ghostly bust pauses, eyes focusing on her audience, as clever and spry as in life.

I know what's coming next. Still, it's a shock when Marsyas gazes out at us with those sightless eyes, no longer amused and ornery. They're accusing.

"My truth is this: I have taken my own life."

Even though I understand her endgame—destruction of the Four Lines, destruction of all of us—a pang of guilt still chimes in my gut, unbidden but undeniable.

"To those hearing my truth, know this now: my death was an act of self-defense and should not be punished."

Auden squeezes my shoulders, and I tuck my cheek into the crook of his neck. His pulse a steady, calming rhythm. This boy I met two days ago—who I lied to because of this woman who is dead now before us—is the anchor I have in what is real and not. Still, my heart breaks as Marsyas's truth unfurls.

"It must be said that this outcome was a decade in the making. The day my son, Marcos Aurelius Blackgate, was executed at the hands of Ursula Elvire Muscatel Hegemony, High Sorcerer of the Four Lines, was the day I chose this path. A path that had only two possible ends when I began it: with my death, or with Ursula's. My destination wasn't control, it was revenge."

Auden exhales as if he can't believe it. A truth that provides answers rather than fuel for more endless questions.

"I plotted alone for almost ten years before I pulled the others in. Luna, who knew it was a coin flip between Erasmus and Marcos for who took the fall for Ursula's three-pronged grief. Hector, who would do anything to squeeze more from Marcos's death than his own survival and a never-ending stream of guilt to compound the furnace of inadequacy that drove him. But they were never my partners. Those who lived when my son did not were as much my enemy as Ursula."

The rabbiting of my heart slows as the inevitability of what comes next falls into place.

"The plan we agreed upon was simple. Take out Ursula at the very beginning of her traditional speech. I would exit the moment she prepared to speak, a red herring on the outside, two marks left on the inside. Disposable, non-magical decoys."

That confirmation burns all the way down as it plops in my gut. We're the marks. But we also survived this long.

"Luna didn't care for power; she simply wanted her master relic and an exit. But the moment Hector saw what was truly at stake, the plan began to dissolve. He was blinded by vengeance and accessible power, eager to right a wrong that he'd been born with. By the time I'd returned to the game as agreed, he had unshakable designs on holding the High Sorcerer title. I immediately stole the Celestial relic, and when I found Hector bargaining to hold the Elemental master with Winter, I knew he had to die."

Hex punches out a breath, from his spot on the ground. Ada's head lolls. Winter is stone-still as Infinity turns to look at her, even as they don't abandon their embrace.

Evander and Auden both want to ask but it's the patriarch who does it. "Win, is that true?"

Tears pool in her eyes as Winter nods, her whole face crumpled together, shoulders quaking. "Yes. I thought giving Hector our master would just end it. Without violence or bloodshed. I meant it when I said I didn't believe it was worth it. Evander, don't—"

What she tries to say next is cut off by Marsyas, her truth still marching on.

"But Wren beat me to the confrontation, and was enough of a distraction that not only was I not able to snatch away the Blood master, but I couldn't gain the Elemental relic either, as Wren had stolen it to activate Ursula's spell and protect herself. Winter must have heard the commotion, came back, and found the mess. She heard the Cerises' soul's truths. I will admit, I could have tampered with their shrouds right away but did not, hoping the remaining

364 + SARAH HENNING

witches would finally condemn the imposters I had hired, which would give me more time to set up my final push for vengeance."

Auden's arm tightens around my shoulders. I squeeze my sister's hand.

"I wasn't going to be happy with control, I was only going to be happy with annihilation. Of Ursula, of all the Hegemonys, of the other High Families. I wanted to leave here with my granddaughters, and scorched earth. Instead, I will leave as ash."

I think that's it, but the projection's gaze finds Ursula's body, Marsyas's gaseous lips pulling into a cavernous Blackgate smile as storm clouds crowd her dark eyes.

I imagine her seeing red.

"I will end my truth by telling you that when I reached for the Death essence within the body of Ursula Hegemony, I connected with the last minutes of her life."

Auden inhales sharply—surprised.

"Ursula knew what I had planned. She knew for months. I do not know how she knew, only that she intended to address it head-on and would have if the poison had not done its work. She'd meant to out us, punish us, and leave our successors to take over—this was precisely why she demanded two generations at dinner when she'd been lax before, especially with my own line."

Evander's green eyes flash between Auden and Ursula's corpse. He nods to himself, jaw flexing.

The soul's truth continues.

"Ursula knew it was a gamble to confront us instead of chaining us up the moment we arrived on site, but she wanted to surprise us, shame us, and keep the Four Lines intact for younger generations. She truly believed she was doing good work, rooting out bad behavior, but it was her iron fist in leading the line that led to her life's biggest tragedy—and the final road for both of us."

That's the last word.

The soul's truth shimmers, flickers, and then disappears, evaporating into the silver clouds above.

Hex and Evander stand, backing away toward us.

There won't be a victim's shroud this time. She wasn't murdered. There's no evidence to preserve.

Still, Evander holds out his hands, and together, six witches and two regular girls watch as the body of Marsyas Blackgate is wrapped in magic, finally at peace after a decade of unimaginable suffering.

My heart twists for Marsyas. For all she's done—to me, to them, to their *unbreakable, unusual family*—a piece of me still aches for her losses and the way they've shaped her, motivated her, and, finally, betrayed her.

In the silence that follows, the carnage is strewn about, much like the shattered remains of the meal that started it all, still littering the dinner table.

The bodies of Ursula, Luna, Hector, and Sanguine lie inert, rotting heaps crumpled at odd angles, falling in convenience, not any natural manner.

One by one, Evander covers their bodies in the same frozen protection. A temporary shroud, a temporary rest. The skeletons receive no such grace, heaps of bones that they are. I wonder if the Hegemonys will be able to determine who they are and where they belong. It strikes me as something that will need privacy—sorting out the last of ancestors and stowing them away like pieces of a board game tipped over.

The forms of the real Lavinia and Kaysa stand like new statues among the refreshed topiaries, bubbling fountain, the onyx splendor that is Hegemony Manor.

Evander returns to us, jaw set in a tight line, his strong arms hanging at his sides, wrung out. "It's done."

"Not yet." Auden shifts, squeezing my shoulder once before removing his arm entirely and stepping out of my grasp. Despite the rising summer heat, cool air hits me in the loss of his body next to mine. But as he takes that step forward, and gathers one of the two chains at his throat and pulls it over his head, a new warmth spreads through my body like a shockwave—relief. "You have one more thing to do."

The High Sorcerer's ring glints between us all, the gems glowing red, black, green, and white.

Evander freezes. Winter gasps. The twins gape. Infinity stiffens.

"You—you didn't destroy it?" Wren asks, quietly, in awe.

"It's not possible to destroy the ring with magic as long as all of the master relics are tethered to it." Auden's gaze meets Evander's eyes. "Something Marsyas clearly didn't know."

"But you did."

It's not a question, but a statement from Evander.

"That, I did know."

Something passes between the cousins, wordless but worth a note within their shared history.

Evander swallows. Auden raises the ring higher and looks each one of the remaining witches in the face. "If any of you have objections to Evander Hegemony wearing the High Sorcerer's ring, say it now."

"I do."

Infinity has removed Winter's arm from their shoulders, stepping forward—but it's not their voice in objection.

It's Evander's.

We all stare at him. "I do," he repeats. "Our parents tried to change the lines to make things better for us, and they all suffered because of it. We suffered because of it. Our parents were right to question how we govern the lines, Infinity and Luna were right to question it too. I think perhaps we need some time away to really think about what we want as the future of the Four Lines, no matter what that looks like."

Then, Evander reaches into his pockets and pulls out the Celestial and Blood relics. The vial of Nostradamus's blood glints in the light as it sits in his open palm, while the box is heavy and solid. Both, an offering, one extended toward Infinity, the other toward the twins.

"Take the relics and your dead—and all the time you need."

In that moment, Evander is every inch a leader as Ursula seemed to be in the short time we'd known her. He gestures to the whole of the group—even Wren and me. "We're the future of the Four Lines.

We'll be here when you—when all of us—decide if it is together or apart."

Infinity and Hex accept the relics, and face their loved ones, broken upon the grass. Winter moves to join Infinity, and they let her.

My heart lifts at that.

But it falls just as quickly when a small sound catches my attention and I see Auden and Evander have moved to stand before us now. They're tall and clear-eyed, shoulder to shoulder, facing where Wren and I cling together, fingers still entwined.

I can still feel the warmth of Auden's body pressed against mine. See the fear in his eyes when Marsyas held my life in her hands. But that was then and this is now.

And I'm not one of them.

I never was.

This is it, then. The moment when our status as liars, as outsiders, as regular people can no longer go unaddressed.

I tip up my chin, and wait for him to say it.

For the words to come out of that too-perfect mouth. The one that kissed me only hours ago.

That the Four Lines can't let us leave with what we know. For their magic to flood my senses until I don't remember a thing. I'll awake with Wren somewhere near here, dumped on the side of the road, expected to point ourselves home.

But then, Auden's hand slips into mine—the one stained with visual proof of my lies. The one he healed. Those magical eyes of his crinkle in the corners, and for a wingbeat of a second I have hope.

"Now it's over, Ruby. Time for you to go home."

CHAPTER 42

AUDEN

When midnight comes, the three remaining Hegemonys station ourselves once again in the solarium of the manor that bears our name. It no longer smells of Luna's blood. Magic and darkness obscure what happened here hours ago.

Our houseguests are gone for now, the quarantined workers attended to, the magical and mental cleanup underway. There are still miles to go, but tonight, after everything, we fall into the comfort of our usual motions on the nights we must be Hegemonys—now this night and every single one forward, perhaps.

Evander, drinking—the amber slosh of scotch against crystal as he settles next to the fire, High Sorcerer's ring glinting from its chain atop his shirt. The ring is unattached to the relics and its original use—for now. Our relic is stowed away in the safe in Ursula's study.

Winter, preening—the day washed away in rosewater suds, her hair wet, clean, and halfway through a braid, her deft fingers making quick work. She almost didn't come back to us, ready to take off the moment Infinity asked. They will. Soon.

Me, reading—not one of my father's coveted editions, but my own memories like things to be noted, examined, analyzed, as I recognize the moment I should've known we would be here.

The memory is as strong as any soul's truth in my mind's eye.

I can picture Ursula in her study chair, prim-backed, fingers threaded together and set atop the leather blotter of her desk, the High Sorcerer's ring catching the light from the diamond-paned windows over her shoulders. Her mouth set in a firm line, cerulean eyes as fierce as a fire's heart and demanding that I look into them.

"We will crack and bleed, and fester until we're healed," Ursula continues, her gaze unwavering. There is magic in that, a thread of power that means what she says in this here and now will never fade from my memory. "Some will see this as a game to be won. What *you* must see it as is a set of instructions. Auden, it is crucial that you do exactly as I say. Is that understood?"

"Yes, Ursula."

A stiff nod—curt, hard, decisive. "Now, here is what you must do."

Next comes a deep, steadying breath. So unusual—so commonly *human*—I nearly fall out of my chair.

She dips her chin, gaze still fierce as her carefully chosen words.

"We are an unbreakable family." Ursula nods, almost to herself as much as to me. "But to live on, we must shatter and bind ourselves back together. This is why when I die, I want you to destroy the master relics."

My lungs shudder to a breathless halt.

The master relics whose wards killed my father. My aunt and uncle. That made us orphans ten years ago.

"To survive, the witches of the Four Lines need to remember why we came together in the first place. I want you to ensure the magic is no longer tethered to the master relics nor my High Sorcerer's ring. Our special family will know what it is to be apart, so we can remember why we're together."

The memory recedes, what actually happened layered beneath. Ursula was right—of course she was—on all of it, all but the final piece.

And I don't know that we will survive this. Not yet.

Evander says my name. He's moved from the fire, seating himself in a wingback chair pulled beside the settee where I'm situated, blinking away the deep violet pockets crowding my vision from staring into the crackling flames too long.

"What?"

Evander answers with a long pull from his glass. Unhurried, calm, all his coiled strength at ease and peace in the aftermath of cleanup, goodbyes, promises, plans.

"Auden," he finally says in the same tone he must have used to get my attention. "How did you know the ring wouldn't burn when you set fire to it? In all my training with Ursula, she didn't tell me that."

"I really thought you were destroying it," Winter adds from her spot, curled like a cat in the settee across from me.

We all had our conversations with Ursula, learning our roles—our places. I may not have been the oathed heir, despite her preferences, but I was the one that she apparently entrusted with what I'm about to say.

My secret. My lie. Every other one spilled out between the cracks and into the light during Ursula's final task.

Every single one except mine.

I sit up, lean forward, my heir's key catching against the collar of yet another Walton-Bridge lacrosse shirt.

"Because," I begin, "when Ursula gave me my title, she also gave me a set of instructions for what to do when she died."

"Instructions?" Evander asks, lowering his glass. "As her executor?"

"Not exactly," I amend. "I was to destroy the master relics, then the ring."

It's as if all the air is sucked out of the room. Even the fire seems to smother and wane.

I nod. "That was her directive. Ursula had come to believe that by breaking the bonds that tie us, the Four Lines would know what it was to be unmoored and consequently recognize the benefits of being united, reconvening stronger than ever."

Cupped into fists, my hands fly apart and then back together, knuckles meeting in a knocking crunch, illustrative.

"She told me the masters needed to be destroyed first because the ring is unbreakable while tied to the relics. No amount of magical or physical manipulation can destroy the ring as long as the masters are tethered to it. She wanted to make sure that I destroyed them properly and was very detailed in exactly how I must do it to succeed."

Winter's brows furrow delicately, while Evander's slam together like a pair of prizefighters.

They can picture it, I know. That same pose of Ursula's, at her desk, the instructions aimed as true and deadly as a sheath of arrows. She always hit her mark, buried her point deep, made it impossible to get away.

It's Evander who asks, "But you didn't?"

"I didn't."

The expressions that follow say it all. *We deserve to know.*

"I planned to do it. That was my job. That was my secret. My lie. Another of Ursula's directives, another test. Not to mention with what Evander saw and knew—it's what our parents seemed to have wanted. To cleave apart our *unusual, unbreakable* family. Shattering it in hopes that it would be better for the following generations, our lines, the witches tethered to us and our choices." I smile at my oldest cousin. "And then, you did it anyway. The outcome was the same as Ursula wanted, but the path was unexpected."

"But you didn't know I would do that. You offered me the ring, the title, and the power. What was that? Some sort of reverse-psychology bullshit, then?"

I nearly laugh, though he's dead serious, because of course he is.

"No," I say, exhaling, "it wasn't reverse psychology. I offered you the ring, the title, and the power in good faith, because in the end, I couldn't do it. I couldn't destroy the relics. Not because I didn't want to acknowledge her wisdom. She thought breaking them was the only way to rebuild the lines, to make us strong enough that what happened to her would never happen again. But when I had the chance, when I could've attacked Marsyas myself and retrieved them just as Evander did, I knew it would be unnecessary. The way we fought together, for our lives, for our legacy, for our family . . . I couldn't."

My cousins' attention rises from their thoughts to my face.

"But you could." Evander rubs his still unshaven jaw. "We broke apart anyway and untethered ourselves from the ring. We did the deed—I think that says something, even if I don't know if the Four Lines will reform. We're not the same as those who came before us. We won't make the same choices. We won't navigate our challenges in the same way. We'll find our own way to thrive."

In that pause, it's a smile that touches my lips.

"Ursula was right, I suppose, when she said I was most loyal to who we are. Maybe she knew that in the end I would defy her if it was the best for us. Maybe she knew Evander would question his right to the title if he had to work for it. Maybe she knew Winter would make sure we considered if it was actually worth it. I don't know. All I know is we ended up here, just as she'd planned."

Winter ties off her braid. Her fingers sweep to the key on her choker, no longer obscured, and she glances into the fire as if our grandmother's face will appear, haughty, hawkish, and full of opinions. "She didn't miss a thing."

Evander gulps down the rest of his scotch in a single swallow. He presses the back of his hand to his mouth until the burn passes. "Well, she did miss one thing—two, actually."

Indeed. Ursula saw and planned for many scenarios, but most definitely not for the imposters. Ruby and Wren are entirely our problem.

One we haven't yet attended to properly.

We could've spelled them to forget what happened—it was what we did to the waitstaff, after all—but we didn't. We just let them leave. In that moment, after all we'd been through together, retention of the truth seemed like a kindness rather than a burden.

Yet, we can't ignore what Ruby and Wren saw. Shock might keep them quiet for a while, but trauma is not a spell.

Winter arches a brow at me. "I don't suppose the instructions Ursula gave you included protocol pertaining to literally the worst con artists in the history of the world?"

I sit forward, elbows resting on my knees. "No, but I do have a couple of ideas."

EPILOGUE

RUBY

SIX WEEKS AFTER

The invitation arrives with a sense of déjà vu.

Cream-colored cardstock. No envelope. Set neatly in the cubby marked "Ruby" in the back room of Agatha's Apothecary & Paperback Emporium.

The penmanship is neat and as sharp as a knife tip.

Saturday night. Formal. Wear whatever color you want. I'll be in touch.

I flip the card over.

Tell no one.

From the ashes of what I'd snuffed out and locked away as we left the grounds of Hegemony Manor, something grows wings and lifts. Since returning home, Wren and I haven't talked about what happened. Not about how we'd walked away, intact but changed. Not about the people we left behind. Who they were, what we knew, what we'd seen.

And yet, we'd still walked away.

No threats. No memory-wipe spell. No magic binding us to secrecy.

I'd burned Marsyas's card. Deleted the file she'd sent that I had stored on my phone. Checked Wren's phone to make sure she'd done the same.

It felt too clean. Too unfinished.

And this is proof.

Immediately, my phone buzzes in the back pocket of my jeans. Wren's name flashes up at me with a FaceTime request. I scoot into the stockroom, flip on the light, and close the door. When I accept and her face fills the screen, I don't even get out a greeting before she's squealing in my ear.

"We're going shopping! Bring your savings account and the good sense to let me dress you."

There's not an ounce of hesitation in my sister's voice. She's just as impulsive as ever, despite what we've been through. Her hazel eyes are round, the bangs she's let grow curtaining that thrilled gaze and grazing the apples of cheeks flushed with excitement.

"Are we sure this is a good idea?" I ask in a whisper. "To go back there?"

"Oh, come on, you saw how it was worded. It's a callback! An inside joke—it made you smile or at least gave you warm fuzzies because it was done *with care*."

Somehow, my voice is even quieter now.

"We haven't seen or heard from *them* in six weeks."

I don't feel like I can say the Hegemony name out loud. Not yet.

As usual, my sister is undeterred. "You saw the mess we walked away from. The actual cleanup is the easy part. The politics? Those loose ends might take years to sort out."

"What if *we're* a set of loose ends?"

"You mean what if it's a trap?" Wren rolls her eyes. "Rubes, we've been there and done that. This isn't a trap, and it isn't a game. It's an *invitation*. They want us back."

I picture Auden's face the last time I saw it. Exhaustion flooding his blue-brown eyes, a smudge of blood on his jaw, throat bruising purple. His hands dotted in thick black ash—proof I'd held them after everything went to shit.

"If they wanted us back, they apparently knew where we were this whole time." I wave my invitation in front of the phone camera for emphasis. "Why do it this way?"

Wren is quickly losing patience with my hesitancy.

"Because it's special. And clever. These people trade those things like currency." She rattles this off like it's a common—and true—fact. "When you're rich, it's more fun to be creative than not."

I blink Auden away from the backs of my eyelids. He was my ally, my protector—coming to my aid even after I had lied to him. And before that, when he thought I was someone terrible he'd known in a past life. But we don't truly know each other. And if anything, I am—we are—a threat to him, his family, his fellow witches. His way of life.

I can't forget that. I won't forget that.

I'm the practical one. The big sister. And this time, even with Auden's form still outlined in the deep purple of every incoming blink, I have to reinforce what going back to Hegemony Manor would mean for us.

"Wren," I say, adjusting the phone so that she can see the entirety of my face in the terrible storeroom light. I can't let her write off the seriousness of my expression. "I would not associate 'fun' with what happened the last time we accepted an invitation like this."

"Well, yeah," she concedes, which seems like a momentary win until she brushes her too-long bangs back into the rest of her dark hair and a daydreamer grin spreads across her face. "But don't you want to know what they want? What happened to the Four You-Know-Whats?" Wren leans in close, so I can only see that upturn of her mouth. "What a certain pair of cousins have been up to since we left? You know they haven't been able to stop thinking about us. We're the ones who got away."

That's precisely what I'm afraid of.

◆ ◆ ◆

"Well, at least now I can say without a shadow of a doubt that it's *fucking haunted*."

That's the first thing Wren whispers to me as we step out of the Uber and walk up the drive to Hegemony Manor. We could've driven ourselves, of course, just rolled up in our beater sedan like it's nothing. A breadcrumb in lieu of breaking the invitation's final instruction.

Tell no one.

I didn't, but I do have the receipts. Literally. An email from Uber with proof of our ride sits in my personal inbox in an open tab on my unlocked computer. In addition to this single step on a digital trail, I may have also left my invitation card in the top drawer of my desk, very prominently available to Dad or Karen if they come snooping should we, say, not be at home when they return from Colorado Springs on Sunday.

And though I consciously did these things in advance of a worst-case scenario, I'd be lying if I didn't admit that a large part of me hopes my preparation means literally only the best things will happen here tonight. The very exciting and romantic things Wren pictures while chasing adventure, not the potential crises that I can't seem to shake.

I wind my arm through my sister's as we aim ourselves toward Hegemony Manor.

It's the final weekend before the school year begins, and August looms heaving and angry over the Continental Divide above the home's gothic roofline. A controlled burn races across the turrets and eaves, the color of which is nearly the same as the tangerine dress Wren picked—a summer day in silk she truly couldn't afford even though this time she ripped off the tags anyway. Meanwhile, I've recycled my prom dress, light blue and extremely basic, because I'm still working to add to a college fund that never got its boost from Marsyas's promises.

The last time we arrived at Hegemony Manor, I'd wished to walk up those tombstone steps and through the double doors, thinking of Mom's love of the place from afar, the new view up close, and the rumors we'd heard about the kids who lived inside.

This time, as we navigate the bricks, the massive doors unlatch before we've even diverted to the path leading around the side of the house to the garden. Evander appears first, slipping into the dusky night, clean-shaven in a crisp white button-up—no suit jacket—and sharp pants.

"You came—welcome."

He seems genuinely delighted, and Wren—the traitor—drops my arm, and runs right up the steps and flings herself at him. No hesitation, no fear, just straight into his arms.

Her mouth connects with his, and Evander stumbles back into the doorframe, surprised but quick enough to catch his balance and both of them before they careen onto the marble behind him. They pull apart long enough for him to say something to her, and Wren laughs out an answer but I don't hear the words as they disappear into the foyer.

Which leaves me face-to-face with the person holding the door—Auden.

Unlike his cousin, he is wearing a suit. This one is expensive and gray like the one he wore so many weeks ago and fits his lean athleticism in a way that has heat rising in my cheeks before I even truly gauge his expression. His skin has the healthy flush of the end of a summer spent outside, and the hue only serves to make his eyes more stunning as they meet mine.

My breath hitches, just like the very first time I saw him. It's possibly even more mortifying this time around.

"Hi, Ruby."

My knees soften, my eyes unseeing anything but him as that initial meeting pages through my mind. The one where he truly thought I was Lavinia Blackgate. Where his very first words accused my sister of lying while telling a story he thought was actually something I'd done, but in actuality was a lie all the way around. Then I burned his hand with a magical relic I'd just thought was an ugly bracelet, and nearly face-planted in my nerves about the whole damn thing.

Here and now, Auden's brow furrows, confusion breaking across the handsome planes of his face—I've been quiet too long. He takes a step forward, down the first step, but then holds himself back, hesitant. "What are you thinking?"

I've scared him—he thinks I'm about to scamper away. Instead, I'm literally stuck on what Wren said days ago about how these people trade cleverness like currency and instead of only worrying about what would happen if things took a turn, I should've considered what would happen if the best possibilities were waiting for us.

Possibilities such as this boy, standing here, looking at me—the real me—like this.

I press my hands to my face and squint at him through the slits between my fingers. "That I can't greet you with some sort of cute and clever callback to our first meeting because the whole thing was absolutely atrocious."

Auden jogs down the rest of the steps until he stands right in front of me, sturdy and solid and smelling of sandalwood and smoke. Like he'd been hiding the summer away in the reading room with a candle and books, not doing whatever has him so suntanned.

"To be fair, I would've laughed if you'd told me we'd gotten off on the wrong foot and reintroduced yourself as Ruby"—God, he's right, that totally would've been the sort of thing I would've read in a book—"but considering how it all went after that, let's not touch anything from that night with a ten-foot pole."

He peels my hands off my face, one by one, and holds them tight between us, peering down at me with the beginnings of a new, wry grin tucked into the corners of his full bottom lip. It's so beautiful, my first instinct is to look down at his hands holding mine to confirm that this is real. That he's actually touching me, that his grin and his words, and everything else are for me.

"Ruby, I don't need you to be full of pithy callbacks to the worst three days of my life, and probably yours." It might be purposeful, or it might be pure coincidence, but his thumb rubs a loop over the curve of the index and middle fingers he'd healed that terrible night. "I'm just glad you're here."

It's not what he said to me when he thought I was Lavinia. But it's close enough to flash my memory to what happened after—to our kiss.

Swallowing, I raise my eyes to look at Auden, my heart picking up a steady rhythm sure to flush more than just my cheeks. He's so beautiful. He's holding my hands. All of this is real.

"I am too," I say, and I realize I mean it. "I didn't think I'd see you again, to be honest."

He arches a brow. "You think we'd just let you walk away?"

My pounding heart goes silent and drops like a stone into my gut. Wren is inside, with Evander—where is she? *Shit.* I let this boy's suit and smile lull me into a safety net that was actually a trapper's snare—

"Oh no, not—I didn't mean that to sound ominous." Auden stiffens, horrified. "Jesus. No. Ruby, I'm sorry."

He runs a hand through his hair, and because it's absolutely perfect, it falls back into place over a surprisingly harried expression that looks all wrong composed of his patrician features. Auden collects both my hands again, this time with the fervor of someone hoping to be both heard and understood.

"I just meant—after what we went through together, of course I'd want to see you again." He squeezes both my hands, and dips down a couple of inches to plant himself at my eye level. "We all do."

I blink. My heart slowly rises. I believe him. I believe them. I swallow again, aiming to center myself. To stave off the parts of me that are terrified of the good I purposefully tried not to expect.

"Is everyone—did they come back?"

His face lights up anew like the western horizon in that selfsame moment. "Let me show you."

Then, just as he did that night, Auden offers his elbow. Like the gentleman he is. He was raised to be this way, and still is and always will be, despite no longer being under strict instructions from his grandmother.

This time, I don't hesitate, but instead of taking his elbow like the lady I pretended to be, I slip my hand into his and tug it to hang between us. Stepping into the rhythm we held before Wren and I left the grounds six weeks ago.

Inside, the chandelier glows merrily in the foyer, Shadrack's beautiful wilderness in watercolor striking against the hard-as-nails shine of the marble floor and walnut staircase. Auden keeps us on the first floor, winding us down the hall, through the tearoom, and, rather than out onto the garden, we turn a hard corner, and there's a door to the courtyard, open wide to the falling night.

Magical fairy lights circle the space, a dinner table newly set in the exact center, round, and fully surrounded by faces I know well now, no cheat sheet needed.

The Cerises stand tall and together, their tattoos visible, opalescent black as they ladder their arms. Hex's sleeves rolled up, and Ada in a sleeveless dress as red as the blood they both wield.

Next to them is Winter, striking in a cerulean blue the same shade as her eyes, as warm as tropical waters.

At her shoulder is Infinity, their hair now a raven black, as shiny as polished onyx, smoothed into slick, short waves.

The Blackgates are not here. Not the sisters. Not their mother.

I set eyes on Wren, who's clearly just finished a round of hugs, one hand smoothing down the fall of Winter's mane as she latches back onto Evander's side.

Auden and I arrive at the table, and he surprises me by placing me beside Wren, and then stepping away. Evander does too, until the pair of them are bracketing Winter—and everyone is facing us.

Evander folds his hands in front of his body, massive shoulders rolling forward. "Before we start this reunion, we have family business to touch upon."

Family business. As in the three of them, or . . . ?

Auden accepts a verbal baton. "We have a proposition for the pair of you, one we have all agreed to and we hope you'll consider."

"Okay . . ." Wren ventures, as my eyes seem to go everywhere, scanning the table, the faces, the space, for some hint as to what's coming. Instead, it's a blur of images too cursory to be of any use, as Winter produces a scroll from a hidden pocket in her peasant-cut dress.

"Over the past six weeks, we have worked together to create a new and rebuilt structure for safeguarding the magic of the Four Lines within North America. This document is your copy to read as you like."

Winter holds it out and I accept the scroll, unfurling it as she continues.

"In my capacity as Liaison of the Lines, I can tell you that the high points are this. We have come to the conclusion that while we can't carry on as the generations before us, we cannot in good conscience fully separate the lines. If there's anything we learned while uncovering the masters it is that we are and always will be connected, no matter our individual lines. The lines are not silos of magic; they are branches on the same tree." Here, her gaze slides over to Infinity, who squeezes Winter's arm. "Thus, we honor our parents' sacrifices and their vision for something new and fair regarding the balance and control of magic. We trust ourselves to know the limitations of our power and control in regard to returning the magical relics to each family member without binding them to a single point of control, but ultimately we refuse to reward dangerous agency to those who would and have used their power against us very recently."

The Blackgates.

Handing them their relic and self-governance would be dangerous not just for the people standing here, but to every witch on the continent. And plenty of non-magical people like us too.

"As such, we have made the collective decision as a High Family majority to create a system of checks and balances not previously in place. The consolidation of the master relics was meant to stabilize and amplify our magic, by funneling the original lines through a central location to keep each line fed and safe from any unsavory designs by witches under our aegis."

One look at the paper in my hand confirms Winter is reciting it nearly word for word.

"To preserve the stability we need for our witches, yet to provide the flexibility and balance we all would like to see going forward, we needed to come up with a piece of the pie for everyone involved." Here, she smiles, going off script. "And, actually, that solution ended up being way more elegant than expected."

Winter fishes a familiar choker out from beneath the high collar of her dress, and there, beside her key, is a ring. I would've thought it was Ursula's, if not for everyone standing around the table, revealing their own rings on chains around each of their necks. The four stones are there—red, black, green, white—but there's an additional flourish on every ring. An extra beveled line encircles the gems.

"Giving credit where it's due, Auden, the genius, was able to magically multiply our High Sorcerer's ring. All of us have identical copies, all equally tethered to the four relics, which each family holds, per the agreement." Winter drops her necklace and gestures to the other families assembled. "Though the relics aren't located in the same place geographically, we've found the multiple tether points keep the magic stable and safe in the same way a woven fabric is stronger than a single strand alone. In a way, we believe this is how the original masters were created—each of them mixed two lines of magic or more, perhaps proving that we're stronger together than we are apart."

Wren wriggles in joy next to me. "Oh man, the band's staying together? I love this for you!"

Evander's lips twitch. "You'll love it more if you keep listening."

That's when I realize Auden is holding out a ring on a chain to me. I blink at him, somewhat aware that Evander's hand is moving in the same revealing motion before Wren.

"We invited you tonight not only because we wanted to see you," Auden says, "but because we want to include you."

My sister flattens her free hand over her heart. "No. Way!"

"Yes, truly," Evander says. "It's right there in your copy of the agreement."

Wren wrests the paper out of my hand and furiously scans the bottom at an angle I can't read. I nudge it back, flattening the page until I can read the words.

Lines. Arrangement. Ring. Masters.

"If you accept the terms of the proposal, the procedure is exactly as it was in Ursula's study. Your signature will be a thumbprint in your own blood." Winter produces another parchment, unrolls it, and flashes the bottom. Six thumbprints shine a magic-infused shimmering crimson in the firefly light.

"And then both of us will be tied to the new lines," I say slowly—not a question but a confirmation.

"Yes. You will be our fifth line."

It's right there, in the very last sentence.

". . . hereby tying myself to the Five Lines as agreed to in terms one through twenty-one above . . ."

The Five Lines.

"Wait." Wren holds up a hand, trying to process. "Will we be witches, like, can you do that?"

"Only biology can do that," Infinity answers in that soft, erudite voice we've come to know. "What you will be is a safeguard. An additional line to keep us in check by providing an outside perspective we don't have and, frankly, sorely need."

My stomach flips.

A way to be one of them, even though we will never actually be witches.

This is both a gift and a shock. Wren must think so too, because not only is she silent beside me—for once in her life—but she slowly curls her hand into mine, pinky twining in the same promise I gave her over and over our last time here.

"We'll have to redo all our internal branding." Winter sighs, at first appearing annoyed, but then the corners of her mouth tip up as she looks straight at me, "but you know, it's worth it."

She taps the table and that's when I realize for the first time that it's not round, it's actually five-sided. A pentagon. Five sides, one for each family.

Including us.

The Fifth Line.

We're the ring around the four stones—the extra flourish on the outside, protecting the inner circle. I take a steadying breath and force myself to face the most recent iteration of my fears. This one—what they will do to us if we say no.

"And if we don't accept?"

Auden's gaze flickers across my face, an answer at the ready even as something that might be disappointment flashes in his eyes.

"Well, I'd hope you'd stay for a nice meal, and then afterward—or now, if you think it best not to draw it out—a simple spell is all it takes to make you forget you were ever here. Tonight, six weeks ago, at all."

They can do exactly what Wren thought they could and would do. I'm not surprised, if anything it's a testament to the bond we forged that, despite all the deceit, they didn't do it before. Six weeks of us knowing. Six weeks of them trusting we wouldn't tell. We didn't.

My vision clears as I read every line of the contract as closely as possible. I want to know exactly what it says. No lies. No omissions. Nothing hidden.

As I do, my sister prods the elephant in the room. Or, perhaps, the missing elephant.

"And the Blackgates?" Wren asks.

Evander answers. "The same terms, though we have agreed to hold their master in escrow until they've made their decision. Though if they do accept, we will still hold their master relic for the next five years in accordance with the punishment of Lavinia and Kaysa Blackgate for their part in Marsyas's plot to steal the master relics and High Sorcerer's ring."

It's a relief that Lavinia, Kaysa, and Athena Blackgate don't currently hold the magical relics that moved the dead and nearly killed us all.

Wren's head tilts. "And if they don't accept?"

I look up from the contract, curious, and, well, a little fearful.

Winter grins, tight but true. "They know where to find us."

"But they won't beat us!" Hex interjects, with a confident laugh. Ada elbows him hard. Honestly, he should've seen that coming.

"Let's not invite any further animosity," she tells him.

"So, will you join us?" Winter asks, circling back. "Do you accept?"

For once, Wren glances at me—waiting for my opinion first. Her decision is written all over her face, big eyes round, cheeks flushed, lips pressed together as if to keep her answer from bursting forth like it always does. Then, she surprises me further by grabbing my hand. "We need a second to talk it over."

She tugs me a few steps away, toward the wall where we found the Great Bear and the Celestial relic, shadows falling like they did in that moment of triumph before it was shattered by Luna's death. The green ivy brushes the backs of my arms, soft and so very alive. Wren lowers her voice and her wide eyes to mine.

"You know my answer—of course you do—but if I've learned anything it's that your instincts are always better than mine. And I'm not incapable of some growth, especially with all the very large mistakes I made on this property. *So.*" Wren flicks her gaze over my shoulder to the table for the briefest of moments. "This is me saying, if you want to bolt, I'm here for the memory wipe and a ride home. We're in this together. Sisters over witches."

Despite the heaviness of it all, that last little bit makes me cough out a laugh.

"Sisters over witches every time."

I flip our grip, twining my pinky around hers.

Holding fast to my sister, we turn to face the table below. Five sides, three full, two empty. Two chairs pulled out, waiting. One black rose in the other spot, marking the Blackgates' absence.

Auden and Evander both palm the rings, chains dangling at their sides, the metal glinting under the lights, the night sky coming on fast over the high walls.

"We accept."

There's a flurry of movement, everything that had been stowed away the last five minutes in the name of maturity and propriety bursting free. Winter side-tackles Infinity into an embrace, the twins applaud, their family rings twinkling, and Evander and Auden approach, rings offered, the signing of the contract saved for later.

Wren squeezes my hand and leaps away, barreling straight for Evander just like she did when we arrived. This time, though, he's ready, catching her by the waist and twirling them both in a way that has her sun-fire dress unfurling like the most beautiful of tropical flowers.

And then she's a swirling background as Auden steps into my field of vision, hope in the cut of his mouth and furrow of his brow. That suit is liquid silk on his strong frame as he extends an arm, palm up, my own relic on offer.

I push my hair to one side and dip my chin in silent instruction, my eyes never leaving his. He slips the chain around my neck, gently arranging my hair back over both shoulders.

Then, for the second time in my life, Auden Hegemony holds me like I might disappear.

His hands cup my face, thumbs on my cheeks, eyes reading mine for permission. He's close enough his forearms press warmly into my collarbones, the buttons of his shirt kissing the fabric of my dress's bodice.

Instead of giving permission, I take what's offered. Because I can. Because it's true and sure and right in front of me, everything out in the open for once. I slide my arms around his waist, smoothing them up his back, and pull him in until his lips touch mine. I can finally close my eyes.

The lie wasn't ours when we arrived here.

But this truth is ours. It's literal magic. And I'm not going to let go.

ACKNOWLEDGMENTS

I dedicated this book to my awesome agent, Whitney Ross, for always being in my corner and helping me make magic (pun fully intended) one book at a time. Without her, this book and all but one of the others I've written wouldn't exist. Agents are an author's partner, and she is truly the best. I cannot tell you how many iterations of this story she read. My hard drive is a graveyard of samples and synopses, and she combed through each and every one of them before we found exactly the right way to execute the book I've been calling "*Knives Out* with magic" since 2020. I'm honored to have the chance to work with her every single day.

Books aren't made in a vacuum, and they take so many more people than just an author and their agent to make it into the world. Luckily, once Whitney and I hacked through all my early iterations to this one, this project landed in the lap of the talented Sanaa Ali-Virani. With an enthusiastic vision and a magically inclined eye, Sanaa championed this book from start to finish and it benefited at every turn from her thoughtful work. She also introduced me to Malaysian-style Milo French toast, which I'll daydream about for many years to come.

Thank you to the rest of the amazing folks at Tor Teen/Macmillan who cheer me on from behind the curtain. To publisher Devi Pillai for making four(!) books possible. To Lesley Worrell for yet another amazing cover design and artist Elena Masci for bringing it to life. To Giselle Gonzalez, Saraciea Fennell, Anthony Parisi, Isa Caban (who also came up with our fantastic title!), Sarah Pannenberg, and the rest of the terrific publicity, marketing, and social media team. To the sales reps, school and library reps, and everyone else at Tor and Macmillan who have supported me along the way.

And, of course, a huge thank-you to my writer friends, who have been there for every step I've taken in making it to the shelves with this book. To Amanda and Julie for our Thursday writing and lunch sessions at T. Loft. To Natalie and Tess for pinch-hitting with their Ren Fest knowledge and for always being on hand with loads of experience and level-headed advice. To Jennifer for being my sounding board via text. To the rest of the Kansas Writers' Crew and the folks at the Writerly cabin for the conversation and carbs. And to everyone who has squealed about this book in person and on socials at a time when it feels like we're all yelling into the void (LOLsob).

Finally, I'd like to thank my family. To Justin, who holds down the fort (aka the regular salary and the health insurance) so that I can argue with fictional characters all day. To my parents, Craig and Mary, who are always there to help with the kids when I'm mired in work, remind me to buy lemon cake to celebrate my victories, and provide treats at regular and much-appreciated intervals. To Nate, Amalia, and Emmie, for being my muses every day just by being awesome kids. And to my furry coworkers—Dash, Pearl, and Camo—who are never above a good cuddle.

Thank you for reading!

ABOUT THE AUTHOR

Fally Afani

SARAH HENNING is the author of several books for young adults, including the Indies Introduce selection, Indie Next List pick, and Junior Library Guild Gold Standard Selection *Sea Witch,* and its sequel, *Sea Witch Rising; The Princess Will Save You, The Queen Will Betray You,* and *The King Will Kill You;* as well as *Throw Like a Girl* and its companion book, *It's All in How You Fall.* She appears in the girls-in-sports anthology *Out of Our League,* and wrote the middle-grade book *Monster Camp.* When not writing, she runs ultramarathons, hits the farmers market with her two kids, and hangs out with her husband, Justin, who doubles as her long-suffering IT department. Henning lives in Lawrence, Kansas, hometown of Langston Hughes, William S. Burroughs, and a really good basketball team.

sarahhenningwrites.com
Instagram: @shhenning
X: @shhenning